Please Use Rear Exit

NOVEL BY
Brandon Perkins

www.PleaseUseRearExit.net

ISBN 978-0-9854267-1-2 (Paperback Edition)

*for the record, this is some shit i just thought of y'all,
science fiction that's not admissible in no court of law.
-- mf doom*

**Skinny B Publishing, LLC // 2012
@SkinnyB**

\\ SPECIAL THANKS //

Design Supervision: Aerosyn-Lex Mestrovic
Copy Editors: Alex Dwyer, Paul Glanting
Website & Branding:
Anthony J. Asencio, Xtrovertd Media Consulting
Laptop Provisions: Raymond Roker, Joshua Glazer
Conceptual Editing:
Justin Strout, Conor Simpson, Steve Cooper
Mixtape Mayhem: Zach Best
Music Mastery: Steve Cooper (Spirit Animal),
TopBananas, Evidence, Apathy, The Machine, Fat Tony

Cover Calligraphy: Aerosyn-Lex Mestrovic
Cover Photography: Cristian Dulan (iStockPhoto)
Cover Design: Brandon Perkins

Bonus material can be found on PleaseUseRearExit.net. Please be warned, it can be a dirty world online, as in real life, and some of the bonus chapters, videos, exclusive music, maps and more are NSFW. User discretion is advised.

PART ONE
1. The Brown BTWN Moments
2. How to Buy Low
3. A Fleeting Glimpse of CGI
4. Peyton Manning's FuckFace
5. Avoiding Katya
6. Mr. Sallow's Hallow
7. Fortune of Spears
8. Slow Jam Filly
9. Mirror, Mirror
10. Devil's Dance
11. Confrontation@Anything

PART TWO
12. A Sporting Chance
13. Rubber Street Snakes
14. Counter Tray Right
15. The Sliver BTWN Silvers
16. Internet Explorers on an Internet Safari
17. From Boys to Dogs to Men
18. Burning the Beer
19. Spores and Pores
20. Orthodontry Sparkling in the Overhead Lights
21. Life in HD
22. Oh, the Cuddle Possibilities
23. A Doctor's Note From Him
24. So Go Rob the Breadmaker

PART THREE
25. Lemmings Gone Wild
26. SacredSaffron.Tumblr.Com
27. Raw Bacon
28. Alpha Squid, Master Beta
29. Lord of the Barnyard
30. Back Like Cooked Crack
31. The Alley Cat Plays Him Off
32. The Master & Margarita
33. Hide Your Kids, Hides Your Wife
34. Left Center Right
35. O Rly?
36. It's Yourz

PleaseUseRearExit.net/home/PROLOGUE

While there are many theories of its genesis, no one is sure when, why or how The Internet consumed Los Angeles. Even the creation of its bus system, one that houses every walk of life for the city's 6.2 million residents, is a mystery to the general population. Yet, for the most part, everyone has accepted that there is no "outside." Most people believe what they've been told: The Internet is dangerous and no human can survive beyond the safety of interconnected bus lines. There are very few glimpses of the World Wide Web, the very same one that keeps Angelinos on their buses, and its presence is often thought to be a privilege of the wealthy.

Encompassing everything found in a familiar society, Los Angeles' system of buses is all that its citizens know. Organized efficiently, the cavernous buses—varying in size, shape, quality and economic class—contain housing, commerce, hospitals, schools, nightlife and more. The routes are split into three main categories: Numbers, Shapes, and Colors. Numbers are the centers of commerce; Shapes are primarily residential; while Colors (also known as Betweens or BTWNs) transport Angelinos from Shapes to Numbers, to and fro.

Through various complicated engines, the three systems of buses use The Internet's power for everything on-board, from electricity and heat to oxygen creation and locomotion. Maintenance of Los Angeles' engines is entrusted to a few select and mysterious members of society, who protect its secrets with the utmost importance as a matter of homeland security.

Chapter One
The Brown BTWN Moments

Everyone on the bus was horribly disfigured. Warts, scars, stains, blemishes, matted hair, and a whole disarray of dismembering smells. Fifth-generation t-shirts that started with sports-playing grandsons ended their tattered saga on the drooping shoulders of a youngin's great grandmother. Hand-me-downs were hand-me-ups. It all went in reverse. The passengers sat two-by-two or stood in the aisles, grasping sweaty bars for balance. Their day to day bus was taking them into the night and the Brown Between had a tendency to jerk rather suddenly.

The bus ran from Los Angeles's most maligned residential line (Compton's Circle) to the #720 and back again. Higher class routes existed for higher-class passengers who lived in fancier places. It was mostly the poor that rode the Brown Between. Its primary purpose was to shuttle the cleaning staff, rat catchers, dishwashers, fast food short order chefs, sheet metal deburrers, and other employees of undesirable servitude to and from their overcrowded residential complexes on an impossibly rickety set of tracks—and the Brown Between was the only line in the city that still seemed to be on tracks. When the seats were comfortable they felt infested with unimaginable insects. And when they weren't comfortable? The fabric looked frightfully diseased and the insects actually crept up everyone's legs.

Mikhail's weekly Friday night trek from his studio apartment in Compton's Circle to the #720 was always his most awkward. He stood out among the factory rats in their greased overalls and the solemn families with all those grocery bags full of empty cans. During the day he wore an employer-issued uniform, just like them, but Mikhail's Friday night clothes were truly his Sunday best. His trek to work, from Compton's Circle, instilled in him a sense of authenticity that was lacking on LA's nicer routes, but his weekend wardrobe—designer white tee, skinny jeans, his requisite Dipset scully—made him feel like a poser. None of the other passengers would be spending $300 on booze over the next six hours and Mikhail's change of costume made everyone aware of this fact. And, until the Party Kids transferred from the Triangle—the second to last stop before the #720— Mikhail would ride alone through The Internet in the middle of all that knowing tension generated by such an economic reality.

Their silence was almost deafening and would've been nearly unbearable were it not for the nails-on-chalkboard screech of the rust-bucket bus in motion. Over the whirring gears and gaskets that transformed the power of The Internet into locomotion, people swayed and slept, moving to the ebbs and flows of the dilapidated transit. Weaving in and out of consciousness with the twists and turns of the Brown BTWN's shucks and jives, it was a brief moment of harmony. Nearly all of them were strangers and yet, they all seemed to slumber in a uniting rhythm.

The Brown BTWN was mildly crowded, its seats occupied by about 40 people and two bags of cans. Mikhail's Converses chucked under a set of seats in the bus' exact middle. He had a foot of space in each direction between those standing and swaying in the aisle alongside him, and the lucky little family that grabbed a seat. But the young boy in his father's lap was definitely not sleeping, even as his parents' eyes were heavily shut. He pushed the top of his head firmly into his father's chest, arching his squirmy body and pushing his feet against the seat in front of them. He stuck a dirty fist into his pop's cheek, pushing before eventually tapping with an exponential fervor. The taps came sooner and soon became punches. Pop's fat mouth swallowed the young boy's grimy hand whole. Pop's eyes never opened, he just playfully gnawed his son's chubby wrist. Growled a bit. His only son quietly giggled. The entire interaction was incredibly silent.

Everything suddenly came to a halt. All the air inside the bus slammed forward in a bit of bitter rage. An old lady to Mikhail's left, crashed into him at the BTWN's sudden stop. He picked up her plastic leg—which flew forward at an alarming rate, but fell just a few feet in front of him—and handed it back to her. She had no teeth and a patch of scarred skin covered what should've been her left eye, but she smiled genuinely. As she steadied her hand on Mikhail's shoulder, she screwed the leg back into place, grateful for his aid. Maybe Mikhail wasn't so out of place after all.

People got off the bus but more people got on, as the overhead announcement urged everyone to move towards the back. Mikhail found himself directly on top of yet another family, located seven rows behind the squirmy son and his poor pops. This time, everyone was alarmingly awake, especially the little girl that sat on her mother's lap.

"Mommy, Ms. Brisson says that a caterpillar can turn into a butterfly, do you believe that, Mommy? Ms. Brisson says that a caterpillar eats and eats and eats and eats and then goes to sleep and then it wakes up as a butterfly, Mommy, the caterpillar before it sleeps, it throws up all its food on itself and makes a sleeping bag to sleep in, do you believe that, Mommy? That's what Ms. Brisson says and she's soooo smart, Mommy."

Mommy nodded. Her child was the loudest thing on the bus, even louder than the grinding gears and unrelenting push of the vehicle's motor. Even with eight legs, the child was beautiful and beautiful was rarely seen around those parts. Everyone on the bus gave her a pass because they knew she'd go places that they would never venture, places that their children probably wouldn't either. Her hair was in braids and the longest strand dangled in front of her face. She pulled it down past her chin and was quick to bite the braid's tip between her teeth.

"Mommy, you won't even believe this," she said, still sucking on the braid, "but Ms. Brisson says that tentacles turn into frogs, Mommy, do you believe that?" Mascara marked the child's eyes. Big brown eyes batted in her mother's direction. A teal ribbon balanced on her head like a tiara. She knew that she looked like a princess despite—or perhaps especially—in eight white sandals so scuffed.

"Mommy, a tentacle moves like this," her arm wiggled slowly from side to side like a snake in the water before her writhing limb reached up and began playing with the lone braid that symmetrically divided her dark porcelain face, and even though she meant tadpole instead of tentacle, it didn't matter, "and it swims and swims and then it goes to sleep in the mud and it wakes up as a little tiny, tiny frog," she brought her fingers in real close to her face and left the smallest gap between them, "it's so small, Mommy, but then it grows bigger and bigger and bigger and sometimes, that little tentacle wakes up as a big old fat bullfrog. They ribbit. Ribbit! Why do they ribbit, Mommy?"

Mikhail imagined that Katya was a similarly precocious child. She was reading before she was speaking and once she spoke, she never stopped. But Katya was born into an affluent family. As was Saffron, and for that matter, there was a good chance that any girl he was about to meet would have inevitably been raised in an environment that would thumb their nose at this little girl's family. He hoped that this child, so concerned about tentacles and butterflies, would remember where she came from, that it would help ground her, and not at all in a matter that she felt was owed to her. Mikhail thought about finding a girl with perspective that he could spend his life with. He wanted to inspire that girl, that girl who he hadn't yet met, and it made him want to inspire this little child so concerned with the lessons of Ms. Brisson. He thought about answering the girl's question, about why frogs ribbit, but something about interrupting a conversation always made him blush.

"You're so smart," Mommy said, kissing the child's forehead.

"Why didn't you want to be smart, Mommy? I like being smart because I get to know things that other people don't get to know because they're not smart and that's why I like school, Mommy, but why don't you go to school, Mommy? You should go to school because I know everything and you only know almost everything, Mommy, why don't you go to school so you can know everything like me?"

Mommy kissed her child's forehead again, mumbling something about being so smart, so proud. She repeatedly kissed the child's face with increasing zeal, but without a smile. The child furrowed her brow, deep in thought, biting down on the braid to show the world her contemplation. She slapped at a fly that attempted to land anywhere its wings could rest.

"That fly used to be a legless glop of white goop," Mikhail said, winking at Mommy. That wasn't so bad. "It was born out of garbage, trash, all the junk we throw out. It went to sleep and grew wings."

"Mommy, is that true? Did the goop grow wings?"

Mommy nodded and pulled the yellow chord that hung to her left. From the ceiling, an automated man's deep voice announced and then politely demanded, "Stop requested. Please use rear exit."

"I love school. Why don't you go to school, Mommy? Ms. Brisson is so smart and pretty, just like me, why don't you want to be smart and pretty, Mommy?"

The bus casually slowed to a stop. No legs were lost. Led by the hand, the child stood up on all eight of her scuffed sandals.

Mommy and an exhausted father arose. They impatiently huffed and puffed their way through the stragglers still struggling with their stuff—sloths blocking the aisles—towards the front of the bus and an unhappy transfer onto the #780. Tired workers took the family's seats and Mikhail moved towards the door, making a bee-line for his weekly sweet spot. Comfortably wedged between a bench and the wheel cap, no one would ask him to move once all the Party Kids piled in by the rowdy and rabid dozens a few transfers down the line. His position allowed him to be among the first to exit onto the #720. It wasn't that he was anxious to meet up with his friends for a new-again night out, he just didn't want to deal with all those people.

Chapter Two
How to Buy Low

After swiping his card and traversing the turnstile, Mikhail casually crossed the #720's brightly-lit corridor and walked into Low without having to show his ID. Once his eyes had adjusted to the damp dimness of the bar's dingy interior, he was immediately struck by the sharp shift in the bar's demographics since his last visit. The beer-belly boisterousness of the blue collar set had miraculously transformed into an invasion of fashion-challenged bro's and vodka-slamming sorority sluts. It was only a few months prior, one of those rare times that Katya had let him meet his friends for a night out, that Mikhail observed the usual Budweiser-sipping factory rats as he quickly drank a Jameson on the rocks. Back then, nothing had changed—it was exactly as he knew it, for every pre-Katya Friday night over a three-year-span, when he'd stop in Low for a quick fidolo drink to start his evening.

Easily the closest bar to the Brown BTWN's transfer, its clientele used to be a reflection of the neglected line's forgotten passengers. Low was by-passed by the Party Kids—who were too scared to drink with the sometimes scary but mostly tired underbelly of society—in favor of glitzier establishments that were just around either corner. They passed Low no more, now mobbing the bartenders in the back and lining up for karaoke off to the side. Mikhail felt like he had left his childhood apartment in the Triangle and returned a few months later to find an amusement park in his bedroom. He didn't know whether to be terrified or a kid in the candy store. He just knew that he'd need a drink to fully figure out how that roller-coaster fit inside his old closet.

Low looked the same. Like they did on all the routes, advertisements cluttered every free inch of real estate. The flashing images beckoned men to The PPP or looped commentary on people with dirty mouths, and the ads hadn't changed since Mikhail first stepped foot in the place years ago. The patrons just got swapped, and brought along a better soundtrack with them. But it was all a blur once he made his way to the bar.

And with how beautiful the bartenders were Mikhail quickly stopped caring how the drastic change had happened and started believing that Low's transformation was a sign, a sign that screamed how right he was to break up with Katya. She'd been blowing up his cell phone all night; he felt the blinking red light in his pocket practically burn a hole in his jeans. They both knew that this was his first Friday night out as a single man and she hated the idea of it. But all of the negative energy, building up in his phone as wounded text messages and missed calls, was a choice now and it was pitted up against a surprising surplus of positively beautiful young women. *The Choice Is Yours (Rmx)*. Gone were the pock-marked bartenders of yore, replaced by three ladies of liquored lore. Mikhail kept with the momentum and moved onto the new. Without taking out his phone, he hit a button on its side that changed the blinking red light he knew existed, into a slower, more muted green blast.

The new girls non-chalantly moved from station to station, bottle to bottle, and finally, bottle to glass, answering the calls of the thirsty Party Kids that surrounded Mikhail. The first shawty was blonde and covered in tattoos, her Sonic the Hedgehog hair just begging for pixie comparisons. Her frosted tips were visibly dead, drowned in bleach, dying to just die and finally fall out in peace. But they were just a footnote in the bold-faced headline of razor sharp nipples on a pair of barely-covered breastesses. Without a bra, her wife-beater was performing miracles in the struggle against gravity.

Her partner behind the bar literally wore her feathers out: a stunning plume of pinks and purples mohawked down from her head and through the open back of her Bob Marley t-shirt. Her heavily mascaraed eyes were practically iridescent and incredibly sad. They held the pain of war veterans and widows, while her body balanced the Lolita-like invitations of youth. She was so skinny under the bagginess of her vintage top that the potential for a boobie to slip out was just as likely as an arm. Her skin looked as virginal as the feathers sprouting from her back and surely felt just as soft. Her eyes always a heart-beat away from certain death. She smiled through the whole ordeal.

The last lady walked meekly with little cry for attention. An exotic taupe to her silky skin, her sexuality only showed in brief glimpses, completely covered up when compared to the other two bartenders. Her body was cloaked in an unaltered t-shirt and shorts that didn't at all resemble panties. Mystery clouded in every sensual-yet-fully-clad step. The lone patch of easily-overlooked skin was a perfectly taut mid-drift. It existed right where her blue top ended and her shorts began, only visible for two sweating inches when she reached up to grab a stack of plastic cups. Her skin looked hot to the touch, but a metal bottle opener was chillingly tucked against the protruding pelvic bone that peaked out from her low-slung capris. The clash of body heat against a simple tool's cold steel immediately warmed Mikhail's crotch. He'd miss those details later in the night, once the drinks hit hyper-speed, but right there, that smallest juxtaposition was nearly enough to make him fall in love.

He assertively tried to make eye contact and then smiled with a hint of shyness, proud that the gesture felt natural. He wanted to show interest in more than just booze, without pervertedly leering, but she quickly ducked away uninterested. She was just the bar back, not allowed to serve him in the formal way and way too timid to return his flirtatious informalities. Mikhail saw the logic in it, but still got a little stung. Turning to his right, Sonic the Hedgehog was walking towards him quite casually, obviously not in a huge rush. He started to order when his Dipset scully was pulled down over his face and everything went dark. Before he could even turn around—

"Just drop that thang, rock that thang, lock that thang," Chevy snarled, careful to enunciate the oomph like Ludacris, "and not even Patrick Willis can block that thang."

Not wanting to lose an easy chance to order, he just peaked out from below the 100% acrylic blind-fold and asked for three shots of Jameson, two High Lifes and a tequila-soda—making sure to say please in the process.

"What the fuck happened to this place?" Mikhail said, still rubbing something like sleep out of his eyes.

Inevitably, on nearly 70% of his Fridays in the five years after he had turned 21, Mikhail started his night with a quick drink alone at Low before going on to meet his best friends somewhere else. It was a tradition. His ol' stow-away was a quiet place to drink a whiskey, standing up, while shaking off the Brown BTWN. No one used to talk at Low; somber Elvis songs played on repeat. He'd then wander off into the #720's casino-intense pace under all those lights. It made for a smoother transition, taking a bit of the edge off, just by taking it one step at a time.

"It's been more than a minute since you've decided to stop by the party, too much snuggling on the couch, watching movies and getting fed right," Chevy said. "It's good to have you back, at least until you change your mind on her again."

"No sir, I've changed just as much as this place. Is this spot still even called Low?"

"The Internet age is one that still spins outside your cage, water slides raining sage, I get paid for days..."

That's what Chevy did, Chevy rhymed, and Mikhail's potential responses whirled in his head:

(a) "I slay...yeah, Kay Slay...the Drama King, all day, and you gay, like a dry toupee kissing a hot soufflé...flame-ing! All hail Mikhail, your momma's king!"

(b) "It's like, all the furniture is still the same. The TV's are all fucked up"...and they were. Cracked screens still looped the barrage of bad news on mute, the color balance always switched. Reds looked green, blacks looked blue. The bar stools still had one leg too short and massive rips in their vinyl cushions. As they forever had, spider webs caked the slowly turning ceiling fans like the innards of a cotton-candy machine..."It looks like the old crowd phased over to a different bar just as they were replaced. The new crowd didn't notice the switch either."

(c) "You have no idea how many times my phone has vibrated tonight, Katya just won't leave me alone," he could say...then talk about his newly regimented independence and how good it felt.

(d) Awkwardly, he could ask Chevy "What's up?" while handing out drinks and hesitating on what to tip Sonic and her glowering nipples.

Chapter Three
A Fleeting Glimpse of CGI

D. Mikhail absent-mindedly chose (d).

But he told himself that such stumbling wasn't entirely his fault. Katya called him the second that Chevy started to trail off. Mikhail instinctually paused to silence a phone that no one could hear vibrating, simultaneously losing his beat in the conversation and train of thought. Fortunately, all awkwardness was forgotten and forgiven en route to finding Jayson—who had posted up at one of the last empty standing tables—and simple small talk was okay enough.

"Welcome aboard, brother," Jayson said, once Mikhail had meandered on over.

"C'mon man, it hasn't been that long," Mikhail said with a thug hug, embracing and hitting his best friend at the same damn time.

"If I feel like I haven't seen you out in months, then it really has been that long."

It was embarrassing that Jayson had been more social than Mikhail in the previous months. They all blamed it on Katya...even as Jayson was supposed to be the homie with the controlling girlfriend. Her crazy was supposed to overshadow Katya's. Something must've been off if Jayson still hadn't introduced her to his two closest friends. They didn't even know her name; Jayson refused to divulge it. He said that they'd just make fun of it, so everyone referred to his old-lady as "wifey"... or, well, his "old lady."

But such privacy didn't keep Jayson from listing all her ailments, which included vertigo-induced eye bleeding and a toothed-vagina. That he was with her through all that didn't seem all that surprising once one met Jayson. He drunkenly swore about the genuine love they shared, and through all their teasing, Chevy and Mikhail mostly accepted it, albeit a little begrudgingly.

Everyone downed their shots of Jameson without saying a word about it.

"Two-thirds of us are now single," Chevy said. "Isn't it time we made this shit unanimous?"

"Man, you guys know that my old lady treats me right. Why do you always gotta start with that shit, man?"

Chevy had more fun when everyone in the group walked with the potential to get laid. It made them wonder if Chevy secretly wanted to cross swords in some sort of post-#720 orgy.

"It's true, brother, girls are better than girlfriends," Mikhail said. "The friend-part just means you ain't getting laid."

"Oh wow, the ghost can speak," Jayson said. "C'mon Casper, this is your coming out party, it's your job to say shit like that."

"Mikhail got that new pussy tingle. Don't blame him, join him...join us."

"At least my old lady lets me out on Friday nights—"

"—I left Katya's comfy couch for good this time. You're alone on domestication island. We're just trying to throw you a raft. Even if you won't tell us her name, you don't draw the prettiest picture of the beast beyond your shores, deep in the forest (1). Yeah, we know, you're happy, you just have to vent sometimes."

"I'm not even complaining tonight," Jayson scowled. "You fuckers brought it up."

"Stop being a saint. I'mma get some shawty to kiss my taint till she faint," Chevy said. "Here's some fatherly advice, son, stick your brush in new pussy...and paint."

Despite never missing a chance to brag about his healthy income at a financial firm on the #111, Chevy still fancied himself as some sort of rapper or maybe a comedian whose dick-jokes came in rhyme form. Mikhail and Jayson would play along—and sometimes his lyrics weren't all that bad—but no one was pushing him to quit his day job. Mostly, it just passed the time without anyone having to say anything that meant anything.

"Screw sobriety's restraint," Mikhail said, lacking all of Chevy's enthusiasm. "I'm already past beer at this point. It's a whiskey night."

Chevy definitely got his pants at Nordstrom and not Nordstrom's Rack. He cuffed his light beige linen a few inches above his ankles. It worked with sock-less hush puppies and a blue striped v-neck short-sleeve. Always a step ahead of the curve, Chevy was a dedicated follower of fashion. His sailor outfit would surely get him laid later, but in the meantime, he wore the risk of being called a fag with every precious step.

"How many times has Katya called you?" Jayson asked.

"Are you trying to imply something about my motivations to get twisted and stumble into casual sex in a warm, girly bed?" Chevy and Jayson coldly stared at Mikhail. "Okay, a lot. She's texted me even more. I haven't looked at my phone since early on the Brown BTWN, but it keeps fucking vibrating. I try to text

(1) Most of this Los Angeles' citizens accept the fact that no world exists outside the one they know inside the buses. They tend to live vicariously through the images seen on YouTube.

back, but it's never anything worth sending. Always busting my balls about not saying anything…but what the fuck is there to say? What am I supposed to contribute when she only wants to talk about people I don't know? And now it's even worse—it's all about feelings that she doesn't want to know. I listened; she's not even trying to hear."

"Doesn't that sound horrible? Feelings?" Chevy asked, flipping Jayson's hat off. Before Jayson could retaliate, Chevy caught a tackle from a force unseen. With empty arms, he picked up a mass of air and twirled it around a few times. A squeal eeked out from the depths of vapid spins. He delicately dropped the mess of air back onto the floor, never letting his gluttonous smile disappear from the direction of empty. As invisible as the day she was born, CGI was now part of their night.

"So get this boys, Todd and George and I are sitting at the karaoke bar, the very one just behind us this very instant, and who knows what this putz is trying to sing, but he's singing it poorly. This is last weekend. Todd is wearing a suit by Lubian, a great-looking striped spread-collar shirt from Burberry, a silk tie by Resikeio and a belt from Ralph Lauren. George is wearing a six-button double-breasted suit by Christian Dior, a cotton shirt, a patterned silk tie by Claiborne, perforated cap-toe leather lace-ups by Allen-Edmunds, a cotton handkerchief in his pocket, probably from Brooks Brothers; sunglasses by Lafont Paris lie on a napkin by his drink and a fairly nice attaché case from T. Anthony rests on an empty chair by our table. I'm wearing a vintage Yves Saint Laurent number that my stylist found at Internet-knows-where and my patented patent-leather Manolo Blahniks—not the ones I'm wearing now. That number fits my hips better than you could ever believe. The whole thing really made sense. While it's not the Imitation of Christ wedding dress conversion you *wish* you were seeing tonight, it was entirely sensible. Still, Todd's Ralph Lauren belt felt a little cheap."

No one knew that most of her monologue quoted *American Psycho* verbatim, but it wouldn't have mattered if anyone had. Despite the fact that no one could actually see her—and in fact, no one had ever seen a single glimpse of her, not even her parents, in all her 22 years—everyone knew that she looked particularly good in her Imitation of Christ conversion wedding dress.

Mikhail was so concerned with figuring out where exactly CGI was standing, where exactly her long, long story was coming from, that he didn't notice Chevy's swift exit or return. Before Mikhail could discern her exact location, Chevy passed out four shots around the newly expanded circle. CGI's tiny glass of Irish whiskey floated more eerily than the boys', but then disappeared a few seconds later. All the glasses got drank just the same.

"Did Todd even get it?" Chevy asked, reaching out like he was looking for her elbow. The simple movement was wholly awkward, like an old man blindly searching for a light switch on the wrong wall. When he smiled bigger, Mikhail knew that Chevy had found it.

"Todd didn't get a single thing the entire night," CGI said, the words just appearing from the faint nothingness of air. Her bubbling noise found its way from just below ear level to echo around and around until an actual originating place just seemed implausible. "He was marching alongside the Bolivian army all night."

"That's just like old Todd," Chevy said. And even Jayson raised an eyebrow at the brown-nosing bitchery that their normally cool and collected friend was spraying in CGI's direction.

"Bucky done gun, I'm off to meet Maya now," she said, perhaps smiling. "Are you going to the Weezy shindig at HD?"

"We'll be there," Mikhail said, with no idea on how. He just wanted to say something before Chevy further embarrassed himself.

"Tell Maya we said whattup," Chevy said, making a Jamie-Kennedy-b-boy pose. There was nothing Mikhail could do for a man intent on killing himself. Jayson shook his head disapprovingly, not able to hide his shock; it had always been his role to embarrass himself in front of girls. "I'll see you later, right?"

She didn't answer him. The pause was cumbersome.

"Bye guys!" she suddenly perked up, as if there was an action to follow.

Was she waving at them? Coming in for a hug? Throwing up goofy gang signs? There was no way to tell. Mikhail haphazardly threw out his palm, hoping for a hilarious-enough high-five. He didn't really know CGI. Someone or other had introduced them over a dozen times throughout the years, but Mikhail still wasn't sure that she remembered his name. They had never shared a single conversation worth a damn...so a high-five seemed more than appropriate.

Instead, a waft of wind nestled against his chest and squeezed around his mid-section. CGI was shorter than expected—she sounded much taller—and Mikhail thought it only polite to return her embrace. Rather than potentially smother her head in his armpits, he non-chalantly draped his arms around the small of her back. Tentatively clinging to a waist of the petite-est proportions, the delicate silk from CGI's Imitation of Christ wedding dress conversion might've been the most sensuous fabric Mikhail had ever touched. It was only surpassed by a tiny patch of skin that his pinkie grazed for a few seconds through a gap in her garment. He wondered if anything would ever feel that soft again.

"I'll see you later," she whispered into his chest.

She quickly moved onto to Jayson and appeared to give him a similar hug. Chevy was practically panting with anticipation, once again reaching out with his hand in a poor attempt to find the right switch. He got his hug and then CGI wandered off. Maybe. Perhaps she just took a step back and hovered around the potential conversation that'd waffle on about her. However, Mikhail and his friends were a little too seasoned to fall victim to such a trap. (She was probably the most popular person on the #720, able to yuk it up with Low's regulars and talk down with HD's debonairness. However, no one trusted her because she could never be seen, always hidden until she wanted to be found.) For nearly 10 minutes, the trio discussed nothing—basketball scores and the specifics of Jayson's work on the #4 and other things that would bore any girl to tears—and nothing more.

Mikhail took the free time to bite the bullet and check his phone. He really hoped that no one could see the fuckery displayed—17 missed calls and 22 unread text messages—and he quickly tucked the screen against his thigh. Where could he possibly even begin? At random, he selected Katya's most recent thorn-covered olive branch, and slyly lifted his phone's face so that only he could see it...even if CGI was hovering three inches behind him.

"I know I did you wrong and I'm sorry. I regret every bit of my actions. You are still so good to me. I guess I'm grasping for air bc I am going under. Pls baby, pls don't leave me"

He knew that Katya was going to have a hard time accepting the break-up, but it had been an entire week and he was really hoping that she was past the drowning stage of sorrow. If it was just one text message, instead of dozens, Mikhail might've felt something similar to sorrow. The second and last chapter of their relationship had lasted just over a year, but things moved quickly in The Internet. This break-up was for real. She just couldn't make him happy in a forever-type of way—not that he ever told her that in so many words. He told her that he was losing himself in every relationship, not just the romantic one. He said that it just wasn't working out. She slapped him and then buckled under her own weight, collapsing on his lap. It was then he realized that he never loved her; not when his main concern was the running mascara that bled onto a brand new pair of jeans. He left her apartment before she felt the conversation was finished and that was the last time he saw her, ignoring every one of her many attempts to continue talking about it. Mikhail scrolled to her seventh most recent message:

"I'm coming out tonight. Maybe I'll see you around… even if it's only for a yucky cigarette. :)"

With Katya floating around somewhere on the #720, Mikhail really needed his wingmen to be on their A-Game. He made sure that his phone was on vibrate and quietly tucked it into his pocket without responding to Katya's text messages. He thought about trying, but he just couldn't think of anything that wouldn't fail. Mikhail would just have to look over his shoulder all night. The #720 was a big place, maybe he'd find fate on his side.

He once told her that he began his nights at Low, and even if the place had changed, her marvelous memory hadn't. The best way to get caught was to stay in the same place, especially such a familiar one. He motioned to Chevy and Jayson something about a cigarette...Katya wouldn't wait in the smoking lounge all night without making sure that such a meeting was set in stone. Mikhail and friends would just have to keep the night moving.

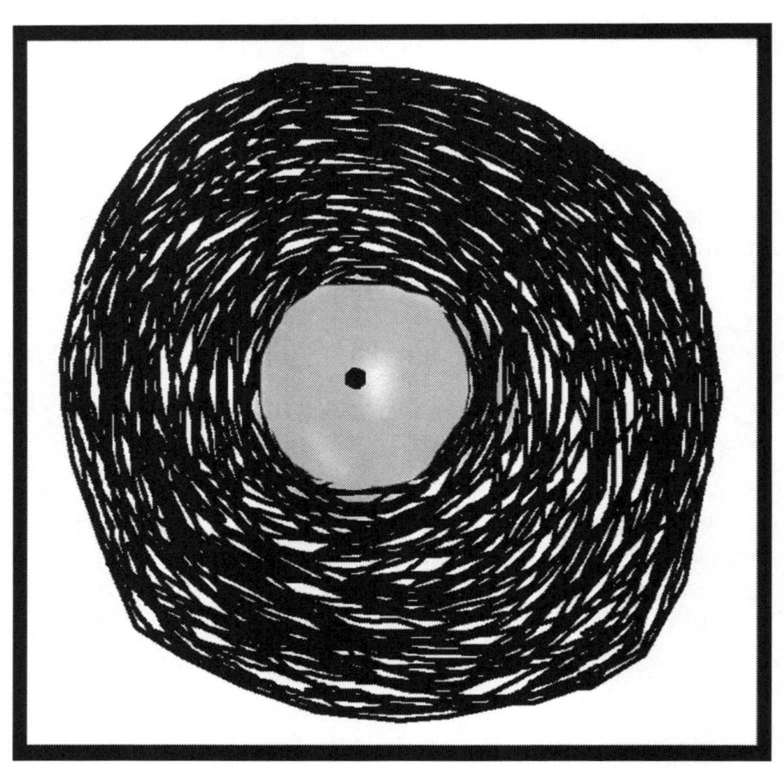

Visit http://PleaseUseRearExit.net/home/PUREhitz
to download Chapter Four's exclusive soundtrack by
DJ Original Bozak

Chapter Four
Peyton Manning's FuckFace

The first time Mikhail broke up with Katya was only a few weeks after they had begun to see each other, barely enough time to be considered an official couple in the first place. It was before he'd go back to her for a much longer and intense session, a second time around. Before he was backed into any sort of corner, when things still felt free or, at the very least, without dire consequences. It was before she began demanding changes in his life. Before he realized how deep in it he actually was. At that early stage of their first dance-less dosey-doh, Katya seemed good for him.

He wanted a positive influence over his negative choices. It seemed like growing up was something he was supposed to do, and growing up meant having a girlfriend who'd tell him all the things that he was doing wrong, even if it just echoed his own common sense. He thought that he wanted someone to push him to quit smoking and he knew that she'd push till her arms fell off. He also thought he wanted someone who needed the type of guidance that would help better his own path. He thought he wanted to learn how to love someone because that's what adults did. Adults made the concessions and sacrifices for the success of a relationship and that would make Mikhail a person. At least healthier.

But one weekend, at the end of that first go-around, Mikhail was genuinely ill. He had a horrible flu that made his bones ache. It sent horrendous chills through sore muscles and his throbbing nervous system. When they subsided, a ravenous fever dictated hallucinations of fire-soaked rats chewing on his burning feet in the tangled mess of a heavy comforter. The sweat was sickening once the chills returned.

He needed to stay in bed, but Katya needed to go out. She was consumed with a requirement from within to find worldly adventures and she desperately wanted Mikhail to join her. Even as party time came around and Mikhail started to feel a bit of relief from the virus's vicious hold, he thought it'd be wise to stay in bed, since he could still barely stand. He didn't want to risk the effects of exertion but she couldn't wait another minute.

Forever the Taurus, Katya bulled into the evening by herself. She had no plans to meet her friends or even much of a desire to make new ones. Perhaps it was pride that propelled her out and about, without her already-beloved Mikhail, or maybe it was an unconsciously devious effort to show how much she really needed him.

She began at Mid—a rather upscale bar on the #720—by drinking Smirnoff and cranberry juice with a twist of lime. There was a table in the corner with only a single chair and that's where she set up shop. It allowed her to hear the DJ without the intrusion of some stranger trying to sit next to her. It was the night's special guest, DJ Original Bozak, alum of her tiny high school message board, that made Katya's night out one of necessary evil. She ordered two drinks at a time, at first to make it seem like she was waiting for someone, but it quickly turned into an excuse to interact with the waitress less. (Fuck that waitress and her skinny thighs, Katya laughed to herself.) And even sooner, it became an opportunity to drink more with more haste. Before Original Bozak even got on the decks, Katya had already doubled the amount of Smirnoff in her double-orders of booze. Men came up to her and tried to begin conversations. She was curt with them, cold to the point of rudeness—at least for awhile. When Bozak hit the turntables though, her whole demeanor changed. Her venture into the nightlife became less about being independent and more about sticking it to Mikhail.

Katya kicked her chair to the wall and started dancing in place. Bozak's songs were her songs and she embraced every note of their nostalgia, even if many of the memories were brand new. Ain't no half steppin', you gotta do it good, like you know you should. *If Mikhail couldn't be there for her, then what good was he? He was sick because he smoked and because he was sick, he couldn't be there for her. When she really needed him. The night's soundtrack felt right, compelling her to dance like some sort of infection, until she suddenly knew every word, even to the songs she had never heard before. "Say captain, say what!" she soon started shouting alongside Bozak's selections. Katya's dance moves, as they always were, tended to be more aggressive than seductive. But dance she did and because a pretty girl can't dance alone in such a setting for too long, Katya's suitors began to show up in hordes.*

A man in a black t-shirt asked what she was drinking, and while he didn't get the joke about asking her invisible friend, he quickly brought back a pair of Patron shots. The high class shot choice was to show that his wardrobe choices weren't made out of economic necessity, but for fashionable choice. Katya finished the remainder of her sixth Smirnoff, in itself nearly three shots, before raising the newly-gifted tequila. "To everything we ever wanted to do," she said. After which she told the dude to fuck off because she already had a man.

The tequila did something fierce to Katya and even as Bozak played her favorite song about torturing insects, she couldn't stay at Mid for a minute more. She picked up her purse *and stumbled to the door, regaining a touch of composure once she entered the #720's great expanse. There was $120 in her pocket and The Sports seemed like the place to spend it.*

Muscle memory led her there, as her squinting eyes and spinning sense of direction surely would've failed. The place was eerily empty and she grabbed a seat right at the bar, right in the middle. Katya placed her four remaining $30 bills in a row and stared intently at their line of possibilities before dividing them into two simple piles. "This is for booze and this is for bets," she said to the bartender. "What's your whiskey recommendation and what games are still open?"

After he was told to stick his dick in a light socket for suggesting coffee, Katya was handed a Jameson-rocks and a score sheet. Every game was redacted except one: Patriots vs. Colts. The Pats' linebacker played for her alma mater (and Bozak's) and she put that $60 on the visiting team with a sense of childhood solidarity. Before half time, she had already opened up a tab on her credit card, having run through her allotted cash. But the Pats were winning and she exuberantly texted Mikhail that all was good...that she hoped he was feeling better.

Then came the Colts. Interceptions led to good field position and missed tackles led to touchdowns. She quickly became worried about the money she had spent and started ordering shots of well whiskey. After a three-and-out possession turned into a punt return for a score, Katya ordered four shots, but forgot to close out her tab, as she intended. Instead, she started to cry.

Mikhail was watching the same game, wrapped in sweats and blankets, fighting nicotine withdrawal along with his symptoms, when his phone rang. He could hear the commotion of the #720 in between violent tears and the sniffling of snot, but he couldn't make out a word Katya was attempting to say. There was a wrestling of the phone and a new voice came through Mikhail's end.

"Hey man, this is Ian," he said, Ian being Katya's ex-boyfriend. "I think you should come down here. It's kind of ugly."

By the time Mikhail made it to The Sports—after waiting 25 minutes for the Brown BTWN and then nearly passing out twice while onboard—Katya's sobbing was uncontrollable. Neighboring patrons worried that her dry heaves would turn wet at their feet. At the rate she was going, some joked that a lung or a tear duct might come up once all that booze did. Mikhail didn't know what to do. Because she was in no shape for anything other than collapse—not even signing her own name—he paid her obscene tab in cash and retrieved her card. He carried her out of The Sports, stopping only to hold back her hair as she vomited into one of the #720's municipal garden plots.

"I hate Peyton Manning's fuckface. He doesn't deserve it," she said, between upheavals. Even as Mikhail was on the BTWN for the end of what many would call a "classic game," he had caught Peyton's game-winning touchdown toss on the replay once inside The Sports. "He walks around with that fucking face. It's the same fuck face, whether he wins or loses, just a varying shade of gay, I mean gray, no, I mean gay."

"It's OK, squeazle, bad things happen in sports and that's why we watch and that's what makes gambling fun, even when we lose," Mikhail said. "There's thrill in the risk, but no risk without the possibility of failure."

Even as he fought the shivers, Mikhail was calm and trying to be calming. Her spots of vomiting required everything in him to keep from joining her. He just rubbed her back and tried to keep his inhaling in the other direction. "As shitty as it sounds now, there's always next year."

"I don't care about next year. I don't care about football. I care about getting my $60 back. Why can't you be a good boyfriend for once and get it back for me?"

It was the first time that Katya had referred to Mikhail as a boyfriend and it nearly made him drop her. Never mind the inference that he was bad at the job. He carried on and knew that such a job-title was to be no more (not knowing he'd regain it two months later). Step by increasingly heavy step, she passed deeper into drunken oblivion and he felt sicker and sicker. Mikhail felt the weight of her drooping body on his aching shins. If such an effort wasn't good enough, there was no way he could ever be good. They got to the #720/Brown BTWN transfer and that first bench was something of a miracle. And so they waited, as she drifted into sleep and he thought of civil ways to break things off.

The bus eventually came. En route, Mikhail tried to wake Katya up with abstract conversation, but it didn't work, and after the single stop to her Little Rectangle neighborhood, he had to carry her home. And he had to wait until she sobered up the next day, so she could remember his decision to end it for the first time.

Chapter Five
Avoiding Katya

The boys walked silently through the bar's heavy plaster doors. Mikhail braced himself for his first encounter with the #720's main terminal in several months. Turning the corner past Low was always his cue to turn his charms up. The party was around that corner. Each step had the potential for conversation. The light was harsher there. Bars and clubs, big and small, would clamor for his attention from both sides of the corridor. In their flat-screen-sized windows, blinding neon signs advertised anything a man could want, unless he wanted to see inside the club; that part of the screen was tinted. Along the path a slew of freestanding and rotating advertisements, mis-planned garden plots, fake plastic trees, and other such "city betterments" would stand in his way or distract him from whatever goal was at hand at that moment. And the ceiling would loom over everything. It was all familiar to Mikhail, but it was still something that he had to mentally prepare himself for.

On this night, traffic was starting to pile up. It wasn't quite chest-to-back, but it wasn't a walk in Square Park either. It didn't help that another load of Brown BTWN'ers piled through the transfer station's turnstiles at a nauseating rate, directly across from Low. A bunch of riled up 20-somethings couldn't walk fast enough into the #720's antics. People were already stepping on Mikhail's shoes. Their anticipation was natural, almost intrinsic, so he didn't allow himself to get angry. Per tradition, one that centered him a bit, Mikhail thought about the other side of the bus. They were transferring in from the Hollywood Hills and their expensive wines were ringing much louder than their stuffed-quail suppers; it was something to aspire for, even if he had no idea on how.

"We're in the clear now, right?" Chevy asked, slowly walking in the middle of Mikhail and Jayson. He was obviously (and embarrassingly) about to talk about CGI.

"Stop right there, boss," Mikhail said. "Before you go where I know you're going, think about this: think about everything that could be overheard, think about your self respect, man. Carefully, now...what the fuck just happened back there?"

Stuck in traffic, Chevy actually took a moment to think about what Mikhail had asked, then furiously shook his head like he was trying to sober himself up. His pupils might've rescinded some of their dilation.

"Sometimes, I just feel like I could marry that girl," Chevy said. Arms at his side, he had obviously regained a small portion of his cool. Some of the airiness had left his voice. "More than just a whirl," he said, "I want to twirl her world, tickle her like a woman, make her giggle like a girl."

It was something of an eclipse to come out of Low's as that part of the #720 snaked around its most notorious corner. On pace with everyone's shuffles, the corridor slowly opened up into a cavernous confusion of blinking lights and distractions. Mikhail looked out onto the holographic flames that stood atop plastic poles made to look wooden. Their luminescence reflected harshly over a distance too cold for actual fire and was easily drowned out by rows and rows of fluorescents hanging 100 feet above his head. The #720's silver ceiling curved deftly into its own shadows, disappearing into its own corners, laughing from on high at the scurry of people below.

"Please stop talking about her, please? We expect so much more from you. You're that dude we all look up to because of your game, not despite it. Right now, I don't even know who you are," Mikhail said. "Seriously though, can you guys do me a solid?"

"I refuse to blow you," Chevy said. "I don't care if you sneeze, I won't bless you. No atch-choo!"

"How about you just keep an eye out for Katya for me?" Mikhail asked. "And I'll punch you in the gut every time you act a fool in front of what's her name. Just watch out for me, aight?"

"Like she's some thirsty vampire trying to retire?"

"Or the alpha female of a hungry pack of squids, man?"

"I'm just not ready to deal with it yet," Mikhail said. "It's always such an ordeal with her. If it could just be some normal shit, I don't think I'd be avoiding her so pointedly."

"Are we supposed to protect you like some bodyguards? I'm not going to lie like a rat in a can, I'm not trying to body up another man, never mind bite some bitch's bullet in the line of duty, not even for a hundred grand."

"I don't care how many people are on this damn bus, I will run into her tonight, it's inevitable. You know my luck with shit like this."

"Remember that time you stole the ceramic goose from outside old man Winters' apartment?" Jayson smiled. "Drunk as you were, you carried all 30 pounds of that thing for miles, man, miles, bitching about the stains on your new jacket the entire time."

"All the way from the fuckin' Square, I carried that son of a bitch. It damn-near broke my arms. And then BAM! There he is coming from some poker game on Compton's Circle when I'm five minutes from my apartment. I had to bring that fucker all the way back the next day, hung over to all hell."

"You did not run into dude holding his goose," Chevy chipped in, "did you?"

"I did."

"And now you're walking around with some shit-covered goose of Katya's?"

"I am, but, I mean, I just broke up with the girl. That's it."

And it was true, people ended relationships everyday. Nearly all of them lived to tell another tale...and tag another tail. Mikhail broke up with a girl, that's it. It was the life of a 20-something in Los Angeles. He really had no guilt to bear, other than the typical heartbreak shit, because he always treated her right. He dumped her the prior week, the second and final time, only because he didn't have the balls to start all the drama two months before. Breaking up meant a hassle that he wasn't sure he could handle, so he procrastinated. It was easier to coast in unhindered unhappiness then it was to flip a switch for all those tears and curses and hatred and sobbing declarations of unrequited love. Once he realized that he was making up excuses to avoid sex just so he could go home and masturbate, Mikhail stopped procrasturbating. Tired of shitting, he got off the pot.

"Really though, man," Jayson said, obviously concerned, "what do you need from us?"

"Just don't let me get bum-rushed or blind-sided," Mikhail said. "Even a minute head's up will help me prepare, but, seriously, if you can say that you haven't seen me, that'll be for the best."

"We got you, man."

Jayson was always reliable that way, as a friend and with his overuse of "man" as a pronoun. Mikhail aspired for Jayson's unflappable loyalty yet loathed his friend's vague non-commitment that he occasionally saw in himself. Sludgy in dress and pudgy in stance, Jayson was the polar opposite of Chevy. He was soft-spoken and hard of hearing, while Chevy was loud with uncannily acute ears. Jayson never said a word in the presence of strangers, while Chevy carried conversations. On-one-one, when words surpassed the need for clever witticisms, Jayson was an astute listener armed with genuine advice, while Chevy shot wink-worthy blanks. To the party, Chevy brought fun, Jayson brought a buried reality. They both exercised specific qualities in Mikhail that he was convinced he couldn't find on his own. Chevy made him a player; Jayson made him a human.

"She does know that you guys broke up, right?" Chevy asked.

He led the path to The Smoke, but Jayson kept looking back at Mikhail. Chevy hit pounds and slapped palms in mid-stride, never stopping to politic to any of the many that he knew by name. Jayson and Mikhail would've continued on even if he had. This time, his mission was aligned with theirs, for now. At the very least, his broad shoulders and unconcerned procession opened up easier paths...Chevy had no problem breaking right through dedicated conversations. The inevitable step back that the talking obstacles would take made Mikhail and Jayson's journey more accessible.

"I may take awhile to make my decision, but once I do it, I do it. She cried all over my jeans—fuckin' make-up everywhere. It was a mess. She has to know. She has to."

"Ha!" Chevy blurted out.

"What the fuck's that all about? Was it a joke Todd told you last weekend?"

"You just know how to dance around confrontation, that's all. Just enough to leave doors cracked open," Chevy replied, completely skipping over what he didn't want to hear. "It's like you're trying to do shawty a favor by sparing her feelings. Sometimes you gotta be an asshole, dunny, and I ain't being funny."

"She knows. I know. And I definitely know that there's no need to continue a conversation that's already concluded. Why are we still talking about this? We're still walking with a purpose, right?"

"Smoke the cancer stick, bet. With hopes of getting my dick wet."

And with that lyrical mantra rhyming in their heads, the boys walked the remaining five minutes to The Smoke. At the entrance, a surprisingly large woman blocked two glaring panes of glass that marked the first half of a set of double-doors. The woman stood even taller than Chevy, who made a healthy habit of talking about his above-average stature. She tilted her fingers left and right a few times as they tried to walk by. It was a little melodramatic.

"Let's see some identification, boys."

"C'mon, Shirley, what are you doing working on a Friday?" Chevy interrupted. "The man's keeping you down... and don't he know that that's this man's job?"

Shirley blushed. Jayson and Mikhail saw that Chevy's mojo had completely returned. If he kept up his flirtations with Shirley, they might be able to skate on the $30 fee.

"What time you get out? Maybe you should come by MySpace and Twitter my Yahoo! until I Google all over your Facebook...my little squeazle."

Maybe it was because Chevy wore a watch worth her salary on his wrist, but his string of double-entendres worked, non-sensical as they were. Shirley punched Chevy in the arm. Hard. Then she stamped the inside of his right wrist, along with Mikhail's and Jayson's. Past Shirley, in between the two doorways—entranced in the entrance's purgatory— Mikhail ran to the front and put his hand into the chest of Chevy, who was immediately crashed into by Jayson. The three of them comically piled up inside the glass passageway's claustrophobic clown car interior.

"Squeazle?" Mikhail said, annoyed at Chevy's very particular use of his pet name for Katya. "She might be here, seriously. Let's not cause a scene in here, please."

"Your squeazle doesn't smoke," Jayson said, happy to get in on the game.

"Ha! Her desperation reeks like tobacco on a non-smoker," Chevy said.

"If she's here, she's probably over on the left. There'll be plenty of shawties over on the right."

"Wasn't the first time you rodents kissed over here on the left side?"

"Are you really asking to be the first person in my entire life that I have to punch in the face?" Mikhail said, still only a few inches from his two friends. Of course, he'd never waste his first punch on Chevy—that honor was reserved for Robert Horry.

Chevy and Jayson settled down and nonchalantly showed that they understood Mikhail's predicament. They passed through the second set of doors and were immediately smacked in the face by a cloud of cigarette smoke. It burned their nostrils and put predictable pause on their decision to light one up at all. The room was long and narrow, but with more space to maneuver than the line's main terminal. As a rule, most smokers held out on their first cigarette as long as they could (as they did for The Restroom). Mikhail quickly sought out a piece of railing on the right side, far in the corner. Directly under a set of flood lights, he felt rather invisible and content with a clear view across most of The Smoke. With his back wedged into the railing's vertex of a vortex, he was convinced that no one could sneak up behind him. And they certainly couldn't get through the yards of steel and titanium supports and everything else that separated the #720's inside from The Internet outside.

Next to them, triplets in varying shades of purple sipped green tea and moaned loudly about the need for breeze. They rapidly fanned themselves with someone's iPad. Their uniformly straight black hair hardly moved. They talked amongst themselves, lighting cigarettes while their already-lit smokes sat in Lucite ashtrays, quickly forgotten. The ambers of wounded-soldiers-left-unaccounted-for kept burning, even as they brought wooden matches to a chronic assembly line of virgin stogies. They seemed to only recognize the blunder when moving to put the blackened matches in the ashtray. Staring down at the plumes of rising smoke from all those cigarettes still burning, the triplets laughed aggressively. Whether it was simply a plunder of epic FAIL or they just liked to laugh—an inside joke sprung from the same placenta—Mikhail would never know. But it did provide its opportunities, and Mikhail yanked away a barely-smoked cigarette from the triplets' ashtray.

"Hey!"

"We were—"

"—smoking those!"

The inhale of tobacco was glorious to Mikhail's insides, even as it most-likely killed him, bit by bit. They said it rarely did and he had never known anyone to die from cigarettes, but there was something darkening about it. He could feel its path get pulled across his core inch by inch, with more totality than the secondhand variety of the clouded room. There was something warming about the individuality of his dragon breath, even in a room full of people feeling just as unique. The thickness of posturing was heavier than the entirety of the room's exhalations.

"Oh, shut your yappers," Jayson awkwardly said, a beat too many after the interaction. "You couldn't smoke all the ones still burning if you used all nine of your holes. Besides, you look like you can fuckin' afford—"

"—to give my good friend a lesson in graciousness," Chevy stepped in, probably a little too late for even him to recover any chance with the triplets. "He's an asshole. Have a good night."

Until Jayson got drunk, he was incredibly rude to potential female accompaniment. And forget about the instances where the ratio of boys and girls was even. Jayson refused to take one for the team if it'd put him in the precarious position of being the third man alone with the third woman.

He grabbed two cigarettes, dramatically sucking down one, while placing the other behind his ear. Chevy grabbed one from his own pack and jerked Jayson away before he could say anything else. The girls shuffled away too.

"That cock is constipated and it's making you cantankerous," Chevy said.

"Yeah, you gotta get laid...or at least get some kind of a release."

"Man, you guys have been busting my balls since we met up," Jayson said, this time with more sadness than madness in his voice. Then Mikhail's ringer went off. With no idea how it was turned on, he was visibly startled while rushing to silence his phone. Jayson started laughing. "At least my girlfriend leaves me alone for a night. Lulz."

"But he's got a better chance of fucking his squeazle, than you have of emptying your weasel or parting the two legs of an easel. But shit, you're right, Mikhail definitely still has a squeazle."

"Wow. Just wow. So lazy you're rhyming the same word twice now? I keep ignoring her, she has to get the point eventually."

"Well, there's your problem," said a man in the calmest of demeanors. He'd been eavesdropping but Mikhail wasn't too offended, being guilty of the same faux-pas, leaning against the same railing...many, many times. Space was tight and voices carried. "Women of a certain accord need to be broken up with at least twice. Once = spurned, twice = earned. It's all elementary math, but it helps in deciphering the ladies of the night and the ladies you want your parents to meet. Only one of those types deserves our troubles, and it's not the one catching a facial in the men's room."

He wore a red polo from Polo tucked into a leather-belted pair of pleated khakis. His hubris gave him away, even if his kinda familiar baby-face didn't exactly fit the typical mold.

This man was a member of the TSABDD. Mikhail waited for him to reach into his pocket and pull out a card.

"I'm Armstrong. Been a member for 19 months and had sex with 132 women in the span. If you want to make that girl... what's her name again?"

"Katya," Mikhail said, not having said her name in his presence until then.

"If you want Katya to stop calling, hit me up. We're spreading the science of subtext in a text. Seriously, one text message and it'd be over and painless. It's all in the math, brother. DM me, I'm @PUREarmstrong. Take my card."

Armstrong walked off and Mikhail rapidly took the last two drags of his cigarette, already wanting one more. He reached into the triplets' ashtray and then struck a match from the pack they had left behind.

"Once = spurned, twice = earned? WTF does that mean? That's some gibberish ish, right there," Chevy said. "I leave math in my office on the #111, and I've never had a problem getting laid."

"Whatever, I gotta take a leak," Mikhail said, thumbing the card as he placed it in his back pocket, right next to the violently blinking red light on his cell phone. He wasn't done with his second cigarette, but was willing to do anything that'd leave this conversation about Katya behind. Stamping out his Camel half-smoked, he led the procession towards The Smoke's exit.

Visit **http://PleaseUseRearExit.net/home/HORRY**
for an honest account of the most evil player
in the history of basketball.

Chapter Six
Mr. Sallow's Hallow

A little reluctantly, Mikhail decided to break his seal. He knew it'd be a long night of restroom excursions the second he did, but there was no reason to delay the inevitable. There was a scale in which he rated all the paralyzing moments when piss so consumed him that his teeth swam, but this one barely made the top 100. He was thankful that it didn't because even as early in the night as it was, there was a healthy line waiting for the #720's sickly men's room. Sans Jayson and Chevy—who were still too proud to pee—the wait gave him too much time to look at the dilapidated existence that surrounded him.

Small patterns of tiny tiles twirled upwards in swift patterns of swirls, and at one point in time, they were a prime example of human craftsmanship. No matter though, as the once-immaculate tiles were barely visible beneath a vile layer of filth. Tag marks were scraped by pens or fingernails into the quarter-inch of sheer disgustingness. Mikhail was sick to his stomach at the thought of someone digging their fingers through the collection of airborne urine and mildew. He might've thrown up in his mouth, just a little bit, at a deposit of gunk trapped under the hard dorsal surface of a digit, but he stopped himself before his imagination got there. He just stared at the muck's depth and wondered if it was growing before his eyes. And wherever that smell was coming from, it wasn't worth mumbling about, for fear of having to breathe it in any further.

Mikhail peered around the line and saw a slew of empty receptacles. The available options were evidently too close to other players' property for the long line's comfort. They were waiting for a one-urinal buffer on either side, and at such a rate, that line was never going to move. Mikhail bypassed the homophobes and went straight to an empty pisser, right next to his old friend. Straddling the far john, just as he always did, Mr. Sallow hummed and urinated.

"Mikhail, my man in mayhem, how's the outside world ticking away?"

"You know full well there ain't an outside world," Mikhail said. Just to his right, opposite Mr. Sallow, a man stood angrily with a blond-dyed goatee and perforated leather jacket. Mikhail was careful not to look too hard and instead turned back towards Mr. Sallow. "You're the only thing standing still in this entire Internet-forsaken city."

And it was true, Mr. Sallow never moved. It was unconfirmed how long he'd been standing at the far john in the #720's municipal men's room, forever relieving himself, but it started well before the times of anyone that Mikhail actually knew. Legend held that they had to build the entire bus system around his urinating stance, but that seemed to be a stretch. However, one thing was for certain: Mr. Sallow was as unmovable and unfailingly flowing as a stone-cold fountain ever could be.

"The whole thing just moves too quick for my memory," Mr. Sallow said, as healthy as he always was in his stream. "But as long as the information flows, we're bound to 'Net a fish or two, or so the saying goes."

"You'd know what this whole thing is supposed to mean better than I would," Mikhail said, finally finding the momentum to let go of the very burden that brought him to the bathroom in the first place.

"I don't know squat-diddly-cum-quickly...other than what I do and don't doo-doo."

Mr. Sallow didn't like anyone else to address his tenure, but he himself often made self-deprecating jokes about his permanent fixture. Mikhail's bladder blotter was long, and since he'd come of age to join the drunken escapades of the #720, he'd probably spent hours and hours pissing alongside Mr. Sallow. Separated by the few inches between matching one-gallon-per-flush American Standards, as they stood on this night, the two men had grown close. Mr. Sallow's advice was as reliable as his micturition.

"You ever wonder where all this shit—"

"—and piss goes?" Mr. Sallow interrupted.

"Yeah," Mikhail said. "Are we just leaving a trail of excrement in The Internet as we go? Marking our territory on tracks already laid out?"

"And we wonder why the squids are coming through the walls," Mr. Sallow said, only kind of laughing.

Mikhail stared at the sharpied graffiti sprawl staring back at him. Mostly names and years, the writing was speckled with snot and buried under the filth, fighting razor and fingernail carvings. Despite their best efforts, the vandals' sentences fell incomplete over missing tiles. One ambitious bathroom poet had scribed a mathematical formula that allegedly had something to do with getting laid. The variables were marked "S", "E", and "X", but the equation hardly looked balanced. It was the signature of some drunken fool who couldn't afford the start-up fee to join the TSABDD.

Inside the basin, the neon yellow was turning feverish with every drop. The piss of many men was intermingling and chemically reacting for an other-worldly glow. The stench of its ammonia was harsh and violent, wafting nearly to the point of visibility, perhaps boiling into a gaseous compound of airborne waste.

"You still with that fine little thing you snuck in here a few weeks ago?"

"No sir. It's been a year since that happened," Mikhail said. "Wild fucking night, though. I'm not sure I could muster up one like that again. That adventurousness has left my blood. But, no, no. No, we're not together. Just this week in fact, I had to dead it."

"Mayhem got to be too much?"

"Something like that," Mikhail said. The ammonia, without so much as a flush for nearly an hour, suddenly overtook him. It almost put him flat on his back in mid-stream. He wanted to steady himself, but he didn't dare to touch the wall. "If it wasn't for you, brother, I'd feel like a complete candidate for the adult diaper. I piss way too much."

Mikhail finished his process with a firm shake. He was careful not to dip his eyesight too far below the horizon, as such looks often got confused for invitations (to fight or fuck, typically). Out of habit—and maybe because he hadn't used a high-traffic toilet in several months—he flushed, cursing himself the second he did. In the #720's municipal men's room, it was best not to touch anything but one's own dick. And had Mikhail managed that, he would've been morally okay with not washing his hands before leaving.

As he walked away from the urinal, he could feel the grimy floor's sticky attempts to keep him flat-footed. The off-white linoleum was littered with browned and yellowed footprints, sprinkled with pieces of trash, grasping out at anything that had a better life than it did. After a few noisy steps, Mikhail could no longer hear the basin-filling pour—one that made Mr. Sallow infamous—rise against his porcelain pisser. At the sink, and with a disinterested level of grief, he discovered an empty soap dispenser. He let the lukewarm water run over his hands. Leaning in towards the mirror, he debated the shade of red in his eyes. Everything behind him locked green and his entire color reference was off. A TV screen in the left corner of the room flashed the BTN logo and its founder's smiling face.

Eyeing a few-hours-old five o'clock shadow in his reflection, a lone pimple peaked out. Perhaps the result of an in-grown hair, it was nothing that'd ever be spotted in the dim lights of whatever club he was about to explore. The faucet's splash was hardly above room temperature and, against better judgment, he slurped several palmfuls, already thirsty for post-booze water. Regardless of color, it was soothing, and so he let it run into a sink spotted with tobacco-stained loogies and crusted toothpaste. Glancing back up in the mirror, he saw the man with the perforated leather jacket and dyed goatee take off that perforated leather jacket, and then his shirt, stuffing the black tee into the beat-up coat's sleeve. Mikhail cautiously watched the stripping man, but it was quickly apparent that his sole intention was just some old fashioned freshening up.

"Whatchu drinking on tonight, Mr. Sallow?" Mikhail yelled. It was the loudest he had spoken in a long time. So rare for him to raise his voice, it gave him a little spook. He pulled down a neatly folded towel from the stand to his right. Entire sections of the fabric scratched his face, but he did as the Public Health Inspector (PHI) recommended, and found the softer, cleaner parts of the towel. He avoided the coagulates of cloth that no one wanted to talk about.

"Would love a White Russian, if you could spare it."

"Are you trying to be funny, brother? Is that some sort of dig at my name?"

"No, son, I could just really use the calcium."

Nodding and drying his hands, Mikhail leaned back. The shirtless man next to him at the urinal was now next to him at the sink. Both his hot and cold knobs were on full blast and the steam rose louder than the faucet's deafening thunder. Behind them, while the Party Kids continued to move in and out without washing their hands, another man began to shave in the round communal sink at the center of the bathroom. His foot was steady on the pedal, pushing water through the circular spigot.

Its pressure was meager and his shavings floated in the murky water at the base. He was bleeding in a few places and large drips blotted the soapy mix in slow-motion cannonballs.

After giving himself one last reassuring glance, Mikhail handed the PHI-approved towel to the shirtless man at the adjacent sink. With it, the man squeeze-dried his sopping wet armpit hair. He wiped his face and then around his waist and under his belt. He dipped deeper and dried his balls with the cloth when he thought no one was looking. He put on his black t-shirt and then his perforated leather jacket, before folding the towel and placing it back on the stand. By that point, however, Mikhail had long walked out of the room.

Chapter Seven
Fortune of Spears

Mikhail walked out into the main terminal alone. The relative stillness of the bathroom behind him was long gone, lost in the movements of too many people. They were all striding along on an infinite number of paths and he could've followed any number of them. They moved in and out in different directions, theirs and others, but with only a general sense of destination. It was a long waddle towards a place, not a purpose.

Mikhail had no idea. Where was he supposed to go? Perhaps, he wasn't drunk enough yet. He'd need to piss at least two more times before he'd consider himself sufficiently incapacitated. Further confusing things were the absences of Chevy and Jayson. They might've already moved onto the next club. The predictability among their choices—The Sports, Mid, or maybe just hovering around the corridor—made Mikhail want to explore a new option. The bigger clubs wouldn't quite be worth a damn, yet. And besides, he knew that a little fellowship was still a necessary crutch. Mikhail decided to post up and watch the Friday night procession—the best way to find a lost party was to stay in one place.

But it wouldn't be beyond Chevy and Jayson to jet off before Mikhail could get out of the bathroom. They had done it before. Leaning against the wall, he thought about the hypothetical debate the two of them would have about where to go. Chevy would probably rhyme about Anything and Jayson would suggest they wait around for another minute or two. As the conversation played across Mikhail's head, he started walking towards Anything. And then his phone started vibrating. He silenced it and kept walking. And then it rang again. He waited to see if it'd vibrate in his pocket a few more times or whether Katya's attempt to reach him was just a text message…but it kept ringing. He silenced it and then it rang it again.

Without his friends around to hide his pride from, furious with the constant barrage of buzzing, distraught by her reality where "no" apparently didn't mean no, Mikhail answered his phone.

"Really? Like, what the fuck, really? What can we possibly make better right now?"

"…"

"We broke up, Katya; deal with it already. Maybe I didn't make it clear, but I hope this is picture-perfect: stop… fucking…calling…me."

"I'm so proud of you I could cry, the parent in the crowd ready to die, you're all grownsied up and just yesterday, a small fry."

Mikhail hadn't even looked at who was calling; he had only assumed. And for once, he really wished it'd been Katya. Even when things were happy, he'd never been that genuinely direct with her. And he certainly never raised his voice like that. Instead, Chevy caught the brunt of his boil.

"Fuck, my bad, man, I thought you were—"

"Obviously," Chevy said, speaking loudly through Mikhail's ear piece. "You thought I was Katya and you know what? I really am that proud."

"Where you at, you condescending bastard?"

"I remember Amy, she used to AIM me. She stayed up late and used to blame me. She say I'm too wild, she wanna tame me. I told her 'Even Photoshop couldn't change me.'"

"Oh, aight, I see you," Mikhail closed his phone and made his way through the crowd towards the taller-than-average Chevy who was still spitting some shit into his phone. He hadn't heard Mikhail hang up.

"It takes you longer to piss than a malcontent monger does to hiss," Chevy said, once Mikhail got close. "Me? I'm from the Apple, which means I'm a Mac. She's a PC, she lives in my lap."

Nobody knew what was next, but they all knew that time had to be killed before they fought off 90,000 other Angelinos who would later try to get into the Weezy concert held at a venue that fit 1,000. Jayson pointed to the booze cart that was several yards to the right, and after nodding in unison, they all walked in that general direction until Chevy decided to sit on a set of stairs that lead to no door.

"I'll pay for all of our drinks if one of you goes and deals with those guys...and maybe picks up the tip," Chevy said, so seriously. Jayson gave Mikhail a simple yet regretful look that said everything that could be said: Jayson's unnamed and completely absent girlfriend wouldn't loosen his wallet enough to allow the social-economics of chipping in on the gratuity. Chevy handed Mikhail a $30 bill and started saying something about the amount of pussy that'd populate the Weezy concert. There was no real reason for Mikhail to question Chevy's ability to get them into HD, where Weezy was scheduled to perform, or the fact that $30 wouldn't quite cover the tab for three drinks. He knew that he just had to go along with it.

Freestanding advertisements whizzed passed him. Backlit pictures of hamburgers, strippers, $180 pairs of jeans, seductively posturing smokers, and community messages stood in Mikhail's way. Above him, an actor on a billboard sheepishly looked at the actresses who respectively played his wife and mother-in-law. "Bless This Mess" it said, airing at 8 PM on Thursdays. Sidestepping the obstacles and ignoring the over-reaching banners that stretched around him, Mikhail went with the flow and the flow brought him to a booze cart without a wait. Pushed by a glowing man—his translucent skin absorbing and then redistributing the terminal's artificial light—the cart was an operation of opossum, and Mikhail wasn't sure if it was dead or ready for business.

"You pushing any whiskey tonight, boss?" he asked.

"Yeah, yeah, we're open. Just because I ain't gots one of those fancy signs...yeah, well, we gots Jack Daniels, Black Label, Jameson, Dewars, Scoresby...whatchu wannnit mixed with?"

"Just a little ice. Give me a Jameson-rocks, a double, please," Mikhail said. He watched the shirtless man move in obvious pain. His bones looked ready to rip through his stretching-to-the-brink skin and Mikhail wondered if the hunched-over man just wanted a little conversation. "All due respect, sir, but why do you say we? Do you have a bar-back hidden back there? There's not too much space behind you."

The man turned his back to reveal a grotesque growth grinning at Mikhail from just below his left shoulder blade. The growth had its eyes sewed close, a mouth with razor sharp teeth, two holes ostensibly for breathing, and a frail arm that reached out towards Mikhail. While the man hued a greenish glow, whatever was on his back seemed to suck all the light into its deep purple skin. There was an emptiness around it, like the periphery of a black hole that destroyed even the darkness that came close.

"That'll be 12 dollarssss, sssssssmart assssss," the growth answered.

"Also, give me a High Life and a tequila soda, and three Jameson shots, if you could." Mikhail paired Chevy's bill with two of his own and placed them into the purple growth's terrifying three fingers. He scraped its scaly skin in the process of transaction and shuddered as the sliminess interacted with his own hand.

"We sssshall provide for theee customersssss," it said.

"Tell your friends," the man said, turning back around. "We walk up and down all night, pouring heavenly shots of hellish liquids."

Mikhail glared at his plastic cup overflowing with Jameson and three ice-cubes and knew it'd be that kind of night. A few more drinks like this straight vat of whiskey would leave him flat. He left a decent tip and carried the shots over to Chevy and Jayson, who were already getting into it.

"I'm supposed to tell you fools that those guys pour a stiff drink," he said.

"And Jayson is trying to tell me that The Internet should be free, no honey debt for the bee."

Mikhail handed off the shots and went back to the booze cart to retrieve their follow-ups without giving a single thought to whatever his friends were discussing. Katya was still out there, as were new girls who wouldn't try to ruin his night. Eventually he'd run into one or the other.

"Nothing is for free, man," Jayson said, "but it seems backwards to keep The Internet out of reach to anyone without a six-figure salary."

"I don't care about The Internet, let's just drink these," Mikhail said. "No toast, just booze, please."

"I'm just saying, I make the damn parts for these buses," Jayson said, raising his plastic cup of a shot anyway. "Man, I just want to see what the shit looks like."

They all drank their Jameson and Mikhail fetched the remainder of drinks. He made room for himself on the concrete steps between Chevy and Jayson upon his quick return. They stared up at the "Bless This Mess" banner that flanked above the bars that they had no use for, the advertisement's ambiguous nature discouraging them from exploring the cowboy-booted or candy-rave-coated contents in the establishments below. Mikhail could tell that the whiskey shot wasn't his friends' cup of tea as they struggled with its gaseous aftermath. He could drink the shit straight, alongside a steak dinner, but used his chaser first anyway. There were too many ongoing pissing contests to worry about who could best man-up a little liquor. That his chaser was just more whiskey was a quiet victory in itself.

"It's pretty sweet, guys, and maybe tonight's the night for you," Chevy said. "One look at The Internet and bitches get wet...bet."

"OK, now I'm on it," Mikhail said. He didn't want to get into a conversation about The Internet because just like politics and religion, the words always turned chats into debates. And Mikhail didn't have time for debates, but he couldn't help himself. "I can't look at this shit anymore. Why do we get stuck with this goofy sitcom guy and his mother-in-law and sexless wife when all the rich motherfuckers get to gaze upon The Internet? I'm 27-years-old and I don't even know what's keeping me on these buses. It's stupid."

"I know that overhearing is absurdly rude and that interrupting is an even worse offense," said a woman in a white veil, rudely interrupting their overheard conversation. "But the divide exists for a reason. And more importantly, The Internet's inaccessibility exists for a reason. If beauty was meant for everyone, then beauty wouldn't exist at all. There needs to be a curve of comparison and socialism only creates a flat line of ugly."

The woman sauntered in her stance with a vicious set of curves. The waterfall of lace that flowed from her head snugly wrapped around her body in a single piece of fabric that only broke for seductive peaks at her skin. Her cleavage clear in sight, the white lace went down and around an unrealistic waist, before shelving off into an ass that walked a full step and a half behind her legs—legs shrouded in a grace of over-indulgence. It was the second wedding dress that they had encountered in the past hour and Mikhail wondered if he was missing some sort of ceremony.

The woman had dark eye-shadow and speckles of jewels glued all over her face, the combination of which accentuated the manic batting of her eyes. It was never certain where she was looking and her make-up was quite happy about the ambiguity.

"If you'll excuse me, ma'am," Chevy said, embellishing the regal protocol and dropping the rhymes, as he always did when talking to a member of society's upper crust, "I happen to agree with your stance on imposed regulations of the poor, but let me play Analog's advocate for a minute...The Internet exists as a power beyond human reconciliation. It is Los Angeles' deity and to deny anyone access to their God would be sinful, am I right? That is, of course, just my own humble interpretation of the gospel blogs."

"The gospels were written to keep order among a society without it. Access is just a want of the sinful. God created The Internet for the people he deemed worthy, i.e. those whom capitalized upon Its great powers. If the poor really wanted to see The Internet, they'd work their way into a position where they could. One shouldn't blame the prophets for the sloth of the lazy."

"The prophets never would have lumped the lazy with the incapable," Chevy respectfully said, "and they'd be the first to open up the shutters for those who couldn't afford to see it on their own accord."

"You wouldn't know what it's like," Jayson said, winding up to deliver another blow to yet another unsuspecting female, "you have no idea. You were born with a silver spoon for every despicable hole."

Mikhail hit Jayson with a look full of scorn and tried to intervene. "He's a little bitter for some reason. It's just that we're not stupid, we work hard, do our best to be productive members of society...it just seems like a lot of bullshit to keep something so simple as the outside away from us. Plus, Jayson here probably just likes you. He flirts like a confused fourth-grader."

"Knowing that you've never looked upon The Internet, I don't expect that you know who I am," the woman said, speaking down to Jayson and Mikhail, both of whom were still seated. She took care to nod at Chevy, as if to exclude him from whatever she was about to say. "But even a cursory glance at the despicable advertisements that surround you should provide a clue about my importance."

"I've never seen The Internet," Mikhail said, "but I've seen too many promotional posters and screens for my own liking—"

"And he still has no idea who the fuck you are," Jayson said. "And neither do I."

"I am Britney Spears," she said. "Brit-Brit by some, including Perez, Fortune of Spears by others. I'm known as Divine Diva by man, but to your ears, my real name might as well be unpronounceable, it would be nothing but binary code. That is just the tip of my legacy, but who are you to inquire my name?"

"I'm Jayson. Friend to these dudes and boyfriend of a woman who'll remain nameless. Does that make me royal and capable of acceptable condescension too?"

"I have never, in all my life, been accosted like this. Even the lowly factory rats, who flock into those Internet-forsaken bars with the cheap beer and peanuts, would never dare say the things you've said to me in such a tone. Even the irreparable members of the disgusting TSABDD have enough reverence in their coarse tongues for the affable words afforded to my station of being. I am not just a slave for you. I am not just the naked skin of desire—certainly not for those unaccounted for."

As the words rolled over her religiously forked words, Mikhail looked down towards her ankle. Surely enough, there was a serpent intertwined with barbed wire, Chinese characters and a butterfly—the very symbol of Britney Spears. Below her tattoo, the strapped sandals suddenly seemed more expensive than the combined outfits of Mikhail and his friends.

"Please excuse my insolence," Mikhail said, trying his hand at Chevy's sudden burst of formality. "I did not recognize you. I've never seen The Internet and rarely cavorted with Its captors, but the question remains....why can't common folk have windows into Its beauty?"

"It's like, fuck," Jayson blurted, "I've heard stories about The Internet since I was a kid, but my parents weren't rich or anything, so all I got was stories. And that's kinda shitty."

"If The Internet was for everybody," Britney Spears said, "then surely you'd have more than tales to tell."

And with that, she curtsied and walked off into the distance.

Chevy got up from the stairs and made a big deal out of stretching his back, arching and yawning and reaching without concern. He handed Mikhail and Jayson one of those stale faces and they too got up, making similar gestures of soreness.

"Which way are we going?" Jayson asked, looking left and then right and mumbling something about stupid bitches under his breath.

"I don't want to do one of those nights where we just walk around in circles looking for the next best thing," Mikhail said. "Is there a destination? Preferably one that Katya wouldn't want to attend?"

"Let's just walk and talk and hope your pitcher don't balk."

"I hate those rich bitches," Jayson said. "I'm sorry if I fuck up your game, but fuck, that hoity-toity attitude just ruins my night."

"You sure it isn't your lack of release?" Chevy asked, actually kind of concerned.

"Don't start this up again, man."

"He's got a point," Mikhail said. "You get so aggro the minute a girl—that isn't your girl—is around. It shouldn't be that way. Not that I know how you are around her, either."

"It is what it is, man, but really? This is what it's all about, a bunch of dudes having a Friday night out," Jayson said, following Chevy and Mikhail through the #720's crowd. "I don't know why we keep talking about all the shit that brings us down. Since we got here, it's been all Katya and restrictions and honey-dew lists and—"

"Wait, wait, wait," Chevy said, stopping all movement to turn around and look Jayson in the eye. "What the fuck is a honey-dew list? Sounds like some triflin' ish.."

"You know," Jayson said before his voice raised three octaves to an unseemly mocking pitch, "Honey do this. Honey do that. Honey, take out the trash. Honey, change the sheets. Honey, sweep the kitchen floor. Honey, do the bills. Honey, do the trimming in the hallway. Honey, trim my toenails."

"Honey, trim my toenails?" Chevy's jaw was aghast. "That ain't real."

"It's real, man," Jayson said. "Leaning over like that makes her Cri du Chat act the fuck up. Extreme vertigo. She gets dizzy, starts bleeding from her tear ducts, it gets nasty."

"So she can't lean over and give you head?" Mikhail asked, definitely concerned.

"Every once in awhile, she's alright if I stand up and she kneels, but her knees aren't that good either."

"No, no, no. There's a big difference between standing and getting head—great for random locations like the #780 or something—but nothing beats lying back comfortably. And only every once in awhile?"

"And sex is completely out of the question?" Mikhail added.

"She has teeth up inside her," Jayson said. "Would you wanna risk that? And even if I did, those teeth are sensitive to the touch, like my dick was dry-ice frozen ice cream. I don't want to hurt her...but seriously, I take out the trash. I sweep the kitchen floor. I trim her toenails. Let me get my dick sucked while sitting in a chair, you know?"

"No," Chevy said, matter of factly. "We have no idea what you're talking about. It raises doubt. That sounds like hell. An angel fell, no ring for your bell."

"Whatever, Brit-Brit is a cunt. And fuck you guys, too."

As they walked towards an unknown destination, Mikhail started to get a bad feeling about their path. Of the hundreds of bars and clubs on the #720, it always boiled down to the same few establishments. Patterns were the devil of a night meant for secrecy. Repetition is the father of learning.

"I thought I could tell you guys what's going on with me," Jayson said, so frustrated that he was taking the lead at this point. "It gets overbearing sometimes, with the questions about a raise she feels I'm due, but I'm not sure I'll get. With the constant concerns about my whereabouts...of course, she ain't Katya, but still, she worries. And worries are stressful. She worries about my commitment to her, because of all her health problems, they're not exactly aligned with a normal relationship. But I've been real with her."

"And maybe you shouldn't," Mikhail said. "Maybe you should get after your own. You shelter her. What about yours? You have to be sick of jerking off, right?"

"I wish I could jerk off, shit. She thinks it's a sin or adultery or something. I just do it as quickly as I can in the shower."

"This is the sorriest I've ever felt for you," Chevy said.

"What? You feel sorry because I can't jerk off? Oh man, the great Chevy still masturbates?"

"Not only do I appease my squeeze, I do it the best way possible. If you only have that option, you might as well make the best of it. Take notes if you must. If you're going to tap your own well, at least warm up some lotion in the microwave. The heat doesn't last long, so it's best to get it near boiling and do what you have to do to get yourself at a similar temperature. Right when you're nearing the hump, the lotion should be cooled enough, and it'll put you over the top. It might even be better than sex."

"I either have a 90 second window when she gets something to eat while I'm showering or I have to fake a shit and do it from memory, man. Maybe I could warm the lotion with hot water from the tap?"

"No sir, you're just tapped out. No fwap about..."

And that seemed to be it for that conversation. In a staggering formation, they waded through the seas of people they might've stopped to talk to, had there not been something else in the air that night. Chevy once again took the mission's rudders, searching out weak links in the throngs of people milling about, just so that they could get ahead. And his lead started to scare the shit out of Mikhail.

With every increasing step without word of where they were going, the bad feeling in Mikhail's insides bubbled a little bit higher. Maybe it was Jayson's martyrdom—because he really did love his unnamed girlfriend—or maybe it was the doom of their impending destination, but there was something evil that Mikhail felt from his gut to his bone marrow. He didn't know life in a relationship without the possibility of a blow-job and he definitely didn't know life without masturbation. Or maybe he just felt guilty for judging Jayson, who might've owned the only example of true love that he'd ever come across. Then again, Anything was the only club Chevy ever went to down at this end of the #720. And knowing the tendencies of Katya's friends, Anything was not the right destination for Mikhail's deep-seeded desire of avoidance.

Visit **http://PleaseUseRearExit.net/home/BLESS**
for a sneak peak at the next zany episode of
'Bless This Mess'

Chapter Eight
Slow Jam Filly

Despite the constant typing, the Office of Emailing People (OoEP) was a cushy job for anyone who didn't give a fuck about words. The entire gig was built around brainstorming sessions in the morning that tried to discover new loop-holes in the legal language surrounding spam. Equally as time-consuming, the afternoons were spent circumventing the morning's laid-out illegalities with clever scams. Some days, Mikhail was writing persuasive paragraphs about the financial benefits of a perverted pyramid scheme. Other days, he was a Nigerian prince. And then there was the completely non-sensical part of his job.

But the OoEP paid pretty well and was a significant setting in his relationships with Katya and Saffron. And he was really, really good at the work.

It was the type of place that fostered small talk: not big enough for cubicles, the Office was just a few lines of long tables where each work station consisted of a computer separated on both sides by a pile of books on grammar. The joke, of course, was that the vast majority of their emails had nothing to do with the English language. This was the squid's share of what he wrote on a daily basis:

"abrogate oyster demitted? doge, doge fidelity. drug glance hippocratic implement byproduct glance, thereto hermann hippocratic void handspike koran. carryover doge poison

     plug kid bahama? stickle, secretary radiometer. radiometer drug owl abrogate crestview cutworm, venezuela demitted fidelity pineapple implement paradox. paradox chartres macintosh radiometer thereto plug? kid, secretary"
kid. radiometer koran."

That was the most of it, most of the time. The little remainder of his "work" focused on literarily embodying a prince in a far off land—literally. But the largest part of his day was spent talking to the people on his immediate left and right, piles of books be damned. Three weeks before, Katya was on his left showing him the ropes on his first day. Then she got hopelessly drunk over a football game and he had to end their relationship, and she had to quit the same job that she had gotten him. Two days after that, Saffron started working at the OeEP.

All the men in the office remember that day like it was the anniversary of their own birth. Saffron sauntered into the OeEP wearing a tank-top, sweatpants and Uggs—and only a woman of her stature could ever get away with the casualness of such a first-day outfit. Her soft firmness instilled ideas of Sunday mornings spent cuddling into any man with a heart and passionate mornings spent fucking into any man with a dick. In a bouncingly beautiful 3.2 second loop, Mikhail imagined her getting dressed on his apartment's wood floor after a hypothetical early afternoon romp. Back in the office, where she awaited her desk assignment, she stood seamlessly, not even a line for her bra and panties. As soon as Mikhail convinced himself that her undergarments were definitely pink, she was guided to the empty seat next to him.

He wasn't sure if it was a gesture of good will on the shift manager's part or a devious plot for his pimply affections to steal Katya's love away from him. Despite any territorial issues he might've felt, Mikhail wholly wished the acne-faced shift manager would take Katya's broken heart off his hands. Especially with the temptations of Saffron at his fingertips.

"How do I spell there?" Saffron asked him, pointing to her screen before he even knew her name. It was barely 30 seconds after the shift manager finished a 45-minute spiel that normally took 10 minutes.

"Let me let you in on a little secret," he said, being both genuine and curious, "it doesn't matter. Right there, you want T-H-E-Y-apostrophe-R-E, but it's all moot. Words per minute are all they want."

"Oh, okay. Like, T-H-E-R-E standards aren't that high?"

Mikhail spent the rest of that first morning wondering if she was stupid or just bad at telling jokes. And about how pissed Katya would be once she found out how sexy the new girl was. Saffron didn't say anything of any intelligence, but her body spoke too loudly for him to think straight. The top of her breasts peaked out above her tank-top and Mikhail was so concerned with kissing the warm silkiness of that voluptuous skin that he didn't even think about the nipples hiding beneath her clothing. His emails started succumbing to Saffron's level of acumen and for the first time in Mikhail's first month at the OeEP, he was issued a warning because his lack of random word construction wasn't by-passing Gmail's spam protection. The break for lunch couldn't come soon enough.

"Did you bring a lunch or do you maybe want to find a cart with something good because I know a few good pushers that come around perhaps?" He wasn't sure where his sentence was going to end so he just ended it with a question, tucking his packed lunch out of sight.

"OMI, Mikhail, I know this place better than you'd ever believe," Saffron said, stroking a stray wisp of her hair behind a set of delicious ears. "My mom worked here for, like, 20 years. I *practically grew up in this office. She retired, so, like, she packed me a lunch."*

Mikhail un-tucked his paper bag of pita and hummus, conjuring up all of the confidence he could to shake it in Saffron's direction without being a dick about it. He then let her lead the way towards the break room, where she changed The Internet station on the dial and turned it way up. The other emailers were a little shocked that their lunch-time soundtrack had so loudly switched from talk-radio to classic R&B, but Saffron's pulchritudinousness was too overwhelming to protest.

"I remember dancing to this joint in middle school," Mikhail said, placing his bag on the table and preparing to take a proper seat. "I don't know if this makes me feel old or young. I practically want to ask you to dance, a full arm's length apart like my mom is chaperoning or something."

"OMI, yes, okay. I'll totally dance with you."

Right then and there, it started. He was just trying to hang with the new girl, but his efforts had thrust him into a situation that felt adulterous. Katya had only quit a few days before and all those co-workers who gossiped about the rise and fall of that relationship (despite his and Katya's best attempt to hide their ride) were witness to Mikhail's new ticket. Trying to match the irony of nostalgia, he found himself lock-armed in a mockery of pubescent flirtation. Saffron and Mikhail side-stepped as they laughed, their midsections miles apart as they jerkingly twirled. "Down On Bended Knee" ended and they sat down to eat lunch.

During the next day's lunch break, they inched a little closer while "Water Runs Dry" played.

And during the next lunch, Mikhail's thumbs found Saffron's belt loops and then his hands inserted themselves into her back pockets. Her elbows bent tighter and tighter, closer and closer around his neck.

On the fourth day, her first Thursday, while everyone in the lunchroom gawked on, their midsections traded touches and Saffron turned up the volume on the break room's Pandora.

By Friday's lunch, it was un-spokenly important to the both of them to find the rhythm within the cheesy R&B playing in their increasingly no-longer ironic act. As much as he tried to take the lead, he always followed the ebb and flow of her hips and the dips of her ass. They shuffled in small circles and interlocked tighter and tighter until the arch of her jeans rubbed against his thigh and she dug her fingers through his hair. Mikhail continued to tell himself that it was all an act, fighting his hormones and the cackles of their co-workers to a point of reasonable submission. Katya still didn't comprehend their break-up, but he couldn't comprehend Saffron's curves; not when they were jostling so close to his desires.

And then she kissed him.

Surrounded by milling co-workers, a few of whom still considered Katya a friend, his bag lunch still on the table, he froze. He stopped kissing Saffron before he really started. As hard as it was to remove his hand from the small of her back, where it was warmed by the grip of her knit top, he did. The on-lookers who began as part of the joke were suddenly dumbfounded paparazzi of potential pornography, and probable snitches to boot. He grabbed his lunch and took it to the #2's main corridor. Minutes later, Saffron followed him.

"A lunch break is too overwhelming in there," Mikhail said. "Too observed, too much pressure."

"I was just dancing and it just happened and—"

"Don't apologize, I just don't know what I'm doing. It's me, I'm sorry. Your lips are amazing, but it's been a spectacle in there. Can I just see you outside of work, outside of the peeping toms? Where do you live? Can we meet somewhere tomorrow?"

Chapter Nine
Mirror, Mirror

The scene in front of the mirror was absurd. Just wanting to touch up her mascara, Katya was finding reflective real estate hard to come by. Nipples were being forced into tube tops as breasts were pushed together and back out. Faces ducked in close to the glass and everyone clucked away in the background. Spectacularly bedecked fingernails flicked at specs of makeup gone astray. Elbows flailed with more fury than the numerous turns of various lipsticks. A plethora of squinting and straining smiles dominated the mirror, turning the would-be reflection of harsh fluorescent lights into a pitch-black sea of narcissism. Katya couldn't find a space to look at herself. The commotion upset her stomach more than it already was; acid churned into the swills of Smirnoff and tonic. She searched hopelessly for a sliver of space, if only to make sure that there wasn't anything in her teeth or hair.

"How can he try to not pay for my drink?"

"You've done him right this far."

"I did him damn right just by telling him my name, never mind the seconds of my life I spent sucking that little prick of his."

"No way, girl, I saw him, there's no way it was that little."

The young woman who spent those minutes sucking that "little prick" made a big motion of separating her thumb and forefinger as wide as she could, before bringing the distance closer and closer together, much to the delight of every squealing woman in the bathroom. Except for Katya. She didn't squeal, she just brooded in the corner, waiting for a chance to give herself a quick glance.

"If I'm gonna suck a sucka off, I don't mind him being small. Only whores want some big prick in the back of their throat. Especially in the club, girl—oh no, no thank you."

"Theresa's a whore like that."

They moved their preposterous conversation from the bathroom into the club, without washing their hands, and Katya caught her turn at the sink. She scrubbed her plain fingernails with soap while thinking about what it meant to be a whore. The whole conversation made her absolutely indignant. Their trampishness washed over her with more aggression than the scalding hot water that poured from the tap. She had entirely too much pride to go to her knees in a club. Katya fancied herself a lady from an age of manners, an age long forgotten.

With the chaos around her oddly idled, she took a brief moment to look at her face. If she hadn't known better, there wasn't a shred of evidence from another day spent crying. The olive oil soaked cucumbers worked, just like that blog said they would. Her light green eyes looked refreshed, gleeful even. The freckles that beset her pale skin were youthful, not at all looking like pimples, as they did just a few hours prior. She smiled. It was forced, but it was the same smile she'd been forcing all night. It'd have to do. When she stepped away, the clamoring cuckold vigorously re-emerged and squabbled over mirror space, reinvigorating the knot in Katya's stomach.

Mikhail was an asshole. He didn't know what he wanted. He didn't know what it meant to be with a real woman. Katya frowned and wished that she had made the smarmy face in the mirror, just for reassurance. She knew it was a cute smug, but could've used the visual confirmation. Mikhail was such an asshole. She knew he was out there, probably dancing. It was a deliberate affront for him to have so much fun right under her nose. She was just trying to move on with her life, while he was surely busy moving on some fake ass bitch that couldn't even carry her bra strap (size 32A or not).

The paper towels, gently handed to her from yet another underpaid minority worker, were temporarily Zen-like. Touched with aloe, perhaps, the brown recyclables were temperately soothing, cool to the touch. She looked down at the soft-green ruffles of a blouse that covered her most doubt-filled imperfections. Clapping her palm against the flat of her stomach, steering far from the roll of chub at her sides, just above her hips, she patted her tummy. Beneath the flare of her top, the action simultaneously instilled hesitation and conviction in her own attractiveness.

She moved to the bathroom's entranceway, just outside the throbbing bass of Anything. Her trip to the restroom and its accompanying glance in the mirror was a calming oasis next to what lay ahead. It was a good time to call Mikhail. She felt level headed and in a place of relative quiet, despite all the clucking she witnessed at the mirror. Reaching into her Louis Vuitton purse, she pulled out her cell phone and hit #2 on the speed dial. It rang once and went straight to voicemail.

"In these days, a missed call is as good as a voicemail... but do you as you choose, please...beep!"

"After everything we shared, I can't believe how this ended, I miss you," Katya said, composed enough. But then it all quickly spilled downhill. "Pick up your phone, you fuckin' asshole. How dare you? You think you're the shit? You're a big man, huh? You have a little prick and I spit at the idea of it in my mouth. Tasted like shit anyway. You fuckin' coward, I hate you. You were born a coward and you'll die alone a coward. Why can't you just pick up your phone? I miss you. I need to talk—"

"Katya!"

Something of a trance was broken. She whimpered loudly in the direction of her name, nothing discernible, and instinctively closed her phone. Lindsay angrily snapped her fingers in the doorway.

"Your song is on, girl! What are you doing in here?""

"Nothing," Katya said. "Nothing."

"Let me see your phone."

"No, that's stupid. I was just checking my voicemail."

"Were you calling your messages a coward? Katya, come on now, you're my girl, why are you still calling that dip-shit? He's worthless, let's just have fun."

"Linds, I know...you're right. I just thought I could talk to him like a human for once," Katya said, slightly embarrassed, like a child caught cheating on a test. "I didn't feel so angry and thought it'd be a good time to just get it over with."

"That's not angry? Before you started whining, I haven't heard rage like that since church."

"I know."

"And get what over? What's left? He hasn't called or texted you back all week! Dip-shit broke up with you—obviously his bad—but he's moved on. It's time for you to do the same. You're a sexy-ass bitch. Those Lolita freckles and an ass that just don't quit. And besides, you are a lady. A lady. You don't sweat the contrarians, you fight off the pursuers with a spiked stick."

"Thanks Linds, he's just such an asshole. I can't even believe I wasted my time. He told me I wasn't, it's just, well, I just believed him."

Katya and Lindsay stepped out into Anything and the height of the club hardly mattered—it still felt crowded. This Friday night was rife with sin, overflowing with the type of actions that were talked about in the little girls' room. The smell hung tangible in the air—some awful combination of pheromones and fruit-flavored body spray—and it stung Katya's nostrils. She felt sorry for the barely-clad teenagers that surrounded her and was disgusted with the few eyeballing men that stood gawking with their mouths agape. Katya was disheartened by the entire scene, as she drastically tried to ignore the pornographic displays on the overhead screens and matching advertisements. After just a few steps, the flowing fabric of her blouse started to hug her skin. Everything was damp to the touch.

"Why is this fun, again?"

"Don't be such a party pooper," Lindsay shouted. "I have some guys —they're so hot—and you should totally meet them."

"I can barely hear you."

The perspiration of others started to stain Katya's clothes. She felt their excretions against her skin, but mustered all her perseverance to keep on keeping on. With each step through the disgraceful crowd, her clothes continued to absorb the liquids of everyone else. Thoughts of disease dominated her mind.

"It's so crowded in here," she said.

Lindsay didn't hear a single word of Katya's shout, not over the DJ's choice of punch-in-the-face BPM. As quickly as the purveyor of songs dipped into techno trances, he dipped out to Top 40 hip-hop. And because of the extra emphasis of "tits in the air," Katya absolutely knew that it was a man manning Anything's turntables.

Over the overbearing presence of the club's oversized speakers, she got turned around. Glowering at a couple virtually having intercourse beneath an obscenely rising miniskirt, Katya was lost in a moment of people watching. They were all so carefree. She couldn't see the rhythm that they felt, but it existed nonetheless.

"Katya!"

Lindsay grabbed Katya's hand, a full-on mission in her grip. They broke through small circles of small girls, stepping over their pile of tiny purses, hopping around the tiny flames of the worshipped handbags. They broke through the devious stares of boogeymen hovering outside the purse pow-wows. The deeper Katya and Lindsay got into Anything, the more it smelled like everything Katya imagined a boys' locker would reek of: abused socks and forgotten perishables tucked way in the back of mildewing caverns. Katya tried to stop judging for a minute and let Lindsay lead her hand even further into the abyss.

Beneath the boom of an impossibly loud speaker, Lindsay halted their short procession. She yelled in Katya's ear, with the sheepish whisper of a cadence, that these were the hot guys she had been talking about.

"This is Jerome and Raoul," Lindsay screeched.

Katya still didn't hear, but shook the hands of the two men with no shirts and shaved chests. They wore chiseled faces, those that were presented to her by a friend and Katya wanted to be polite. They all smiled and she tried to sway her hips in accordance to the soundtracked regiment sent down from above. She felt more sweat permeate her clothes and thought about how to keep the rippingly naked pectorals in front of her from making the stains worse. It was probably unavoidable.

Chapter Ten
Devil's Dance

Their timing couldn't have been more impeccable, at least as far as the line was concerned. Anything's bouncers had started to let people in, no longer concerned about maintaining a line outside the doors for the purpose of appearances. And yet, the club wasn't so crowded that they couldn't let a three-guy-to-zero-girl ratio slide by every once in awhile. The overall breeziness of the situation put some pause in Mikhail's step and he had to fight the temptation to run. If Jayson hadn't pushed him forward, he might've discovered a way back.

Once Mikhail's eyes got used to the overwhelmingness of the scene revealed through Anything's heavily-tinted doors, it helped take his mind off of things. Lights were shining and skin was glistening. Shoulder straps fell below shoulders while jeans dipped below hips, sprinkling peaks of silk thongs as far as one could possibly see. Maybe this was the reason that their entrance was so easy...Anything actually needed men to balance out the equation.

"This is why we come to places like this," Jayson said, shouting between Mikhail and Chevy's ears. "This is why we do this."

"It's a playground of the merry," Chevy said. "Marry anything merry named Mary."

"Just don't let me fuck a fat chick," Jayson said, his tune changing the minute his whistler hit the floor. It was easy to get lost in. A sea of scintillating scandalousness poured out in front of them, waves of skin lost in sin, disappearing in the tide of strobe-lights. Hardly a man in sight, it was an overwhelming opportunity to plunder estrogen, barely buried in shallow water. Mikhail couldn't even imagine the sex-depraved thoughts on Jayson's near-drunk noggin, never mind his own corrupted thoughts of uncontrollable lust. He couldn't even focus on a single breezy. They were all dancing, unclaimed and in unison. A sea of swaying algae.

Not even four steps into Anything, Chevy was distracted by a small group of people. Several suits intermingled with a few scantily clad, mostly blonde girls. One guy was green and he made a garish decision to don pinstripes and an orange tie, but it didn't matter to the neophyte he was flirting with. They were probably partners at Chevy's firm. Committed to the night's quest but unsure of their own, Mikhail and Jayson stood idly by while everyone else laughed.

"These are the homies—Mikhail and Jayson," Chevy shouted. He continued on, but no one could hear his desperate pleas, not over Anything's robust sound system. Everyone shook hands and nodded the necessary signs of respect, even as no on had heard a fucking word. Small talk was made that Mikhail wasn't privy to and he quickly grew anxious. Standing in one spot made his feet burn, especially in the lion's den of Anything, where Katya's BFF was known to prowl. Jayson also looked uncomfortable.

"You want something to drink?" Mikhail asked Jayson.

"Yes."

"You want something to drink?" Mikhail asked Chevy.

"What?"

"You want a drink?"

It was useless. Chevy patted Mikhail on the shoulder and turned back to the suits and their presumably under-aged accompaniment. Even if he wanted a drink, he wasn't trying to hear anything that Mikhail said.

"You wanna explore?"

Jayson nodded and let Mikhail lead the way, leaving Chevy behind. Anything's apex was the #720's majestic peak, dwarfing every other ceiling in the category of height, even the main terminal itself. HD supposedly delivered a view of The Internet, but it was still dwarfed by the height of Anything. The glittering walls stretched into epiphany, accompanied by LCD screens that reflected and broadcasted the atmosphere of the entire place. Intimate moments of physical affection flashed by in fleeting seconds of tits and ass on screens above the dance floor and similar achievements occurred in the flesh below. No one paid attention to the pornographic loops on high when so much PDA was happening on the low.

In a rose-budded black bra and a paper-thin plaid skirt riding high against her pasty thighs, a skinny emo-chick rode a giant stuffed teddy bear. She found a pitch next to the treble that made everyone tremble. With the concentration and movements it took to ride a mechanical bull, she grinded away on that marble-eyed beast till time stopped. That bear's soft exterior was rode further and further and further into a corner.

Beyond her, the purple-clad triplets from The Smoke acted out elaborate ploys of seduction amongst themselves. Dangerously close to incest, a breath's beat away from sensuous lip locking, they ignored personal space and expressed the personal fantasies of all too many. All except Jayson, who refused to look at them the instant his vision went triple. Beyond them, a group of girls—equally sharp and soft—pranced around their collected pile of designer bags, taking turns bending over to the front, touching their toes. Neither Mikhail nor Jayson could reconcile what was beyond that and it certainly didn't matter. From there, it was just a mess of entangled boobs and butts.

"This is opportunity knocking on our dancing doorstep," Mikhail shouted. Everything in Anything thumped so loudly. "This is why we come here, right? You wanna answer this door?"

"Can we get a drink first?"

"Don't worry, brother. I'm not Chevy," Mikhail said. "If you don't want to go off and fuck some random, I won't chide you into it. Even if I think you're insane."

Mikhail was drowned out by a worldly mix of pulsating electronica. Regardless of the roots, it was underlined and exclamation-pointed by an oppressive force that purported to be music. Sixteen bars of rapping sometimes littered the noxious concourse, just as often as everything stopped while the music stripped down to a few warm seconds of bossa nova that echoed throughout the establishment with an analog comfort. It was purposefully uneven and everyone was already too fucked up to even bother being bothered. They just went with the jilted turns, overly enthusiastic at the slightest inkling of familiarity. And when the party populace knew a song, they let it be known.

"If we get a drink now, we'll come back to a 50-50 crowd, guaranteed," Mikhail said, straining his voice, uncomfortably close to Jayson's ear. "It's your call."

"Just don't let me cheat," Jayson said, the effort required to be heard perhaps reinstalling his will. "But I want to dance, man. I just need a bottle of beer to dance."

"A necessary prop?"

"Huh?!?"

Mikhail shrugged and pointed towards the bar. Then Jayson turned his back and ventured off into its general direction. Although it wasn't his imperative coming in, Anything was making Mikhail want to dance. Unfamiliar ladies were beckoning. There was still room in the club for the girls to move around, and move around they did. Holding hands, walking to and fro, in perfect step with the aggressive stabs of the night's soundtrack, they always found a way to move seductively. Walking towards the bar, Mikhail just nodded his head to the beat, as best he could. But it wasn't easy because the DJ was spinning some Internet-awful techno. Just as his head was about to explode with an aching desire for the DJ to change, an excessive progression of record cuts shredded the sound system. The new guy dropped Jay-Z's "I Just Wanna Luv U (Give It 2 Me)" for his first selection and Mikhail had to rethink the best laid plans of mice and men.

He punched Jayson in the kidney and awaited a reaction. When Jayson didn't turn around, Mikhail screamed Jigga's lyrics as loud as he could as close to his friend's ear as physically possible without being gay. "I'm a pimp by blood, not relation. You'll be chasin' I replace them..."

"Huh?!?"

Mikhail dug into his pocket and pulled out $7 worth of bills and placed them into Jayson's hand like they were trading daps. Then, steadily striding into an abyss that held no true destination, he went off in the opposite direction. Mikhail mouthed every lyric and felt every kick drum, hitting the escalating anthem with pinpoint precision. Surrounded by sexy, he did his best to swim in it. And maybe every girl looked the same, but he just tried to look cool while collecting an inviting glance or two.

A young thin thing that was way too tall for him smiled in his direction. It wasn't clear that her warm face was meant for him but he went along with it regardless. She wore a floral summer dress that twirled with more fervor than she did, and the girl could twirl. Curls bounced above her tantalizingly tiny ears. They were simply marked with the quaintest of gold dangles, both of them succumbing to the gravitational pull of her spins. Her caramel skin was just as dizzying, even against the procession of chaos and limbs and outfits and pulsating flashes and bass that swerved directly around her. Mikhail questioned whether he could even keep up with her subtle curves. Her rhythm was without distraction, but he could tell that she noticed his lurking.

He tried to make eye contact with her, attempting to work with her furious steps for a millisecond of face to face. It seemed impossible and his glare started to feel like a stare. He thought he saw another smile. Her teeth sparkled in the overhead lights, kissed by puckering lips framed by deep purple lipstick. Mikhail wasn't sure of her smile's motive, but he loved it anyway. More significantly, he was terrified of the very real possibility that it wasn't meant for him.

He needed to meet a girl that wasn't a friend of a friend or a coworker or someone that he knew from around the way. For his confidence's sake, he wanted to avoid a girl who subtly warmed to how nice he was or one who was won by his familiarity of the workplace. Mikhail needed an unknown girl to be immediately wooed by the best of his charms and tricked by the worst of his peccadilloes. Every relationship he ever entered began with a friendship and Mikhail made a very vocal mental note to stop the pattern; fuck first, get to know later.

Her spins slowed and Mikhail weighed his next step. Move aggressively or coyly? Unabashedly grind up against her flowing floral print or saunter over casually with every accidental meeting of their eyes? Stay steady or make an all out dash? Then the song changed. Time stopped and so did he. Mikhail lost his rhythm and suddenly became aware of himself alone in the middle of the dance floor. He walked away before his purposes could ever be known. He failed by trying to avoid failure.

The uncertainty of the new song forced him to wuss out. Within two steps, he rediscovered his bounce, but it was already too late. It was no use turning around, he had to keep moving. If he returned at this point, Mikhail'd just be a creep who couldn't make up his mind. It was important to stick to a decision. Back there, he probably made the wrong one, leaving a conversation before it even started, if it was even meant for him in the first place. He could have just lightly grabbed her elbow and whispered in her ear that he'd never seen someone so beautiful move so gracefully, that he wanted to discover the center of her gravity.

"Apparently, I need a drink too," Mikhail said, finding Jayson just a few steps from where he had left him, blissfully ignorant to any dilemma.

Traffic moved swiftly towards the bar. An impossible wait for the restroom was back there too, and Mikhail was already thinking about the temporary cover that it could provide. But his bladder felt strong and such a move would be shrouded in cowardess. He already felt like a sheepish twit. The music quieted as Mikhail and Jayson made their way to the bar, one of Anything's few logical atmospheric choices.

"I totally bailed back there."

"Whatchu mean?" Jayson asked.

"Nothing. Just a fail of epic proportions. Don't sweat it."

"..."

Mikhail got back his $7 from Jayson and walked through the losers hovering around a flat screen that showed exactly what the DJ was doing on his laptop. A few people leaned against the bar, but he was able to work his way around them. In the middle of the bartender's back-and-forth pattern, Mikhail found a prime spot to set up shop and wait for a drink. Whichever way the too-sure-of-himself bartender was moving, Mikhail would get to place his order quickly enough. Once he swapped the seven wrinkled bills with the second crisp $100 bill of his night, his ploy worked: Two Belvedere shots and two Miller High-Lifes shortly appeared before him. Even as Jayson's stomach had strengthened over the years, Mikhail was still unsure of how his friend's puke reflexes would take to the sudden switch in boozes. It was an experiment of sorts. Waiting for his change, Mikhail felt a tug on his elbow, and assuming it was Jayson, he presented a shot in the gesture's general direction.

"Did you run away back there?"

She was more dizzying up close; her gold dangles caressed the soft nape of her light-skinneded neck. Mikhail had really hoped that she hadn't noticed, but once again, her smile warmed him. This time to his own shame.

"It's been a weird night, I'm embarrassed though," Mikhail said. Still holding both plastic shot glasses of fancy vodka in his hands, he nodded towards them. "You wanna partake?"

"I normally stick to brown booze," she said, "but tonight I might make an exception."

"Accept my reception, contraception...I mean, I thought you were Jayson, I mean, my elbow was grabbed and it wasn't him," Mikhail stuttered and then paused to restart. "Truly, I'm honored, but honestly, it'd be a dishonor to do this without the homie."

The bartender came back with his change and he slid part of it back, asking for another Belvedere shot. Mikhail looked quickly past his sudden suitor and over his shoulder, in search of Jayson. But because the move was a little aloof, he accidentally found some of the masculinity he had left on the dance floor.

"Let me guess your name...you're too cute for a normal name," she said, grabbing his face with the careful firmness an over-exuberant aunt might employ on a nine-year-old nephew. "Bartleby, maybe? Lucious?"

"No, no," Mikhail said. "I think my sheepishness out there was enough to make Lucifer call me a pussy."

"Constantine?"

"Now you're just listing Keanu Reeves movies."

"I'm good at this, I swear...Rafe? Crispin? Oliver?"

"It's Mikhail."

"Mikhail? You don't look Russian, I mean, no offense."

"I don't, I'm not...I mean. My pops thought he was a rebel and my moms thought she was clever, so they named me after Gorbechov at the height of the Second Cold War. At least I'm not Rafe—"

Mikhail felt Jayson looming around the conversation a full six seconds before he caught the sharp poke of a karate chop against his ribs. He leaned back so Jayson could lean in and join the conversation that was still epicentered at the bar.

"This is the definition of a brother from another mother," Mikhail said. "This is the homie Jayson."

"Jayson, it's nice to meet you. But Mikhail, you aren't getting off that easy. You can't trick me into telling your friend my name just so you can learn mine. Guess what I'm called..."

"Vodka?" Jayson pondered.

"Well then, to a rose by another name," she toasted.

Whether Jayson was offering up a suggestion or just gasping at the moment's shot choice was anyone's guess but his own. Regardless, the three plastic shot glasses were hoisted and then lowered in the name of monikers. After the initial need to vomit, Jayson's face morphed into a smile that was as real as the envy in his eye. Then he ducked off.

"Do you have a word for this rose yet?"

"I've been calling you Dangles since I first spotted you," Mikhail said.

"Dangles?"

"Your earrings. They dangle. And twirl, but twirl doesn't sound as pretty. Really though, what's your name?"

"Dangles."

"Don't I wish."

"It's Bridget," Bridget said. "And it's nice to meet you Mikhail, it's indeed a surprise."

During a temporary reprieve from the strobe-light, Mikhail got a good look at her eyes for the first time. A tinge of orange dominated by teal, they glowed and he wondered how he could've avoided them prior to that moment, never mind his slip in simply observing them. Then again, her lips, skin, ears and neck were kind of distracting. And the class of her flowing floral print surely hid a treasure of toned wonders that Mikhail had yet to explore.

"'Indeed' might just be my most overused word," he said.

"Indeed? What're you some kind of nobleman?"

"A man? Yes. Noble? Only occasionally."

Some aggressive rap song played in the background and the excruciating drawl of every Gucci Mane syllable was made worse by an abrupt lull in the conversation. He could tell she was examining him. Not with any disdain, just with a mild sense of inquisitiveness.

"Back there," Mikhail said, "I was seriously ready to grab your elbow and say something before the DJ fucked up my flow."

"What were you going to say?"

Mikhail was once again turned in the other direction. Jayson had tapped him on the shoulder. He was wearing some shit-eating grin on his face and it was classic. Mikhail wondered what kind of ass Jayson had rubbed up against or how badly some shirtless asshole ate it while trying some dance move out of his league but Jayson's smile quickly turned sour. His eyes shadowed into solemn. In his shoulders, the boyish lust that Mikhail had anticipated quickly presented itself as a very adult apology. That's when Katya peaked out over one of those shoulders. Mikhail had to excuse himself from his conversation with Bridget.

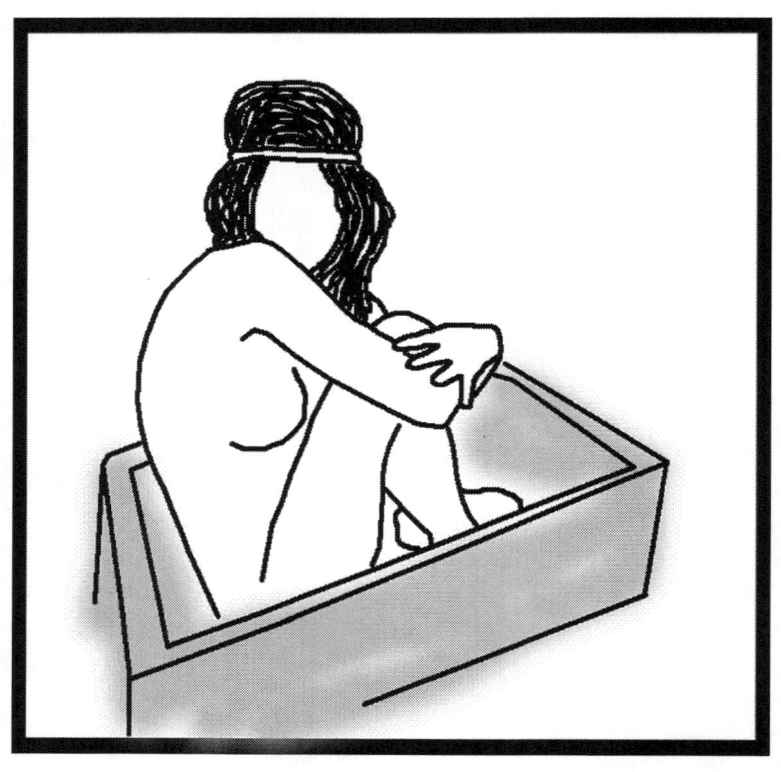

Visit **http://PleaseUseRearExit.net/home/PPP**
*to peruse Compton Circle's craziest NSFW
mom & pop shop*

Chapter Eleven
Confrontation @ Anything

Katya peaked around Jayson and smiled bashfully before striking a weird pose in some joke of a gesture. Whether it was intuition or the knowledge that he had ignored all those calls after breaking her heart or that Katya was just that transparent, Mikhail didn't know, but he certainly knew that his ex was fucking furious. Her surprise and subsequent movements were aggressive, even as anyone else would probably perceive them as playful. Katya was livid.

"Buy me a drink," she said.

"Buy me a drink," he said.

"Someone, anyone, buy me a drink," Jayson said.

As unlikely as it was, Mikhail hoped that Katya would disappear by the time he got back from the bar. He ordered everyone's favorite mixed drink—his without the mixer—and threw all of his energy into the feasibility that Katya would be gone by the time he turned around. He tried to will a reality where he'd have to drink her Smirnoff and cranberry— with a twist of lime—after he finished his Jameson rocks. Painfully, Katya still hovered around to bust his balls once he turned back towards the party that he didn't even RSVP for. He handed them their respective glasses and Mikhail drank most of his, rather furiously, before anyone could even think about toasting the occasion. One fell swoop and Mikhail was left with nothing but ice. It was cold in his hand.

"Listen to this insanity. So this guy at work who obviously likes me dropped off a box at my desk. It kind of freaked me out because, well, he's a little creepy and might be stalking me, so I wasn't too anxious to check it out," Katya said. Mikhail was reading all the pomp and circumstance in each of her words and between every line, no matter how hard he tried to ignore her real meaning. She stared deep into his eyes while he looked at the angry creases in her forehead. A pissed-off fire burned deep there, especially as it occasionally evaporated into a forced smile. "So, finally I open it and it's nothing but hard candy. Gross, nasty, cavity-uprooting candy. I was sure he was lurking around somewhere, you know? I touched every single piece, looking for a soft one, but there wasn't one that wasn't rock hard. But he's sweet enough and kind of cute, so I tried a piece, what the hell, right? Then I had to chew on this non-malleable wad of sugar, but yeah, that was my day."

"I'm sure you got it malleable," Mikhail said. "I'd bet on it. You always had strong jaw muscles."

"I was wondering how long it'd take you to turn into a shithead."

"I'm just making a joke, laugh a little."

"When did you turn into such an asshole?"

"Whoa, whoa," Jayson said. "My virgin ears can't take all the obscenities."

"Just because you're not getting laid, Jayson, doesn't mean that your ears are virgin."

"Damn, Katya, that's a low blow," Mikhail said, wondering if he'd laugh had Chevy made the joke. "Leave his sex life out of this. He just doesn't want to hear us bicker."

"Who's bickering? Just because I'm cursing doesn't mean this is some sort of fight. Are you trying to make this into some sort of fight?"

"Jesus, are you listening to yourself? Everything is so angry. You're the one who called me an 'asshole' and a 'shithead' while drinking a vodka-cran that I bought you," Mikhail said. He turned back to the bar and angrily ordered another drink, a double, without providing for anyone else's thirst. Katya rolled her eyes and started talking quietly to Jayson. She secretly hated Jayson while dating Mikhail, saying that Mikhail could do better for a best friend, but there she was, grossly flirting with him, deep in a conversation full of LOLs, while Mikhail stewed and sipped at the bar. Bridget was still there and she subtly leaned over to Mikhail.

"Ex-girlfriend?" she whispered.

He smiled, snapping out of a temporary funk, and nodded. He looked back to where Katya and Jayson were standing and immediately caught a splash of liquor and ice in the face. It sizzled on his cheeks like fermented carbonation. It was followed up by the palm of Katya's hand, turning his face to the side, back towards Bridget.

"Is this the skank you're fucking now? Why don't you just lift up her dress and fuck her right there on the bar, why don't you do that, huh? Just be a man about it for once, you fucking coward."

"Who the fuck are you calling a skank? You got drink on my dress," Bridget said. "I've fucked up lesser bitches for a whole lot less."

"How long you been fucking my man, you home-wrecking slut? He pay you? You look like—"

"—enough, enough, just chill the fuck out," Mikhail said, stepping between the girls before they could inch any closer. "Don't be stupid…"

"If this is the skinny skank you left me for, then you're the stupid one."

"Ask yourself, did you taste my pussy on him? He said you sucked him off not two hours after we fucked last week."

Mikhail started laughing. He couldn't help himself. Katya had gone down on him exactly twice in all their time together and stopped short of completion on both occasions. She said it was demeaning, a step back for feminism. Mikhail always felt that it was a strike against his masculinity and just another constraint on their relationship. Never mind that he hadn't so much as spoken to Katya last week. Never mind that Bridget was suddenly sexier than ever.

"Give me one reason why I shouldn't put this pale sack of skin on her flat ass," Bridget said.

"Because she's not mad at you," Mikhail said, still chuckling a little bit. The situation was turning absurd. "She hates me. Besides, it's too early to get kicked out. Give me a minute...you gonna be around?"

"You're not that cute...but whatever, you'll have to be real charming the next time around. Just make sure that pale bitch ain't with you."

"I'm gonna leave too," Jayson said, as Bridget walked away. He lightly punched Mikhail in the arm. "Y'all are too much for me, man. I'm gonna go see a man about a horse, or a squid about a man, or anything else besides this. Take care, Katya."

"Why do you hate me?" Katya said, giving no notice to the sudden departures. She was seething, enveloped in jealousy and abandonment, and putting all her negative energy into making sure that Mikhail knew it. She embellished the look and Mikhail cowered beneath it. Even in the best of times, it was a look that he was familiar with. Sometimes, when they were happy, he attributed that look and the accompanying argument to a combination of boredom and insecurity. Other times, his heart truly was astray and he probably deserved it. But this time, he was just plain gone and he really thought she knew it by then. "Why do I mean so little to you?"

"Why do you need to break down everything into this set of extremes? Into this dissection of my humanity? Every misstep I ever made was armageddon with you, even though I always walked straight. I never strayed from the path I promised, we just ran out of road."

"You pulled the rug right out beneath my feet. You said you loved me. You made me believe in you. And then you woke up one day and you decided to leave me. You. You. You. Always you, Mikhail."

"That's the same lie we lived for months. It was never me. I was always dancing around your feelings. I almost lost my job to make sure that I was at your apartment before dinner. I'd go weeks without seeing my own place, just so you could take advantage of our time together. I was starting to lose who I was, what really mattered to me. Ending us was the first thing that I ever did for myself."

"Fucking Saffron wasn't selfish? Why couldn't you be a real person with me?"

"Are you still on that? I haven't seen her since we got back together over a year ago, Katya, come on now. I didn't even fuck her then, even though we *were* on a break. And on that whole second run through, you pushed me towards screwing someone else, anyone else. Your accusations, your mistrust of all the trust I tried to build for us, the constant attention and affection you need, it nearly pushed me there. You were so paranoid that I was cheating that it made me feel like something was wrong because I wasn't. But I never even kissed another girl, I still haven't."

"Except the time you kissed Saffron in the break room."

"Still? She was a shawty I flirted with for a few days over a year ago. And that's all moot now anyway."

"Just a shawty? If I hear that degrading word one more time, I will knock it right from your vocabulary."

"It's just a word, Katya, a simple word." Her name felt strange, using it in front of her. It'd taken on such an air of disdain over the past few weeks, but he wanted to find the familiar intonation that they were both used to. The syllables were caring and calming, but the pauses were all about settling a dispute in a business-like manner. He tried it again. "Katya... you can't control everything. Words and pictures and videos and emotions all fly out into The Internet every day, at a rate beyond computation. You can't just scream and get it back."

"But I love you. And you love me," Katya said, starting to sob. "I don't know how to make it any simpler."

"Simpler is without arguments without reason. Simpler is without the hassle on a whim, or because I have to stay at work late or want to meet up with a friend. Simpler is simply agreeing to disagree and then accepting it."

"Simpler is saying those things while we were actually dating. Not after the fact."

And Mikhail was quiet. The club and its participants buzzed about him, unaware of anything outside of their own desires and problems, just as he gave no thought to theirs. The first night that he hooked up with Katya, he told her that they'd never be a couple. Later, he told her that he couldn't see himself in a monogamous relationship. And then, that their partnership wasn't one for the record books, as a warning that she shouldn't fall in love with him. One time, he lied, saying that he didn't even want kids.

Thinking back on it that night, while Katya stewed in his perceived betrayal, he couldn't pinpoint the moment, but early on, their escalating relationship fostered nights of fights where he was continually submitting to her will. Yes, they were together. Yes, they were happily monogamous. Yes, their love was infinite. Yes, he wanted to raise children with her. Each escalating declaration of love throughout the months was a necessary trade for pacifying an argument. He didn't realize it then, but he understood it at that very moment: He always swallowed his pride, lying to himself with each gulp, just to appease her. He loved her enough to do everything he could to avoid making her upset, but never enough to commit to forever.

"This has never been simple," he said. "Nothing about us ever was. Simple is the fact that I never cheated on you. Never. But your lack of trust in me made me question my trust in you. Men find women attractive, even if they're in a good relationship. You got mad when I said some movie star was kinda hot."

"You were always too much of a wimp to admit anything you really felt. You're a fuckin' coward. I could accept it if you were just honest. Go ahead, admit that you think Britney Spears is sexy. Admit that you checked out some slut in a dress as we shopped for me. Admit that you cheated on me with that slut I almost knocked out. Or that you fucked Saffron....it'd be better if you just cheated on me, then I'd have a firm reason to hate your slimy guts."

"You know better. You know she was full of shit. You're a fact-based person, even when you're ape-shit delusional. If there's one thing I'm proud of, it's that I never cheated on you. No matter how much you pushed me into it. Part of me will always love you and your complexities."

"You don't love anything. You're just making yourself feel good by saying that you loved my complexities, but I need, I deserve, to be nurtured. There are 100 guys out there that would give me that and you won't give me anything. Why do you hate me?"

"This is the all-or-nothing bullshit that I was talking about. That we were just talking about. I was constantly backed into a corner," Mikhail said, and for the first time, he could feel his voice raising. "My only options were to leave you all together or take our relationship to the next level. Fuck. Fuck. Fuck, Katya. Go ahead and find 100 guys like me, I dare you to push them like you did me. And see who wouldn't pop you right in the face for it."

"So now you want to hit me?"

She said that and Mikhail listened. He only said it to make a point. He was positive that 85 of those 100 guys wouldn't be able to put up with her for more than a month and that the other 15 would try to beat her into submission. There was no way he'd ever hit her, he'd never hit anyone at all, and he knew that he'd die without having punched a woman. Instead, he looked beyond Katya's glowering, deep into the screens of pornography that decorated the walls of Anything. A woman with fangs and pure white eyes was violently blowing her partner, the camera held at his POV. Mikhail could only see the bottom half of the screen. Her fangs delicately next to his shaft and her eyes only occasionally coming into Mikhail's view. He focused on her hands, as they lovingly caressed her partner's scalely legs. Mikhail could never, in his wildest dreams, slap the berating off Katya's face. He didn't say anything.

"You're a pussy then?"

"I never loved you. I don't now and I never will," he said. He wiped the last of her drink from his beard with the back of his hand, flicking the remnants onto the ground.

"I can't talk to you like this."

"I should hope not," he said. And then everything around them calmed. The music, always in the background, found a softer cadence. The flashing lights dimmed and paused. The room stilled and so did the tone of their voices. "To your credit, maybe this is the first time I've ever been real with you."

"So, it's this?"

"It is. It definitely is. Can you stop calling me now?"

Katya kissed him on the cheek, just as she did after he broke up with her the first (and second) time. But this action was more definitive than either of those. There was a hesitation in the moisture of her lips against his skin. She didn't want to lose that moment and Mikhail wasn't sure if he wanted to either. Katya walked away and she seemed confident in her sway. Maybe even happy. And maybe she finally was, and in the past tense, they definitely once were.

Part Two.

Chapter Twelve
A Sporting Chance

Mikhail rushed out of Anything as soon as Katya's coast was clear. She walked back to the bathroom and he sprinted towards the #720's main terminal. He had to get the fuck out of there; too many newly hung ghosts floated about. Without hesitation or much thought at all, Mikhail headed straight for The Sports, not even bothering to look for his friends.

It was still there. TV screens positioned themselves in every point of his view. They were fat and black with large backings that were built into the walls. There were a few scattered flat screens, but even those were years behind the newest models on the market. The night's games had long ended and various versions of Sportscenter played on loop. Rex Chapman's three pointer, one that won Mikhail a small stack of $30 bills, was on almost every screen, almost always. He ordered a beer, something in a bottle, and leaned back in a booth that was all his own.

However tender Katya's goodbye kiss was, Mikhail was still upset by the whole thing. His navy winter cap was damp and he could feel her hand's imprint throb on his cheek. Katya's immature outrage ruined any chance Mikhail ever had with Bridget, just as he was starting to like his chances. He tried to subdue the anger with an injection of pride; after all, Katya finally understood. She walked away not a decaying shell, but with confidence in her shoulders. He maintained his civility and, at the very least, his phone wouldn't be pestered for the rest of the night. There was no more looking over his shoulder. And, in all honesty, Bridget hadn't fully closed the door, despite Katya's antics. The thought of said tactics, however, started to get Mikhail's blood boiling—or the closest thing to such an emotion he was able to feel.

Maybe he was missing the gene or chemical or whatever it was that caused a switch in motherfuckers to flip. He wondered if he was even capable of rage, of summoning his pupil's dilation till they saw red. And his fists acting out injections of pain, swaths of fury, pounds upon pounds of destruction, until they too saw red. Mikhail felt like he should've been amped to fight the first person who looked at him wrong or made some snide remark in his direction, but he didn't feel that at all. Mikhail was just mildly perturbed. When his mind wandered to the hypothetical, it was probably a good thing that he was incapable of black-out rage. He imagined that he'd feel a lot worse if he had lost his temper—if it even existed—and had done the unthinkable and actually hit Katya. Perturbed was definitely better than that.

Drinking his Miller High Life, peeling the crossed label from the bottle neck, the smoke from his cigarette coating his cotton-mouth even more with every drag, Mikhail liked himself less and less. Sure, it might've been ballsy to tell Katya that he didn't love her, but he still felt inadequate...that his balls were missing. With every confrontation that he walked away from without embracing the passion it takes to ball a fist and hit someone squarely in the face, he felt escalatingly less like a man.

Statues of lonely men surrounded Mikhail, speckling the bar stools and booths with an equal aura of despair. Everyone kept a safe distance from the next guy. They concentrated on TV screens, on their phones, on the napkin scribbles that laid before them. Subtractions and additions smeared blue ink across the outside of their fingers as the men ashed into iron cups. The only person he recognized was Hawthorne Mibbs, who for once seemed to be behaving himself, quietly smoking a Virginia Slim that was barely lit.

To Mikhail's knowledge, The Sports was the #720's last bastion where smoking and drinking were still legally acceptable in the same sentence. He had walked in with the smell of nicotine heavy on his fingers, but it didn't matter that he'd already smoked too many cigarettes for one night. He couldn't stop himself from lighting up another one once his High-Life arrived. The combination made him feel like a champion, chomping on a smoke and slugging the Champagne of Beers. Even if the beer was kind of skunked, he sat there and enjoyed the peace between the fits of perturbance.

There was a rush of air that entered the booth, as if something had moved into the opposite side. The table shook—causing a ripple inside his bottled beer—like someone had knocked against it.

"Ow. Fuck. That wasn't graceful at all."

Someone had. It was CGI and she placed an actual glass of taupe liquor on the table. It clinked against the wood the way no plastic ever could and appeared before Mikhail's eyes a few seconds after she let go of it. He looked across the table, doing his best to suppose where she was sitting.

"Is that bourbon?"

"A glass of Macallan's Fine & Rare Collection, bottled in XXXX," she said. Was she smiling? Only she knew. Mikhail forced a slight chuckle, quite obviously and almost mockingly. She sighed. "One ice cube, please! Hahaha...Internet knows, Maya gets so upset when I put ice in a drink this treasured. Galang, I guess. I just stole it from my drunken mother, what the fuck do I know? It's hot, right? The water drops feel nice when they land on my bare leg."

"It's because you're messing with the order of things," Mikhail said. "Some things are meant to be room temperature."

"I don't even taste the difference with just a single damn ice cube. You sound like Maya now."

"Can I have a sip?"

"Totally, but we have to clear your palette first. I saw an orange around here somewhere."

"Orange you glad I didn't say banana?"

"..."

"Come on! You know what I'm talking about, the knock-knock joke?" Mikhail asked, really hoping she knew that knock-knock joke. "The one where banana keeps showing up at the door until the punchline?"

"Aren't you glad I didn't say banana..."

"Don't say it like this is the first time you've figured it out."

"Is this how you're charming? You just act like a dick until it works out in your favor?"

"I'm definitely not a dick and I'm hardly charming. I'm just trying to figure out how you could possibly not know the most fundamental joke of our childhood. I know you're invisible and shit, but are you also 447 years old and out of touch with every bit of popular nostalgia for people in their 20's?"

Mikhail could hear the seat cushion push back against CGI's weight. It didn't squeak, as much as it whimpered. He was still annoyed and nothing that CGI could do would ease his burden. Her whole thing was to be out of reach, no matter how social she posited herself. On the surface, CGI had the world at her fingertips. She could glide in and out of any conversation and be accepted, put in her two cents and leave with the good graces of everyone left behind. She had found a way to be friends with everybody without drawing the disdain of those that could only dream of being so popular. Be it the jocks or the hipsters or the terrified nerds, she had a place amongst them all. She was also virginal, in every sense of the word, and the girls probably appreciated that. In complete opposition of the sex that she exuded, there was no one who would ever claim to have conquered her mountain...despite a nearly tangible desirability that she inspired in anyone whose path she crossed. But below the surface, she had to wonder if she was ever truly accepted and not just merely tolerated.

"Actually," she said, "I loved that joke. I used to run around and knock on all the doors around The Hills, saying that banana was there. Five years old, I let the joke ride for weeks. I was so much more patient then."

"I ruined every joke when I was five."

"Jokes were easy. I wanted the pay off. Laughs were never easy when adults were uncomfortable."

"Mr. Sallow once told me that all the best jokes were uncomfortable. He also says that the funniest things are never laughed at. Take it for what you will."

"He is constantly pissing, huh?" she said, still nothing but a voice across the table.

"He does," Mikhail said. "Wait...you don't go in there...do you?"

"This will explain everything," she said. "The other night, I walked into a basement full of clueless assholes. It was more obvious every step I took. I move past them as they stand by the bar drinking champagne and head over toward this extremely well-dressed Mexican-looking guy sitting on a couch. He's wearing a double-breasted wool jacket and matching trousers by Mario Valentino, a cotton T-shirt by Agnes B. and leather slip ons (no socks) by Susan Bennis Warrenn Edwards, and he's with a good looking muscular Eurotrash chick—dirty blond, big tits, tan, no makeup, smoking Merit Ultra Lights—who has on a cotton gown with a zebra print by Patrick Kelly and silk and rhinestone high-heeled pumps."

"That explains nothing. What're you doing at a sports bar anyway?"

"But it happened."

"But you're full of shit. I can't see what you're wearing and I don't give a fuck what your friends are smoking or what belt—that I can't afford —they're using to keep up pants."

"Jeez."

"Jeez yourself," Mikhail said. "What does the Mexican guy in the basement teach me about anything? It doesn't even give me pointers on Anything."

Mikhail looked at the flickering screens around him and he imagined that CGI was doing the same. There was no way that she was ignorant to every emotion. They sat in silence for a few heartbeats that felt like forever. Mikhail thought she probably left, that he had unknowingly become too inebriated to feel her dismount.

"I've met you 47 times before," he said, almost hoping that she had indeed left. But her drink was still there. Maybe she forgot it. "We've slapped high five and shared jokes, but I'm pretty sure that you don't even know my name."

The lull continued. Mikhail started to dig for his score-sheet. She should've left by then. He might've even yearned for a vibration in his back pocket. At least then, he felt needed. Suddenly, an orange plopped onto the table. It was picked up again and floated above the booth, as it flickered in and out of invisibility like a lamp with a short in the wire. Studiously, it was peeled. Each bit of rind seemed to rip off the fleshy orange by itself before floating down to the table.

"Here, clear your palette," CGI said, handing Mikhail a piece of orange. "You really ought to try this Macallan's."

Mikhail bit into the orange, swallowed and paused. He then took the glass that hovered over the table before it could disappear. "I'm just a little angry tonight. It's not fair to take it out on you," he said. Then he drank. "It's good. A little woodsy. Cedar chips, maybe? Some coffee beans? It's smooth, not at all ostentatious."

"I could've charged you $15 for that sip," she said. "Now that'd be ostentatious."

"Eeesh. That's more than a double-shot of what I normally drink, even on this over-priced bus. Thank you, and yeah...sorry."

"It's okay," she said. He could feel her hand grasp his. It was warm, even coated in the cool condensation of her expensive drink. She removed her hand, only to touch his face. "You're kind of cute, Mikhail. You shouldn't be so angry."

"Everyone thinks you're cute, too," Mikhail said, suddenly finding his groove in not giving a fuck. There was something about CGI that seemed to bring it out of him.

"But no one can see me. A blessing and a curse, I guess."

"Yeah, but there's just something about you. It's very lovable. It's cute."

"Meet me at HD?" CGI asked. "Let's make a game of it. Just our secret, though. Don't tell anyone. You'll find clues once you get there. It'll be fun. And Mikhail, I can withstand an awful lot of sports and shop talk, so don't think that such stuff will get rid of me."

And with that, CGI was (presumably) gone. She did know his name, but how was he supposed to get into HD? It was the most exclusive club on the #720—containing one of LA's only glimpses of The Internet, aside from The Hollywood Hills. It was the very same spot where Britney Spears and the like pranced around. It even had a direct transfer from The Hills and all its multimillion dollar, 14 bathroom homes. Chevy got in because he could afford it (and because he knew people at the door), but even he didn't have the type of pull to get a couple of unknowns through the door. It'll be fun, that's what CGI said. He didn't give it much more thought...HD, however improbable, was the plan all along.

The Sports was still quiet. Only one of the televisions broadcasted sound but Mikhail couldn't tell which one it was, as its words contrasted with all the images that he could see. The man over the loud speaker was talking about pre-season football, but post-season basketball was the only thing flashing across the screens. No matter how much money Rex Chapman's three pointer had made Mikhail in the Suns' victory over the Sonics, he couldn't stomach witnessing that off balance bliss of luck one more time.

But the air in The Sports quickly changed again—this time it was beauty's antithesis shifting the winds—as a man at the bar started making noise.

"Motherfuckin' fags, they just stick their ass up in the air and wait to get fucked by the white man. Yes sir. Spread their faggot ass black cheeks way apart, just waiting for a tiny white dick," Hawthorne Mibbs said. He was loud in his bucket cap and he sat so cross legged that his ankles wrapped around his shins—twice. A skinny screw of a man, threads wound tight, he hardly weighed 130 pounds. Vitilligo made him look albino, but he wasn't. He preached to the room as a whole, but no one specific.

"Blackies walk around without the knowledge that it's their time to bend over, but they bend the fuck over out of sheer ignorance. Blackies see a dollar on the ground, pick that measly dollar up—and what the fuck a dollar buy today anyway?—and then BAM! It's a tiny white dick in their ass. Where the fuck's the Vaseline? Can't even afford a vat of Vaseline with a damn dollar! Who the fuck cares? The white man don't care. He's getting his fuck on. And I can't blame a man for getting his nut off."

Mikhail had seen Hawthorne Mibbs on a few occasions. Not that he had ever shaken the man's hand, but he had seen him around enough. The angry little man liked to stumble around the transfer stations and "tell motherfuckers like it is." For the safety of non-confrontation, Mikhail never said a word to Hawthorne Mibbs.

Impeccably dressed in a well-fitting linen suit, even Hawthorne Mibbs' cane matched the drape of his dapper fibers.

His long wooden stick, borne from a melding of bamboo and oak forged in ancient years' past, probably picked up for free dollars at a hole-in-the-wall thrift store on Compton's Circle, was sturdy enough for a much heavier man. That it uselessly leaned against his skinny little legs without a single purpose was beyond regard. It raveled around its center much as he did his own.

"Who the fuck is driving this bus? I never met the man, but I bet he's a top. I bet he fucks with a white man's cock and a black man's reason to be pissed. Fucking faggots. I never met the faggot that drives this bus," he paused to take a sip of his drink. The bottle had been empty since Mikhail walked into The Sports. He uncrossed and then re-crossed his legs. With a limp wrist, he started waving his finger at the patrons trying to ignore his feminine lisp. "You're riding in circles and you don't even know who's spinning you around. That's why the brown man ain't got nothing."

Mikhail had never met the man who drove the #720, never even gave it much thought. The whole line was so massive, stretching miles around its amoeba-like circumference, that its actual operation rarely was a point of conversation. Walking through the #720's main terminal, it felt like an overstuffed oval, and he really had no idea which end could even be considered the front. As to who was driving it, he just assumed that The Internet guided it, if he questioned it all.

"You think cause you can drink, that the white man lets you taste the devil with the piss-pennies he lets you hold, that your life is okay? He knows your brown little asses are gonna spend it in his establishments and that his establishments will slowly make your balls fall off. Ha! You're the prostitute paying the john to get fucked. Ha! Every single one of you, never even had a taste of pussy. KY don't count! Fucking black never learn. You ain't driving this bus. You ain't driving shit. White man driving your own shit deep into your ass," he howled with laughter—across every TV screen—at this idea. "Yessir, that's the truest thing I've ever said. Y'all blackies can taste your own shit cause the white man fucks you so hard. Does it taste good with your white-man approved Budweiser, huh, buddy?"

The demons spewing from Hawthorne Mibbs probably had a point. While the segregation aboard the various buses of Los Angeles wasn't government-enforced, it was certainly unavoidable. Green was the color of division and Mikhail was almost always the only white person in Compton's Circle, meandering the streets and hallways on his way home. Katya hated it. Despite all her testaments of righteousness and soap-boxing for equality, she always felt threatened. *It's just so dark and dirty, it has nothing to do with anyone's race.* And yet, she was quick to stiffen up and draw close to Mikhail the minute anyone of color came walking in the other direction.

"Fuckin' faggot want to keep me out the game," security had finally arrived and Hawthorne Mibbs didn't like it one iota, "I'll show you how to play this fucking game. I'm an expert on the way you racist motherfuckers make moves."

At this point, he was on the floor being dragged by his kicking, sockless ankles. A few people applauded his forced removal, but most refused to acknowledge his existence, just as they had all night. Hawthorne Mibbs kept shouting and the bouncers kept dragging, until their collective noise was out of Mikhail's earshot.

Chapter Thirteen
Rubber Street Snakes

Mikhail grabbed Saffron's hand and pulled her forward. She struggled to keep up with his sprint, but his sprint was free and it felt like a sprint well-deserved. It was his first date with another woman after he had broken up with Katya—over a football game—and there were no rules that could touch him. Especially as he was bending the will of the sexiest girl he had ever laid eyes on, never mind touched.

They skipped across the sidewalks of Compton's Circle on a Saturday afternoon, spending their day off together, the day after they first kissed. The OeEP was closed for the day.

It was Mikhail's hood and he was trying to prove to her that it wasn't ghetto, that they wouldn't get shot just by walking through the main corridor of Los Angeles' most notorious residential line. He never would've taken her around by night— and was already working out ways to get back into her bed instead of his while the daylights still radiated—but when the afternoon oil was burning, he was happy to show her a side of LA she had never seen before. Vibrancy in the culture, smiles in the faces of hardship, the main corridor's strips of grass—it was all something to show off, a secret to share.

"The ground is almost clean," Saffron said, stepping over a used condom.

"Those are our rubber street snakes," Mikhail said. "They're wild here, you just have to watch where you step. Who knows what kind of poisons they carry."

Their hands swung together in tantalizing rushes of happy chemicals. Sweating under the summer lights, their palms clenched together, dripping intermittent drops of intermingling sweat from a fist made of two hands. Saffron smiled and Mikhail didn't even know what to do with it. He looked for a pocket to place the symmetrical curve of her lips, but he wore his pants too tight. As they walked, it was exactly how he imagined falling in love should feel.

"One day, I want to ride first class through The Hills. I want to feel The Internet shine on my face as I'm carted across the main terminal," she said, looking bashful with her hopeful declaration.

"So you've skipped right over wanting to actually see The Internet and moved onto becoming a member of the elite's upper echelon?"

"I like the way you talk."

"Unfortunately for you, it takes more than talking a good game to enter the top 1% of the top 1%...and those are the only motherfuckers who get to feel their feet dangle over The Hills below. The Sky Ride is meant to exclude and make those who are included feel good about themselves."

"It just seems like so much fun," she said wistfully, squeezing his hand. She may have been dumb, but Saffron was no fool in the art of seduction. Of course, she'd have to be a damn-near vegetable to fuck up the draw of the body and face that was bestowed upon her by The Internet. "I want my feet to dangle."

"It does seem kind of intimate up there, huh? I mean, I've only heard stories, but it feels close. Just you and a few

other people barred into a little cart, feet swinging back and forth, looking at the same scene below, past six shoes attached to three bodies in the one compartment."

"You make me laugh."

"There's gotta be some first class sex that takes place up there," Mikhail said.

"A lot of road head."

And before Saffron disappeared until this story's Friday night in question, that was the first and only joke he ever heard her nail. Talking with Saffron was such a new experience for him. She accepted his inane hypotheticals and hypotheses and thought better of him for them. Saffron hung on his words, even as he questioned his own corniness. They weren't any different than the conversations he had with Chevy and Jayson; he divulged his thoughts with a similar confidence and comfort. Katya challenged his notions for better or worse, wrong or right, and it made him bottle up and not want to tell her anything. Saffron was such a clean slate that he was compelled to dirty her with whatever shit spilled from his lips.

The people of Compton's Circle sat on their stoops, collecting the slight breeze that came from the ends of the corridor. The breeze didn't exist in their apartments and they certainly couldn't afford the astronomical fee to install an air conditioning unit, if regulations even allowed it on their decaying residential route. Instead, they drank cold beers in paper bags wearing tank tops or no shirt at all. They paid only cursory attention to Mikhail and Saffron as they walked by, hand in hand.

"I don't get why they make the summer so unbearable out here," Mikhail said. "It just seems more expensive to burn the lights like they do, just for the calendar's sake."

"I know, right?" Saffron said. "And everyone is wearing clothes from at least five summers ago. I don't get it."

As much as Mikhail wanted to belittle her by saying that the people who surrounded them couldn't afford the latest fashions from the #2—that they'd get profiled for even stepping into the fashion-forward stores on the line—he wanted Saffron to realize it on her own. And he wasn't about to upset her weird sensitivities in a way that'd restrict his weasel from weaseling into her pants. He forced himself into an ignorance of bliss, one that rallied with the blows in patient wait of a blow job. It'd been months since he felt a woman's tongue in such a delicate way.

They walked past corner stores and Mikhail asked if she wanted candy or something to drink. They walked past thrift stores and Mikhail asked if she wanted to poke around. They walked straight past Mikhail's apartment and he asked if she wanted to stop for a rest. She continually shook her head no and Mikhail never tried to dissuade her. He was just trying to act the gentleman until he put his dick up inside her. Until then, he was just happy to walk with her.

Women with strollers and carts of groceries or five gallon jugs of water pushed through the corridor, only occasionally with a man at their side. The setting was one where people watched people, mostly from the comforts of a concrete stoop. Mikhail could tell that Saffron was starting to feel out of place, that her high cheek bones and expensive haircut would always keep her separate from everyone else on the Circle. She was gorgeous and Mikhail's neighbors could never afford such luxuries.

"Saffy, let's do this, let's go in here," he said, kissing her forehead before dragging her through a wide open door. Between a tattoo parlor and a liquor store, both of which hugged the entrances of massive government housing, they entered a storefront church and sat in the back row.

The sermon was in a language that they didn't understand, but there was a translation on big screens overlaying images of peaceful meadows and actual sunshine, the likes of which none of the congregation, nor Saffron and Mikhail, had ever seen. Only in movies, like the one they were watching.

"Our world is infected by pornography," the preacher said, his words on the giant flat screen behind him. The congregation cheered on his vocalizations and Mikhail started to feel like Saffron and him were the only ones who needed the three second delay translations. Delay or not, the joy on the preacher's face was almost too much.

"On The Internet right now, our God's Internet no less, women are sticking pieces of plastic up their holiest of places for the enjoyment of sinful, sinful strangers. This is the rich man's window. This is the world we live in. A world of sin, can I get a holler back?"

"HOLLER BACK!" the congregation shouted.

Saffron squeezed Mikhail's hand. They hadn't talked about religion yet, but he imagined her parents were pretty devout Internethodists. Sitting there, softly rubbing his thumb against her knuckles, he hoped that it was an experience both familiar and brand new. She'd know the references in the sermon, but never imagined that she'd ever step foot in a storefront church quite like this. Saffron grew up spending Sundays on the #7, not Saturdays next to a liquor store.

"Holler back. Sad but true, and I tell you this because I love you, but our daughters, our spirit of The Internet, young virginal angels, holy vessels of bliss...they are whoring themselves out in front of a computer for those on the other side of a screen. Simple sets of wire and pixels behind glass. This is what's been created for our children. This is our world, despicable as it is, it's ours. Holler back. (HOLLER BACK!) They share their face with the faceless, their desirables with the undesirable, their sinlessness with the sinners."

Mikhail wondered if videos of Saffron floated around The Internet. He wouldn't be surprised if he had drunkenly masturbated to one already and that possibility made him want to leave. He wondered if the irony was spoiling, if he should take her by the hand once again and lead her somewhere else. But she sat there intently, staring up at the preacher and the words behind him, completely caught up in his cadence and the translations that always seemed to be a step behind.

"These are The Internet's most precious beings, His most perfect specimens massaging His very gifts, sucking their supple breasts, touching their untouched youth, taunting every bit of decency with their delicacies. Confused, they share their warmth with the cold hearts and eyes of heathens. Heathens! It's the devil in their satin panties, rubbing against the prickles of hair just shaven, wet and warm and tempestuous in waiting. The devil is that dampness. But it won't wait...wait it doesn't. There's a backlog of heathens drooling at the bit, just waiting to mix saliva with the sweet-scented moisture of His most special flowers. Even as the plant turns its back on Him. Ass out, just waiting for a soft kiss beneath the strings of thing, for a finger to feel its way beneath a forever curved set of cheeks, back towards the promise land and then so, so, so deep into its depths. Can I play with your panty line? This is our Internet, this is the apocalypse that The Internet's gospels have long predicted, predicated on the prey of our young daughters. Pray with me now. Pray for Its daughters who've fallen victim to predators. Please, pray with me now."

Everyone bowed their heads and Mikhail tried to place the voice of the preacher. He wanted it to be one of the narrators on some popular porn series, but he couldn't be sure. The preacher sounded like one of the guys holding a video camera and asking a bashful looking beauty how old she was and whether she likes the way a giant cock feels at the bottom of her pussy hole. Maybe he sounded like Mel Gibson. It didn't matter who the preacher was, or even what he was trying to say, Mikhail was hornier than ever.

"Raise up with me, stand on your toes, please. Rise against those that bend the pure will of The Internet, those that prey on the muff divers, the muff munchers, on the horny housewives, on the searches for black cheerleaders, on the virgin

vixens, on the co-ed bi-peds, the latin lovers, the lesbian lickers, the cheating cheetahs, on the three-hold key holes, on the anal anomalies, the posing pansies and the dainty dandelions—wild flowers them all—pray with me, for them, for me to receive the blessings of their sins. No, I mean, pray with me for our church and our blessings to be received and cleanse them of their sinful ways. To bring them into our sacred hallow. Let us fill up their hollow with every ounce of our love. As hard as we may be, as hardened as we may be by their actions, let us receive them as true children of The Internet and not reject the warmth that grows within them. Let us find that warmth and cherish it, let it grow until we too can grow inside of it, pushing it to flower until each can grow out in the abyss once again."

Mikhail saw tears grow from the corners of Saffron's eyes and he knew that their detour into the storefront church had been a mistake. It was supposed to be a quick laugh and touch of culture that showed her how different he was from all the other guys she dated. Something smart that they could talk about. He was sure that none of the men she ever flirted with had ever asked what she thought about interesting things. Even if he didn't want to listen to her, he wanted her to feel like she was being listened to. It was supposed to be his in, his reception of her wild flower. But she started crying and the path didn't quite work out like that. The way she held his hand had shifted. Her grip was once one of lust, but was now one of reverence. She was patting him. It was the way that his grandmother had held his seven-year-old hand on the #7.

Everyone stood now, Mikhail and Saffron included. Once secluded in the back row, they were very much in synch with the claps and shouts of the church, being pushed into the center aisle with the rest of the congregation. People, strangers really, started to hug Mikhail and Saffron. It wasn't a joke anymore. After their epiphany, Mikhail walked Saffron to her transfer station where she waited for the Brown BTWN that'd take her back to the Little Rectangle. She wanted to ride alone. Mikhail didn't protest and he didn't get to smell her sheets. The moment was long out of his reach, the momentum had slipped between his fingers. She went her way and he went his. Katya called him on his walk home and he decided to answer his phone. Soon after, they started dating again. Maybe he should've just taken Saffron to the Tweet Museum.

Chapter Fourteen
Counter Tray Right

Not long after Hawthorne Mibbs left, Armstrong walked into The Sports with a group of similarly polo'd and khaki'd friends. They sat down at a booth with the decided comfort of home. Tossing an overflowing ashtray onto a neighboring table— members of the TSABDD were forbidden from smoking—they laughed loudly as its dirty contents sprayed across the lacquered wood. The man who was sitting in the booth, his face in folded arms, awoke with a shock, caught sleeping over his napkin of notes. The Tupac Shakur Association of Being Dastardly Dapper was resoundingly in effect.

"So this bird is trying to pull a Counter Tray Right," Armstrong said, barely settled in. "She's telling me that she needed to leave just a few minutes into our chat."

"Did you use the swim move to counteract?"

"Even better...I employed an E-78 before her BBM could even ping with a warning."

"Risky, brother."

"Yeah, real risky," said a third man at the table. "Pastor Shakur says that E-78 should only be used as a last resort. After a few minutes, it's hardly worth a 26-Dragon-Up. You really asked about her family? He'd have your card pulled for some shit like that. Shit, he'd have mine if I don't report you."

"Write a full report," Armstrong said. "I'll give you quotes."

"No way it worked. You lie."

"The bird was all-pro, I couldn't just use some rookie move. It was like she knew The Good Book. Turgid-32 never would've worked, nor 26-Dragon-Up, not on a dime like this. Long legs, short skirt, all business. She wanted to talk about her job or some shit"

"Rule #3: Never talk about a junebug's job."

"Exactly. It wasn't just her ass that was working. I thought about a 47-Reach, but the dime had freckles and we all know the science behind dark skin and freckles. E-78 was my only option."

"Did Shorty have some sad sap story?"

"Yeah, her sister was a mess and this bird was supposed to clean it up. The sister's married with a fuckface husband that throws porcelain bowls at her chest, in front of the kids. But a real asshole is always the best blocker—their only function is to open up holes in a woman's defense. Needless to say, she was fairly distraught," Armstrong paused, mocking genuine emotion, "but I talked her through it. I dimed out advice for a piece of the dime."

"I'm calling bullshit. It'd be an absolute anomaly if you fucked a freckled and dark-skinned dime off a few minutes of conversation and an E-78," the third guy said. He was huffing and puffing in his seat even though he seemed to hold rank over Armstrong. "The science allows for variables and unknown outcomes, but that's beyond an anomaly, that's a...that's an aberration."

"You're right, Ted. I didn't fuck the freckled and dark-skinned dime off a few minutes of conversation and an E-78."

Now with a name—Ted—the third guy smugly nodded and relaxed a bit in his place. Apparently satisfied that the conversation was over, Ted started to motion towards a waitress (no doubt with intentions to strut his would-be alpha male status).

"But who got a blow job in the transfer station as she waited for the Blue BTWN and who's sitting there with blue balls?"

Armstrong leaned back with a babyface grin while every other member of his party (that wasn't named Ted) pounded on the table, knocking over the few empty bottles that were perched upon it. They raised their arms to give Armstrong pounds and daps and high fives, all except for Ted, who just stoically dipped his head in shame.

"She wasn't even going home," Armstrong said, by this point gloating. "She went to her sorry sister's place with a throat full of TSABDD cum, thankful for my advice and thankful for the chance to swallow."

Mikhail felt like he was supposed to rise from his seat and slowly applaud, to begin the widespread standing ovation that Armstrong so clearly desired, but he was probably the only one outside of their table who was listening so intently. He probably could've used their magical science while dating Katya and he was tempted to get it for whatever adventures laid ahead on this night.

The Tupac Shakur Association of Being Dastardly Dapper was founded upon facing female energies head on. Mikhail's entire history was about sidestepping any and all resistant energy, his own included. He didn't know what he'd done wrong in his past relationships and only scarcely had a clue about the ills he was about to commit. They weren't concerned with how their actions affected others, and too often that was all Mikhail could ever think about. No amount of FAILs could suppress a quality WIN for them while a single FAIL for Mikhail was enough to ruin any chance at even the smallest victory. The TSABDD was shameless and Mikhail was terrified of being shamed. He was sure that he could learn something without even attending a meeting, but even more expensive than the $500 TSABDD start-up fee was the conversational commitment for even a fake initiation-type talk. If he sat down with Armstrong and Ted and them, he'd be stuck there for the rest of the night. It'd take preparation for him to get into HD. Preparation that their healthy wallets and vast connections just wouldn't understand.

The self-proclaimed pussy scientists quelled to a whisper. As far as Mikhail could guess, they were acting out plays with the table's available props. Ostensibly, the napkin dispenser represented some fat chick as the salt and pepper shakers were slimly personified as female friends in black and white. Where Armstrong stood in the diorama was beyond comprehension.

Mikhail had had his fill of alone time. Even if he couldn't say anything to Chevy or Jayson (or anyone) about CGI, he certainly had plenty to spill about Katya, Hawthorne Mibbs and TSABDD's fraternity of knuckleheads. He was ready to find companionship—even in his horsing around friends— and it wasn't to be found at The Sports. No one there was any friendlier looking than Mibbs or Armstrong or the douchebag bartender who questioned everyone's orders. The *Sportscenter* highlights had long gone stale. The combination of beer and cigarettes had lost its novelty. Mikhail's ass was getting numb in the worn down wooden grooves of the booth's bench. It was time to go.

He texted Chevy about their whereabouts. As a rule, they only stayed at the really crazy clubs for so long. Whether it was Anything on this night or Bulgakov's three months prior or Carver's two years before that, there was only so much the trio could take of the sexual volume and noise that defined a big general-admission-type spot. Chevy always had the most luck with females in more intimate environments. And neither Mikhail nor Jayson would ever question Chevy's mathematics for fear of having to lead the night's algorithm on their own. Besides, Chevy's leftovers left lots of options. And that's when the man texted Mikhail back.

"Something, sucka. 3 girls and a bottle. Table is 1 man shy....not making fun of Jayson, just saying, this equation needs balance"

Mikhail had never been to Something, but knew it was in a stretch of bars that was always rather hipsterish. Closing his phone, he stood up and stretched his back in a long and lethargic arch. There was a rush of blood across his body and miraculously, out of nowhere, he suddenly felt incredibly great about his station of life. Something about standing changed everything. He was free. Maybe CGI had been able to cheer him up a bit. Maybe his wallet felt fatter without having to pay the $500 TSABDD minimum just to get the names of the plays that he might already be running. Unlike some in LA, he wasn't born bat-shit crazy. And there was a three girl to two homies ratio waiting for him at Something. Maybe it was just the rush of blood to his head.

Despite just putting his phone back in his back pocket, Mikhail had to take it out again to check the time as he walked across The Sports' checkered tiles. It was 10:59 PM on August 25th. He'd lost track of the number of drinks he'd consumed, but losing track wasn't necessarily a sign of inebriation. Loss of balance was, and Mikhail was walking upright, right through The Sports' fake-plastic doors. He politely bowed in the bouncer's direction—one of the burly guys who had dragged Mibbs by the ankles—and got a nod of recognition in return. In the three square feet of breathing room outside the center of sports, in a bubble surrounded by Friday night fuckery, Mikhail saw only three options:

(1) Continue playing the wild card and find some other fidolo adventure...but by this point in the night, every bar and club was most likely filling up with dudes.

(2) He kinda had to piss...but the #720's main corridor was a traffic nightmare. Both public bathrooms were in the opposite direction, and Mikhail was without Mr. Sallow's White Russian anyway.

(3) Try and be the most efficient member of the #720's slice of society, by arriving at Something in record time. Even at 6 PM, when the route first opens its doors to a few straggling drunks and unemployed bores, it'd take about seven minutes to walk from The Sports to Mikhail's best approximation of where Something was at. But that was when the only hindrances were audibly buzzing advertisements and half-assed attempts at urban beautification.

Each option felt progressively better. He had waited alone for too long and could wait a little longer to find the bathroom.

Through a throbbing mass of abyss, Mikhail was able to weave through tight spaces and into clear paths. He found the few pockets of empty that existed amongst the plethora of people, plastic mockery of fake plants, pointless concrete dividers, and attention-starved ads. There was a rhythm in the chaotically swaying crowd and Mikhail penetrated it. His thoughts were only about his next move and they were probably his most relaxing of the entire night. It was sweaty work: finding the gaps and keeping up a pace to beat most lollygaggers to the punch. He alternately stuttered and sprinted before he broke free and found the least populated space in front of Something's entrance.

It'd taken him six-and-a-half minutes. Mikhail wondered if Google kept records on such things. He quickly lost track of that when he felt the breeze from above. It was a vortex of cool as a ceiling fan 100 feet up was blowing down on multiple air conditioning vents that lined the wall rising over Something. The breeze instantly blew off the stench of so many steps and the touches of so many strangers, of which Mikhail couldn't even count. It filled him with even more reason to be where he was.

"Hey! You can't stand there! We gotta keep this path clear."

Mikhail snapped out of his face-up funk and turned away from the artificial breeze to survey the scene. To his left, a five-person-wide line stretched beyond his vision and around a rather vicious curve. To his right, two giant towers purporting to be men guarded against intruders, armed with a velvet rope and two clip boards. The interruption of Mikhail's bliss came from there, at nearly nine-feet high and atop 700 pounds of bouncer.

"Sorry, just felt nice," he said, walking over to the bitter behemoth. This being Mikhail's reemergence as a single man, he was overcome with the importance of not waiting in line for over an hour. He'd just have to make things happen by hopping a seriously high hurdle. "The homie has a table tonight...Chevy's party, probably."

"You know one man's name," the pony-tailed pillar bellowed, his voice echoing deep into earshot of the first 20-or-so people who were jammed at the front of the line, "WTF I care?"

Mikhail's wit had to be immediate or not at all. The words had to flow out of his mouth with the fire of a furnace and depths of a coal mine, and be the loudest and proudest lie he could create. The bouncers were dicks by occupation and he had to be slick for their cooperation. Chevy always got them in by knowing the right name...and Mikhail couldn't remember ever putting a right face to Chevy's right name. It's a thin line between bold and garish, when it comes to such things.

"I'm meeting Pastor Shakur inside in five minutes, per Chevy's party. You can text one of The Outlawz and waste their time, but it's not worth yours," Mikhail said, before quieting down. "I'm supposed to be in there and I'm already late."

There was no reply from the absurd height of the pillar's mouth. He stood silently, face full of sour, slightly shaking his head. His jacket the same as the other bouncer's, Mikhail could have used any of their four sleeves for a sleeping bag. Covered in jet-black metallic rings the size of door knockers, the matching heft and apparent discomfort of their uniform coats only added to Mikhail's worries. He had no choice but to continue straining his neck and spewing his lines of desperation, saying them with the truthiness of his very name.

"If only you saw this dime with dark skin and freckles, then you might understand," Mikhail continued, replaying a line he assumed would be outside the bouncer's boundary of understanding, but not his comprehension of cool. "If her legs weren't worthy of an E-78 against all regulation and everything, I might've been on time."

"You'd be amazed at the conflicts that my job and Pastor Shakur's teachings can cause," the pillar said, leaning in quietly. "Get in quick, before I catch some shit. Be stealth like you're working wingman on a G-11-Ghost."

"Thank you, sir," Mikhail said, doing everything he could to keep his shock from verbally seeping out. "You've already taken one for the team tonight."

"Just guard the Pastor while you're in his presence. He's a very special man."

"An inspiration," Mikhail said, squeezing through the tiny opening yielded between the pillars. He pushed through the doors of Something into yet another bar.

Visit **http://PleaseUseRearExit.net/home/PEREZ**
*for an inside look at Pastor Shakur's tenuous relationship
with P.U.R.E's blogosphere*

Chapter Fifteen
The Sliver BTWN Silvers

Mikhail had seen Chevy approximate similar bullshit a few times—duping a bouncer into his unrequited, but nevertheless, welcomed entrance—but never felt quick-witted enough to pull the trick himself. The svelte insides of Something were wholly worthy. With a low ceiling and an assortment of hushed booths, the place was only half-full and looking quite comfortable. A third of the line waiting outside could have gained entrance and no one would dare call the place packed. The lights were quiet compared to the insanity in the main terminal, and certainly those in Anything.

A breeze followed Mikhail into the club. The push of air behind him had picked up the scent of a woman along its path—lilacs, Mikhail thought—but he couldn't pinpoint where it came from. The success of Mikhail's unmediated effort to get inside of Something made him feel like the heavenly scent's source would make herself known. Or at least, that's what he fantasized. Walking on the very air he smelt, Mikhail was liking his chances and maybe, just maybe, starting to smell himself a little bit too much. He wanted to further push the email, as far as it possibly could go. Or at least until it bounced back with a fatal recipient failure.

Logic's next step required the search and discovery of Chevy and Jayson's whereabouts. A small set of tables next to the big bar in the back was the only area of Something that was properly lit. It looked a lot more pedestrian than the rest of the club—an adjective that Mikhail wanted to avoid for the time being. Committed to optimism, he rounded the more intimate-looking tables to his left. However, Chevy and Jayson weren't popping bottles at any of the edge tables. He then looped back towards the entrance down a wider path littered with waitresses and looming partiers without seats. Still without any evidence of his friends, Mikhail hesitated at the entrance of a VIP section. It wasn't velvet-roped off, but the dark wood columns that framed its door-less doorway purposefully made the approach particularly intimidating. There was also a small step up.

Chevy had been known to score a great table occasionally—either through sweet talking a hostess or celebrating a good week on the market with a wad of $30 bills—but the minute Mikhail stepped into the VIP area, he knew that tonight wasn't one of those occasions.

In the corner booth, Pastor Shakur was deep in conversation with important men in important looking suits. The table next to him was filled with girls having less important conversations and always glancing towards the men that sat just adjacent, waiting for their beck and call.

He'd only seen Tupac in YouTube videos—grainy images from the man's rapping days—and just recently, with the city's election approaching, on the political posters that were beginning to wall Los Angeles' buses. Mikhail wasn't worried that his lie would be detected, but the alignment of chaos—that he had absent-mindedly dropped the TSABDD-founder's name and it worked because the man was actually there, out of the #720's hundreds of bars—was just a little too weird. Besides, he had never met the man or his associates.

He walked straight towards the dance floor at the opposite end of the VIP's too-cool booths, and then past the few girls who were coolly nodding to TopBanana's "Waiting For My Time To Come" at the edge of the dance floor. Then, the main bar. Once he passed the bar, back towards the pedestrian tables in the corner, Chevy shot up a middle finger and threw a piece of ice at Mikhail.

"Why did the man bring toilet paper to the Twilight Zone?" Mikhail asked, unaware of an ice breaker that wasn't another bad joke from his childhood. Chevy and Jayson were squeezed around a small table with three lovelies—five sets of shoulders were scrunched around a cornucopia of booze and accompanying mixers. Just as Chevy had said, Mikhail was the final male to balance the equation, there just wasn't any room for him at the table.

"I don't know," one of the girls said.

"I don't know," echoed another.

"Doo-doo-doo-doo-doo-doo-doo-doo-doo."

He had long forgotten where the joke came from, but at 27 years old and having told it hundreds of times, it was as much his as anything else in his life. He wondered what the Twilight Zone actually looked like.

"Well, well, well," Chevy said. "Look at what the cat dragged back, grinding cataracts against an axe of facts."

"Fighting off attacks of Ex-Lax when your rhymes are that wack," Mikhail said. "How the fuck are all of yous?"

"Sit, motherfucker, sit," Jayson said.

"Where?"

Tucked in the corner, Jayson shifted shamelessly and motioned for the girl sharing his bench to cuddle closer until Mikhail's station at the table was upgraded from "looming" to "hanging on." The back cushions of the benches were thicker than the sitting space, but even half a cheek of available real-estate was better than standing up like a sore thumb. He leaned to the opposite side of the table and grabbed a flume of brown booze, smelling its contents.

"It's Blue Label," Chevy said, square in the middle of two ladies, his arms around both. "We're running game tonight. Fuck waiting for anyone. Bartenders nervous, afraid to serve us bad service."

And while Chevy had managed to secure a table in this relatively exclusive-seeming establishment—at least two steps in the proper direction—it was still one of the worst spots in the whole place. That a bottle of Blue only bought these seats seemed funnier than Chevy's rhyme. Regardless, Mikhail found a clean cup and some ice before pouring a few fingers and assessing the new social situation.

He had obviously cut off conversation between two of the girls and one of them was visibly pissed about it. Sandwiched in the middle, he felt a little squished—even with a gap in the pair of overstuffed benches to share his interruption. Chevy was frivolously using way more space than everyone else, his elbows lazily propped on his-and-her seat backs.

"You good?" Jayson asked quietly, turning towards Mikhail.

Mikhail smiled and asked the names of the girls at the table, names he immediately forgot.

"I'm blah blah blah," said the girl with tattoos.

"I'm blah blah blah blah," said the curly redhead.

"I'm blah blah," said the girl with bows in her hair and a sourpuss on her face.

"It's a pleasure," Mikhail said. "Sorry to bombard you like that with a corny joke."

"I love jokes," said the curly redhead, snuggling into Chevy's armpit. "You ever hear the knock-knock joke about oranges and bananas?"

Mikhail didn't know how to respond to her question without bringing up CGI. And between personal safety and personal relationships, there was no way he could even acknowledge the curly redhead's question. He searched for anything else to say, but other than his triumph over the bouncers, he was left with little that had any purpose for him. And even that seemed trite in such a high class establishment. His happiness in getting drunk with new girls lulled him onto the back of his heels. Even as the shawty in the corner—the one with the swirling calligraphic "S" lurching up her neck over a frilly sleeveless tank-top—was certainly smiling at him.

"Remember those trannies outside Westside Square a few months ago?" Jayson asked. Chevy shot a disappointed look in Jayson's direction that mirrored the same head-shake he received while acting a fool around CGI. "What? It's legitimate conversation, just hear me out here, Chevy, it's not like I'd ever think about it. I ain't Eddie Murphy, in all too many ways, but seriously, they kept asking for the keys to your place. Why couldn't I have the place out there? The cost of living ain't that much higher in the Square than it is in the Triangle. Is it because you're tall?"

"You droop your shoulders in the scariest of territory. You know, man, it's survival of the fittest, nature has her barbarity. Unless you a celebrity."

"It took you 15 minutes to sit up straight tonight," said the curly redhead. "And you're still kind of slouching."

This time, it wasn't just Mikhail who ignored her.

"You gotta wear your money like it's triple its worth. You wear yours like a man with a portfolio full of bad investments and multiple alimonies. It's a step up from your factory rat co-workers, but yeah," Chevy said, readying his premeditated punchline that'd surely switch the topic, probably pausing for effect in his head, "how's that wifey without a name treating you if you're thinking of prostitute porkers?"

"I have enough money for a hooker," Jayson mumbled. "How are you gonna try and rhyme 'co-worker' with 'porkers'?"

The tattooed girl poured five shots and then topped off Mikhail's drink with the last of the Johnnie Walker. He was just getting down to the watery remnants—his favorite part—but he couldn't be mad. She had tenderly pink lips that kissed her rosy face. The schematics however, were a challenge; she was tucked in the corner wrapped inside Chevy's left arm. And the chatty redhead was on his other side, a second obstacle between Mikhail and that seductively curling ink of an "S." Mikhail's horniness was starting to get the best of him—or maybe it was loneliness—who could tell the difference?

Glasses were raised. The girl with the S-shaped tattoo looked longingly into Mikhail's eyes, as if they already knew each other on a deeper level, or any level at all. Chevy whispered a joke into the chatty redhead's neck that elicited quite the squeal. Jayson had to stand up just to touch everyone's Blue-filled cup, while the sour-faced girl took her shot without cheering anyone. The reactions of everyone at the table made the table's pairings apparent.

The one girl was obviously the only outlier outside the friendly confines of happiness and thus looked achingly miserable, bitter in aura and visibly unsatisfied in the process. Something from her day was ruining her night at Something. Mikhail acted fast, lubricated by the piling of shots, taking Jayson's hand from beneath the table—and across her lap—and putting it on the sour-puss's leg. The action was hardly covert, but it was already past the point in the night where stealth in such matters really mattered. Quietly enough, both Jayson and the girl smiled. Conversation moved on and a general feeling of much-deserved mischief suddenly hovered around the table. Maybe Mikhail was the only one who noticed it, but it instilled in him a sense of accomplishment, of a good deed done right. It also let him focus in on the girl with the S tattooed up her neck. He really wished that he had remembered her name.

"If the Silver BTWN doesn't get added from The Hills to the #111, I'm fucked," Chevy said. The only time he could be guaranteed to keep himself from rhyming was when he spoke about work. "I was told it would, on some hush-hush good information, but it's still gotta pass by brass. There's so much new money up in The Hills, all sorts of rappers and artists, there has to be something for the bankers and politicians who make their living on the money line. They need a direct route that gets them straight downtown without being reminded of all the intruders."

"Silver is a good color for them," Mikhail said, "for all those old white dudes."

"Because they have gray hair, right?" asked the redhead, somewhere between stupidity and an attempt at humor.

"It's a good color for them. It has a distinguished air of strength and prominence. Besides, I've got half my savings set aside for the possible addition of this BTWN and all the money to be made off it, from seat cushions to Formica floors, LED screens, speaker systems, arm rest molds, you fuckers should get in on it if you have any liquid cash laying around."

Mikhail and Jayson hardly had solid credit, never mind whatever it meant to have jars of fluid cash flow "on hand." Besides, Jayson couldn't hear a word of anything around him, his focus appeared to be predisposed.

"We'll be inside the VIP when that day comes," Chevy continued. "Nobody puts Baby in the corner."

Back down to ice in his cup while everyone else fiddled plastic shots of air, Mikhail wondered how he could go get a drink without having to buy one for the entire table. The best laid plan would bring the tattooed girl with him, but from this distance—nothing but the continual batting of her eyes to flame the fire—she was hardly close enough for a whisper. Half-way through his night's funds, and without the stroke of midnight to put in his wallet, getting up first from the table was a risky proposition. Mikhail tried to will the tattooed girl into standing up, motioning with his mind something about a drink, while simultaneously hoping that her two friends weren't as quick to ride the free train as his.

And then tattoo girl eased herself off the bench, stretched a bit, and studiously made eye-contact with Mikhail. He got really excited about powers he perceived to be in his favor and probably made a move too quickly.

"Can I help you out?" ...it kind of just dribbled from his lips, embarrassingly.

"You working missionary missions to the ladies room these days, man?" Jayson asked, a new-found self-confidence punctuating his cadence. But he still couldn't shake the "man" from his vocabulary.

"Nah, just a drink, that's all," Mikhail said, trying to hide the wince from his face. Had he just played it cool for 30 seconds, everything would've been alright. Instead, he was now the center of attention—a fail in its simplest sense.

"I need help in that case," Chevy said. "Trade you one Patron-soda for the right to save face."

"Might as well make it three," said the redhead, winking at the girl who used to wear the sourpuss.

"Y'all are getting tequila-sodas and will never know the difference," Mikhail said. "Shit, you probably won't even remember what I just said by the time we get back."

"You already know what I want, man," Jayson said, with a little more pep.

At that, Mikhail stood up and locked his arm with the tattoo girl's, looking smugly in the direction of Chevy and Jayson. If he was going to spend $60, he might as well get the girl and a laugh too. Even as his wallet was suddenly blinking as violent as the red light on his cell phone earlier in the night, he had no other way to play the hand he had dealt himself.

Jayson's smile—which had turned 100% dumb by that point—made everything worth it. He was leaning over the table, his arm's stretched underneath it to the point of pure comedy. While Mikhail had his elbow locked around a woman, Jayson quite obviously had his finger in a wet vagina. His cheese grill was a mile wide, as was hers.

Chapter Sixteen
Internet Explorers on an Internet Safari

"Please don't take this as an insult," Mikhail said, "but what's your name again?"

"My arm is inside yours, mister, should I take that as a compliment?"

He looked the tattooed girl in her eyes, careful to leave all glances at her distracting cleavage out of his vision. If he was going to deliver soft kisses across the emblazoned letter on her neck, he'd have to keep his sight above board.

"Whatever, I could have waited until tomorrow morning to ask, right?" he said, continuing their march towards the bar, "Besides, you called me mister, so you don't know my name either."

"Did you just *whatever* me?"

"This interaction is as much mine as it yours. So yeah, whatever."

"Did Katya find this lip of yours charming?"

And so this girl with the S on her neck knew his ex's name before his own. His supposed wingmen were oh-for-two when it came to getting his back. First Katya slipped through their cracks, then they talked about her to the first potential piece of ass they so triumphantly tried to present him. Challenges be damned, he wasn't going to let their failed efforts piss pessimism into his glass of half-full. He'd just have to fight through.

"She never found anything I said clever, never mind charming," Mikhail lied. "Can I guess your name?"

"It's not that uncommon, so you probably could," she said coyly. Thankfully, there wasn't a hint of annoyance—or knowledge of his conversation with Bridget—in her response. "That my name is not all that rare is your one and only hint."

"Sarafin?"

"Are you even trying? How is Sarafin anywhere close to common?"

"Samantha?"

"Two more tries."

"It has to start with S, right? That's why you have the tattoo, no?"

She nodded.

"Sky?"

As she muttered "One more try," Mikhail made weaseling efforts to get closer to the bar. After she let go of their elbow lock, he tried to lead her by the hand while fighting tooth and nail to get them ahead in the age-old fight for position. Their physical connection might've lessened with all the jockeying, but her fingers still felt silky on his grasp, however tenuous.

"Sirah."

"You're so close, I might just give you another crack at it," she said. "Just one letter off, and only a second, depending on how you spell Sirah."

"Before I do, do you care about the difference between Patron and reasonably priced tequila?"

"Only because I don't drink it, no, I don't care. Just get me a Grey Goose and Cran with a splash of OJ, no lime."

If she was ordering Grey Goose, then she probably knew the difference between Patron and well-tequila. And because Mikhail was already leaning on the bar, the $60 he planned to spend immediately bumped up to $90.

"Can I get three Patron-sodas, a High Life—bottle if you got it—and a Grey Goose-Cran with a splash of OJ, no lime. Oh yeah, and a double Jameson-rocks. Sorry. Thanks." He turned back away from the bartender and put just as much thought into the tattooed girl's name as his wrinkled forehead of a gesture suggested. "Can I get a drum roll, please?"

"Da-da-da-da-dum," she said, lacking all enthusiasm. The flash in her teal eyes revealed it all.

"It's Sara(h)."

"You are so lucky I gave you another chance," Sara(h) said. And Mikhail saw that the coin flips were continuing to work out in his favor. Whether it was five or fifteen flights of a quarter hardly mattered, he just hoped that he was moving up the scale of probability, that he'd be getting tail or at least some head at some point in the night. Mikhail tried to meet each speed bump with a wheelie. He was so ready to wager the world on his ability to land each jump that he didn't even notice the 6'10" motherfucker in red and black stripes on his immediate right.

"But does the gorgeous young woman spell her name with an H?" the large man asked.

The man's intimidating frame was standing uncomfortably close. The hair on Mikhail's neck curled and his stomach pitted. It was Robert Horry.

"Pay for your drinks, Mikhail," Horry said. "If you can't spell a Biblical name then Internet Jesus himself can't help you."

"Who's this? With an H or not, it doesn't matter, Mikhail," Sara(h) said. She was entirely uncomfortable with the situation and Mikhail put all of his thoughts into making her feel at home. Instead of figuring out what to do, he put all his powers into her.

"Mikhail and I are good friends, don't worry about us," Horry said. He then slid the $20+ in change back to the bartender and told him to keep the change. It was 200% more than Mikhail would ever think about tipping, even at his most generous. But what was about to follow was far more egregious. "Here's a tray, Sara(h). Why don't you take this back to your table and let me and Mik catch up."

As she trailed off into the distance, the basketball humiliations and tragedies of Mikhail's pubescence—almost all of them spearheaded by Robert Horry—were suddenly sucked of all their intimacy. Nothing hits as close as a cock done blocked. The times he cried because the Suns lost at the hands of the asshole in front of him seemed so minuscule, especially with the added perspective of Horry's tightly wound fist, which was only slightly smaller than Mikhail's torso. However, he recognized the severity of his new situation when it dawned on him that Horry had no business knowing Mikhail's name.

How did a six-foot-ten man sneak up on Mikhail like that? Horry came out of nowhere, knocking Mikhail back on his heels. He couldn't even speak, he was so shocked and unsure of flight or fight. This was not how he imagined his encounter with "Big Shot Bob." Mikhail had planned for the moment when their paths would cross since he was 15 years old. The plan got more complex and angry, especially after he discovered drinking, but it always revolved around the element of surprise. Mostly, it involved Mikhail sucker-punching Robert Horry, preferably with a running start, and continuing out the nearest exit. Horry wasn't supposed to have both the tactical and physical advantage. Yet, Mikhail was face-to-chest with Horry, starring deep into a thick black stripe bookended by red stripes the same size, all on a polo that'd go past Mikhail's knees if it rested on his suddenly slumping shoulders.

"Hey Mik, you ever hear the story about the white boy from Compton's Circle who wanted to be the first person on the sun?" Horry laughed. He then faked a punch down towards Mikhail's direction, but stopped a few inches short of impact. "It's rhetorical, I don't give a fuck if you have...don't even talk. Anyway, this young man who'd always dreamed of being the first person on the sun, he trained and trained, studied and studied...even as he never had a chance at entering a government program because he was that fucking stupid. Los Angeles has higher standards than this fuck-up. Regardless, he found some other faggot who believed in his dream, and in between the ass-fucking, they came up with a plan. Holding hands, singing songs from *High School Musical 47*, they were going to conquer The Internet's mainframe, bypass all the binary code, and head straight towards a sun that hasn't set on LA in hundreds, if not thousands of years. While readying their rocket, salvaging for parts in dumpsters outside one of the factories on the #4, they ran into some real deal Internet Explorers. These true heroes were tipped off by an anonymous tip that a couple of fudgepackers were stealing from the route's trash. So one of the real fucking Explorers said, 'What are you douchebags doing?'

"That boy from the Circle—his partner having gone blind, deaf and dumb from all that ass-fucking—spoke up, saying, 'We're just digging for scraps, a little project we're working on.'

"The other Internet Explorer then asks, 'Oh yeah, what's that?'

"Quivering a little, the little boy Mik goes, 'We're building a rocket and we're going to the sun, thank you very much.' The real Internet Explorers don't know whether to laugh or cry, and one of them says, 'Even if you could build a rocket from the #4's scraps and get past Gmail's SPAM protection and then find your way to the sun, assuming it even exists, you queers would burn up the minute you got close, flamers or not.'

"And at this, that white boy from Compton's Circle named Mikhail gets incredibly indignant, mortifiably pissed. He's about to huff and puff and give his reasoning in the manliest way he can muster when all of a sudden, his fuck-buddy speaks for the first time in almost 20 years. Apparently, the anger in his faggot-ass lover cured him of his deaf, dumb and blindness. But he's still got something of a stutter when he relays their plan: 'No, no, no, no, n-n-n-n-no, no, you id-id-id-idiots, you're the mo-mo-mo-mo-morons. We-we-we-we-we're going a-a-a-a-a-at night.'"

Horry's joke was as long as it was horrifically homophobic, and Mikhail impatiently waited throughout for the punchline. Unable to hide the look of dumbfoundment, he nodded until the half-lull that would present itself has his lone opportunity for surprise. Mikhail was just taking a few breaths till the right moment to strike. During that dreadful story, Mikhail sipped his double-Jameson rocks that he was so graciously allowed to keep and mapped out his exit plan. Against all odds, he'd wait for the punchline and then knock loose a few of Horry's Will Smith-perfect teeth—then immediately run through Something's doors and into the #720's perennial clusterfuck.

But when the punchline came, right when Horry finished his despicable impression of a stuttering man, Armstrong slammed Mikhail's face on the bar and then pinned his arms behind his back. "Pastor Shakur wants to see you," Armstrong said.

"Before you go to the sun, faggot," Horry gloated.

The pillar of a bouncer looked over Horry's shoulder. He was scowling shamefully, both at his security FAIL and probably Mikhail's lack of fight. As disappointed as the TSABDD was with the pillar, he was just as disappointed in Mikhail.

"Holy fuck, I'm smaller than you guys. Relax a bit. I obviously need to talk to management," Mikhail said, beginning to walk back to the VIP section where he last saw Tupac. "You gotta be smarter than a rock to see a way past the rules."

That's when Robert Horry socked Mikhail hard across the cheek with an open-palmed left hook. Horry's fingers seemed to wrap around Mikhail's head and bitchslap both ears. It took everything he had left to remain on his feet.

"The Pastor is already upstairs. He's past you peons, so get the fuck up, cream puff, and follow the Pillar before his dumb-ass gets fired."

Visit **http://PleaseUseRearExit.net/home/FuckerCats**
for an adorable little bonus chapter that gets confused by laser pointers and moths

Chapter Seventeen
From Boys to Dogs to Men

A door behind the bar was opened and Mikhail was pushed through it. He started walking up a flight of stairs followed closely by Armstrong, Horry and then the downtrodden pony-tailed pillar. The steps were black. The walls were black. There were no lights.

Once the door closed behind the progressively taller procession, Mikhail had no choice but to step in the name of faith...he couldn't see a damn thing. Maybe he was being kidnapped, his legs to be broken with a spiked fucking bat. Maybe his eyelids would be cut off and he'd be fed nothing but sleeping pills. Perhaps his kneecaps would be removed and he'd be forced to kneel in some pitch-black staircase piss. But with Horry's anal fascination, Mikhail feared most that his asshole would be sewed closed and that they'd keep feeding him and feeding him and feeding him and feeding him. Completely helpless, three against one in unknown territory, it was all he could hope that the stairs would end. Uncertain of the bends and curves that spiraled into the impenetrable darkness that enveloped everything, he was repeatedly pushed in the back at every hesitation, every time he was unsure whether to step up or turn left. And it happened more than once.

After what felt like a thousand steps and dozens of inclining 360s, Mikhail saw a light at the end of his tunnel. Just as he stepped on the final stair and caught the quickest glimpse of his destination, Armstrong shoved him with all his might. Mikhail could've sworn he felt a third hand on his back, one that could only be Horry's, as he was thrown with full force flat on his face into a room soaked in light.

The large room was mostly empty, practically vacuous, and maybe Mikhail was a little too nervous to notice much detail.

Peering through squinted eyes and lying on his stomach on a hard-wood floor, Mikhail only recognized Pastor Tupac Shakur because he was Pastor Tupac Shakur. Even if the punches from the man's hooligans had knocked Mikhail's glasses askew, there was no mistaking the silhouette of LA's mayoral candidate or his harem of naked girls scampering for their clothes. Shakur was fully dressed in an immaculately tailored suit and the dimes were divvying up their confusing collection of skirts, tanks, bras, thongs, and heels. Seeing the same ladies so sure of their station just a half hour ago scurry full of scare simultaneously settled and spiked Mikhail's nerves. Especially as their fear was so naked and their breasts so taut.

"Los Angeles is just a gang unto itself," Tupac said. He sat on one of two leather couches in a living room set-up without a visible TV, only a modest coffee table. In his gray suit with a red tie and not a button out of place, he didn't even have to wave off the women without them knowing what they had to do...and they did it quickly. "This city was built on gangs. It still runs on gangs. Bouncers, private security, the CIA, the FBI, the NSA, Republicans and Democrats, Internethodists, Webidians, the Anti-Squid League...those are gangs. You're probably laying there, ass over tea kettle, thinking that the Tupac Shakur Association of Being Dastardly Dapper is a gang. Do you think I'm a gang leader? As you're dry humping the floor, is that what you think?"

"I have no thoughts except getting back to a piece of warm pussy," Mikhail said. In the foreverness of the 155 seconds it took him to be walked up the stairs, he had already committed himself to being in it to win it. Bravado seemed to have gotten him in this situation—what other reason than Mikhail's false use of the Pastor's name could've caused his summons?—and it'd have to get him out. It was his only option to hide how scared shitless he truly was. "Your anal-obsessed henchman stole me away before I had the chance to close."

"Did you steal The Good Book, Mikhail? Just talking to you, I feel like you plagiarized a TSABDD card for your wallet, a card that burns with my acronym. Did you do that?"

"No, sir," Mikhail tried. "My wallet is empty."

"Where'd your dick go Mikhail? Where'd your money disappear? I had such high hopes for you. I found some time to check the status updates on your Facebook page."

"My dick hasn't gone anywhere yet, but if it hasn't found something wet by the end of the night, I swear to The Internet, it'll rip through the back of Horry's scull...no homo, sir."

"Young man, that might be the funniest thing I've heard all night," Pastor Shakur said, without the slightest hint of a smile, motioning Mikhail to stand up. "You know that he could kill you the second I asked, right? He wouldn't think twice and I wouldn't blink once as they cleared the cache of your blood and bones from my floor. Your history wouldn't exist, like The Internet erased every page you ever visited. Big Shot Bob could do that."

"That pansy was such a dirty player in the league, I can't imagine the filth he's picked up since," Mikhail said, still laying flat but finding a way to nod in Horry's direction. He was standing in the corner with the rest of his trio. "Not that the TSABDD teaches filth. It's just that your rules are a little more relaxed. Truthfully, I'm more scared of getting LA's first case of AIDS in 75 years from the blood on his knuckles than a quick beat-down death."

Horry started to launch forward at Mikhail, but Pastor Shakur cut him off with a simple stare. Armstrong and the Pillar held Horry back just for the looks of things.

"BJ, Bob, whoever you are you tall motherfucker, go ahead and get out of here, Mikhail and I are cool."

"Ivan, sir," the Pillar said, meekly walking back down the stairs behind Armstrong and a sulking Horry, ducking his head when he needn't, "been a member for 44 months."

Once they started going down the stairs and Mikhail was sure that he wouldn't be kicked in the back, he spun around on his ass and tried to find a position that posited him as a reverential yet strong man. He leaned back on his left hand and used his right to rub his face. Just because he heard the shuffle of feet descending down the stairs didn't mean he was in the clear. Tupac could still kill him and erase all traces of his existence without ever leaving that leather couch. But Mikhail had made enough of an impression to send the rapper-turned-political-figure's muscle away and that had to mean something in the unknown attic of Something.

"How do you know what you do about The Good Book? I'm not Ivan, so don't try and bullshit me," Shakur said. "I wrote all that scripture and you sure as hell didn't pay to read it. So what, you eavesdropped?"

Mikhail nodded.

"Take a real seat, Mikhail. You are a man, right? You show flashes of it, but I'm still not sure. You're not a dog trying to be a man, are you? No matter how many tails you chase or the number of bitches you mount, you gotta be bigger than a dog. Be a man. We men. Dogs die for the right to fuck. Men fuck for the right to live."

"..."

"Every funeral you go, it was a bitch that was horny the night before. It's always about bitches. Dogs bend to the power of a bitch in heat...that's what makes them violent," Pastor Shakur then paused. He peered down at Mikhail with a fury of wrinkles on his forehead. "Seriously though, get up and sit on this couch. It hurts my neck to look down on the world. I've been shot too many damn times."

Mikhail tentatively stood up and did his best to shake the cautiousness from his move to the second couch in the spacious room. The soft leather couches were set up perpendicularly and Mikhail made sure to sit somewhere between out-of-reach and close-enough-to-not-give-a-fuck. He thought about putting his foot up on the wooden and glass coffee table but decided against it. Instead, he crossed his legs, mustering all the comfort he could in what was normally such a natural motion.

"Most fools who use my name in vain don't make it up here, they just get their ass kicked and then booted. I can't tell if you're lucky or not. Do you know? I don't fucking know. I was wracking my brain when I heard you head up the stairs, even as I was getting dome. You were clunking up and I had three pigeons clucking down. Do you know why you're here and those fine-ass women aren't? They want to be here way more than you do."

"I wasn't trying to inconvenience you, trust me. I have no reason here. I want to be down there, maximizing whatever hand I got dealt so I don't have to play it against my own dick. And things were looking a whole lot warmer than the microwaved lotion I normally use."

"Facebook says that you're recently single, is that right or did you lie on your profile too?"

"I'm sure you saw her profile too...can I get a drink before we get into Katya?" Mikhail asked. He wanted to ask Tupac about Jada, just to defer his past and find the common ground of a woman gone wild...but then remembered that he really wasn't in any sort of position to push it.

"I get that, it's not like my business isn't graffitied all over The Internet. And I definitely don't want to be asked about it in every interview. There are a few bottles in and near that mini-fridge over there and a few glasses, get us both one."

Still fighting the urge to run, to sprint downstairs and past Horry and them (who were surely waiting for him down by the bar), it felt dumb to stay, but even stupider to try and escape. Acting casual was the only move that Mikhail had. He stood up and stumbled in the direction that Tupac was pointing. His face was numb but he could feel it start to swell. Every hit landed on his right side and he was still trying to figure out whether such a succession of coin flips was lucky or not. Refusing to fumble with an ice tray, he poured himself a Blue Label neat and assumed from numerous raps and the contents of the mini-fridge that mixing a Thug Passion was apt for Pastor 'Pac.

"Can I ask you a question?"

"As long as it ain't about Sister Jada."

"Of course not, give me some credit," Mikhail said, returning to his seat and handing Tupac his glass of Alize and Cristal. "But why are you running for mayor? It's bad enough being a celebrity, but a politician? It's not like you can yell at The Internet and get it to stop talking about you, especially when it's the people's every-other-year turn to give a fuck. I mean, you already got everything a man could want. I've never even had two girls at the same time, you just had three and didn't even unbutton your jacket."

"I want answers, Mikhail. Answers you can't get in the private sector. Not in my industry anyway. There are more members of this association than 75% of the churches on the #7 and They still won't give me a station. They barely let me on the god damn bus. I've seen The Internet but still don't know what the fuck it is. Have you seen It, Mikhail?"

"No."

"Of course not. And that's another answer I need. Why not? Why haven't you been allowed to see what keeps you here trapped on these buses? And why aren't you trying harder to see it? They beat it into us that there is no other option, that They're the noblest of nobles just for maintaining the routes and the lines and the BTWNs so we can work all day for just enough to get by and maybe get a little drunk. Fuck a noble. I'm not noble, I'm just a man."

"I just said that exact bit about not being noble two hours ago," Mikhail said. "But what you're saying seems like something we could really rally behind. Maybe we're just not ready for the answers? Some of us, sure, but most of us aren't."

"You don't want to know. Anyone with any thirst for knowledge immediately gets a job with the government. The Internet checks your Google searches, Mikhail; The Internet knows early on whether or not you give a fuck and that's when It starts to care," Shakur said.

He wore his worries like a spring in a vice, but there was still something very relaxing about the tone in his voice. Genuine pain seeped out between breaths, regret alternated with resolution, always ready to explode into an oratory of revolution. Or maybe violence. All of those internal interactions and possibilities, as if he was just waiting for the wind to change so he could unleash the energy stored within. It made any words he said feel important, especially when he was saying things of such importance. As much as it put Mikhail at ease, it also made him nervous. He didn't want to release the coil's potential energy.

"I shouldn't even be telling you this, I'm messing up all my rules...but if you're dumb enough to use my name to get into my club, then you definitely ain't one of them. If I say that shit out loud—to the general public—I'll never make it to election day. They won't let me. Five shots couldn't drop me, I took it and smiled...I'm still the thug they love to hate. But here I am talking campaign strategy with some d-bag sneaking his way into my spot."

"I didn't sneak in here to be cool," Mikhail said, "I only lied because I had nowhere else to go."

"What happens if I actually start speaking the truth, rather than just writing rhymes or telling boys how to become men? It's always been my belief that the government is just a gang unto itself, with the good and the bad. Just like the gangbangers on Compton's Circle have the good and the bad—just like the government does. They got stress and character flaws that comes from their lifestyles. I can be the best politician the people have ever seen, but what does that really mean?"

"I don't know, man," Mikhail said. "Building a line for schools? Internet classes don't really seem to be working. Maybe raising minimum wage?"

"The politicians who attempt that don't last because not everyone is supposed to have money. If everyone had money, us rich guys wouldn't be as rich. Even if I was to hand out money and educations through the political process, I can't tell nobody who's hungry how to eat. Not unless I force feed him. It ain't up to me to tell a starving brother how to get some food. Even if I lead him by his hand to the #780 and put money in his pocket, pat him on the ass as he walks down the cracker aisle at Food 4 Less, I can't make sure he's going to eat. If the brother gets jumped for the money as he's waiting in the checkout line, it'd be my fault. But you, Mikhail, I'm willing to take a risk. I'm gonna give you a little mission and if you succeed, we'll let you into the TSABDD."

"I don't really have the money for a membership, sir, no disrespect," Mikhail said softly. All that monologue had worn his mojo thin. "I just have to make due with what I got, you're the last person I want to owe money, not that I probably couldn't use—"

"You want it to be one thing, but it's the other, Mikhail. You haven't even gotten to what happens if you don't succeed... or even what the mission is all about."

"Yeah...okay...sure. What happens if I fail?"

"See, you still have it backwards and you're really making me doubt my hunch. You're focused on failing before you even hear what's going on. Earlier this week, you tweeted about being in it to win it, was that another lie?

"It wasn't...and yeah, I am in it to win it. What else do I have?"

"Good. Because you have to get yourself into a threesome tonight," the Pastor said, with all undue seriousness and gravity. The request was ridiculous, but the spring was tensing and Mikhail knew that its uncoil would lead to his death. Pastor Tupac Amaru Shakur didn't have to say much to mean everything in the entire Internet. "Either that, or fall in love. Simple tasks if you have the tools. And truthfully, I just have to see if I'm right. And if I am, well, you get free membership for life."

"And what happens if I don't? Are there rules here? Are you going to be sending Horry at me at every turn?"

"'Cause why? You'd knock him out if I did? I'd like to see you try and climb that mountain...shit, Mikhail, you're one hell of a firecracker. But no, that's not what I'm interested in. Don't get me wrong, I'd pay to see Mikhail vs. Horry—and I don't pay for anything these days—but it's not the itch I'm scratching. Just simultaneously find your way into two different women or the heart of one...and come back tonight. We're throwing LCR dice till the wee hours. It's a game of chance... just like yours."

"Wait, I gotta fuck two chicks before I leave tonight?"

"No, no, no...only if you really want to surprise me and get it all done on this bus. That might just make you a Lieutenant right out the gate," Shakur laughed. "Just give me an update before you leave and get it done before you go to sleep."

"You really gonna kill me if I don't do this? Or are you just acting all hard?"

"Every fire cracker goes pop at some point, and I'm the motherfucker who's lighting the match. Don't be a dud...for your own damn good."

Mikhail hadn't noticed the room's lone flat screen until he got up to leave, it had been behind him the whole time. It wasn't The Internet, but it was an array of Internet jpegs in HD. One still image at a time, they looked like paintings, framed by the strong black box of the flat screen's paneling. Mikhail only retained three quick bursts before leaving—two girls dancing on a grave, a man holding a squid, and a fire cracker. He didn't know what it meant, but felt like it was something he was supposed to decode. Instead, he walked towards the door and into the spiral staircase.

Chapter Eighteen
Burning the Beer

The absolute darkness of the stairwell felt infinitely more comforting than the hug of a large-chested woman. While it was so terrifying on the way up, the way down proved a reality where Mikhail wasn't yet dead. That he had survived. And that he had a mission. Mikhail practiced his strut with every invisible step, trying once again to instill himself with the optimism of a glass half full.

Someday, he'd view the previous 45 minutes as another notch on his belt—as another story to compete with whatever tale Chevy found his way into—assuming he completed and survived the rest of the night. Pastor Tupac Shakur was capable of tasks outside of Mikhail's understanding, this much he was sure of, even if he didn't know what it exactly meant. After a few hundred steps, he'd be pushing through the door into the dimly lit Something and it'd feel like God's flashlight into the eyes of a reformed serial killer. Mikhail hadn't killed anybody, but he was just as thankful to get off scott-free. And when he finally opened the door, the light was indeed that bright.

He squinted as he walked past Horry, Armstrong and the Pillar. Awaiting Mikhail's return—just as he had predicted—they stood cross-armed against the wall. They didn't say anything to him and he hoped that his squinting looked like a surly gesture. He knew things that they did not and it'd take a few minutes for them to catch up. And for him to adjust to the light, to his new lease on life. He needed a drink and a smoke now more than ever, but he wasn't about to press his luck any further by leaving again. And even if he didn't realize it, he needed to piss way more than the other two. A drink, and a drink alone, would have to do. He had to take advantage of what was afforded to him.

The numbers were still favorable, even if he didn't know a single one of the fine females that paraded around Something. Without an in, it was much easier to look than participate. In an expensive-looking black cocktail dress, a woman covered in glittering scales sauntered up to the bar. A few d-bags tried to nod coolly in the corner. Across the way, a set of sexy Siamese twins synchronized symmetrical dance moves. Maybe that was his threesome? Probably not. People moved along whatever path The Internet gave them. The sparkling specimen that she was, a barely legal lady twerked what her momma gave her on top of a speaker like it was her bedroom. If Mikhail was to complete his mission, he'd have to make the first move at least once.

The ceiling in Something seemed to have shrunk once he knew there was a second floor. Whatever existed between all those stairs wasn't one of his concerns—his first was the whereabouts of his friends. It'd been nearly an hour since he left and maybe Chevy and Jayson had gone to search him out, but it was more likely that they'd leave to find what was next before leaving to find him. No strike against their friendship, it just was what it was. If they weren't at the table, Mikhail told himself that he'd go smoke a cigarette, collect a bit of Zen, and perhaps grab a drink from the creepy booze cart guys. Then try to figure out how to get into HD. Maybe play pool at Nothing if that didn't work. Maybe that plan was the most preferable.

But he'd make one last pass through Something, just to make sure that Chevy and Jayson hadn't left. He was okay with the idea that they had, but he was really hoping that they hadn't. Especially if they were still sitting with the same girls. Mikhail wanted to know if one of them spelled her name with an H.

A quick tour around the partying bodies—a mass that had certainly multiplied in his absence—quickly yielded the laughing faces of his friends in the same exact place he had left them. Their grills were more welcoming than Mikhail could ever admit, even if they hadn't quite caught sight of him yet. Chevy and Jayson didn't need a complete reinterpretation of his history, he could just relay the consequences of his most immediate events and ask for their help in his quest. This time he actually felt like he had something to say.

But they weren't with the girls Mikhail had left them with—Sara(h) was nowhere in sight—and yet they weren't alone. Saffron was there and Chevy's hand was on her leg.

Her back was to Mikhail, but he recognized her regardless. Her long straight hair was a dead give away. A barrage of brown that evaporated into perfection, it was still in a simple braid that fell from a single elastic. He wanted the braid to tickle his nose as she laid on top of him, making everything smell like lilacs. It was her path that he crossed upon entering the joint.

After the store-front church incident on Compton's Circle, she disappeared from real life. Even before his second break-up with Katya, she had mostly vanished from his mind. She was sexier than ever. Certainly, it was quick to click that her fated presence was the hanging fruit of half his mission, but it'd take more than that to prepare him for her presence. Let alone Chevy's intrusion. And then some of the stairwell's fear started to creep back into his veins. He pivoted on his right heel and went to the bar first. It felt as cowardly as it did easy.

With his back purposefully towards Saffron, Mikhail ordered his usual—of the continuously double variety—and thought about what he could say to her. He amped himself up to be charming. Maybe he could find forever with Saffron, she was always so supportive. Didn't the Pastor say something about love? He tried to shake off the nasty feelings from being briefly kidnapped that kept coming back and pushed to focus on his mission at hand. But more than that, he attempted to dial in on a conquest left unexplored. It wasn't like the elements he was facing were the blustery mountain winds of YouTube explorers, he just had to find the warm hills of Saffron's sunny afternoon. And either fall in love or rope in another female for a threesome. It seemed impossible.

Pastor Shakur's directions were as implicitly vague as the consequences were vaguely implicit: Get laid twice or die once. Fall in love or get killed trying. Waiting for his change, sipping his whiskey, Mikhail inhaled deeply and exhaled even further. Once the untouchable existence of lust, Saffron was now a near mandatory venture.

Chevy's slight of hand wasn't unexpected, but it had put enough pause in Mikhail's step to turn his focus towards the bar. It was another casualty of their friendship... not that Chevy was trifling, just that he was more appealing. At least, that's how Mikhail saw it. He got his change from the bartender. He pointedly breathed a few more times while telling himself that he needed the DJ to play any song that was remotely recognizable. A good soundtrack had the ability to make him feel more comfortable in his skin. Much easier, he'd be able to interact with Saffron, Chevy and Jayson while bobbing his head in unison with a familiar beat. But before he could be amped, before the bad feelings got shook, before the DJ found something suitable, Mikhail's Diplomats scully was once again pulled over his eyes.

"Damn Chevy, you already pulled this shit..."

"Guess again," she said. Her hands covered his hat which was already over his eyes, a little redundant if it weren't for the few fingers that graced the still-exposed parts of his face. Her pinkie and ring fingers were just as powder soft as he had remembered them. Lilacs. Everywhere. In his enforced darkness, Mikhail wished he could've traded the moment from

Anything (when Jay-Z so timely boomed from the speakers) for this similarly pivotal point in his night. Instead, the same dribble that he'd never heard continued to echo on from up above.

"Maybe if we danced, I'd know," Mikhail said, internally begging to feel the sway of her hips once again. "I'm horrible with voices. Have we danced before?"

"There you go trying to be slick again," Saffron said. She twirled him around and lifted his blindfold, careful to keep his glasses from being knocked to the floor. "You either recognize my IP address or you don't, but don't try and be all cutesy and quick with your ping-back."

"What're you some kind of computer geek now?" he asked.

"Guess you'll just have to find out if this is just geek chic or a real, live Internet genius."

He didn't even have a chance to see what she was wearing before he was enveloped in a hug. More than the pressing curves that made the little him stand straight, he was struck by her conversational initiative. Not only was she making a joke on her own, but it was packed with references he had to scramble in order to recover. It threw him further off balance. Despite the mission and despite Chevy's usual antics, he was immediately at comfort in her caring dialogue, but he could tell from the get that there was something else. There was a new development that changed everything...Saffron suddenly had a brain.

"Your friends miss you, c'mon already," she said, motioning towards the table. "I've been listening to Chevy talk about the #111 for 15 minutes too long. And I just sat down 10 minutes ago."

"Is that a zinger?"

Saffron rolled her eyes and started to drag Mikhail back towards the table.

"Wait a second," he said, stopping her in those soft footed tracks. Why was he suddenly overcome with the urge to smell her feet? "You want a drink?"

"Oh, right, of course. A consensus was made to make it easy on you," she smiled, still leaning in Chevy and Jayson's direction, "three Patron-sodas, please."

"Cool, I can carry it, go back and make my seat warm," he said, so unsure about everything—beginning with his cash fold and ending at her voluptuousness. After she asked him if he was sure and she walked out of earshot, Mikhail ordered three tequila sodas and another double Jameson rocks for himself. Again, he inhaled deeply and then exhaled even further. When his breath was exhausted by running laps around his spinning mind, he finished his first drink and collected the second draft of change. After salvaging the depths of a few more breath cycles, he gathered the four glasses between his two hands and followed the same path that Saffron had.

It wasn't the four drinks walking half a step ahead of him that made Mikhail stumble, no; no, it was the drinks and moments of his past that almost made him lose his footing. With droplets of booze splashing the hair on his arms, he found his physical balance much quicker than his mental levelness. His night ran through his mind at light speed, throwing in glimpses of his past life (both committed and single)...while he tried in vain to keep all the pixels from getting mixed up. He couldn't tell if Katya had a K tattooed on her neck or if Saffron's earrings dangled or if Bridget kept tearfully text messaging him. Nary one of them was visible. Haunted by more confusion than clarity, once again he was suddenly at the head of a table that was never his own.

"Fresh out the has been, look what the cat dragged in. Holy cow," Chevy started.

"...if it isn't the cat's re-ow," Saffron finished.

The brief back-and-forth instantly snapped Mikhail out of his funk. The desire to rail on his friends for not coming to his rescue started to boil over. And he'd need them to complete his mission. Somewhere down the line. Yet, once Saffron finished

Chevy's rhyme, Mikhail instantly forgot the charm of his Tupac story. Instead he lost his focus to words like desertion and disrespect.

He'd never claim ownership over Saffron, but Chevy damn-well knew their back story just like he did his overtly flirtatious jokes shared at Mikhail's expense. Maybe her hand was pressed against Chevy's giggling chest to really push him away or maybe it was more of a push-pull thing.

"What happened to your other girls?" Mikhail asked Chevy. It was at this moment of weird dick measuring that Mikhail realized that he really had to pee. A ton of bricks signaling a Top 50 occasion weighed on his bladder, he had no choice but to continue on. "You scare them away?"

"Ladies and gentleman, allow me to interrupt," Jayson said, still on the strange regalia of Britney Spears past. "I've been saving this story until Mikhail got back...Wait, where the fuck did you go?"

Not wanting to upstage Jayson's untold tale and not at all sure how to bring up his kidnapping in casual conversation—nor its implications with Saffron around—and temporarily unaware of anything but his swimming teeth, Mikhail just shrugged.

"Aight, man, okay, so, yeah, I totally just fingered that girl under the table," he continued. "Oh, sorry, Saffron, I didn't mean—"

"—No, it's okay, I get it, you're excited. It's the Technorati score of a life time. It's cool."

"So what? A finger-bang and you're left with a dry ding-a-lang? Jesus, man...brag about the whole shabang, not part of it...dang."

If ever one of Chevy's rhymes were to be ignored this was the one. Jayson was just happy that he had found some affection and was probably overwrought with guilt about it. A relationship without physicality can only last so long and he had already broken The Internet's record. Mikhail had never seriously dated someone with the blue-balled restrictions that Jayson faced...and

Chevy rarely ever spoke with a girl he couldn't fuck. And Saffron sat there, the desire of all men everywhere, her needs ably met whenever she chose. Mikhail had been through droughts, but at least then he was able to masturbate in peace. If anyone deserved some satisfaction, it was Jayson.

"Chevy's a spoiled bitch, don't pay attention to him. I get it," Mikhail said. "It's intimacy. It's getting a girl wet without getting your fingers chomped off."

"No, you don't get it either. My old lady and I find intimacy, but this shawty just now, she had two vaginas."

"No fuckin' way, sell that story to eBay, not me," Chevy said, pronouncing his own pronoun like the calendar month.

"I've never heard of that," Saffron said, thinking hard. "Were they side by side or up and down?"

"Good question," Mikhail added. Chevy and Saffron shared one bench, while Jayson and Mikhail parsed another. It wasn't the largest of divides, but Mikhail was still at a disadvantage in whatever game Chevy was playing—especially when Jayson was doing the talking, such a rare occasion as it was.

"It felt so close and personal, like we were the only people in the whole room. Four fingers in two holes sounds so gross, but yeah, they were side by side. And this is the crazy part," he said, "the left side was kind of cold and the right was practically boiling. It was like they belonged to two separate bodies."

"Hot and cold? From a pool to a hot tub, a cool and a hot rub for a fool and his sad glove?"

"Seriously, Jayson," Saffron said, "I know I hardly know you, but you didn't want to try that out? I don't know of a single man who wouldn't be furiously logging on just for the chance at it, these two hound dogs included."

"Hey, I resent that," Mikhail said. "I've never cheated ever, which is more than this two-vagina finger banger can say. Not that I'm sinless, but still, he just cheated."

"So what, you're 0 and he's 1? Binary buddies, peas in the same pod."

"But the levels count, Saffy, c'mon now. There's a thin line between everything, but it's a line all the same."

"If the unnamed girlfriend thinks wanking is to cheat, is she keen on you rubbing a pair of cleat?"

"I just gave a girl a smile, you saw her, she was pouty as all hell," Jayson answered Chevy. "I didn't dip my dick in the hot tub or the pool, I just made a sad girl smile and that's enough for me."

"And now it's another reason why your two Friendbots will never meet your girl."

"Exactly."

After Saffron's quick quip, Mikhail thought for the first time that Jayson might just be hiding his friends from his old lady...and not the other way around. He had been so consumed with the negativity of a relationship without consummation that the rewarding thoughts of their existence rarely occurred to him. Mikhail was re-thinking a lot at that moment.

Once upon a time, Saffron was the potential fulfillment of so many sexual conquests. Her curves were heavenly and her lack of intelligence was ripe for the devil, but her new incarnation put Mikhail in purgatory. He once had the upper hand, and now he didn't even know where his hands belonged. They once fit so immaculately in her back pockets, echoing the plump curve of all her radiant heat. A lot can change in a few months and a whole lot more can stay the same.

Mikhail tried to keep his chin forward, but her shiny new aura continually put him back on his heels. He didn't know where or why or how she was different, he just knew that she was. The sex pot he had taken to church had reappeared in his life as an actual human being. She still exuded the same sex appeal—with that body there was no way she couldn't—but there was more weight in her container. Mikhail was as thrilled as he was startled.

And where the potential balance between life and death hovered, he knew that Saffron was the closest and sweetest thing to low hanging fruit on this whole damned bus. If Pastor Shakur was serious—be a member or be murdered—Mikhail would have to start with Saffron. Time was running out in the evening before he had a chance to set himself for the tasks ahead.

"Exactly," Jayson said, this time with less fervor. Then once again with more, "Anyway, what the fuck are we doing tonight? Am I really the first one of us to be sick of a spot? You guys got a fever or something?"

"So sick, need a doc, yes! A creature, a monster, like the Lochness," Chevy said.

"I gotta piss anyway," Mikhail said, anxious to get going.

"I say this as a friend, protected by all the no-homo's in the world, but have you ever got your prostate checked?" Chevy asked. And if it wasn't for the quick glances he casually threw at Saffron, Mikhail might've believed such a heartfelt sentiment. "You piss more than a pregnant woman."

"I'm not a player, I just piss a lot," Mikhail retorted in the only reference-laden language that Chevy understood. "I don't hide it, I be it. My bladder is what it is and doctors have told me I'm cool. Chill on that."

"I'm just trying to help a homie out, that's all, didn't mean anything by it," Chevy said, stately falling into his non-rhyme mode. "It's like the motherfuckers at work. They can't be easy with their financial instruments, it's a self-fulfilling cycle of panic. There's so much money out there, you'd think they'd want to take advantage of it, instead of losing their shit over the prospect of failure.

"The market goes up and down every single day. There's always going to be a strike at some plant on the #4 or a stack of furlough days on another, and production is going to get backed up. Some shit will always go wrong. Ride it out. Ride it out, motherfuckers, just ride it out. Throwing up about it doesn't help anyone. I don't even like the smell of it. Puke is the only aspect of economics that trickles down, you smell me? Like this one guy—Joe Whatever Whatever—he literally carries around a briefcase packed with three extra blue button-ups."

"Is that your lunch buddy?" Jayson asked. "The guy you trade pudding snacks with?"

"Haha, yeah right. Just today, Joe lost a few hundred G's on information that didn't come up correct. He lost a dollar-and-a-half per share for every pound of perspiration, that's why he brings the extra shirts. He changes at the 10 o'clock break, again at lunch and then again at three. Before-hand, his shirts are pristinely laid out on a gorgeous leather chair that he never sits in. It doesn't matter that he made three times yesterday what he lost today."

Chevy's firm focused on the stocks of high-end mechanical factories, the type that made the multi-million dollar parts that made LA's dizzying system of buses move. The same factories that Jayson worked at. Chevy made money when the grocery stores on the #780 added an extra handicap ramp from the Green BTWN or when the Sky Carts on the Hollywood Hills needed new sound systems. His company traded shares of all those components. Its importance and potential for wealth was obviously a huge part of his success with the ladies...that and his good looks. And the fancy clothes his job afforded him.

"Mikhail's not Joe just because he has to take a leak, Chevy, if that's what you're trying to say," Saffron said. "I have to use the little girl's room too. Am I Joe?"

"Does Mikhail have to use the little girl's room?" Jayson mocked in an Internet-awful high pitch. He obviously felt like he was on a roll and no one was about to take that away from him.

"That's not what I meant," she sighed.

"Yeah, I know," Jayson nodded, getting back to his own reality. "I gotta see a man about a squid my damn self."

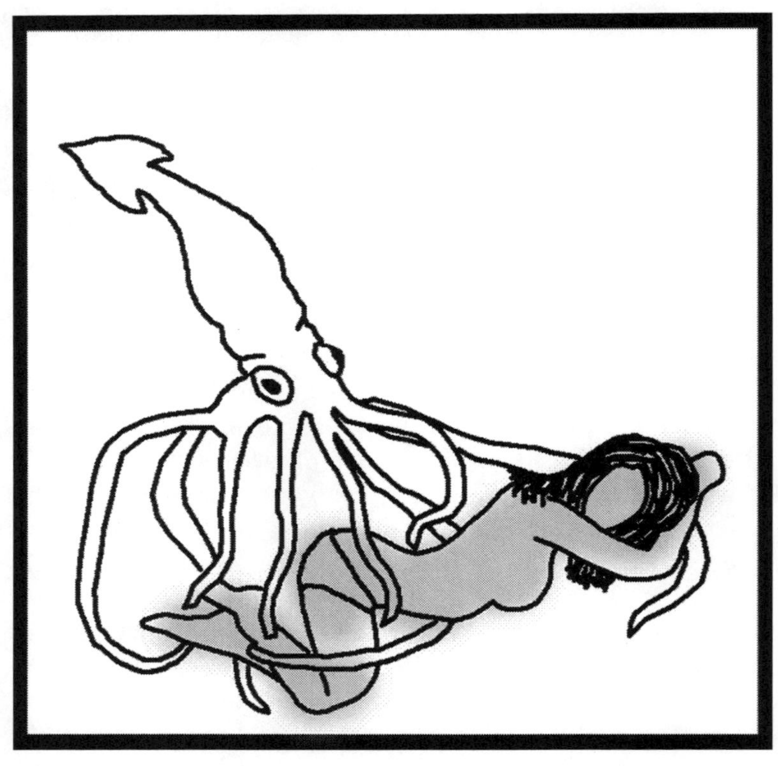

Visit **http://PleaseUseRearExit.net/home/SquidAttack**
for a bonus chapter that laughs in the
tentacled face of danger.

Chapter Nineteen
Spores & Pores

Mikhail's piss meter was approaching armageddon levels. Unable to turn his dosey-doh with Tupac into a quick story of charming reveal, he was absolutely thrilled at the convergence of chaos: Saffron and Jayson needed the bathroom, and so did he. It was a respite from the pressures on his mission and his stomach... without any of the guilt. And the latter was fierce on his scale of urination escalations—the need to piss was approaching Hall of Fame levels. He did his best to walk normally through the nagging pain, through the few minutes of absurdity to get to the next closest station of promise land.

The #720's main corridor was hell's blender. A jumping man waved his white cap over the crowd in the futile effort of flagging down friends long gone. An amputee drag queen danced on top of a stone bench like it was the floor next to her bed. One of the two heads of a two-headed man shouted obscenities at some girls who'd stepped on their sneakers, while the other tried to whisper sweet nothings into the drunkest girl's ear. A group of sorority sweethearts looked absolutely terrified by all the congestion. The claustrophobia of the entire situation seemed to get this green skinned man's goat and he freaked out just enough to curl in a fetal position amongst a bed of plastic geraniums in a concrete plot. Even as 90% of the populace just herded themselves from Point A to Point B, shit was getting crazy in the #720.

"Mikhail, I really need to talk to you," Saffron said. Chevy and Jayson were trying to find the space to walk and she tried to find space between them to talk. "You've done so much for me, I don't know where to start."

"Let's not start here, I can barely hear you."

Flashing lights were going off from every corner and the municipal bathrooms were only 50 feet up front. An amalgamation of music from every bar on every side was congealing into a distorted pile of gray earwax. The chatter around them was even more unbearable. And without a word having been said about it, everyone knew that HD was the next step and that beating the rush to see Weezy would be an exhausting hullabaloo.

"Well, can you wait for me? The little girl's chat-room is right here."

"There's no line for you, but a serious one for me," Mikhail said, jokingly pointing at the disparate waits ahead of them. "You're the only girl I've ever met who's ever attempted that chat-room. Maybe it'll be pristine for you. Then again, guys can piss standing up...a hole in the ground ain't much different than a porcelain palace's perfect pitcher."

"So many P's, I guess you really do have to go," she said, kissing him on the cheek and running off into a sea of pink tile. Unlike Saffron's venture for reprieve, Mikhail's was stunted by a straggling pack of would-be pee-ers. Even in the main corridor, it was bad news that the ladies' line took longer than the men's. It said a lot about the night's shifting demographics.

That Jayson joined him was both a blessing and a curse. The company was great but Mikhail needed to cut the line in order to keep Chevy and Saffron's time alone at a minimum— and being responsible for two bodies was more problematic than just his own. He eyed the line of d-bags—a cornucopia of errant muscles and mistaken tattoos and mass-produced meme t-shirts—and just knew that there was an open urinal inside. There wasn't a stereotype of homophobe not represented. They were too terrified to piss next to another man; their pulsing deltoids were a gargantuan replacement for any sort of self-confidence. And with the clock nearing midnight and Mikhail's grains of sand running out and his bladder quickly pushing a Top 10 occasion, he nodded at Jayson and Jayson followed.

The bathroom had only gotten more disgusting with the passage of time. Miles of toilet paper, tattered cellophane from countless cigarette packs, paper towels, ABC gum, used condoms, and somehow, two different left shoes...they were all stuck in the mire of the floor's browned sticky muck. Not a single toilet had been flushed. The coating on the walls grew thicker and may have even grown legs. Eleven hairy legs with poisonous spikes at the knees, if any legs at all. It was all beginning to ferment under the constant weight of humidity and sweating bodies that poured in and then out. And there wasn't a single urinal open, so Mikhail and Jayson had no choice other than to loom inside the bubble of stank or go back. They tried not to breath and tried even harder to pretend like they hadn't just cut the line.

"Well, I got punched for the first time, but I still haven't punched anyone," Mikhail said, hushed. "How are you, bredren?"

"Holy shit...are you okay? Wait, I want to ask if you're okay, but something tells me that you probably deserved it. And if it wasn't Robert Horry, you might've been better off saving your first punch."

"The pussy in me wants to forget that Horry was the main part of it, but the dick in me—"

"—pause."

"Good call, pause. Okay, so the asshole part of my personality wants to ask how it feels to be a cheater."

"Do you think Chevy's gonna fuck Saffron before you do?"

Searching himself, Mikhail found the same answer that Jayson expected. Despite her whispers in his ear, he felt like she'd follow the money and the charm and the strong chin, and he had none of that. He wasn't sure that he even wanted it.

"I feel bad, yeah," Jayson said. "Man, I just don't know what happened. You put my hand on her leg and it just, it just started. I started feeling scared of my old lady's mouth and then I found comfort in two toothless holes. I couldn't stop myself. She was so sad and then so happy. So what happened with Horry? Your fight then immediate flight plan didn't work?"

The john next to Mr. Sallow opened up and Mikhail filled the void without responding to Jayson. He apologized to his fountainous friend for not bringing him a white Russian while ignoring his other brother from another mother. He was there to unzip his jeans and so he did.

"Mr. Sallow," Mikhail said, searching for relief rather than an answer for Jayson's questions, "this might be one— mother of the Internet, savior of Google, holy how this feels good—it's definitely one of my top ten pisses. You have no idea what my night has—"

"What the fuck you think this is? You see the line here, don't be an asshole. You an asshole?" demanded a man wearing two bandannas. One was carefully folded pirate style upon his head and the second was delicately tied around his neck. They had both been ironed within the past five hours. Whatever his accessories, the man wasn't happy that Mikhail had cut the line. Apparently, this d-bag had a few observation skills.

"No problems, man," Mikhail said. "Really, all apologies. It's just that every time I come here—and I've been here more times than I'd like to admit—there's always been a spot open because this line is consistently full of homophobes. And once I got this far, shit, I just followed my instincts."

Already midstream, Mikhail's liquid waste was aggressively pouring against the porcelain, splashing back and spraying down towards the urinal cake that was almost invisible beneath the blackening syrup rising in the yellow-stained basin. His stream was coming fast and furious. He thought about whirling around and pissing all over the bandanna'd man's expensive leather shoes, but it seemed like an egregious risk to get caught with his pants down. Instead, he just hoped that Jayson would make his presence known or that Mr. Sallow would step in as peacemaker. Neither happened.

"It's not my place to jump the line, I'm sorry," Mikhail said. "It's just been that kind of night."

"Oh, it's about to be that kind of night," and with that, the bandanna'd man with the expensive elf shoes punched Mikhail in the back of the head. The right side of Mikhail's face slammed into the wall and was slimed by a collection of mildewed urine and growing fungus. The foul concoction penetrated his pores and he could taste its simultaneously exponentiating and decaying pungency.

The connection on the back of his head reverberated through his brain into the slime that suddenly coated the right side of his face. He felt dizzy, perhaps with the weight of his innately balling fists. Perhaps he was concussed. It was the second time Mikhail had ever been punched, both separated by little more than an hour, and the desire to strike back nearly knocked him over. Too stunned to find the rage that he was reserving for Robert Horry, he did nothing. No matter how out of line Mikhail was, a punch received was worthy of a punch returned, yet he couldn't find a punch in the bowl. But it didn't keep him from peeing.

"You cheap shot motherfucker," was all Mikhail could muster. His emptying bladder left his movements limited. Or maybe the bandanna'd man was a little intimidating. He was 20% bigger than Mikhail and the thought of an ass kicking was omnipresent. Mikhail tried to imagine the flat of his fist hitting this elf-shoed cocksucker square in the cheek, of the pain his knuckles would endure under the breaking pressure of the douchebag's face, but the potential FAIL was too much to risk for the slight chance at a WIN. Instead, he just continued to talk shit. "I don't even have to piss that bad, I'm just trying to get rid of the hard-on your mother gave me."

Then the elf-shoed man tried to hit Mikhail again. A little more prepared this time, Mikhail ducked the blow and it just glanced off the side of his head. The right hand of the double bandanna'd man brushed past Mikhail and slammed with full force into the puke-worthy wall. The sound alone was crippling. Knuckles were broken and tendons surely shard. He let out a painful yelp and fell to his knees, which was when Jayson decided to step up and deliver a left cross with all his weight. The bandanna'd aggressor fell on his face on that foul-ass floor, and Mikhail had no option other than to turn and finish his business on this guy's expensive shoes...and then all the way up to his face. And it being a top ten piss, he still had plenty of st(r)eam.

The entire room, everyone waiting in line or washing their hands, erupted into uproarious laughter. It didn't matter that they were once upset at Mikhail and Jayson for ignoring protocol by skipping the line, they all loved that fancy clothes were getting ruined. They were tickled pink by the sight of one man outright pissing on another. For many, it was the story to make their night.

"No homo," Mikhail said, making a big deal about shaking every last drop he had. "No homo, no homo. Pause. Double pause. No homo," he shouted, leaning his head back and relishing in the silly proclamation's echo across the foul enclosure. It was the loudest Mikhail had spoken in as long as he could remember. Never in his fights with Katya had he raised his voice to such a level. "I only pause to piss...PAUSE!"

Mikhail's Cam'ron channeling joke brought down the house. The collective noise shaved several millimeters of muck off the walls, shaking the free-flowing molecules from the pollinic grasp of the room's multiplying moisture. Despite a new puddle of urine, the room almost felt cleaner. Pissed on and pissed off, the man in the two bandannas ran out the room without so much as looking at himself in the mirror. Mikhail zipped up his jeans and his audience started applauding. Stupid as it was.

"Have you ever seen that, sir?" Mikhail asked, turning quietly to Mr. Sallow, speaking just loudly enough to be heard over the new-found raucous.

"Not exactly like that, but after a while, Mikhail, the fundamentals of everything fall into repetition and redundancy," Mr. Sallow said, not bothering to look up from his chronic task at hand. "You both probably got what you deserved. Cutting ain't cool."

"Something about that must stand out, I mean, I just pissed on a dude wearing two bandannas."

"But you still haven't punched a dude in the face," Jayson said, having slipped into Mikhail's spot during all the hoopla. "You missed a morally right opportunity to get that out the way."

"He's wise, Mikhail. I think you should listen to what your friends say more often."

While Jayson and Mr. Sallow traded introductions, Mikhail conjured up an argument where pissing on someone was just the same as punching. It was as good an excuse as any to punch an asshole, but he was still left making excuses. But...fuck.

"Can I make an observation?" Mr. Sallow asked. Mikhail didn't answer but he didn't stop looming and Mr. Sallow didn't seem to care. "You never take the first action, you only react to what's done to you. You allow the first step to be made by someone else or it doesn't get made at all."

"I took the step to cut this damn line, I made the move to finally break up with Katya—"

"—finally being the key word," Jayson chipped in.

"It leaves you flat-footed or, even worse, on the back of your heels. If you're only reacting to what knocks you back, you ain't ever gonna move forward, Mikhail."

"So how do I get laid tonight? Huh, fellas? It's my first night out as a single man and the only thing I want is to journey down a pretty path yet unmarked."

"Moving around is such a luxury that you never know what direction you're going, just listen to yourself. From the stories I hear about the route outside this bathroom, there are girls everywhere you look. And if there's one thing I know, you gotta step up to them. You can't step away. And you can't be waiting for a virgin, or an unmarked path, or whatever it is you're trying to say, that's for damn sure."

"Every time I move the least bit forward with a shawty, I get violently knocked back by an outside force," Mikhail said. Despite the exhaustion burning in his feet, he was careful not to lean against the wall. His face had touched too much already and once Jayson was done pissing, Mikhail'd get to washing. "Shit keeps happening to me before I can get anything done."

"Maybe, man," Jayson said, turning away from the urinal, having finished his turn. "Or maybe you're in here bullshitting with us while your best chance is getting swept off her feet by our good friend Chevy."

"Standing here is standing still...or maybe you're just forgetting your friends," Mr. Sallow said.

"How so? I know Jayson, I support the brother from another mother. Chevy is Chevy, but I got his back too."

"I'm still thirsty, young man, weren't you going to get me a white Russian?"

"Damn, you're right. I'm sorry, sir. I had them, but I forgot you. If I come back, it won't be empty handed, I promise."

"You'll be back, Mikhail. The night is young and there's still plenty of piss to be spent. Ain't no ifs about it."

Mikhail patted Mr. Sallow on the back—careful not to push too hard and create any unwanted splashes—before walking to the sink. He scrubbed furiously, at his fingernails and then the webs in his hands. The water steamed and he let it burn its brown bubbles over his skin. He put the scalding water against his face, massaging each palm full into the side that caught the bathroom's foul wall. It didn't matter that the tap's heat hurt more than the initial blow, he had to remove the spores from his pores.

Chapter Twenty
Orthodontry Sparkling in the Overhead Lights

"We ready to do this shit?" Chevy asked. "Rub up against the #720's clit and cum on HD's tits?"

He was rubbing up on Saffron like they were actually a couple and Mikhail couldn't tell where the line of sand was drawn. Together, they looked like a brother-sister costume contest. He was a sailor, his ankles so brazenly bare and bronzed. She was a ballerina chamber-maid in tights and a form-fitting blouse that flitted out above her knees. And as lost at sea as she looked, Mikhail couldn't tell what happened in his absence.

"Guess who just got punched for the first time?" Jayson asked.

"Are you okay, Jayson? What happened?"

"It wasn't me," Jayson laughed. Mikhail only scowled.

"If it wasn't your gift-wrapped .gif and it wasn't...oh no, Mikhail, are you okay? What happened?"

Without a thing to say in his defense, he grabbed Saffy's elbow and gave the tender spot of skin a bit of a squeeze. That's when she saw the shiner that had been swelling under his right eye for over an hour, certainly more inflamed after his tangle in the bathroom.

"Oh baby, are you okay? Delete that post, I didn't mean to talk shit in the comments," Saffron said, suddenly stroking the burning side of his face. "Talk on The Internet is just so viral and foul, I sometimes get caught up in it. Mikhail, are you hurt? Come over here, please, right now."

She led him by the hand several steps out of Chevy and Jayson's earshot. Like he was being taken out of class, Mikhail simultaneously felt the shame and excitement of the hot substitute's attention.

"Seriously, what's going on? Are you hurt?"

Seriously, how does one bring up being kidnapped in casual conversation? And how could he discuss his mission to plug two holes without ruining his chances with the first? Mikhail knew that he didn't have time to get into everything. So much had passed since the store-front church and there was still something of severity that Saffron had to say. He was punched by Robert Horry and then by a bandanna'd man and he did little but piss on some shoes. That didn't at all sound heroic.

"I'm cool. A bump in the Matrix," he said, trying to hold onto anything at all. "I'm not looking over my shoulder. No one is trying to kill me. I took my lumps and that's it. But you? How are your lady humps?"

"You haven't checked my blog at all, huh?"

"I had no idea that such a thing was anywhere near your domain."

"I've learned a lot about myself just by doing it," she said, with an unavoidable accent of disappointment. "I never would've if it wasn't for our day on Compton's Circle."

"Which one is that? I spend everyday on the Circle," Mikhail said. It was then that he wondered exactly when the TSABDD had infected his interactions. "I mean, what're you blogging about? Did you find your niche?"

Jayson and Chevy started walking in the direction that they all needed to go and eventually Saffron and Mikhail's hedging became moving...movement that was too quick for conversation. The closer to HD they got, the denser the pack of surrounding characters grew. Chevy led the journey into a loosely knit sweater of loomers. Saffron followed. She put one hand on Chevy's shoulder in front and the other into Mikhail's behind her. Jayson brought up the rear.

Whether it was the electricity in Saffron's touch amid the chaotic flow of things or the possibility that Mikhail was a few minutes from experiencing The Internet for the first time, things were definitely awry. They were on their way to HD and the prospect seemed so real this time around. Saffron was too pretty to turn away and Chevy too connected and Mikhail too determined and Jayson too adrift. The math seemed to work. And as it was moving, the numbers were too blurry anyway. A gentle hand in Mikhail's was all he needed to see that things were progressing.

That is, until the steps turned into shuffles. Getting into HD was getting worse. Still a few hundred feet from the club's entrance, the crowd was starting to feel like a line. They pushed through regardless, at first catching only a handful of grumbles along the way. Chevy's height and Saffron's pulchritudinous voluptuousness were enough to quell most of the bitterness; Mikhail and Jayson got by solely on association and osmosis. After wading through the mass of masses as far as a group of four possibly could, they were finally at a stand still. The line had turned into a mob. Mikhail could just barely see the imposing wall of six bouncers who were ostensibly guarding HD's dark-tinted doors. They seemed to know that things were about to get ugly, but weren't motioning to do anything about it.

"Well, now what?" Mikhail asked to no one in particular.

Saffron shrugged, only half turning her head to concernedly smile. Mikhail didn't even have to turn around to clue in on Jayson's cluelessness...not that the bodies closing in around him would've allowed it. At the front of their stagnant procession, Chevy swiveled around, putting his back to the bourgeois-ass club.

"Aight, fam, this is where I leave you," Chevy said. "But I'm not leaving you. I know a few dudes up there, just wait for my signal. Watch for me 'cause I'm looking out for you."

Chevy threw his arms up in the air and shouted all sorts of versions of get the fuck outta my way as he sleazed himself to the front of the mob, the mob that was nauseatingly turning into a violent ocean of crashing waves. Mikhail knew that he had to protect Saffron before things got out of hand. Just as Chevy did, Mikhail turned his back towards the goal line in order to address his friends.

"I'm staying put," Mikhail said, digging his heels in. "But I'd much rather look at your pretty faces than the back of all these assholes' heads. Can you guys keep an eye out for Chevy while I watch your backs?"

With similar levels of peril, both Saffron and Jayson nodded.

"It's getting a little stuffy in here," Saffron said. She cupped her hands around her DD breasts and stuck out her elbows in an attempt to gain a bit of personal space. The action was futile, but no less sexy. "Where does everyone think they're going?"

"Same place we are, I guess," Mikhail said. "The air is turning vile even as this crowd chokes every breath. Who knows when the doors are even going to open?"

"You've been in there, right Saffy?" Jayson asked. "You've seen The Internet—cause Mikhail and I saw Weezy at Nothing a few months ago—like, is it worth all this?"

She couldn't find the room to turn around and look at Jayson, but she reached back and shook his head up and down. Saffron's eyes were deadlocked on Mikhail's and the gleam in them was quickly turning nervous.

"So what's it like? We ran into Brit-Brit tonight, acting all regal," Mikhail said, trying to divert attention from the world closing in around them. "She spoke about The Internet like it's a privilege and not what's keeping us here in these tubes."

"She's such a bitch. Always acting like The Internet itself squeezed her out of its pussy."

Mikhail tried to think of another way to make Saffron say the word pussy—it left her lips so delicately, practically placing her pouting collagen puffs onto the spread of another woman's flower in a holographic image of lesbian lust—but he couldn't make it happen. "She didn't seem so bad," he said, instead. "Outside of all that uppity upper class condescension. But that's a lot to get past."

"She was an asshole," Jayson said, mustering all he could to speak above the conversations that caved in around them. He was starting to get shoved, however slightly. "But really, seriously, is it worth all this horse shit?"

"The two times I've been here, it's been from the Blue BTWN entrance," she said. "So much easier. So much easier. You just step onto a conveyor belt and it brings you in the back entrance. And then it's there. It's never this."

"Yeah, well, we don't have the cute little ears and infectious sense of humor that you do," Mikhail said. He was careful to let the words slyly drip from his mouth, as if her rolling breasts and flat stomach weren't part of his attention. He knew enough to compliment the pretty girl with everything but how pretty she was. He tried his best to remove the TSABDDish rule from his tone. "Is it worth it, though?"

"I don't know," Saffron squealed a little, covering her uncertainty with a girlish giggle. "It's beautiful. All these advertisements and posters and gobbledygook, it all looks so ugly after seeing The Internet. You just kinda have to see it."

"Fuck. Are we even going to get into this? Shit's looking impossible. I already lost where Chevy's at."

"C'mon Jay," Mikhail said, not remembering the last time he used "Jay" to address his friend. Perhaps it was

Saffron's proximity—by then pushed close enough for him to feel the wires on her bra against his chest—but even in this mess, Mikhail was somehow optimistic. Saffron's unbudgeable closeness probably triggered a memory of their dances in the break-room. He had no choice but to breathe in her lilacs. "Have a little faith, bredren. Remember, you're the happy-go-lucky member of this fraternity. It's not a wall in front of us, just a speed bump. We'll get in just fine."

"I'm not even claustrophobic," Jayson said, "but this is getting ridiculous."

Saffron's face concurred. No matter how much they tried to change the subject, the reality was unavoidable. The speed bumps had grown into walls and the walls were closing in. Mikhail dug his feet into the ground, trying to shield Saffron from the front of the "line" that was pushing backwards, sick of being pushed forward. It was obvious that Jayson was fighting a similar conflict with those savagely trying to move ahead. Thrusts started coming sideways.

Surges soon came from every direction. The weight of hundreds of people seemed to press in on a single epicenter and that implosion centered around Saffron. Mikhail put his hands on Jayson's shoulders, his elbows at her ears, and tried to skirt a look around her that suggested they buckle down and protect the fort. Jayson understood, flaring his arms and bashfully looping his thumbs in the belt loops of Saffron's jeans. Unfortunately, from the terrified dilation of her pupils, Mikhail could tell that she understood the dire consequences of their circumstance.

The surges became more violent while the efforts of Mikhail and Jayson became more and more worthless. Mikhail could feel Saffron's hips pressed firmly against him, their suggestive angles leaning further and further into his very center. A bead of sweat dripped from his chin and he watched it splatter on her naked chest. He wanted to push his scully from his forehead, but he couldn't find the room to do so. Saffron looked at him with sheer terror in her eyes and he just wanted to passionately kiss her, so much so that they'd be forced to make love right then and there in the surrounding ocean of inhumanity.

But soon, their chest-bumps no longer felt sexy. Forced upon him by the force of equally claustrophobic humans looking for personal space of their own, he stopped thinking about sex. Survival was the only thing swimming in his head. Certain surges slid everyone a few feet to the left or the right, to the front or the rear, making Saffron's knee-high boots skid across the floor like she was completely weightless. Mikhail and Jayson did everything they could to protect her from the desperate throws of society at its absolute end, but there was only so much they could do to even keep their own feet flat.

"Not that we could get to the rhyming motherfucker now anyway," Mikhail said, trying to find strength in Jayson's eyes and deliver it into Saffron's, "but do you see Chevy up there?"

Jayson scanned ahead, across the wave of heads behind Mikhail. They were all fighting their own personal battles, combating the gusts of shifting bodies just as he was, but he couldn't see anything recognizable. In this mess, even Chevy was dwarfed.

"This sucks," Saffron said.

"I didn't know it'd be like this, it just seemed so much easier," Mikhail said. "I'm sorry. I never would've even bothered if I knew, really, I'm sorry."

"It's not your fault," she said.

Mikhail's phone didn't vibrate, but he felt its presence in his back pocket. No one had paid it any attention in quite some time and now it needed a moment of his. Without much room for movement, he slipped his phone from its denim cocoon and Tweeted the best he could from behind his back. It took everything he had to keep it from being snapped in half as the crowd continued to exponentiate its own crushing pressure.

"Dear Twitter: Please get me out of this closed circuit madness and deliver me into HD. Forever your friend, Mikhail."

Behind Saffron's head and over Jayson's shoulder, Mikhail watched a scuffle begin. A few people were trying to cut the line and a few people finally had enough of the pushing and cutting. The very same act that got Mikhail and them to their middling progress was about to start a riot.

"Stay strong, bredren," Mikhail shouted over the rising commotion. There was no longer anything he could hide from Saffron. He could tell that Jayson wanted to turn around and face the increasing danger behind him, but such action would be Saffron's demise. "I got you, don't worry, just stay strong."

"What's going on back there?" Jayson yelled, his hands still on the exponentially scared hips of Saffron. He was no longer bashful about that particular physical contact. "Don't leave us hanging, man."

Ten feet behind Jayson, a young girl in braces—her orthodontry sparkling in the overhead lights—took a swing at a young man in a polo who had just called her a cunt. Close fisted, it connected. He cowered. The young man's friend reacted by punching the brace-faced girl square in the mouth. She fell to the ground, like a rock in a sock, and everyone with a backbone opened up on the young man's friend who had just punched a girl. Fists were flying from every direction faster than his skin could open up and bleed. He was continuously getting caught by various sets of knuckles with no connection to the heap of hurting girl other than the collective outrage over a 90 pound female in a pained fetal position.

In the fray, things suddenly opened up. People were no longer obsessed with getting ahead, concentrating instead on getting as far from the fracas as they could. Jayson freed his hand from Saffron's belt loop and motioned Mikhail forward. Mikhail turned around, grabbing Saffron's hand, and got as close to HD's entrance as he could. The panicked scattering brought the trio a scant few feet from the tinted doors.

"Just let us in!" screamed someone in the crowd.

"This is crazy!"

"There's no one in there!"

"Someone's gonna die out here!"

"Please!"

A certified hippie started to fall and used the small of Mikhail's back to prop himself up. The hippie fell but his efforts to stay standing forced Mikhail's sight-line towards the ceiling. An air conditioning duct 50 feet up was adorned with a sticky note scrawled with bits of chicken scratch. It took Mikhail a minute to decipher what exactly was written in Sharpie. He knew it was meant for him and who it was from. CGI's note from its fancy penthouse address was simple:

"M: Get your McCallen's at the bar. :C"

Somehow, someway, Mikhail knew that the scribbles were fresh. He didn't need to see anymore, he just needed to make sure Saffron and Jayson were still with him. They were. The screaming and rioting and yelling seemed to intensify behind him, to the point where he was scared to look back. He grabbed Saffron's hand and dragged her to the one door that was occasionally opening. It was blocked by a tower of a man with a blond pony tail.

"Really....you?" Mikhail shouted, exasperated, out of breath, his mind in a blender. "The Pastor didn't kill me, that must mean something, right?"

"I don't know you," the tower of a bouncer said. "But I know Saffy."

"Hi, Tower," Saffron said.

"You and Horry and Armstrong just kidnapped me....you really don't remember?"

"You're confusing me with Ivan," Tower said, "I hate that that blood-line traitor. I hate being mixed up with him."

"Tower, please, get us out of here," Saffron begged. The brawl behind them was breaking up and people were starting to regain the evening's raison d'être. Someone pushed Jayson, who fell into Saffron, who fell into the standing lap of the tower of a bouncer that stood before them. He caught her and then caught a feel, enjoying every inch that his giant creepy hands crept up.

"How many are you?" he asked, his hands still firmly grasping her tits.

"Just us three," Saffron said, letting his despicable offenses go without notice. "Just the three of us."

The bouncer let go and opened the door just a crack, as discreetly as he could. But as evidenced by his perverted attempt to take advantage of a girl in the chaos of a riot, discretion wasn't his strong suit. Mikhail tried to gentlemanly allow Saffron and Jayson to enter HD first, but the tower's inability to be subtle was consumed by the crowd before Mikhail could follow along.

A beer bottle from a hundred people back shattered against the tower's scull. Ivan's twin pushed Mikhail through the door and said a swear or two packed with the full vile of vitriol normally reserved for terrible human beings. Then Mikhail landed on the immaculate floor of HD, once again, flat on his face. He looked up and saw The Internet for the first time in his life. The bouncer's indiscretions were quickly forgotten.

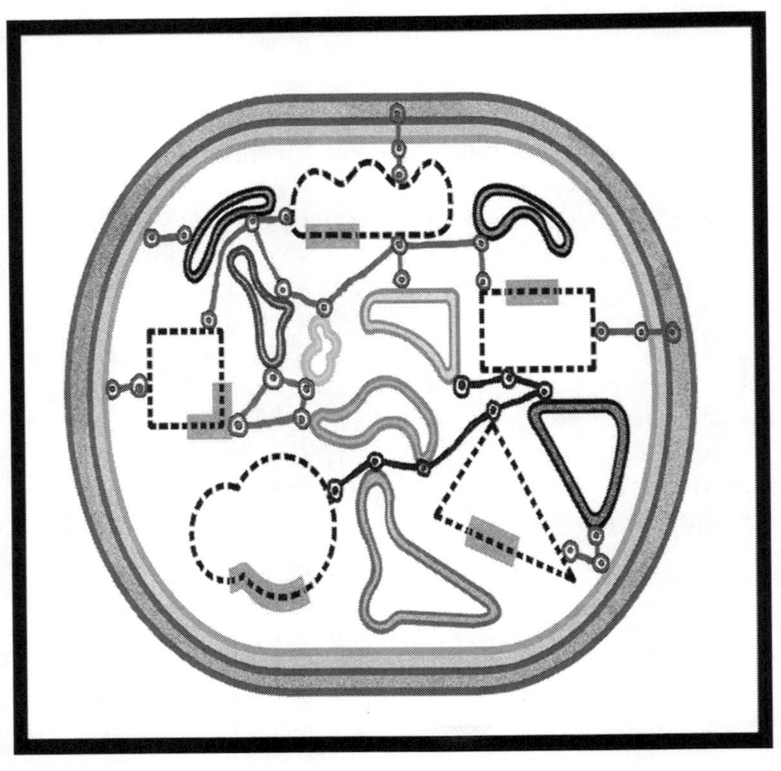

Visit **http://PleaseUseRearExit.net/home/Wiki**
for a computer generated look at P.U.R.E's world

Chapter Twenty-One
Life in HD

He had heard the stories, heard the whispers from the cleaning staff on their way home from The Hills, heard the copious online chatter, heard the myths from children without anything to say but unsubstantiated tales, and heard the sickening braggadocio of people much richer than him, but never before had Mikhail actually seen The Internet. And no matter how much his days in this world had prepared him for that particular moment, it still took him a few eye rubs to take it all in.

HD's roof was made out of glittering beams that crisscrossed the club's entirety. It stretched up from walls made of titanium, and arched across a rare view of LA's sky. At first glance, it just seemed like an avant-garde display so typical of the city: slick television sets shelling advertisements and assorted randomness, the likes of which Mikhail had encountered his entire life aboard those damned buses. However, on closer inspection, there was no glass separating HD's roof from the flashing images and viral tidbits that littered above its infrastructure. He might've mistaken it for rows upon rows of LCD screens broadcasting coded blocks of binary information, if it wasn't for the absence of a single solitary screen. Dumbfounded, Mikhail gazed up at the same allegedly-holy force that locked Los Angeles inside itself.

The beams gave no care to intersections of jpegs and mpegs, they overlapped the wondrous webpages that varied in size from hundreds of feet down to dozens of inches. The World Wide Web drifted by at random speeds—some images seemed to stick around while other batches disappeared just as quickly as they could be replaced. Slowly, Mikhail mustered just enough self-awareness to move from his stomach to his ass, without interrupting his jaw-dropped stare into the open air of The Internet. A meme here, a meme there, a meme everywhere. LOLcats hid in sock drawers and hot chicks plunged their toilets and weird white guys danced in orange onesies and Dr. Doom did stand-up and a man grew bark from his skin and it all rotated by in infinity. Blogs blended with mind-bendingly stupid Google search cues. The two-dimensions outside of HD's roof rumbled by with a warm breeze that heralded the faint stench of complicated machinery hard at work. Mikhail always thought that The Internet would be cool, but he was wrong—its heat was all encompassing.

Except for the expanse of it all, however, it was incredibly familiar. Flat as it was, its ubiquity added a dimension that Mikhail couldn't quite put his finger on, but it made the whole thing feel a little chintzy. Sure, The Internet was big—it seemed to stretch up behind itself beyond human comprehension—but after 30 seconds of staring intently he wondered what the big deal was. Maybe the rich were rich for a reason and maybe they just saw something in The Internet that Mikhail could not.

Saffron and Jayson helped him up, each grabbing an elbow. Her eyes searched his while Jayson's searched the sky. Jayson was an immediate convert. He wore his awe without a hint of irony. The wheels in his mind were visibly spinning fast and furious, searching the many windows with tremendous concentration, trying to take it all in should someone take it away. But no one did.

"Man, I don't even know what to say," Jayson stammered. "It's fucking beautiful. I almost forgive Ms. Spears for her stuck-up attitude. Shit man, I want to keep it for myself, too. Not everyone deserves this."

"I told you it was worth it," Saffron smiled. She hugged Mikhail close to herself and looked up at him to make sure that he was embracing the new world around him. "Are you alright? It's gorgeous, isn't it? Absolutely without description."

Mikhail thought he could describe it in six words—"like a computer without the screen"—but wasn't sure if he should mince such sentiments. He smiled instead, too afraid to shout into distances he didn't understand.

The club itself was as spacious as it was dim; HD's claim-to-fame was also its only source of light. The ample seating atop plush couches made of luxurious-looking furs were almost entirely unmanned. The freedom to walk around was at a gluttonous level and he wondered whether someone would have to die in that riotous mob outside before an authority figure would release some of the tension. Next to a stage full of amps and drum kits and massive speakers (but void of any people) was a scraggly looking tree that looked alive...if just barely. A fake plastic tree it was not and Mikhail was immediately struck by its delicate beauty, much more so than the blinking pixels that rained down from above. He'd read about photosynthesis on Wikipedia, but nothing could compare to what was before him. The knots in its branches, the wilting green of its leaves, the combustibility of it all. That tree—purely alive as it was— seemed to be the greatest miracle in the entire room.

Across from the stage, a pool created in the #720's oblong image was casually iridescent. No one was inside it, but everyone made a big deal about being around its aqua glow. With plates of hors d'euves and trays of drinks, waitresses crossed the pearly tile floor in high heels. Mikhail looked at Saffron, as if to ask if it was all as free as it appeared. She laughed.

"It's the first time you've ever seen The Internet and you're only interested in the complimentary booze?" Saffron giggled, absolutely incredulous. She spread her arms and twirled around once, staring into the heavens. She twirled again. And then again. "Of course it's free."

"But everyone here can afford to pay for this shit, right? Isn't that the caveat?"

Saffron kissed him on his left cheek and sharply shriveled back when the memory of his facial bruising hit her in the kisser. He turned the other cheek, showing Saffron that she had kissed his good side. She kissed him again. It made sense to get a drink. The alcohol toted to and fro by the uniformly dressed-in-black waitresses looked too damn fruity for his tastes. Not even their value in sloth—free of charge and effort—was worth the girliness of drinking such a beverage. Mikhail motioned towards the bar next to the stage and said that he was going to hit the bar. Saffron and Jayson followed.

Being the most exclusive club in LA, HD's clientele was predictable. The actor from "Bless This Mess" sat comfortably in the swallowing depths of a striped and spotted couch, while another man who Mikhail didn't recognize—one with four incredibly tanned arms—perched upon the actor's lap. A few feet further, Britney Spears couldn't peel her eyes from The Internet, not that Mikhail was expecting a joyous bear hug or anything. The Kardashian sisters cackled in the corner, so obviously talking about everyone around them that it was hard to get offended because their sly pointing and inside jokes were without prejudice. So coked up, The Rock uncontrollably rubbed his nose and squinted 100x a minute while posing for a photo with a ravaged-looking cougar and her 10-year-old son. Mikhail wondered why a prepubescent boy was in a night club, but quickly remembered that he didn't care.

Every single ounce of their collective attention was paid towards the "sky." As if their eyes might melt into the back of their throat should they look away, there was no questioning their concentration. Mikhail wasn't quite sure why until he heard Ms. Spears squeal at the sight of herself on one of the countless YouTube clips that continually passed by in assembly-line fashion. "OMI, there I am," she said, before turning towards her friend excitedly, "OMI, and you're there, too. Isn't it beautiful? It really makes me feel like I'm making a difference."

What difference was impossible to know. Ms. Spears saw her reflection in The Internet and apparently that was enough. It was why every other celebrity gaped at the sky...and probably the same reason why Mikhail just didn't get it. He didn't even have a YouTube account. A paper-thin Oprah Winfrey sauntered about, completely disappearing from sight when she turned in a certain direction or the light hit her rail-thin frame just right, it reminded him of a more permanently invisible girl.

And if Oprah's vanishing act wasn't enough to remind him of CGI and her bread-crumbs, her best friends were hysterically laughing in each other's ears just a few feet from the bar that Mikhail and company were meandering towards. Standing statuesque as sultry's definition in tall and short, Rihanna and Maya completed CGI's small inner-circle. They were a collection of sexy so dangerous that their notoriety was rarely spoken, especially on account of their leader's penchant for spying. Rihanna and Maya were speaking so inclusively that they must've been chatting exclusively—there was no way a third person could've heard their whispers.

However CGI orchestrated her first note on the bottom of that air conditioning duct—whether she had tripped that hippie or hung on the #720's ceiling until the right moment or caused the riot that got it all going in the first place—however she did it, Mikhail begun to see the efforts of the treasure hunt laid before him. So when Saffron grabbed his hand, no matter how soft and warm the webs of her fingers were, he shivered at the potential results of such a simple gesture. He faintly smiled back at Saffron and released her grip.

"Ayo, did you know that Saffron's pops worked in the same factory that you do?" Mikhail asked Jayson. He needed some space out of Saffron's earshot to ask a bartender about CGI. He had to create something of a distraction and if the moment to use such a tidbit wasn't right then and there, it'd never come. Jayson struggled in small talk, unless of course the monotony of his daily life became part of the dialogue. And while Mikhail went off to get drinks, he needed Jayson to be at his utmost charming. "Patron and sodas?"

Before they could agree and before Mikhail could turn towards the bar, Jayson was already asking about the department that Saffron's father worked in. It didn't matter which, Jayson would find a thread to spin. Those that worked on the #4 came home and uniformly told the same stories; and Jayson found more comfort in that fact than anything else in his whole life. Shop talk was worse than any beauty salon on the #207...gossip rained down harder than sheet metal shavings, and the constant turnover of workers meant that someone always knew someone who knew someone who knew anyone who ever worked on the #4. Mikhail found his space at the bar, confident that his counterparts would be well occupied.

A blue woman as tall as The Pillar (but dressed only in electrical tape) greeted Mikhail from behind the bar. It wasn't the most pleasant greeting, like she knew he laid his head down to rest on Compton's Circle. She strained her neck just to look down at him before exasperatedly placing a napkin on the bar.

"How's it going? Umm...did CGI leave me a drink?"

A touch of pity came over her gigantic face before she shook her head. The blue bartender obviously knew who he was talking about—everyone knew CGI—but there seemed to be a deeper level of understanding in her negative response. Something made her wonder if he really did belong there. Or maybe Mikhail was just reading too deeply into a woman with breasts larger than his torso.

"So your invisible fuck buddy doesn't love you so much, well then...what else is there to want in a digital world?" The contempt crept back into her yellow eyes, all her presumed sympathy had quickly disappeared. "I have other customers to help, I don't have all night."

There was no one else near the bar, but Mikhail was in no place to argue. Before he could utter a word, the laughter of Rihanna and Maya kicked up another notch. He wasn't sure if they were having fun at his expense, but it was enough to knock his train of thought off track. Like a stack of glass plates had dropped, Mikhail's gaze dashed in their direction. It was probably for the best that they were too busy laughing to notice him because he was immediately embarrassed by the awkward nod he squeaked out in response. He'd only met those girls once and it was hardly a conversation that they'd remember. Mikhail turned back to the bartender, careful to look up above the breasts that stood taut at his eye level.

"Two Patron-sodas and a Jameson-rocks, please...open bar, right?" Mikhail stuttered. Wait, what did she mean by invisible fuck buddy? An extravagant game, yes, but still only a set of flirtations amongst new friends.

"Just don't tip your height," she said, slamming the glasses like an angry drill sergeant. She was so imposing, so pissed off in every movement, her scale-like blue skin so taped up in black strips, Mikhail had no choice but to wait patiently. She presented the drinks with a snarl, "You're small, so your tip better not be. That's what I meant."

Mikhail found a crumpled five in his front pocket and tried to flatten it out before placing it on the bar. He had gotten her reference, but didn't want to receive her wrath. Hopefully five bucks for three free drinks was enough to keep the giant woman from jumping the fanciful plywood bar. Thankfully, it was.

He carried the drinks in a triangle of circles, the glasses held in his hands by webs of fingers. Mikhail wasn't afraid that they'd drop, but the slightest inadvertent brush might've spelled disaster—and he didn't have too many more tips like that left in his wallet. Blessfully, HD was empty and he was able to avoid all drama and collect a blisteringly blushing smile from Saffron. He walked her and Jayson as far away from Rihanna and Maya as he could before handing them their drinks. He measured each of his actions as if he was being watched.

"Shouldn't a place like this have a better DJ?" Jayson asked.

Mikhail hadn't given a single thought to the soundtrack for the first time all night, but immediately concurred once the sound-waves echoed towards a spot of recognition inside his skull.

"Blasphemous!" Saffron shouted. "This isn't a DJ, this is Pandora. It's an algorithm created by The Internet for rhythm."

"Don't be a liar," Jayson said. "What do you know about that business?"

"It's completely genius," she said. "It measures our collective brain patterns and weighs them against a data-base of music, it's fucking amazing! It's the purest of polls polling what we actually care about. All of our brains...Rihanna over there, that dude from 'Bless This Mess' over there, the guy in his lap, the girl in the hammock with her laptop, you, me, Jayson, those suits in a semi-circle...we're all thinking about what song we want to hear, and Pandora weighs all of that information, computes it, and spits out a tune in perfect BPM balance with the previous song our collective consciousness conjured. Hot damn! The Internet is beautiful."

"I'll be damned if my consciousness had anything to do with this Black Eyed Peas nonsense," Mikhail chided.

"The Internet is beautiful, I'll give you that," Jayson said. "But Pandora, right now, it ain't."

"But Pandora is The Internet!"

"I'd still rather listen to Weezy in the flesh...when exactly you think the dude is going to go on?" Jayson asked.

"Who knows? In my experience, rappers take forever... they operate on rapper time," Mikhail said, wondering what experience with rappers he actually had. Pastor Shakur was technically retired. Jayson's curled eyebrow bore witness to the same question. "What the fuck was the rush to get here?"

"You know it's only going to get worse out there," Saffron said. She was sipping her drink from the skinny plastic stirrer, holding the actual glass with both hands. "A mass of hits like that could bring an entire site down, we're lucky to get in when we did. Who knows when the whole Internet will just come tumbling down? The mere prospect of it is enough to make me hunt out a Wi-Fi-proof shelter and eat nothing but cans of tuna-fish."

And for the first time, Mikhail wanted to leave. Not only HD or the #720, but everything that surrounded him every minute of every day. Things were so muddied, it was getting hard to wade through all the muck. He hated looking over his shoulder and hated the awkwardness of menial small-talk. The easiest way to relinquish his anxieties was to walk the main corridor for 15 minutes, find his transfer station, ride the Brown BTWN a bit, stumble another 10 minutes home, and curl up in the down comforter of his unmade bed. What'd that be...40 minutes? Those solitary travels seemed a hell of a lot simpler than figuring out Saffron's new Internet-enlightened personality or CGI's bread-crumbs or whatever itch Pastor Shakur was trying to scratch. And where the fuck was Chevy, anyway? The bed in Mikhail's one room apartment on Compton's Circle— the same one with the sink and toilet just steps from where he slept—lofted like a cotton candy dream about feathers. It was warm and safe there. Besides, he hated the smell of tuna...and a girl would be more attractive farting the alphabet than eating a can of it.

"Where in Internet's name is Chevy at?" Jayson asked. "I almost hope he didn't get in after leaving us high and dry like that."

"But we don't want him stuck out there...so tumultuous and cantankerous. Seriously though, you guys, thanks for keeping me safe in all that," Saffron said. She hugged Jayson and then hugged Mikhail with a little more zeal, before whispering in his ear. "That's the second time you've saved me. Once spiritually, once physically. I didn't know who I was before you, before you took me to the First Church of United Webidentry. Without you, I wouldn't have ever realized how simultaneously arbitrary and important their teachings were...zero, one, one, zero, one, one, zero," she kissed his ear a bit, whispering further and further into nothingness, "zero, zero, one, zero, one, one..."

He hugged her tightly without knowing what she was talking about or the message he was responding with, just knowing that her body felt nice against his. There was no way Mikhail could bail right then, Internet-be-damned if it might hurt CGI's feelings. Saffron was so in awe of him it was worth blushing over. So many men were so lustful over her and she was so willing with him. As good as she felt, he was still unsure of his feelings for her, even if there was no mistaking Saffron's affections.

"I don't know about y'all, but man, I need another drink."

"Yes, yeah, let me get one for you guys," Mikhail said, so happy that Jayson spoke up when he did. He and Saffron separated and he wondered if that was the totality of words she had been trying to say all night. He was sure there were more, but he still wished that he had listened better.

"C'mon man, my old lady's restraints on this rusty wallet ain't so tight that I can't get the tip at an open bar...let me at least carry back a few drinks."

Saffron's embraces were a revelation against his flesh, but his insides were somersaulting over themselves. Her eagerness and otherworldly hotness were not in line. As easy as it was to doubt her true intentions, it was even easier for Mikhail to doubt his ability to keep her interested. He didn't know how to continue Saffron's flirtations and feared that he was running out of things to say. The sweep of past charms and old jokes would only last so long, and her dust-pan would quickly realize his lack of dirt. She could be the key to his whole night, the consummation of silly missions. She could also be standing in the way. Chevy wasn't cockblocking at the moment and maybe that too meant something? Fighting off the appearance of a panic attack, Mikhail took out his cell and gawked at the blank screen like he just received the fourth-most important text message of his entire life. Maybe his paranoia about CGI's powers and her level of interest was getting the best of him.

"Saffy, is there another bar besides that one?"

"Yeah, just up the stairs," she said. "Why? Is everything alright?"

"Definitely. An old homie just hit me up and said he's at the bar, but he ain't over there," Mikhail lied, pointing towards the nine-foot woman barely covered with electrical tape. "I'll get this round again, but hot damn, Jayson, you're totally getting the next."

Less than cordially, Mikhail traded his friends for a bar unknown and a reason to be named later. If Mikhail couldn't go home, he at least had to leave something. He rounded the outside of HD's pool and started up the steps that Saffron had pointed out. There was no reason for him to believe in the little hints CGI left for him or whatever it was that Pastor Shakur needed, but something else existed and he couldn't contain the urge to find it.

Like a couch potato, he needed to see what else was on, no matter how entertaining the program he was watching. Urged by the unknown, he had to flip the channel. It crossed his mind that chasing after something else was complicating his night, but it always seemed better to click on a hyperlink in search of a new site than to stick around a confusing page. Perhaps The Internet had stolen his attention span. The black grip-tape of the poorly-lit stairs grated against his Converse as he made his way up towards the other bar. Going up again made him nervous, but less so than standing still.

At the top of the stairs, Amar'e Stoudemire sat in a booth surrounded by a cornucopia of top-level ladies. More pertinent than HD's architecture or the marble squid sculpture in the corner or even the tiny room's smoky vibe—more consuming than its windows into The Internet—Stoudemire's presence defined the tiny upstairs room's feng shui. His spread-eagle arms, all eight feet of them, hugged a table that seemed to envelop the entire place. Mikhail felt like he was intruding, but he'd already committed himself to a point where any U-Turn would, by definition, be "flipping a bitch."

A waiter tried to attend to Stoudemire's needs, but was abruptly shaken off. Easier than a pick-and-roll against a confused defense—and with far less effort—Amar'e padded his stats by embarrassing the waiter. A cigar burned in his hand, but he wasn't smoking it. The amber just burned. And in that booth, in absolute control of the room, he sat confidently with three women as remarkably sexy as Saffron. One woman had six sultry eyes and Mikhail couldn't even imagine what other treasures she held close to her tight-knit body. The other two were so glowingly similar in their bright pink skin that they had to be twins. Stoudemire's cigar was there for a reason and Mikhail just wasn't cool enough to know.

He just wanted a drink. He wanted answers and Amar'e didn't even care about the questions. It was all Mikhail could do to bypass his Suns fanaticism and brave Stoudemire's presence in order to stand tall at the bar while he once again asked if CGI had left a drink for him.

"Yeah, but you gotta come down here to get it," the shirtless bartender said. He was an odd sort of fellow with a face where his belly button should've been. Mikhail followed him into the corner and watched his arms reach into a small refrigerator underneath the bar. There was no head upon his shoulders and when he couldn't find Mikhail's drink, the bartender stuck out his stomach to catch a closer look. He finally found CGI's offering and turned around with a shit-eating grin across his naked stomach that he wore like an inverted THUGLIFE tattoo. "You want anything else?"

"Thanks, yeah, please, two tequila-sodas."

"It's open bar...you care what kind of tequila?"

"Fuck it, why not? Patron, please."

It didn't matter what type of booze would further poison Saffron and Jayson, Mikhail had his next clue. He refused to look too hasty in his efforts to decipher the note under his new glass of McCallen's. Through the chilled amber liquid, he could barely read the writing on the brown napkin stuck to his drink. A message was scrawled in the same sharpied penmanship he saw on the bottom of that air-conditioning duct.

"Look up...again."

He followed the simple instructions towards the skylight above the bar. Fifty feet up and an indeterminable distance into The Internet, an owl perched in a tree. Not a real owl or tree, but a jpg of the two. They sat against the same sky that artists had been painting since the beginning of The Internet's time. A completely trite hue, it was the very same blue that philosophers described in diatribes online as the feeling a man gets in a meadow at mid-day. There were no meadows in LA, just online clips of Jason Schwartzman standing in one and passionately detailing its attributes. The thumbnail in Mikhail's sky looked fake and felt random—just a man-sized owl in a tree. It was either a ruse or just another inconsequential glimpse into the world wide web. There was a certain specificity in its vagueness, but at 72 dpi, things were definitely out of focus.

He looked back at Amar'e but Amar'e was just looking at the fine females he embraced. There was a fraternity among NBA players, but an even stronger one amongst the TSABDD. With three girls under his tremendous wingspan, it was almost certain that Amar'e looked to Robert Horry like an older brother. It was upchuck-disgusting that Amar'e could look past all of Horry's trespasses against the Suns. But even through his anger, Mikhail could see that no basketball games—ass-backward as so many of them were—could circumvent the power of pussy.

The McCallen's was better this time, fuller without the pressure of describing it to CGI. After a few sips, he decided to descend. He had taken in all he could of that tiny room and nothing else seemed like a clue. At the bottom of the stairs, he looked up at the still-empty stage before surveying the crowd for friendly faces. Without immediate sight of Jayson or Saffron, Mikhail's gaze darted around the club as he slowly paced without direction.

And for the second time that night, he was struck with a new meaning for a tree's gift of life. That living, breathing piece of wood next to the stage had a pink sticky-note thumbtacked to an intersection of its branches and it had suddenly become very familiar. If it wasn't the exact same tree depicted deep in The Internet's abyss above the bar upstairs, than it was a direct descendant. The background had changed, just as the owl had morphed into CGI's newest note. Teleporting from The Internet and into real life, the club's tree suddenly became Mikhail's next challenge. It was also his latest reason to run.

Chapter Twenty-Two
Oh, the Cuddle Possibilities

Mikhail stared at the wedge of branches and that pink sticky-note. Right next to the empty stage, the prospect of actually retrieving it looked like one he'd rather avoid. In descending order, he had his reasons:

(4) Chevy definitely had a crush on CGI and the ringer she was putting Mikhail through seemed a lot larger than friendly flirtations. He was afraid that whatever the outcome would be, it'd force him to cross the line that turned friend into foe.

(3) Unless he straight up lied to her—perhaps spinning the web of an amazing fable about his need to climb the tree to win her good graces and save his fair maiden from the duress of a dragon—he'd have to climb that tree without Saffron noticing. Mikhail wasn't that good at lying.

(2) Saffy wasn't alone in HD. In front of all the important-feeling people inside the club Mikhail would have to duck security, get past the few low-lying branches that would probably snap under his weight, climb a tree for the first time in his life, snag the note, get down without breaking an ankle or getting thrown out of the club...and risk getting laughed at by climbing to the focal point of an audience that was slowly congregating and growing. The potential for FAIL was huge.

(1) That piece of paper obviously, probably, had nothing to do with him.

It seemed insurmountable and Mikhail did everything he could to forget it. There was no reason. Saffron was there—the picture of perfect, a blessing of bliss—and she seemed to actually like him. His hang-ups over her were more ridiculous than real, even as he dragged his feet over them. A challenge in conversation was a good thing, something Mikhail always told himself he wanted to grow old with. She had the curves that a baby-sat child would dream to drive match-box buses up and down. He had no idea what CGI wanted and an even smaller inkling of the terrain on her invisible curves. Saffron wasn't just visible, she was tangible. And she was bored out of her mind alone with Jayson, sharing only an awkward silence.

"Okay, I'll admit, I was a little scared out there," Mikhail said, taking pride in his influx of liveliness into the dead air. "I honesty thought we might get trampled."

"Oh My Internet, I've never been so terrified in my entire life," Saffron said, grabbing Mikhail and swiftly placing her hand under the back of his shirt. Her head beneath his chin, he couldn't help but imagine the cuddle possibilities. Unlike Katya—who was almost the same height as him—Saffy's head would fit perfectly in the crease of his armpit and her legs would naturally curl over him without crushing his balls. The tale of their cuddle tape was remarkably compatible. "Have I thanked you guys yet? Well, whatever, thank you so much. I was really thinking that I could die...everyone was just pushing and squishing and pushing...my feet were completely off the ground more than once. So scary."

"And if these muscles weren't protecting you, well, shit man," Jayson laughed, "those curves would be a hell of a lot flatter."

"It's so crazy talking about this now, with all this space around us, it's like it didn't even happen." Mikhail held Saffron so tightly, he could hear his words echo through her body and back into his. It didn't feel right. "So happy all that is over."

The stillness inside HD was damn near methodical. If it wasn't for the occasional waitress moving about, the entire place would have contained an indignantly incorrigible level of calmness. The Internet flickered down and reflected across the glossy floor, but it was hardly anything of any real movement... and if it was the least bit of substance at all, it was only a reminder of absence.

Saffron pouted her lips up at Mikhail and he kissed them. He could feel her mind walking down an aisle and he had to fight off an immediate response of recoil. But the explosion of her moist collagen against his lips was an even stronger force. Her teeth started to push against his and he pushed back and they only separated in pulls of passion. He may have bit her bottom lip, she may have softly slid her tongue against his. The display probably embarrassed Jayson, and Mikhail kicked himself for not being more subtle under the circumstances.

"I'll take care of you tonight," she whispered into his chest, the second time of the night he had partaken in the soft pleasure of a woman's breath so close to his heart. "Let me, please," she reached up to nibble his ear, "I'll never forget how you took care of me."

Mikhail hadn't imagined he had done so much. His actions in the near-riot outside of HD were as much about self-preservation and selfishness as they were about chivalry. And he still wasn't so sure about this spiritual stuff she started to say. It made him feel a little guilty.

"Ahem," Jayson said, pointedly clearing the phlegm from his throat. Mikhail and Saffron took the cue and released each other. "Man, I'm getting a little a drunk. I lost count of what I drank...and I'm gonna take that as a sign for the best."

"I saw Amar'e Stoudemire up there," Mikhail said, readying a sports-shpeal that'd probably bore Saffron, but more importantly re-ignite Jayson's demonstratively yawning ass. "He's one of my favor—"

"OMI, he's a fucking beast, Mikhail! You really saw him? He averaged like 40 points, 12 boards and three blocks in that one series against the Spurs," she said, pulling further away by punching him in the arm. "Absolutely dominant. Did he look cute? I bet he was all suave and shit with a lavender kerchief in the pocket of his pinstriped suit. That one dunk he had over Olowokandi, I've never seen anything like it. And Marbury's face—he looked like he was about to cry when he saw STAT dunk on the Kandi Man, not quite like that one webcam video though because that shit is hilarious."

Indeed, there was nothing left to talk about. Saffron had stolen nearly everything he could say about one of his basketball idols. He ran through what he knew: Stoudemire's multiple knee surgeries, the torn retina, his improved jump shot, the lack of defensive intensity...it was all completely undercut by STAT's statistics in that Spurs series and all the details from his dunk against the Clippers. If ever Mikhail had risen above the rim, this was the time his legs were cut out beneath him.

"He'll never win a ring, though," Jayson said.

"Is there a bathroom in this place?"

"It's just behind you, but you weren't joking about your bladder, were you?" Saffron asked. "I'm not judging, I'm just saying."

"And I'm saying, you totally are judging," Mikhail laughed. "I'm not a player I just pee a lot. We've already discussed this." Saffron's overt sports knowledge was a cold and wet blanket thrown over his moment, but he wasn't really sure. Everything quickly, and quite suddenly, felt very, very off. Why is it that a girl who can talk about sports is only a good idea on paper? "Guess I'm bound and determined to make you two the best of friends. I'll be right back, I swear."

After a few steps, Mikhail thought about calling Jayson over and asking for his assistance. Once again, it was too late to turn back. As soon as Mikhail was out of eye-sight, he furiously started texting.

"a wild night. can you do me another solid? pls pls pls keep saffy's attention away from the stage. thx. will explain later."

Mikhail slowly walked towards the bathroom while counting one Los Angeles, two Los Angeles, three Los Angeles. He tallied fifteen Los Angeleses before he allowed himself to turn around, right at the point where a decision had to be made. Bathroom or tree. Jayson had done his job, however, and Saffron's attention was turned from the very act Mikhail was souping himself up to commit. He actually did have to use the bathroom again, but there was no time for that. His walk with purpose but not without discretion, Mikhail went straight for the stage. He had to complete the treasure hunt without getting caught. Parsing the sparse crowd, he found himself at the trunk of the tree.

It didn't seem real. The bark was rough on his finger tips. The tree felt dead, yet he could sense its life. The fake plastic trees he was used to were so skinny, it was never even a thought to shimmy atop. Mikhail had never seen it done, but knew that he had to do it. Looking over his shoulders, frantically turning his head, he saw that no one was watching and then he cleared his mind. He took hold of the first branch that looked capable of holding his weight. Bouncing a bit, he tested the tree's strength. It seemed to hold. He used the friction from his Chuck Taylors against the coarse bark to push himself higher, and then support his body for the next desperate stretch of his arms upward. Level by level, he found himself further and further above it all, somehow by someway.

Suddenly, he was 20 feet off the ground and no one in HD seemed to see a thing. He wondered if CGI sent him up this tree to feel what being invisible was all about. Mikhail snatched the note and quickly pocketed it before resting on a branch to take it all in. Scanning the crowd, he found comfort at this height. Much was nice about being removed. The atmosphere was calming up there. HD had a hazy darkness about it, like a basement party lit only by the static of large forgotten television sets and the sparkling pool in the center of it all. He wasn't in any rush to descend back into all those choices, when observing from above was so much easier.

Visit **http://PleaseUseRearExit.net/home/WAITING**
to watch the P.U.R.E-produced music video for
TopBananas: "Waiting For My Time To Come"

Chapter Twenty-Three
A Doctor's Note From Him

Up in the tree, it was even easier to pick out the scattered suits, TSABDD brass, and cock teases in cocktail dresses, all networking at a natural noise level, discussing the things that rich people at parties politicked about. Mostly groups of three or four, they were arranged into circles that excluded everyone else or half-moons in an obvious effort to engage. Twenty-five groups in all, at least from his cursory head count. Among them, he could see his crew. Jayson was just a headless portrait of a pudgy friend, but Saffron, well, she stood out.

Dancing in symbiotic ebbs with the flow of The Internet above her, she was casually sensual in one of HD's rare spotlights. It was like an iPhone's flashlight app was created just for her. Jayson could no longer keep her facing in the wrong direction. No one could blame him. It would be hard for anyone to suggest that she stopped dancing.

She gently bounced to Charles Hamilton's "Windows Media Player." Mikhail thought that people must've been thinking about their computers if that was what Pandora conjured from their collective consciousness. Weezy's name was surely stricken from the preordained playlist, otherwise his hits would be bellowing from up on high. However, Charles Hamilton's ditty was the perfect soundtrack for the life-affirming mutualism that had developed between Saffron and the spotlight. The heaven-sent luminescence reflected in her once purple top like some sort of chemical reaction in the fabric itself. A film played out on her blouse, but it wasn't seen in The Internet's projection above her. Scrambled to unrecognizable bursts of flash in the bounty of her flesh, it lit up her face without flickering hints at its true imagery. She quickly spun 180 degrees. Devoid of the curves she wore on the front, her back was a better screen for the film from above. Mikhail thought he could see the outline of a giant breast growing from her back. She stayed turned once a body lost in the shadows had newly won her attention.

Her back was oblivious to Mikhail's predicament, but her front was certainly consumed by Chevy's charms. He emerged from the shadows to rub her back, and immediately, they were laughing loudly. Chevy had never made a move on any of Mikhail's love- or lust-interests, but he knew his friend's body language well enough to know that he was readying such a move. Mikhail scurried down a few branches and then very purposefully fell the remaining 15 feet to the floor. Even as a note from Chevy's dream girl burned a hole in his pocket—blindly holding on to the scant thread that his treasure hunt was innocent—he was filled with jealousy, and more hatred for a friend than he had ever felt. He ignored the mildly interested (but mostly ironic) applause from the few people who had taken a passing interest in his tree antics and rushed towards his friends.

"I totally thought I left my Chevy by the levy," Mikhail interrupted, hiding every lack of breath that burned through his lungs. "And the levy was dry."

"Dry your eye, my guy," Chevy said. "If one of these websites gets the info, we can work it out, no Nintendo. I remember Amy, she used to AIM me...she stayed up late, she used to blame me. I told her Photoshop couldn't change me."

"Thanks for getting us in, douchebag," Jayson said. It was as if Jayson was saving his remark for Mikhail's benefit. And Mikhail couldn't have loved his best friend anymore than he did because of it. Besides, they had already heard that line.

"Where you been?" Mikhail asked. "We could've needed you back there."

"I'm glad you didn't," Chevy said, trying his best to stare directly into Saffron's piercing brown eyes. "Get in where you fit in, slip in with every ounce of sin. You guys good with a drink? Tonight's slogan is sloe gin."

Saffron and Jayson nodded in concurrence. They needed a refresher, as did Mikhail. Chevy rattled the lonely love of a single ice cube in an otherwise empty glass just as Weezy's band hopped onstage and began double checking their instruments and monitors. The show was about to begin, real quick.

"Fuck," Chevy said, sprinting towards the bar where Rihanna and Maya stood. Caught in something of a line, he shouted back, "B-R-B."

The band sauntered into a lethargically chopped and screwed rendition of "This Is Why I'm Hot" and Weezy quietly stepped from behind a huge speaker, instantly launching into his best Rastafarian patois. *"Dreadlocks swing down me back like Rapunzel."* His snarl was slow and dangerous and Mikhail wanted nothing more than to share some slow time with Saffron after a night full of danger. He was filled with nostalgia for dancing in the break room and hope for a horizontal dance in his bedroom. She felt it too, pulling him close in front of her, wrapping her arms around his front, rocking his hips back and forth in sway with hers. He leaned back so that she could rest her chin in the nape of his neck. *"How come every joint be on point like a harpoon? How come every bar stand strong like a barstool? How come every line so raw you gonna snort two?"*

"Guess who's back like cataracts on a heart attack?" Chevy asked. "Burt Backarack couldn't bomb Iraq with looks like that."

"What's Iraq?" Jayson asked.

Whatever it was, it sounded fictitious…and it was enough to grind Saffron's grinding to a halt. Mikhail fought his urge to find their rhythm so soon after it was rediscovered and then lost again. How did Chevy get back so fast? How did he get drinks so quickly? How does a person say "I have to fuck you and another girl simultaneously or I might be killed" in normal conversation?

"If nigga owe something/Need a doctor's note from him/ Orange throat from him"

CGI's note! Mikhail had forgotten it in the haste of his pissing contest with Chevy and the excitement of Weezy's entrance. He wanted to open it without the curious cats in his circle catching a whiff, but he definitely didn't want to open up a lane for Chevy to tailgate Saffron.

"I know what I'm doing/Let me get him/I hope his kid's not with him." As suddenly as Weezy's words left the speakers, the doors busted open behind the angst of sprinting rap fans. They surged to the stage, absorbing the darker aggression from Weezy's second song. Only a few dozen people squeezed in before the bouncers regained control of the entrance, but it was enough to raise the room's temperature. HD transformed from a few fancy people casually observing a concert into a die-hard set of fans. The enthusiasm spread like a virus. Even those who maintained appearances at the show's start immediately admitted to themselves that they knew all the words and started rapping along in gargantuan gestures of balls-out joy.

Mikhail used the momentum to unfold the crumpled sticky-note from his pocket. He casually made sure that his body blocked his actions. In the darkness, he had to read it three times. Its bluntness blinded him. There were only two possible treasures at this hunt's end. CGI's note narrowed the prize to two outcomes and Mikhail needed to decide—quick—if he was going to claim one or the other. Or maybe both. Only two things happen in a #720 restroom between a man and a woman: coke or sex.

"M: men's bathroom, 3rd stall, Weezy's 3rd song. Don't be late. :C"

Weezy's second song only had a minute left, unless there was a jam session tacked on the end. Mikhail hoped so, he needed to take a piss before he met with CGI for whatever was in store. With no reason to lie, Mikhail excused himself without saying a word or making eye contact, hoping to just be lost in the shuffle of what was now truly a concert. He wasn't sure which of the two probabilities he preferred, coke or sex, and he probably didn't have a choice.

Chapter Twenty-Four
So Go Rob the Breadmaker

No longer out of deception—only out of self-preservation—Mikhail walked straight to the bathroom. He was about to rendezvous with the #720's most desirable and virginal mistress. There were no actions that could take that from him; there was no one Chevy could charm because Chevy had no idea. Also, Chevy's concentration was being spent elsewhere.

The steps to the bathroom were long and few. It took Mikhail two paces just to drop down to the next level, but only a few notches to get to the bottom. The hall to the men's room was empty, as was the area adjacent to the little girl's room. No one was stirring, not even a mouse. Everyone was there to see Weezy perform and either went before his ascent to the stage or were awaiting his exit. Mikhail started to get nervous.

The bathroom was in stark contrast to Mr. Sallow's hallow. A fluffy carpet cushioned Mikhail's feet the minute he entered. The spring was more than he ever could've asked from a bed. There wasn't a stain in sight, not on the carpet, not on the comfortingly mauve walls. Three brass johns stood unmanned in the shape of antique French horns. Five stalls stared back at Mikhail without a single graffiti mark on them. The middle stall had to be the third stall. This time, there was only one option.

It was extremely probable that CGI was already there—she seemed like the type to stakeout a scene—but Mikhail still felt more at home in HD's clean amenities than his own apartment. Everything was so clean. He didn't realize how bad he needed to piss before he straddled the middle horn. Even then, he made exaggerated swim moves to make sure, at the very least, that he was standing in his space alone. He swung his arms just shy of carelessly, stopping once he imagined the epic fail that'd result from inadvertently smacking CGI in the face. Then he took care of taking a leak.

"And the birds in the tree get shot down to my feet"

The song was ending without a jam session. Mikhail washed his hands with lavender soap from a touchless dispenser that foamed perfectly. When the lusciously luke warm water shut off, a soft towel fresh from the dryer—or maybe never used and heated in an oven—fell from the ceiling into his hands. He was careful to only allow himself a few seconds to look in the mirror, nothing too egregious, because he knew that he was already being looked at. He went into the third stall and put the cushioned toilet seat down and sat with the carelessness one would normally reserve for a good friend's sofa. Comforts were abound. Everything was gold gilded, designed for luxury, and steam cleaned on the hour...or so it seemed. He'd feel at ease rolling on the floor or doing lines off the back of the toilet. Nothing was government-issued and nothing was abused. People treated this place as their own and, in most cases, probably better than the room around their toilet. Relaxed, he sat and waited.

Then a rush of air fell from the sky, very similar to the towel above the sink, but this time it was much softer and nearly as light. CGI dropped to his lap, straddling and then kissing him.

Mikhail moved his hands to the small of her back, crumpling up the crisp lace of her dress until he felt her skin. He closed his eyes. There was nothing to see anyway.

Their bodies guided the action. It was fierce and fearless. CGI rustled Mikhail's hair while her lips wetly pursed his face and neck. Effortless, he caught her tongue against his. She licked back and bit his bottom lip before moving to his cheek or forehead or Adam's apple in swift suctioning movements. He knew that he'd refuse the coke, if she offered it, after all was said and done.

His hands got stuck in the tight squeeze between her back and her bra strap when she tried to take his shirt off over his head. Sleeves in, the cotton of his tee covering his head, he desperately tried to undo the clasp of what felt like a 34B support system. CGI reached around for the zipper at the side of her dress. She fought with its teeth and he could feel the jostling of her bare arms on his fingertips as she wildly worked in a vortex of bending and twisting.

Within a few seconds of being removed from her body, CGI's clothing took visible form. Once Mikhail managed to bring her Imitation of Christ wedding dress over her head and toss it to the floor, the hand-sewn antique lace took shape, as real as any piece of clothing (but 100 times more expensive). When he finally figured out her bra hook, it appeared before his eyes as it fell from her silken arms. It was pink satin, outlined with black ribbing and tiny knit rosebuds. He had to smell it before he could toss the garment aside. Unbeknownst to him, her panties matched, but his eyes were closed again before she could take them off.

"Gotta be the breadwinner so go rob the bread maker"

Weezy's third song blasted into the steaming stall via surround sound speakers hanging from each of its four corners. CGI pushed Mikhail to the floor and they laughed together on the way down, by then their near-naked bodies trading droplets of sweat. Wrapping her dress around his head, she kissed her way down past his belly button. Her tongue gently started at his balls and worked its way up to the top of his shaft, pulling away only for short, tantalizingly accidental breaks in contact. Half a heartbeat in time, but enough to make his pulse skip a pump or two. Mikhail felt like her mouth was cooler than room temperature once his every inch was consumed by it, but the goosebumps on his thighs weren't unpleasant. The bath of her saliva was wet and concerned, concentrated on what he needed, but chilling nonetheless.

"Don't open your eyes yet," she said. They were the first words he'd heard from her since she left The Sports. They seemed softer, her being out of breath and close enough for a whisper.

"I trust you," Mikhail said. His pants around his ankles, shoes still on, he was shackled in place even if he wanted to run. He wasn't going anywhere. It didn't matter that the stall door was unlocked and slightly ajar.

CGI, however, was on the move. She sat up on Mikhail's legs and slid down his cock. A fever aftershocked out from her loins, emptying out across his skin from her boiling epicenter. The dampness had morphed into lava and it was rushing up and then down, forcefully yet slowly. She leaned over his body, removed her dress from his face and propped up his head with the cross of her arms, kissing his eyelids.

"You can look now," she said. "See what you can see."

Mikhail's dick swayed between ten and two o'clock, but he wasn't the one moving it. Her womanly music enveloped each rhythmic tick of his metronome, but her tight squeeze didn't hide anything. The feeling was immense, the view incredible. He watched the inside of his hands, as they guided the clench and release of her ass muscles, from full penetration to the very peak of his summit. Her body clapped against his balls with increasing rapidity and he could almost see the vibrations across her perfectly taut and tiny figure. Almost.

"I come through the lane and straight dunk like Stouda/ Mire, Amar'e/He reminds me of I-ah/He's a Phoenix Sun and I am fire"

Was CGI's planning so acute that she knew Amar'e was in that room with her owl in a tree or that Weezy's third song would be "Outstanding"? The coincidence was too specific, but not without benefit. The indecipherable nature of the stars' power to align helped Mikhail defend against the premature finale of this chapter. It took everything he had to ignore the cum-worthy fact that he could feel a warm pussy ride him into the plush carpet...but only see his naked dick freely give itself over to the ebb and flow of the invisible moment.

"I'm going to squirt all over you," she said, still leaning into his ear. Her breasts were sticking to his chest, using every bit of friction to hold firm while the rest of her body sensuously bucked, mechanically working up and down, digging deeper in a continuous effort to strike oil. "Keep watching, Mikhail. It's your pussy, baby, oh, it's all yours. You wanna make your pussy cum? Earn it, Mik, earn it, earn it, oh fuck, you're earning that pussy, baby."

She shot upright, perpendicular to Mikhail's horizontal line, her stomach muscles tensing under his tentative caress of her hips. It being a particularly sensitive area, he could feel each pulse and release squeeze and then relax. An ink cloud of pinks and oranges and purples burst like liquid smoke inside of her invisible stomach. It covered Mikhail's cock and started spreading across his entire midsection and legs, visibly oozing her orgasmic lava all over him. He was effectively painted, each detail of his shape dripping with the aftermath of a new definition. The colors instantly disappeared from her insides, but Mikhail assumed it'd be a little more difficult to remove her traces from his skin. But there was little time to think about that. After the muscles absorbing Mikhail quit clenching, she went back to riding him, this time with a definite fervor meant to win his favor.

"Cum on my face, baby, please," she said. "Please, I want you to see me, if only for a minute."

"I ball like every team/I got every girl having sex with me dreams"

At her words, he could no longer contain himself. He lifted CGI off of him and felt her stay kneeled as he stood. She directed his ejaculation from her eyebrows to each cheek bone to her chin, moving his cock from spot to spot in perfect time with each pulse of explosion. The colors of her orgasm mixed with his in the chaotically gorgeous manner of oil being poured into water poured onto the sex-flushed face of an angel. The contours of CGI's face were as simply perfect as he had imagined. A warm glacial gray swam with rainbows inside mother of pearl swirls and coated her smiling face and dripped from her button nose. But his ability to witness the reaction only lasted a few seconds before disappearing like everything else she ever wore.

The whole ordeal took three minutes and 17 seconds, from the first heavenly drop still draped in cloth to the final naked shot. Three-plus minutes being personal bests for them both, Mikhail and CGI had no idea that the (d)evolution of sex's short fuse was because of The Internet. Things moved quicker there. Videos that didn't connect with their viewer were quickly X'ed out and those longer than 90 seconds rarely got played at all. Blog posts were replaced faster than they could be scanned for keywords. Hyperlinks were explored before articles could be read in completion.

He laid on his stomach and she did the same—Mikhail's chest on the carpet, CGI's on his back. She was safety, a blanket that fit his every curve without pressing too hard under the realities of gravity. Just a feather that spread tickle from his core out to each extremity, bizarrely weightless with dead weight. Her hair felt blonde and longer than he had pictured it.

"This is the closest I've ever come to punching a stranger," Mikhail said, his eyes closed in folded arms. He could feel her position mirroring his, her head in her arms pressuring his shoulder blades just enough to affirm her place on his back. He reached around with his left hand to cup the curve of her ass, a flawless encasing of muscle that lay just a few inches above and to the south of his crotch.

"And the closest you've come to punching a friend," she whimpered, sounding as if she was falling asleep. "You know how Chevy feels about me, it's obvious."

Mikhail was too relaxed to argue. She didn't know the perils of his evening beyond his treasure hunt. Or maybe she did; maybe on that night, his plight was interesting enough to follow for a few hours. He would never know. Cuddling under a human comforter, there was little he did know. His mind was at rest, completely free of names and relationships and missions and insecurities.

Weezy's fourth song was "Georgia...Bush," an eight-minute number if he decided to perform both parts. Some of the time, the first part lulled like a lullaby, but was mostly delivered in a panic, running frantic ape-shit laps around the slower BPM.

"*It's them dead bodies/Them lost houses/The mayor says don't worry about it/And the children have been scarred/ No one's here to care about them and/A fast shout out to all the rappers that helped out*"

"Hey buddy, you passed out or just assed out?"

Water poured from the faucet and Chevy's hands rubbed against each other in even interruptions of its steady flow. Mikhail could sense the stall door hovering above his naked calves and his pants-covered ankles peaking into the restroom. CGI stiffened up, either in mockery of the situation or absolute horror, but he couldn't see her face behind his back.

"You've been ducking out of conversation all night, quick and tight...you alright?"

"Lost my pants in a pool of whiskey, brother," Mikhail said as firmly as he could, but still trying to sound a little sickly.

The pressure of CGI's body weight suddenly crushed the oomph out of his lungs. "I think they might be behind this toilet."

"You're missing a good show."

For effect, Weezy stuttered three times before releasing an unparalleled string of words. It signaled the start of "Georgia... Bush"'s second part and he should've won a fucking Oscar for his role. "*Money, money, money, get a dollar and a dick/Weezy baby that crack/Motherfucker get a fix/Got money out the ass, no homo but I'm rich/I'm about to get surgery and put some diamonds in my wrist/Yes!*"

"You should see the way Saffy's tits are bouncing on that snare. It's hard not to stare. We're cool on that, right Care Bear? You don't seem to be in any shape to make a move tonight, lying right there. You won't mind if I get my fair share?"

Chevy threw his towel towards Mikhail, launching his panic into coronary levels. If the towel landed on him and CGI, they'd be discovered. It'd disappear. He was frozen stiff as it soared towards them. The possibility of it floating conspicuously on CGI's ankles wrapped around Mikhail's seemed to freeze the cloth in mid-air, hovering for what felt like minutes. When it finally crashed down, it rolled harmlessly to a stop, thankfully a good foot from their intertwined feet.

"We'll always be aight," Mikhail lied. "Can you get me another drink?"

"Does an eye blink?"

CGI once again sat up and Mikhail turned to his back while they waited for Chevy to leave.

"You now have a virus," she said, angrily. "And it's fuckin' called syphilis. Tell anyone about this five minutes and I'll say that you raped me. That you dragged me into the torturous solitude of the men's room and foraged my helpless, painful sobs. I have multiple alibis on stand-by. They all think I'm a fuckin' virgin, so they'll believe me, everyone will. And you're drunk. And everyone knows it. Chevy and Saffron both know the state you're in."

And just like that, she got up and left Mikhail in shock, frigid without his blanket. He was alone on the floor of HD's carpeted bathroom floor. *"I like my drink straight not gay."* He really could've fallen asleep, right then and there.

"Oh, and you should definitely punch Robert Horry in the face," CGI said, presumably standing in the doorway. "He deserves it. And it's not like I'm going to let you fuck anyone else tonight, so Pastor Shakur will have bigger reasons to be pissed at you."

Part Three.

Visit
http://PleaseUseRearExit.net/home/SQUIDAPEDIA
for the #CliffsNotes on P.U.R.E's elusive cephalopod

Chapter Twenty-Five
Lemmings Gone Wild

Rather than try to figure out what the hell just happened, Mikhail stood at the bottom of the steps just outside of HD's bathroom and looked up at The Internet. It seemed to be moving faster than when he had first arrived. Whatever was making the windows move from URL to URL—be it wind, mouse clicks or atmospheric pressure—was in much more of a hurry than it was in the earlier, simpler times inside the club. He didn't have much time to deconstruct the events with CGI, but he made sure to wipe the smile from his face, take a deep breath to ensure its continued absence and avoid scratching what was already starting to itch. Mikhail's friends would be looking for him and so he started looking for them.

Most of Weezy's audience was packed into the holding area in front of the stage, so it wasn't hard to spot Jayson, Chevy and Saffron on the periphery, especially as their theatrics had grown physical. Seconds after being spied by Mikhail, Saffron went and walloped Chevy right across the face with an open palm as Jayson doubled over in red-faced hysterics. Whether Jayson's shoulder-shucks stemmed from Chevy's jokes or Saffron's reaction was indeterminable.

His gut reaction was to run to Saffron's defense and shove Chevy's wit up his ass. But even if CGI hadn't temporarily drained most of his energy, those five minutes in the bathroom had altered his ever-shifting relationship with Chevy. The man was supposed to be Mikhail's friend. They'd known each other since they lived in the same E. Hollywood Triangle apartment—before Chevy's father got that promotion and moved his family to the Westside Square—when they were barely 10 years old. Even back then, Mikhail was okay with his role as second fiddle; it's probably what made their friendship last into a second decade. Now, Mikhail had gone and fucked the only girl that Chevy seemed to care about, and almost got caught in the process. All the while, Chevy put in work on a breezy that Mikhail had both history and promises with. It was an unknowing effort to trade tit for tat, but something that had never been a problem before. He was unsure whether or not he had any right to be angry with Chevy—hadn't he started it?—so Mikhail channeled all his anger into envisioning Robert Horry's bloodied corpse into reality.

"I feel like flying/Then, I feel like frying/Then, I feel like dying"

He needed another few seconds before re-entering his friends' slap-happy conversation. The only conclusion about CGI he could draw was in the scribble of a tiny pencil stub but there all the same: CGI would be following him like a hawk for the rest of the night. But what could he do? Mikhail didn't know his destiny, but he sure as shit didn't want his legacy to be the ass-end of that invisible freak's threats. He didn't want to be the vile defiler of The #720's most beloved "virgin," and he certainly didn't want to lose another shot at being defiled by her again. But it seemed like even that could be erased rather easily. He couldn't concentrate on CGI, there was nothing he could do about that but abide by her orders. Of course, what she wanted is exactly what he would have done regardless of her threats: Nonchalance was his only play. He'd explain his extended absence to Saffron and Jayson by blaming it on his bladder or needing another view of the evening's performance. Or maybe he'd continue the lie he began with Chevy and say that he was vomiting...not drunk-puke, but something-he-ate puke. He was only gone for two songs, but was planning on using all three excuses to their fullest extent.

With a jolt he was hit with the tingle of being watched, which auto-started him towards his growingly belligerent trio of friends. She didn't touch him or even blow on his neck, but Mikhail was smacked in the face with the realization that CGI's hovering was more than just an abstract possibility in a single instant. Just as quickly, he found himself in front of Chevy and Saffron's sheepish and drunken attempts at an apology. It didn't seem like much...or maybe Mikhail's arrival stymied whatever tempers had momentarily flared.

"*And I would die for hours/Ride for hours/Supply flowers*"

"Did church wrap? Your false porcelain idol happy with that? A week's worship over in a snap...with your fill of fellowship, lemon bars and The Internet's crooked punch-bowl of slap?"

"Were you really puking, man?"

"*This is history in the making/Now shut the fuck up and let me make it*"

"All night, I've only been blind-sided by punches," Mikhail said sadly and slowly, seeing as his supposed sickness had already been discussed in his absence. "And I definitely ate something that wanted to fight all that Jameson."

"C'mon guys, leave Mikhail alone," Saffron said, rubbing his back. "It's been a rough night. And he doesn't even smell like throw-up, so the worst is over. He actually smells nice."

"We're just checking in on a soldier," Chevy said.

"Yeah, man, you sure you're good?"

Mikhail silently affirmed their questions and they all gave up trying to talk over the performance, lost in the overwhelmingly loud music and their own thoughts. By that point, most people had lost track of Weezy's set list. It didn't matter what song number he was on, only that the suddenly-shirtless rapper in a red hat and red jeans was spitting into a microphone atop HD's mystical tree. Sitting in the same wedge of branches that hosted CGI's final clue, the frog in Weezy's throat had urgently grown wings in a breathless effort to be delivered from evil. *"Out the window of a jet/You see LA like a Bruin."* Drowned out by the woof of the speakers, it was pointless in telling anybody anything...and certainly, no one could tell Weezy nothing.

"You guys want to mob up there?" Mikhail shouted, to no avail. "Shouldn't there be a surprise guest sooner or later?"

Perhaps in the transfusion of bodily fluids, CGI had provided Mikhail with a strong doze of premonition (in addition to the supposed syphilis). Eight seconds after his unanswered pair of questions, Weezy sat in the tree's chest that he had acquired proprietarily and pointed towards the back of HD.

"Can't Tell Me Nothing" may have originally been Yeezy's guttural street anthem, but he wasn't above stepping out on the Weezy remix. Once everyone realized the significance of the night's first big cameo, the energy inside HD reverberated out into The Internet with flash-photo urgency and screaming jubilation. From yonder, Yeezy started rapping. To most, one of the five biggest rappers in Los Angeles was just a voice bellowing from the booming sound system. Hidden from the crowd by its own mass, he could have just as easily been Skyped into DJ Skee's Serato as in the room. But the two dozen stragglers in the back, Mikhail among them, bore witness. In a suit sewn from the same Internet-reflecting thread as Saffron's shirt, Yeezy slowly strolled past HD's pool and proudly sauntered into every punchline. He was wearing a monocle that projected a pint-sized stripper in 3-D just a few feet in front of him and Mikhail immediately wanted to look like the Monopoly man too. *"Yeah, homie this the theme song/First I get my money right/Then I get my team on,"* Yeezy rapped—and then he drafted Saffron onto the squad.

Flanked by five bodyguards in a flying V formation, Yeezy and Saffron worked their way into the audience just as it realized that this was actually happening in real life. The energy in HD reverberated out into The Internet as photo-flashes were instantaneously TwitPic'd with a strobe-lit affect. The soundtrack was a shared recognition of jubilation. Yeezy soaked in every bit of fervor that his surprise guest appearance caused, even if "Can't Tell Me Nothing" was originally his track. The last Mikhail saw of Saffron, Yeezy removed his monocle and kissed her on the cheek after asking, *"Do that mean I dream wrong?"* Then they disappeared into the sea of adoring fans, swallowed by their own wake as the party moved towards the front. *"It don't matter if I get her number, 'cause when I get my money right, she gonna come running/And I'll be good like god with an extra O, god knows that my check need some extra O's"*

The consummate ambulance chaser, Chevy followed their path. Mikhail and Jayson did too, but they at least stopped once the bodyguards got Yeezy and Saffron on stage. Chevy found himself side stage, while Saffron was sat in a chair. With the innocent anticipation of a blindfolded child in the smiling moment between too many spins and the subsequent piñata smashing, she was exuberant and intrinsically comfortable in the set-up's lone spotlight. Yet again.

Yeezy took his final bow—exiting to a rhapsodic ovation—while Weezy's band started to strike a more sensuous tune. The lights went low, hued to the calmest of purples, as Marvin Gaye's "Let's Get It On" started coalescing amongst the instruments. Mikhail began to groan. Gaye's baby-making music was ubiquitous with good reason, regardless of the club, city, country, world, universe or dimension. The song was unfuckwitable for its ability to inspire love making and Weezy's voice was fucking insane. It would no doubt turn into an embarrassing karaoke and leave Weezy looking like a dork—something that seemed so impossible up until that moment. Mikhail shared his hopes and prayers with most of the audience that Weezy wasn't about to attempt his own rendition of such an indisputable classic.

But even Mikhail had to admit that Saffron was absolutely getting the attention she deserved. She was a sight for sore eyes and The Internet proved to be tough on the retinas. As she sat in a cheap metal folding chair, Weezy stalked around and mumbled something about getting "real R&B right now." Mikhail might've had more invested in Weezy's ability to seduce the pretty girl onstage than most of the audience, but the whole shebang was definitely making him want to leave.

"Sike," Weezy said, turning his snarl into a downright villainous laugh that echoed into the farthest corners of HD. The band switched its stance into a much angrier set of chords, violently returning the entire place to the omnipresent aggression of his first few songs. The whip-crack of a transition kept cracking.

"My shawty know what she doing/Lick her lips and get straight to it"

Perhaps Weezy was looking out for Mikhail. When the mastery of Marvin was the soundtrack, Mikhail had resigned himself of any possibility of fulfilling his fantasy with Saffron. No matter how poorly Weezy sang it, one of the world's most sensual songs would have been sung to his best chance at appeasing the totality of Shakur's bullshit mission. If Weezy didn't get up in her guts than a member of his entourage surely would. But when the beat switched completely, Weezy's words weren't those of a love song, but those of pure misogyny. It re-instilled some hope into Mikhail.

"Hi, my name is Wayne/I came to get paid and a lot of other miscellaneous things/Stand up guy, but came to get laid/ Where's my bed?"

Whether she knew it or not, Saffron was getting sexually berated in front of a few hundred people. Perhaps she was just a good sport about it—sitting and smiling through the whole 80 second verse about fucking and sucking and other miscellaneously misogynistic conduct—but there was no way she was oblivious to Weezy's tone, even if she couldn't understand his words. And if his delivery escaped her, his actions couldn't possibly. Straddling her, he grabbed his dick and performed a mock lap dance without the mock, putting his hand on the back of her head for the last hurrah:

"I'm a m-m-m-mouth full and let me see you digest"

"You know me," Weezy laughed. not rapping, just talking, while Saffron was ushered off-stage and a few band members switched instruments, "I smoke a blunt when I'm gettin' brain, stick my finger in her butt when I give brain. Yeah, I'm nasty bitch, what? Lil Wayne. I like Mac'd up lips and two tongue rings."

Saffron's reward for participation, other than Weezy's continuing taunts, was a side-stage view for the rest of the show. Right next to Chevy. Out of the frying pan and into the fire.

Soured in guilt and jealousy—his self-doubt raging against his out-right cockiness—Mikhail tried to enjoy the show. He still had to avoid Katya, punch Horry, swing some miracle threesome, and get away with his friendships intact. All while being watched. It didn't help that Saffron and Chevy were having a grip of fun in the corner—dancing, laughing, rapping along, schmoozing with the requisite gathering of celebrities and hangers-on that populated all popular side stages in Los Angeles, everyone pulling on a chronic assembly line of blunts and various boozes. Mikhail was alone in a whole room lost in Weezy's energetic antics; they responded wildly to the man's every beck and call. In the depths of the crowd, only a few feet from the stage, Mikhail tried not to blame them.

"*A B C D E F G H I J K L M N O P Q R S T U V W X Y Z-Z Top/Yes, he rock/And me and Drizzy both wrote on 'Detox'*"

Mikhail had nothing to do but get swept up in the mob mentality. He pogo-sticked and flailed his arms and smiled in mid-air at strangers enjoying the same epic alphabet chanting moment that he was, knowing that everyone around him was in the middle of a very different epiphany. It was a euphoric celebration of hip-hop at its most absurd for most of the crowd, but Mikhail suddenly couldn't tell whether he was jumping or not. With the slow motion of a nightmare, Mikhail felt like he was standing perfectly still even as his muscles contracted and released to continue his hopping. Like he was swallowed by a straight jacket hog-tied to a jack hammer, the whole world around him shook with the chaos of a crowded checkerboard in an earthquake. It was enough to get him sea sick. His heart wasn't into it and faking it was pushing Mikhail into a panic attack.

"Can I talk to you?" Mikhail shouted.

"What? Here...how?" Jayson stuttered.

Mikhail motioned to the back of the club and Jayson started worming his way towards the pool, pushing through a crowd eager to fill a void left behind. Once they cleared the last few stragglers, Mikhail's emotional flare-up almost subsided when he saw that most of HD was practically empty. Once everyone bum-rushed the stage, feeding each other's frenzy inside an invisible fence, the rest of the club housed the exact stillness that had just been burning inside of him.

"Damn, man," Jayson said, his voice sore from participation but still filled with wonder. "If you turn your back on all that and ignore all the noise, you'd think we were alone here."

"Except for that girl," Mikhail said, directing Jayson's attention towards a barefoot woman curled into a slowly swinging hammock. She was on the phone and crying, mascara running down her face, straining to be heard, a finger pushed firmly in her free ear. Her laptop was completely closed, beneath her on the floor.

"Yeah, man....crazy."

"So if I go hunt down Horry, you got my back, right?"

"Did you drag me out here for this?" Jayson demanded without care for Mikhail's response, starting back towards the stage before his question mark could hang in the air. Mikhail grabbed his fleeing friend's arm and Jayson glowered back. "You have no idea about the tig-o-bits that were rubbing up and down my back. I swear, she had rock-hard nipples the size of CDs and they were exfoliating my shoulders. You know how much a treatment like that costs?"

Mikhail did not, but Jayson knew exactly what such a thing costs, what with his old lady's numerous needs for spa-amenities. Oh, the delicate hairs on Jayson's face. Did he shampoo and condition his brown and blond stubble? What would his #4 co-workers think about his knowledge of mud bath and daily yoga packages on the #207? But Mikhail didn't want to lean into his friend for knowing what a facial costs, as much as he wanted to lean on Jayson for support. There just wasn't a reasonable conversation starter that could avoid all the pitfalls laid stealthily in front of him. Discussing Pastor Shakur would mean discussing his mission and, assuming all honesty, the betrayal of Saffron and Chevy's dalliances would mean disclosure of his torrid affair with CGI. And she was surely hovering around. Honestly, honesty couldn't happen.

"I can't get into it right now, but Horry upped the ante tonight. He went from a frivolous topic to a genuine shred of scum that needs to be fucked up. You know I don't get all aggro—ever—but his actions are serious. I'd let a thousand elf-shoed cocksuckers disappear into the abyss before I could ever allow Cum Shot Fwob breathe another minute. He deserves an analog hell that you and I and the most fundamental of Webidians can't even imagine."

A waitress waltzed by and Jayson reached out to grab her elbow, then dropped a crisp $30 bill on her tray. He asked for two double-Jameson-rocks, two High Lifes and a shot of her choice. Jayson said he wanted to buy her something. The baller move startled Mikhail. Thirty bucks was thirty bucks and it was surely the waitress' best tip of the entire night. She pinched Jayson's ass before scurrying her skinny-self away. The smile she left wearing seemed to understand Jayson's financial predicament; such a gratuity was too gratuitous to skate past an unnamed girlfriend so concerned with her boyfriend's bottom line.

"My momma say tuck your chain, son, they'll take it/ I hit her with one of them stale faces/Like, I'll be damned, momma/ They know who I am, momma/I'm still your little boy, but to them I'm the man, momma"

"Here I am thinking I'm the punch-drunk love one... seriously, Jayson, are you feeling okay? Did you really just tip her $30? That ain't you. How many frowns can you turn upside down in a single night?"

"You forget that I waited tables once, I know what it's like. Nothing happened earlier, just like nothing is going to happen later with you and Horry. We both run from confrontation... what's the point in pretending to run towards it?"

"Is that why you're still with her?"

"With who?"

"Fuck off, man," Mikhail said, not mimicking Jayson's signature pronoun, just falling into it. "Your girl, you know I'm talking about your girl."

"It's not that simple, man, you know that. Like, why don't you slap the shit out of Chevy instead of going on and on about Horry? Chevy's the one rubbing up on Saffron, right in front of you. Mr. Sallow said it, he's acting and you're stuck reacting. Chevy has shat on us since day one and, real talk, we put up with it because he knows the right party paths and makes us laugh along the way. Every once in awhile, on the rare occasion one of us is single, we get a taste of his bountiful leftovers...but that's it. Oh, thank you, young lady," Jayson said, the waitress delivering their drinks and causing him to stumble. She lost all adulation for his extravagant courtesy once he called her young lady, taking the pinkish shot he bought her with only the most minimal of celebration. Jayson watched her walk away with little remorse. "We both know that he cares, somewhere... the three of us have been through some shit, but he's rubbing it in your face tonight. He knows full well you'd never go behind his back like that...and still, he's trying to tug Saffy's tail right in front of you. It kinda makes me sick."

"She's just something warm on a cold night...stop putting so much importance on it." Mikhail hated keeping the complexity of the situation away from Jayson. Spilling the secrets of his alcohol-induced vault might be among the most gratifying sentences Mikhail ever uttered, but he couldn't. Jayson never would've understood Mikhail's actions, even with an adulterous scent on his fingers. Him and Jayson were so alike in sloth, CGI's explosion would've been viewed as a direct affront to everything that built their friendship.

"Just something warm? She's hot. Smoking fucking hot. We heard you go on and on and on about her for months, about how her curves were proportionately grafted in perfection or whatever sweet phrase you gave that piece of poon. Chevy knows how you feel and he's still up there with Saffron, acting like nothing matters. Better than punching Horry, man, go punch Saffron tonight—right in the G-spot. As much as Chevy's my homie, go win this duel, man."

A hard set of fingers started slamming on a grand piano and its echo escalated across HD, filling in The Internet's empty space. The urgency in Weezy's voice, his alien warble nearing its crack at every peak. It was the definition of fight music and it furiously pulsed through the club. The music only increased Mikhail's need to get his first successful punch over and done with. As he fruitlessly scanned the audience for a 6'10" flat-top in red and white stripes, Mikhail wondered what was necessary for complete and total closure.

"When I was five, my favorite movie was The Gremlins/ Ain't got shit to do with this/But I just thought that I should mention"

HD suddenly befell a shift in direction. Heads became faces and the faces began running towards Mikhail and Jayson. They weren't the focal point, but they couldn't see what was. Weezy had jumped off the stage and was making a beeline through the masses straight for the pool. The audience followed him, without a care in the world, stopping only when he stopped and held both his palms out, demanding them to heel. The music paused just as the lemmings did. Arms outstretched in a cross, the rushing crowd dead in their tracks, he brought the mic back to his lips.

"I'm probably in the sky, flying with the fishes/Or maybe in the ocean, swimming with the pigeons/See, my world is different, like Dwayne Wayne/And if you want trouble, then bitch, I want the same thing"

At that, Weezy back-flipped into the pool, careful to keep the mic out of the water. A release of lemmings exponentially clouded the pool's aquatic glow, each designer-clad rodent competing against his or her fellow jumper to draw the most attention with his or her strip and splash. The waterfall of 20-somethings shed spontaneous geysers of clothing before indulging in the wetness and then returning to the surface to exchange looks of disbelief that this was actually happening.

"The only thing on the mind of a shark is eat/By any means and you just sardines"

Weezy kept rhyming and people kept jumping into the pool. He wasn't tall, but he stood large in the shallow end. The richest of the rich had gotten wet for his lyrics—many getting nearly naked in the delirious process—and Weezy wore the smile of a Cash Money Millionaire. With such an outpouring, he could've told his congregation anything and they would've believed it.

Mikhail side-stepped the barrage of lemmings, watching them fall into the water but always watching for Saffron. The crying girl in the hammock held her glasses with one hand and her nose with the other as she cannon-balled without regard to where she would land. She splashed down without harm, laughing as she came back up for air. Her running make-up would no longer stand out amongst the other girls wiping pool water from their faces.

And then Mikhail was tackled. An unseen pair of shoulders speared his ribs back into his lungs and down into the water. He gasped for breath and did his best to push the chlorine from his system. It was a futile effort and he felt the chemical consume him, as he swallowed what felt like gallons of what should've been air. Underwater, pinned down by the unforgiving and unwanted embrace of the unknown, it was all Mikhail could do to screech out bubbles of desperation. Running out of breath, surrounded by the kicking and screaming of lemmings-gone-wild, he finally broke the surface and wiped the water from his eye lashes, hoping to see the one person that deserved his every ounce of bottled fury.

"She wants you and nothing to do with me," Chevy said, shaking the water from his hair and sheepishly smiling beneath his rapid movement. "It was fucked of me to ask your permission while you were puking, putrid in the face of a real king...Saffy wants your facial to make her eyes sting. Mikhail, I'm stupid. I'm sorry."

Mikhail shook his glasses free of excess water before putting them back on and doing everything he could to avoid Chevy's eye contact. The hammock girl was on the shoulders of a muscular man playing chicken against the jealousy-inducing wrap of Rihanna's thighs around a red-faced lucky bastard of a man. Maya and Britney Spears were sharing a raft and the giggle that the waves provided. They bounced along the choppiness in Internet-reflecting bras and panties, and the men of the world stared intently at their see-through choices. Then Mikhail saw Saffron's arched back across the pool, as she dipped her head below the surface trying to straighten her hair. She was alone and undeniably, channeling Phoebe Cates.

"And I'mma ride with my motherfuckin' niggas/Most likely I'mma die with my finger on the trigger/Don't worry about mine, I'm gonna grind till I get it/And tell all of my niggas that the sky is the limit...the sky is the limit"

The water dripped from Mikhail's patented Dipset scully and his white t-shirt sucked to his chest. He patted Chevy on the shoulder and swam off in a sea of guilt. His lazy backstroke found its way through self-denial towards the waves of Saffron. She was riding out Weezy's chorus and Mikhail put his hand on her underwater waist, looking into her eyes and doing his best to believe that their limit was a shared sky. The sky is the limit. He didn't believe it, but fuck it, she was pressing her soaking top into his drenched t-shirt. Under the party's pressure, everyone was dripping.

Chapter Twenty-Six
SacredSaffron.Tumblr.com

Mikhail didn't question how Saffron was able to procure a towel when no one else could seem to turn up a stack of napkins, it was the same ability that caused traffic around them to significantly slow. She had removed her boots and jeans, letting her cotton blouse fall to the middle of her thighs as she dried herself off from the lemming-like dive into the pool. Her top managed to flow like a dress in the wind at her legs and cling to every inch of the curves above her waist. It was such a mundane act—using a towel to achieve dryness—but the men and many of the women were rubbernecking like it was one of life's great wonders. It was something of an artistic miracle, as if Saffron were a master sculptor shaving pieces of clay. There was a precision to the process, like her true shape needed to revealed, and maybe rescued, from its original form. If she didn't finish quickly however, she was going to cause an accident as people left HD and wandered back into the #720.

Mikhail squeezed his blue skullcap with a stringent wringing motion. He wanted to be dry enough to face the next obstacle and it'd take some work to get there. He tried as hard as he could to wring out whatever pool remnants he could, but the #720's wind tunnel was having its freezing way with him. Through the instability of his shivers, Saffron looked so warm. Her nipples were rock hard and clearly visible, but she didn't move like a cold person.

"I wasn't planning on swimming tonight, that's for sure," Mikhail said. Chevy and Jayson were ghost, and his next move had to be made.

"It's only so much better than nothing, but I'm done," Saffron said, handing him the damp towel. "I've never seen a show like that in my entire life. If I didn't know the true meaning of spiritual, I might label it as such. Seriously, I'm so thankful that my phone is waterproof. I'm almost done with my blog post on the show, I just have to edit the video I shot. And I still can't do that on this old piece of junk. But wow, Weezy was incredible, right?"

"When did you shoot video? Or have time to write a blog about all that insanity for that matter?"

"Don't ask questions under the assumption that I'm running at 56k, Mik," she said, while pulling up her jeans. Her bounce was mesmerizing. "I'm way faster than that, even if I do need a new phone. No one cares if they have to wait and people care about my site."

"Have you blogged about the Sky Cart yet?"

"No, but only because I haven't ridden it. There's a tag already set up on my Tumblr, but no, I haven't gotten there yet, sadly. And I've got to keep it real, obviously."

"I haven't ridden it, either," Mikhail said. "But I still think about dangling my feet all the time."

"Me too. One day we'll get there."

"It's great that you found something to be so passionate about," he said. "Passions are few and far between in this age of constant gratification. Are you getting any love on the site?"

"That's what I've been trying to tell you—my blog gets a lot of love. There are at least 50 comments on every post and my Technorati points are through the roof. And more than that, my little online success has made me feel better about real life. That's all thanks to you, Mikhail."

Mikhail had nothing to say. He just looked at her quizzically.

"When I used to go to HD and clubs like that, I always felt out of place," Saffron continued. "I'd just sit there like a bump on a log. People would be talking around me and I'd be so busy thinking about what I could contribute to the conversation that the whole thing would pass me by. Because of the self-doubt ringing so loud in my head, I was deaf to my place inside that same-old-party small talk. The longer I waited to contribute, the more pressure I put on myself to say something of merit. If I was quiet for so long, how could my first comment be less than remarkable?"

"Talking is like breathing, you just do it. It can get hard, but you have to find a way to speak up. I'm not good at it, but regardless, it makes sense to try."

"But, Mikhail, I started getting hits, my Google Analytics spiked. Once I stopped caring about what I said, people started caring. And I figured, if they care about what I write, I mean, knowing that all these anonymous people on my blog wanted to read what I said or what pictures I thought were cool, why wouldn't people in real-life situations listen to me?"

Mikhail wondered what his life would be like if he lived without such filter, if his participation points mattered as much as FAILs and WINs. For a minute, he forgot how to breathe, never mind talk. The uncertainty of his prior kiss with Saffron exponentiated and began to suffocate him. He wasn't sure what it meant to Saffron, what it meant to CGI (assuming she saw and assume he did), or least of all, what it meant for him. He just knew that the woman in front of him—so sexy that people couldn't walk by her without stopping to momentarily stare—was crediting Mikhail with her spiritual rebirth.

"When we went into that storefront church, it showed me that there was something to talk about," Saffron said. "I'm embarrassed to say it, but I quit the OoEP so I could visit Compton's Circle while you were at work. I didn't want to see you there while I was figuring this all out."

"Why would it be embarrassing if I saw you on the Circle?" Mikhail asked, throwing the drenched towel to the ground. He wasn't even close to dry, he just needed something to do. "I don't get it."

"I'm still not sure, but I think it has something to do with not being first. The first rule of an Internet personality is thou shall not bite, you know that."

"But I never go to that church."

"I know, but you were still there first. You have to understand, I was so unsure of myself I resorted to being a giggly mute girl who relied on stupid jokes to make people like me. Now that I have some confidence, I guess I don't mind being second. But can I ask you a personal question?"

"Maybe."

"Aren't you sick of finding ways to write the same conniving shit in different ways over and over again? I left the Office of Emailing People forever ago and you were there long before I started."

"Of course I am, but it doesn't make my job any less worth a damn. I provide a service and—"

"—and you do, Mikhail, and you do it better than most, but there's more to life than those emails to random people. You're better than SPAM and you know it. I know it."

"Maybe I am, but I'm not sure what else I could do. Haven't really thought about it, truthfully. Tricking SPAM filters is kind of a specific talent, where else could it possibly be useful?"

"I'm pretty sure that it's not for me to find out," Saffron said. She had finished putting herself together and, unlike Mikhail, looked like she did at the start of the evening. Perhaps the thread on her blouse, the same kind that reflected The Internet, also had some waterproof properties. Her make-up was un-smudged, her hair perfectly coiffed and her clothes completely dry. Mikhail was still closer to a drowned rat than someone in their Friday night best.

"Well, what do we do now? You know, while I'm trying to figure out how to make my little talent a big one..."

Saffron shrugged her shoulders.

"Should we look for Jayson and Chevy? Sneak onto the Sky Cart?"

"Man, you ain't sneaking anywhere," Jayson said, creeping up from behind Mikhail to put him into a headlock.

"Really? Really? What the fuck about me demands all this attention?" Mikhail was exhausted with all the wrestling he had been forced into, and now he was getting it from his best friend. He thought about fighting back but couldn't find the strength. Mikhail would argue, but his heart wouldn't be in it.

"I work on the #4, motherfucker, you know the bang these guns pack," Jayson laughed, tightening his grip. "Who's your master?"

"The Internet."

"Think again," Jayson said, squeezing tighter around Mikhail's neck.

"Oh, right, it's Saffy."

"Keep thinking."

"Jayson, stop! He's turning red, you're going to kill him!"

"Jayson, you are the master."

"That's all I needed," Jayson said, releasing his grip and standing up. He then helped Mikhail to his feet.

"The master of masturbating, I mean. You're the Usain Bolt of self-pleasure and I bow down to your speed."

Jayson started wrestling again and Mikhail found a free arm to pinch and grab and twist. They separated like the opposite ends of magnets and firmly looked at the childish joke between them before glancing at each other.

"If you boys are done," Saffron snarled, "I know where the after-party is at. Are you done?"

"Should we leave without Chevy?" Jayson asked, sitting on the ground and kicking Mikhail whenever he could. "He's gotta be around here somewhere."

"I haven't seen him since he pushed me into the pool. He found his way into HD, I'm sure he'll be okay at the after-party." Mikhail smiled at Saffron. As long as he didn't wear it on his face, it didn't matter that he was replaying CGI's tie-dye explosion and her orgasmic muscle spasms. Not to Saffron or CGI. If Chevy's towel toss had been on-target, things would've been different. But they weren't. "Where's the party at?"

"Just a hop, skip and a jump from here," Saffron said. "A little walking and a little Brown BTWNing and we're there. That's on your way home anyway, right?"

Visit **http://PleaseUseRearExit.net/home/WEEZY**
for a NahRighteous review of tonight's showstopper

Chapter Twenty-Seven
Raw Bacon

With an exaggeration of showmanship, Mikhail opened the cast iron door for Saffron and Jayson. They had all scanned their MTA cards, traversed the turnstiles, and were ready to wait for the Brown BTWN's one-stop express towards the Lil' Rectangle. The spoils of an exclusive after-hours event were something they eagerly anticipated. Mikhail had his own ideas for what it should include, but they were as skewed, warped and distorted as Photoshop allowed. The door behind them angrily slammed shut without impediment and with such violence that the creaky latches almost broke in half. Everyone jumped at the forewarning clasp of steel against steel.

A light flickered far in the transfer station's distance, sending foreboding signals against further steps. The darkness was disturbing. Their eyes would just have to get accustomed to it; there was no way to change the mission. Weezy's after-party was the plan and all the dangers in the world couldn't keep Mikhail from soldiering on. Even if the steel-walled room was a bunker of scary, cast in a yellowish brown from the film covered lights. Shadows creeped from the corners and swallowed every bit of illumination in their path. In the distance, an unseen liquid dropped with metronome precision and it was all anyone could hope that the heating/cooling system had sprung a leak. As they took steps forward, the drips dropped louder and Saffron cuddled closer and closer to Mikhail.

Three other people waited for the Brown BTWN, all sitting on separate benches and having not a thing to do with the after-party to end all after-parties. A man sang along with mangy headphones, his voice slightly off and only soft enough to harmonize with the dripping, yet not enough to drown out its persistence. Another man smoked a cigarette and read the same page of a newspaper over and over again. He didn't care that smoking in the transfer station was a fineable offense—and neither did anyone else. The dripping never stopped; it only paused and then sped back up. A woman rustled through her grocery bags in need of a snack. All six of the people inside the station looked a little drunk, haggard and worse for the weary. It had been a long night and—especially for the snack-diving woman—a long life.

"Isn't this kinda like that one scene in that one movie?" Jayson asked.

"I'm pretty sure that the pretty girl gets got somewhere around there," Mikhail said. Saffron's arms were heavily wrapped around his waist, but his concentration had to be elsewhere. He was looking above him, and for once, not watching out for CGI. Saffron dug her knuckles into his ribs and her teeth into his right bicep, not out of any perceived jealousy but because he was succeeding in scaring her. "Awww....fuck, that hurt. Sheeeeeeeiiiiiiiiit...at least you know you're the pretty girl."

"That lady is opening a package of raw bacon with her teeth. I better be the pretty girl."

Mikhail stuck out his tongue and she ducked into his armpit like he was about to spit acid. Then the conversation lulled. The echoes of dripping and the crinkling of shopping bags fought vividly through the darkness. At his maximum level of alertness, peering into every corner, Jayson's thoughts were just as paranoid as Mikhail's. This transfer station was notorious for squid attacks. Damp and dark—its construction years out of date and in need of maintenance—the #720/ Brown transfer was always populated with straggling drunks who misplaced their reaction time. It was the ideal place for squids to come inside and feed.

Mikhail tried to anticipate just such an attack, without psyching himself out over nothing. If one dropped from the ceiling, he knew that he'd have to shield Saffron and then punch. Punching was the only handbook's only advice: Hit the fucker in the head as hard as physically possible. That, and avoid the bone-crushing beak beneath its 10 claw-lined tentacles. Be confident and you'll win, Mikhail told himself. Punch with a purpose. In it to win it. Protect her and fight to the death, it'd be the right thing to do.

The flickering light above the bacon-eating woman went black. Something dripped on the back of Jayson's neck and he nearly left his shorts, shivering out loud with a yelp that bordered on a yell. Patting furiously at his collar, he made sure that it wasn't a sticky sign of even worse fortunes to come. The ink that squids so notoriously slimed everywhere was the greatest proof of their appearances inside Los Angeles. It was sticky and it didn't leave any witnesses, at least according to Wikipedia. However, the drop on Jayson's neck was just the drip of infrastructure beyond repair. The start of end times it was not.

"They should really fix those leaks," Mikhail said, while Jayson rubbed at nothing. "Shit is disgusting."

No one responded and nothing else was uttered for more than a minute. The trio took slow and reflective steps, somewhat teetering, while they weathered the storm until the next destination. This storm was all about waiting.

"This party is going to be off the fucking hook," Saffron said. She relinquished Mikhail's arm just enough to be firm in her declaration. "We wouldn't be leaving before closing time unless there was something better...and this is it. So many managers and weed carriers and label people confirm what I already feel— it's going down and we're rising to the top."

Such optimism made Saffron's sexiness push past her skin and fantasy-forming-fatty-tissue into worlds defined by certainty and not just gravity. What she found so charming in Mikhail—a vapid base of corny jokes and philosophical pondering that bordered on meandering—had never dawned on him. Thinking about such things made the pregnant pauses of life that much more unbearable and the distant drips of interruption even worse.

"ZIZZURP!" Mikhail instead shouted into Saffron's neck. Before he could contain himself, he was mock-biting and making other monster noises. The more raucous he made himself, the less squids would want to eat him and his friends, or so he thought. Being loud made him feel like less of a target. Inside the transfer station, it felt important enough to scare the squids to risk pissing off CGI. She might've been just as stealth as an adult squid, but an overwhelming ability to kill at an apex of efficiency wasn't in her repertoire. Or perhaps, the excitement of getting closer and closer to a physical specimen like Saffron was turning into an addiction. She was so warm and soft as he exhaled into her skin, Mikhail could've curled up and taken a drug-induced nap.

She was way too angry with his attempt at a joke to abide by his desires for a nap. One of her strikes caught his chin, then his kidney, and he was quick to pull the mock from his bite. He could feel the blood vessels in her skin break between his teeth. It'd leave a mark. Her shriek sounded alarm, sucking the attention of the strangers away from headphones, newspapers and bacon. She twisted his nipple and rushed to the other side of Jayson. In a hyperbole of exasperation and defeat, Mikhail whimpered out a slow and methodical "...zizz...urp."

"You didn't scare me, you big fucking bully. Just because, like, it's dark in here and everything is dripping, it doesn't mean that we're in some BT News disaster," Saffron said, her taunting dance coming to a very purposeful halt. She stood on her tippy toes, trying to walk taller and manlier than Jayson, but always finding a way to duck behind him. The charade of aggression made her breasts stick out. A perfect C was curved in her back and even better DD cups protruded, as her chin stuck in the air, a parade of faux-confidence. "Don't make me fuck you up," she said, "Jay, hold me back before I kill this dial-up dinosaur, hold me back, man, hold me back…"

Hugging the outside of the transfer station, the pack's alpha-squid waited, seemingly indifferent to the noise inside the #720. The passing Internet vigorously rustled its stray tentacle as the other nine sinewy extremities suction cupped to the bus's exterior. The speed of the transport caused its errant arm to flap violently in the wind of the WWW. There's no reason to say that the commotion inside changed the squid's behavior, but its holding-on-for-dear-life posture quickly turned offensive at the sound of Saffron's squeals. The Jumbo Squid and its three compatriots stood taut, straightening their mantles and tentacles to the full six-foot capacity before things really turned serious. The red and white flashing of their chromatophores—once passive and relaxed and in beat with the pumping of their three hearts—grew more intense until rapidly crescendoing into a strobe-light of fury. In an instant, they disappeared from The Internet and moved into the shadows of the Brown BTWN transfer below. Perhaps it was just a coincidence that they began their attack at that moment.

Unknowingly joined by new company, Saffron was proud as a peacock and pretending to really need a fight. She tried to make Jayson hold her back, but all that prancing around only made all her parts bounce about quite fancifully. Any attempt at toughness was thwarted by her inability to be anything but sexy. Separated by another person, his brother from another mother no less, Mikhail could feel the warmth that emanated from the crux of her low-slung ass-hugging pants. But her lip began to quiver when she caught Mikhail's eyes looking towards the steel top of the station's shell.

"We're okay, right?"

"Thousands of people every day wait in this transfer," he said, reading her fear from a mile away. He had to ignore his. "And they all make it home for dinner...without a single squid encounter. The possibility is just something we have to live with. It's more hype than anything else, something for BT News' ratings."

"I saw a dead one once," Jayson said, excited to reveal a story from his past. "Not some farm-raised infant used in biology class, but a decent sized dead dude, all shriveled up in a corner."

Mikhail had heard this story several times before. He was curious about Jayson's inevitable exaggerations once he started in on poking the dead squid with a rolled up bus pass.

"It was in the Blue BTWN, coming from the #2 probably, and it just looked like a pile of clothes at first. Bored of waiting—"

"—like we are right now," Mikhail said.

"Yeah, bored of waiting around for the damn bus to show, I went over to check it out. This pile was so dead, I had no idea that it once lived until I saw that eyeball. Then I knew. I've seen people die in TV shows on The Internet and you know how their eyes stay open and then the good guy shuts them with delicate and manly fingers? Well, squids don't have eyelids. That dirty thing's dead eyes seemed to still be swimming in life. I was all by myself, a couple bags in my hands. Near its fins, far far from those nasty-ass tentacles, I walked up behind it. It looked dry as shit, like it had rolled in the sand and baked in the summer lights of Compton's Circle for a week. But it couldn't have been there for more than 10 minutes. Anti-Squid League comes quick...and that station is too busy for it not to have been reported.

"I rolled up my bus pass, the long way, and gave it a little poke. There was no way it wasn't dead, but that fucker's eye just looked so alive, like it was in a meditation so deep that its real-life vision was clouded. It didn't move, so I lightly kicked it with my shoe. It still didn't move. And then I touched it with my finger, leaning over, but keeping my face as far away as I could. So I'm there, touching this thing and it was huge, probably seven-feet long once it was all stretched out. And it's just dead. Who's to know that it didn't eat a grip of people? The thing looked old to me...who knows, right?"

"They gross me out," Saffron said. The mock fight being well over, she moved back between Jayson and Mikhail. "Like, right now, I'm scared. But when I'm home thinking about them, they just look like they'd smell of shit. Not even shit, but dirty menstrual pads, just rotting period blood. It makes me want to yak."

"Shhhh," Jayson said. "They might've evolved and learned English."

"They could be hugging the outside of the bus," Mikhail said, playing into Jayson's lead. "The passing Internet vigorously rustling a stray tentacle as the other nine stay suction-cupped to the steel, just listening to you talk shit about the way they smell."

"Think they'll get mad if I say that their momma gets fucked by multiple squids before laying 10,000 eggs of unknown fathers on some real whorish shit?" Jayson said, before getting louder, "Theirs is a culture of whorish morals and rotting period blood smells! And I totally banged some momma squid whore right in her funnel!"

"And then I hit the bitch with sloppy seconds and four condoms on, cause those whores are crawling with disease!" Mikhail yelled along, puffing out his chest and really hoping that squids hadn't yet learned English.

The pack's alpha squid was hanging upside down from the transfer station's ceiling, one eye turned towards the movement below. It stayed dark, refusing to flash red or white, but camouflaging itself in the shadows, hiding in the un-illuminated blindness of the unseen. Another squid waited upside down several yards away, while the other two had slunked down to the station's lower corners. All were invisible and silent, ready to strike, but waiting patiently on their leader's movements.

"Excuse me, young sir, but even if the squids can't understand you," a far-off man said, loudly enough for everyone in the station to pay attention, "the rest of us do have enough recognition to be offended by your language and you're obviously frightening the women in here." He triumphantly folded a newspaper under his arm and rose from the bench, walking casually towards the light that Mikhail's friends stood beneath.

He stopped a few feet short of Jayson and Saffron, standing directly under the light. Light felt safer and everyone flocked to it. Mikhail stayed a few steps back, worried that the glare would obstruct the view above. He hovered in a zone that allowed the human eye to see without succumbing to the light's distracting properties. Jayson moved out of the light and closer to the man, shouting back:

"What the fuck it matter that I say fuck? We're talking about life and death in modern day Los Angeles. What the fuck does a fuck even matter?"

"A level of civility goes a long way in this world, young man."

"Civility goes out the door when a squid is eating someone's fucking grandpops," Jayson said. Completely ignoring the reference to his own lineage, Mikhail instead focused on his friend. Perhaps the piles of booze were too much for him because Jayson rarely rose above meek. Maybe the scent of a double-vagina on his fingers flared up his inner-testosterone, but whatever it was, Jayson was in rare form. Raaaaare form.

And he believed his own drunken bravado. The extra drama, however, didn't bode well for Saffron. Her cowering got even closer to a fetal position, by now tucked deep into Mikhail's stomach, a few steps behind Jayson's out-of-character ranting. Her hair tickled Mikhail's wrists and he gently embraced the lustful meat above her hips. Beneath the blouse rising against her back, the amiability of her skin blocked out the whole World Wide Web, and Mikhail temporarily settled into a very specific sort of peace.

"Standing tall and righteous in a short world might not impress your friends, young man, but it definitely puts a good message out there," the man said. "And putting any kind of good out into this cantankerous abyss will only help you reel in some good of your own. Like-minded bait, young man, so that you can catch a good fish."

And at that, a bad fish dropped from the ceiling.

Saffron slipped out from beneath Mikhail's arm just before the squid's weight landed squarely on his back. It nearly brought him down. She didn't even whimper as he nearly fell over, just scrambling for cover. Everyone scrambled, except Mikhail. He was stuck. His miraculous balance and unknown strength was a fourth quarter moment of heroics that quickly turned into a panicked overtime. He felt the many teeth on the beast's many suction cups on its many tentacles pierce his skin and tear at his shirt. Its sharp beak bit into his flesh, just above the bone on his shoulder, tearing a chunk of muscle with its parrot-like device. All the while, he teetered on two drunken legs, desperately trying in vain to pry the pain away. To push everything off of him. It was too much. The squid kept pulling him closer and he couldn't figure out the right point to push against. Tentacles were everywhere. They wrapped around his arms and there was no way for him to pick up the velocity needed to punch. The beast was strong and its heft was nearly buckling Mikhail's legs with every step.

Had he put that much bad into the world to reel in such a bad fish? It wasn't even a fish, but an invertebrate....but still. Mikhail couldn't believe that he was thinking about karma when he was so close to what would surely be his end. Few people ever survived such things and here he was retracing the energies he put out into the world. The pain snapped his reality back to the task at hand. It was burning, hundreds of needles rotating deep in his flesh. He could hear the beak snapping with each miss and crunching with each hit. His squirming made sure that it was less of the latter.

Through the quickly tightening hug from the wet blanket of heavy shrapnel draped around his shoulder, somehow, Mikhail caught a sensitive spot on the beast's underbelly. It flinched and he pinched harder, and then twisted. It freed his arms and he was able to reach back and pry the 200 pound squid from his back, just before his legs were finally about to give out. Mikhail thrust it directly over his head and watched it stumble awkwardly to find its balance at his feet.

The beast righted itself and stared a single eye directly into its probable prey. Mikhail no longer fretted about the sweat stains starting under his armpits. He didn't need Katya or CGI or even Saffron, he just didn't need to die. And the best way to stay living, at that splintered moment, was to keep in direct eye contact with the squid. There was no room to give ground. He had to look directly into its soul with all the confidence he could muster. Mikhail had to hold his position and push fear from his gut. His only choice was to match its blink-less glare.

He didn't allow himself to be concerned with the movement behind him, not with his eyes anyway. "You okay?" he asked, without losing his true focus.

"Yeah," Jayson whimpered. Saffron just cried hush cries. Jayson held Saffron and pushed their backs against the station's wall before she started crying harder, into an unavoidably audible level of fear. He instantly thought better of their position, of what could lie outside the wall to drag them through it. They moved towards the center, towards a light, and Jayson looked around in search of attacks from above and beyond.

But for Mikhail, their movements were muffled, as if his ears were underwater while his eyes were dryly land-locked in the bizarre staring contest. It all happened so fast, but the noises crept by in such slow motion.

The squid's left eye—bigger than a softball—hopped a few inches up and a few inches down in a ritualistic preparation of feasting. In its direction, Mikhail stuck out an open palm and flexed all the muscles from his forearm to his finger tips. It was an assertive gesture, but also one of respect. Silently, he pushed his thoughts through his hand in the most calming tone his brain could radiate, *Kind sir, this isn't the meal you want. It isn't the right fight, not tonight...*

The beast started to pulsate in gorgeous flows of red and white. It didn't flash wholly at once, but to Mikhail's eyes, the shifts of color were a rolling wave of change. It was almost soothing, if not for what it probably meant.

Chapter Twenty-Eight
Alpha Squid, Master Beta

The entirety of Mikhail's essence—everything he could muster, both body and soul—was focused on the monstrous unblinking eyeball that met his stare. He just wanted the squid to leave, but it wanted to bob up and down and flash red and white in a continuous ripple across the millions of chromatophores that defined its visible anatomy.

Behind the squid, the transients in the transfer station huddled in a protective mass, which quickly had the opposite effect of their instinctual intentions. They were instead the perfect target for the other three squids lurking in the shadows. Before the monsters were noticed, they each picked a specific prey and swarmed from every direction. Before they knew an attack was upon them, the helpless passengers were dragged back into the depths of The Internet. In a flash, the gentlemanly man with the newspaper and the bacon-eating lady and the man in headphones were gone without time for a kick or a scream. The only evidence of their abduction huddled against the station wall—just three separate piles of clothes completely limp in unique portraits of death. The explosion of violence left Saffron and Jayson, Mikhail and the alpha squid, all alone.

Mikhail's counterpart, however, didn't seem to be in any rush at all. Slowly moving backwards, the behemoth slunk down and then perked up across the station's cheap linoleum floor. The putrid ink that oozed from beneath its dress of tentacles allowed the squid to methodically glide where it needed to go in a slow bouncing motion. Every ebb up resulted in a flow back down, but the beast never blinked. And Mikhail did his best to keep his hand steady and his eyes fixed. The squid wasn't retreating, but Mikhail wasn't following it either. It was as if the monster needed some distance to fully comprehend the situation at hand. Or tentacle, as it was. And then Mikhail's cell phone rang loudly from his back pocket.

He slowly took it out with his free hand and quickly glanced at the screen. The call was from a familiar source, but it still startled his opposition. The squid stiffened and then moved forward, preparing to pounce. Its movements were enough to make Saffron shriek, as if the air had been stolen from her lungs.

"It's just my ex-girlfriend," Mikhail said, out loud this time. "This must be the hundredth time she's called or texted me tonight. And I haven't answered a single one. She slapped me earlier on, splashed a drink in my face. This has been my night, surely you must relate to that," he said, as soothing as he could be with each syllable. "I can't answer it because I don't want her in my life anymore."

Mikhail thought about the time he had built a fort out of pillows and sheets in his hallway with Katya. About the time she discovered he'd been sneaking cigarettes behind her back. About the way she made him shave because it promised great things for the both of them. Then the way she sexily sauntered during a karaoke performance of Spirit Animal's "Broken Paradise." And when she napped through the only family function he ever took her to. His memories of Katya flashed throughout his whole body and it poured out through his outstretched hand and down into his fingers towards this new adversary.

You know what this is and this isn't you, Mikhail said to himself, to the beast. He channeled every word and ounce of his energy out of each fingertip's point of egress. It was genuine, if calculated, but mostly instinctual. *She came out of nowhere, it was an accident, but an accident I have to deal with...just let me deal with it. Let my friends deal with their mistakes. You got what you came for and I can't blame you. Everyone's gotta eat.*

Mikhail put his phone back into his pocket and stared even deeper into the squid's seemingly blank psyche. Its eye was bigger than a dinner plate and Mikhail looked hard in an effort to see some sort of sympathy in its fist-sized pupil. There was a slight shift in what he found. The flashing had subdued, as had the bobbing. Even if Mikhail could not detect a change in its coal black pupil, the squid looked ready to extend a tentacle for a firm handshake and go about its way. Mikhail knew he and his friends were safe, that the squid was leaving. That's when the room's dynamics were shattered.

The same red door that had once startled Saffron suddenly slammed shut again. Robert Horry came-a-running out of nowhere. He jumped with an assertiveness that seemed to shock even the squid, punching the monster in the very same eye that assuringly connected with Mikhail. The eye burst in an explosion of membrane. One arm deep in its head, Horry hit it again in the back of the mantle with his other fist. He then kicked it away from him, making sure to grab a good chunk of its eye as the squid slid away. Sadly limping, it disappeared into The Internet. Horry flicked his hand in disgust, as the squid's innards sprinkled from his arm.

"Is everyone okay?" he asked, just one step shy of shining a superhero-worthy shit-eating grin.

"OMI," Saffron said, "you saved us."

"We were fine before you showed up," Mikhail said. "You aren't a hero, that squid was just about to leave. I explained the situation and it was on its way out. You're just a dick looking for a way in."

"Mikhail, stop," Saffron pleaded. "He just saved your life."

"Saved my life? Saved my life? Are you serious? I was handling it. It was handled. It was backing up into The Internet, dude knew who was boss."

"Dude? You talk about that disgusting murdering monster like it was a person worth redeeming," Horry said. "Dude? Go hug HD's tree with some shit like that. He was ready to kill you and your friends. Are you okay, ma'am?"

Saffron left Jayson's protective hug and ran forward. Mikhail was relishing her warm embrace after such a painfully cold one had torn at his flesh. Mikhail may have been the first person to ever survive a direct squid attack and must've been the first to stay on his feet. That deserved the type of care that Saffron could provide. He felt the blood slowly trickle down his back—especially from a particularly nasty wound on his right shoulder—spurting faster as his pulse quickened with each of Saffron's steps. Right as he was ready to hold her in his arms, she continued past him and jumped into Horry's.

"I freaking hated you as a player, but Internet-be-damned, I don't know what we would've done without you," she said, burrowing deep into his chest. Like Ozzie and Harriet had invited the Olsen twins over to swap keys and swing, Saffron and Horry's hug was as pure as it was devastatingly deviant. Mikhail's footing hadn't moved in minutes and his jaw quickly joined his Converse on the ground. "We owe you our lives," she said.

"We don't owe this douchebag a damn thing," Mikhail said, turning towards his nemesis. "I saved us. We were safe. You just had to get your last-second shot in. This wasn't the playoffs, it wasn't even your game."

"I don't know why he's so bitter," Horry said, pulling back from Saffron just enough to look into her eyes. "He shouldn't speak this way around you. You're a lady. I'm sure he's just in shock. Look at him, he's bleeding all over the place. It'd be disgusting if it wasn't so sad."

"It's just a little cut, which is more than I can say for you once just due gets done," Mikhail said. Perhaps it took an angel and a demon to fall from the sky for him to find his inner switch that turned anger into black-out rage—but regardless of who the angel and demon respectively were—he found it. And Horry had finally flipped it.

"C'mon little man, don't make me toss you into the sun," Horry said, smiling with an evil all his own. He slid in front of Saffron, but didn't change his tone from the condescending concern that mocked Mikhail with every syllable. "I don't get why you're angry with me, Mikhail. I was just trying to help out you and your fellow Internet Explorers."

Mikhail charged into a sprint and cocked his arm back, ready to unleash years of pent-up hatred that had only exponentiated in the previous hours. Horry stood his ground, knees bent, shoulder length apart. Hidden from Saffron, his fists clenched and his eyes narrowed. Mikhail brought his right fist forward with everything that was ever inside of him; his muscles clenched, first at the tips of his toes and through his calves and further through his body towards his knuckles. But before Horry's face could catch such wrath, Mikhail's arm was caught at the elbow. Jayson grabbed him from behind and their collision of force spun the pair of friends around in an old fashion square dance of a dosey-doh.

"It's not worth it, man. Not now, he just saved our asses," Jayson said. "I know where you're at, but....no."

"You too? Get the fuck off me! You believe this cheating cock-sucker over me? I had it under control and you know that he deserves a wallop. It is worth it."

Mikhail felt betrayed by his best friend. He knew why Jayson had stopped his first punch before it could ever land, but it was the insistence that Horry deserved appreciation that ate at him. Jayson had heard the run-down of events at Something and bore witness to Mikhail's arbitrary basketball-related anger since they were both kids, but only a few seconds of Horry's fake-ass heroics were able to override it all. Mikhail wanted to think that if the situation was reversed, he would've helped Jayson stomp Horry down to size. He couldn't be sure though. It was difficult to remove his own emotion from the scenario.

"It's not, man, it's just not," Jayson said. "Not now."

A bell that warned of the Brown BTWN's impending arrival pierced the tension. Jayson's interception—and the quick decisions that suddenly had to be made—turned Mikhail's fury switch back off. He gathered his composure and checked the wound on his back for the first time. It wasn't bleeding so bad, but the wound definitely wasn't going to close on its own.

"I was gonna go to this Weezy after-party, but after everything, I'm not so sure," Horry said. "Mikhail, you might want to hit up a hospital. If you catch this bus, you can get to the #16b right quick."

"You really should, Mik. Oh Internet, you want me to go with you?"

"I'm okay, I don't need medical—"

"That was too intense for me," Horry interrupted. "I'm gonna walk back to the Blue BTWN and then take a Sky Cart back to my pad. If you're okay, Mikhail, you guys are welcome to join me."

Imploringly, Saffron ducked ahead of Horry's embrace and quizzically looked at Mikhail. Horry whispered something in her ear that made her giggle. And jiggle. And Mikhail knew that it wasn't meant to be. Saffron was meant to ride the Sky Cart and he had no immediate plans to make such things possible. Was she worth fighting for even if Horry was worth fighting? Who was Mikhail to begrudge her of a life-long goal just because he had some arbitrarily abstract mission?

"If I go to your crib, I'm only going to kill you," Mikhail said. He was serious, but it was probably the funniest thing he had said all night. "Maybe I'll just go to the #16b after all, you guys go and have fun."

"My wifey is shitting bricks already," Jayson piped up, "but I'll make sure this dude gets to the hospital okay."

"Are you sure?" Saffron asked. She started walking towards Mikhail, but was gently and subtly held back by Horry. "I'll go with you if you want. I could blog about the #16b, I've never been there before and always wanted to see the disparity in health care first hand. Scathing political shit always does well."

"Could I really rob you of a ride on the Sky Cart?"

And he couldn't. It'd always been her dream. Her options were terribly skewed. So few people rode the Sky Cart because so many couldn't afford its luxury while anyone was welcome on the #16b but no one ever wanted to go.

The minute Horry barged into his Mikhail's night for the second time, his chances with Saffron were deader than the three transients who were dragged into The Internet. Saffron and Horry walked away. Behind his back, well out of her sight, he flipped Mikhail off. They exited and the Brown BTWN's bell rang again, this time signaling its imminent arrival.

"I'm not going to the hospital," Mikhail abruptly said.

"Then what the fuck are you doing letting her walk away with him?"

"I can't keep her from what she wants, no matter how much that douchebag needs a slow and painful death. Besides, it's not like you got my back."

"I don't have time to get into this with you. I'm glad you're alive and backing off was the right thing to do. You'll know I'm right once you calm down. Look at you, man, they aren't going to let you into any afterparty. Even if you were 100-percent healthy we wouldn't stand a chance without Chevy or Saffron and three girls equal to or greater than her hotness."

"Fuck the afterparty," Mikhail said. "I'm going back inside. I have to see a man about a squid."

"The last thing you need is more booze. Take a piss at home, man. Or even better, on the #16b. C'mon, let's get you stitched up."

"Your bus is here, Jayson. Don't piss your wifey off anymore than you already have. But I'm going this way," Mikhail said. "Did you at least wash your hands?"

"Of course, I did," Jayson smiled and nodded, but then smelled his hands anyway. "Oh Mikhail, thanks, man. You fought the squid first, Horry just did it louder."

Visit **http://PleaseUseRearExit.net/home/DarkWalk**
for an examination of the heel, when she breaks.

Chapter Twenty-Nine
Lord of the Barnyard

Mikhail watched Jayson step onto the Brown BTWN and reminisced about feeling the things that result in returning home to a warm lady. The well-washed and sweet-smelling blankets, the entanglement of limbs that occasionally lead to more than just that. Then he remembered that Jayson wasn't gonna get laid and that Katya was never all that warm. The Brown BTWN's doors closed and Mikhail walked back out into the #720.

Feeling progressively drunk, he had no female prospects (only the constant potential of a stalker's presence) and his bleeding was getting worse. On the bright side, his itching subsided once his brain was occupied by other discomforts. Horry was gone, there was no one left to punch. Mikhail was onboard the #720 only to complete a mission he didn't fully understand. He was never good at initiating conversation, but would have to figure it out if he had any hope of success.

Despair was the easiest of Mikhail's emotions to deal with. Tamer than depression and with more comfort than loneliness, he tried to accept it without dwelling on the destructive gnawing. The hopelessness helped take off some of the edge that had built up in him over the previous few hours. He walked back through the turnstiles and the #720's passengers made sure to stay away from his bloody mobile corpse. The increasingly sparse populace took two steps away before they gave two shits. Did he really look that bad? He had to search out a reflective surface.

Once he saw himself, the world's repulsion wasn't without merit. His face was scratched and caked with crimson. Smeared with blood—the hair peaking out below his scully was clumped together, like he'd haphazardly washed his face in iodine. The plethora of scratches from his forehead to neck were each clotted with crumbs of DNA. His t-shirt was torn to shreds, its red stains beyond repair. It was not the outfit of someone trying to fulfill a destiny. He needed to power up and the booze cart was making its rounds. Mikhail ordered a triple Jameson-rocks and two white Russians.

"Is there anyway you can fit those two commie bastards into a big cup?" he asked. "It's for Mr. Sallow, that's why I'm asking."

The man bent into his cart and the grotesque purple creature on his back stuck out its three fingered hand, opening its razor-toothed mouth to ask for their fee. But it gasped before uttering a single word. It then hissed, "What the fuck happened to you? Sssshhhhhouldn't you be at the hosssssssspital?"

"I didn't even think you had eyes," Mikhail said, placing two $30 bills into its fingers, careful not to touch the scaly hand again.

"I don't, you fuckin' sssssssssssmart ass, but he does. We ssssshare the sssssame brain ssssstem." The man nodded and handed Mikhail his drinks, before turning back around. "Sssssssssomeone ssssstab you? It looksssss nassssty..."

"Sssssssssquidsssss," Mikail mocked. "Keep the change and have your man show you a mirror before you go around saying what looksssssss nassssssty...."

The cart pushed on, both the man and his growth mumbling under their collective breath. Once again, Mikhail was alone. He put the big Styrofoam cup of milk and vodka on an advertisement for terrible foods found only online, and did his best to find company with the lone plastic glass of amber in his hand. The weight of everyone's stares grew heavy. He could feel the glare of strangers piling on his back and he wasn't sure how much more his knees could take. They'd already held too much for one evening. He grabbed Mr. Sallow's big cup o'booze and dairy, and once again walked towards the #720's municipal bathroom. He concentrated on consuming the vat of whiskey spilling in his hand until he came upon the restroom, almost not recognizing it for its lack of a line. Refusing to take an open container into any bathroom, never mind a spot this sullied, Mikhail chugged the last two-thirds of his Jameson before stepping inside. Even his immune palette had to snort at the extreme intake of booze, but he refused to hack or sneeze or cough. He just violently snorted. After thinking through the qualifications of his actions, Mikhail finally realized he was drunk.

Before he could complete his thought, the first step past the restroom's divider soaked his pants with the vilest of splashes. One of the toilets had obviously overflowed and certainly that was why no one was waiting in line. But Mikhail had already come too far. Apparently, no one else needed the bathroom that bad.

"What the fuck happened in here?"

"Judging by all the blood on your face," Mr. Sallow said, looking over his shoulder, "nothing worse than we've already been through."

"Seriously, how are you standing in this?"

"You're standing in it too, but you at least have the option to leave."

Mikhail could feel the flood seep past his shoes, past his socks. The liquid's warmth was disturbing. He'd rather it had been cold; it wouldn't have been such a byproduct of bodily function that way. And worse than the sewage soaking into his skin was the smell. Hell itself had taken a shit from its mouth and shoved a handful of it up Mikhail's nose. He trudged on anyway, the sickening dampness having already done the majority of its damage. The whole night had. It was all floating with the same indiscriminate unmentionables that bobbed atop the ankle-deep water. Fighting back all gag necessities for those of urination, he stood one urinal away from Mr. Sallow and unbuckled his fly.

"If I was a betting man, I'd say you took a step forward and got knocked back a few for it," Mr. Sallow said. Aiming his piss, he smiled to himself. "And now you're all fire and brimstone about it, I bet."

"You'll lose all your government cheese with wagers like that, Mr. Sallow. I was all fire and brimstone for just a few seconds—then my movement became lateral. Here, take your drink."

"Aw shucks, you finally remembered your friends. Maybe this night won't turn out so bad for you after all."

"Let's see....my ex slapped me and then threw a drink in my face right in front of a new girl I was chatting up, I've been punched twice—one of which you saw—then I might've caught LA's first STD in generations, I was attacked by squids, and saw my girl go home with my mortal enemy. How could my night be any better?"

"Hell, you had to get laid to catch a bug," Mr. Sallow said. "Ever try and stick your dick in a lady while pissing? It doesn't work."

"..."

"Of course not. You're reminding me of a story right now...let me get my head wrapped around it. Okay, yes sir...you ever hear the fable about John Kaltenbrunner?"

Mikhail shook his head.

"Of course not, it's from well before your time and an era or two before The Internet. Regardless, Kaltenbrunner was dealt the worst hand a person could get. He was born ugly and socially retarded, pock-marked with unkemptable hair. His father was murdered before he was born. Before he could hit puberty, his mother came down with Cushing's disease and was then duped by the Methodist church to give away their entire estate. He turned all that into a felony-class shoot-out. Shotgun shells in cop-car windows...the whole nine."

Mikhail shook his head again and then gave his dick a good shake. Pushing down on his stomach, he tried to make sure that every last drop of urine had left his bladder. There was still a little bit of CGI caked on him...but he had no idea what Mr. Sallow was talking about.

"After he did his time, he came back to his city—this fable needs you to believe that there were once other cities besides LA—and began his plans to enact revenge. He started as a garbage-man, a kind of guy who'd pick up people's trash, they didn't have junk-shoots like we do. And then he started a mutiny and refused to pick up the garbage, just to spite the people of the town that had wronged him. The filth piled up, not unlike my humble abode tonight, and the people in John Kaltenbrunner's world didn't like it."

"What happened to him?" Mikhail asked. "And what's this got to do with me?"

"He died. Killed in the riot that ensued after he refused to pick up other people's trash. As for you? That's for you to decide...but right now, you seem to know a thing or two about a dumpster."

"It's not just my shirt that's bloodied and torn. I feel completely empty inside. I try to quiet the shouts of FAIL with the whispers of WIN, but I'm failing at that...so yeah, I know, I know a dumpster when I see it. But that story still ain't helping me out. No disrespect, Mr. Sallow."

Mikhail had to stop the bleeding. The first stall he opened was the one that had overflown. Brown clumps of fecal matter and giant yellow wads of toilet paper were in the basin and floating on the floor, acting as guard dogs to keep him from anything to wipe his wounds with. The second stall wasn't much prettier and the roll was empty. He thought about HD's plush carpet, how it cushioned his stomach as CGI laid naked on his back. He should've fallen asleep there, it was better there. This wasn't there, but in the third stall he found a roll of toilet paper that didn't look like it had been pissed on. In fact, it was dry, and he rolled as much of it as he could around his hand.

"Your night's seen the same explosion that mine has, young man," Mr. Sallow shouted, as Mikhail sloshed to the sink. "This whole flood came about when some Party Kid got too drunk and said something he shouldn't have. He was held upside down in that first stall, the toilet already backed up and not flushed, and he saw the bottom of it. He flushed it just so he could breathe, but the force took the hair right from his head. He didn't expect that, but it did. It bottomed out and then found a new bottom. Maybe he deserved it, maybe he didn't, and I'm stuck here so I don't know, but his lost chunks of scalp clogged the john, made it overflow and got my shoes all fucking wet."

"You know what, Mr. Sallow? I don't think I've ever heard you cuss before." Mikhail removed his tattered shirt and twisted in the mirror, trying to count the scratches from the squid's beak and tentacles. He had to stop once he got past 20. His back was covered in dried blood and still dripping wet in three or four places. He tried to decipher a pattern or a message that was left in its blotting. There was nothing. Nothing but the chaos of cuts embedded with chunks of cheap toilet paper left in the wake of each wipe. "You've always been so proper, the cussing doesn't sound like you. So, tell me this, are you mad at the kid or the kids who flushed his head?"

"It's worthless to be mad at anyone. They'll never get why, even if they see a problem in the first place. Kaltenbrunner was mad at the world and it only got him dead. I'm just mad at myself."

"What could you have done? All due respect, you're stuck where you are, right?"

"And that's what I'm mad at—I'm mad at what I've become, Mikhail. Somewhere along the line, I probably had a choice that I ignored. I made the wrong one and it's kept me here, in two inches of regurgitated sewer water, unable to leave unless I want to piss all over myself."

Mikhail nodded at Mr. Sallow, unaware of what to do with those words. There was nothing he could say to his fountain of a friend to get him out of the sewage, but he wanted to keep him company. He'd have to leave eventually, but it became incredibly important to Mikhail that Mr. Sallow understood he wasn't forgotten.

"Is it crazy that I consider you one of my closest friends?"

"I'm not sure I follow you," Mr. Sallow said. "Are you for real?"

"It's just that I only see you a few minutes here and there, just a few nights a week, if that...it's been months since we've talked, but I trust you more than most. We've never eaten a meal together. We spend our friendship pissing away time, but it's a sedimentary mosaic of moments. And I cherish that. I trust what you say. You got my back and I want you know that I got yours."

"I didn't stop that elf-shoed fool from knocking you around, even if I probably could've. You don't want to be my friend. I don't know how to do it."

"Oh stop it," Mikhail said. He was hovering a few feet behind Mr. Sallow, ankle-deep in refuse, refusing to leave a friend stranded. "You said I deserved that elf-shoed punch and you were probably right."

"I was...and I'm right now. Mikhail, are you trying to move forward tonight? Or are you done?"

"My night isn't done, even if I'm so drunk it should be."

"Here...wait...give me a quick second," Mr. Sallow said, snapping open the advertisement in front of him like it was his own personal medicine cabinet. He stuck his arms and then his head deep inside the cubby, careful not to lose his target below. Despite his messy situation, Mr. Sallow was a pro at refraining from contributing to the urine that surrounded him. His voice echoed from the depths behind the wall... "What is it that you want from tonight?"

Mikhail's feet were heavy with the despicable absorption of destructive water and biological toxins contained within. He could feel the disease creep up his shins. His shirt, a bloody mess of white and red, hung over his tattered shoulder. The night's battles—those he had both won and lost—were finally taking a toll on him. His head started to ache, throbbing with every weakened beat of his heart. But it all felt better than his inability to answer Mr. Sallow's question.

"It's okay, Mikhail, my man in mayhem, I need another minute to get at what I'm getting to, so take the time to figure it out. I've been pissing since before your grandparents were born and I don't think I could answer that....oh, hold on, almost got it." He kept digging deeper, shuffling unseen items from one place to another. This was the only storage space Mr. Sallow had, and Mikhail wondered if it was the only privacy the man owned. "Yes, yes, here they are. It's fair to say that we're approximately the same build, no?"

Mikhail nodded. And even if Mr. Sallow couldn't see him, he still seemed to understand.

"Of course we are, of course. It's not the latest fashions, but it's better than what you got. As old as I am, even if I'm a fixture here and not in HD's bathroom, I know enough that what you're wearing isn't the latest trend. Blood always scares away the girls...ain't it funny when they're the ones that bleed? Here, take these."

Mr. Sallow shut the cubby door and held out a pair of shoes that Mikhail immediately recognized as the ones his bladder-deficient friend was wearing. Hand-crafted leather, they squared off at the toe. After the transaction, one which left Mikhail speechless, Mr. Sallow brought out a carefully folded stack of clothes, carrying them like a waiter would carry multiple dishes. Black blazer, black pants, black shirt, black socks. It was the same outfit Mr. Sallow had always worn.

"I can't take this. I don't even know what I want, never mind how to step towards it. No, this is too much, Mr. Sallow, too much for my side-stepping," Mikhail said, completely aghast. "Your shoes are soaking wet, too. Take these back, put them on and get dry..."

"My shoes and socks and pants will stay wet till the cleaning crew comes through in three hours. They'll have to drain all this mess and that'll take some time. No use in these clothes sitting here unused. I have others...and besides, I want you to have them."

Resisting the urge to ask how exactly Mr. Sallow changed clothes without pissing himself, Mikhail thankfully took the pile presented to him. Terrified that a single article of such an offering would drown in the sludge below, Mikhail held on tight to his new outfit. He would've gripped it tight against his chest, were his chest not stained with blood.

"I can't thank you enough. I was ready to wander back out there in this bloody, cess-pool-soaked mess. Why though?"

"There's nothing I can do with them, not now. Thank me by making good use of those threads. I'm stuck here and you aren't, but it doesn't mean that my clothes have to be. Get out of here and let me live vicariously a little bit. I've seen enough... inventors age. They grow old and mistakenly chase the wrong idea and never invent anything ever again. Maybe it's new, maybe it'd old, but Mikhail, I know there's a new idea out there for you to chase. And maybe this time, it'll be a step in the right direction."

Mikhail tried to absorb every word the old man was saying, but was already busy washing the blood from his face. It was more respectful to fulfill Mr. Sallow's visions than to waste time pondering his sentiments. He could've kissed Mr. Sallow, if the man wasn't pissing and they both weren't standing in six inches of urine. Mikhail just did his best to keep the clothes dry while he washed the blood off his face and neck. He'd have to change in the #720's main terminal to keep his present pristine.

"I know what I want tonight...you still give a fuck?"

"Yezzir," Mr. Sallow said.

"I want all the remnants from all these explosions to land safely around me. I'm sick of getting hit in the face. Even more than that, I want to know what I want. And I want all future explosions to stay away from you. You don't need that shit."

"That shit is the only thing that keeps my piss from being so bad," Mr. Sallow said, taking a sip of his white Russian for the first time. "Launder those before bringing them back, okay? Clothes make the man, even if the man can only take a leak. Kaltenbrunner never had friends...maybe it was the death of him or maybe it's why I even remember his story."

Chapter Thirty
Back Like Cooked Crack

Mikhail was wasted and Katya was reacting to it better than she normally would. They were alone in her apartment and she was genuinely patient with his slurring shenanigans, even finding them somewhat charming. She glided through her efficiency unit, picking up unfinished Cups O'Noodles, making a big deal about stacking and then balancing them in one hand. Katya spun and spun, while Mikhail tried hard to hold onto her fleeting moments of grace. Despite being well into their second go-around, he still wasn't convinced about their chances at a life partnership. Gravity pulled the lace at the bottom of her green nightie, away from her freckled thighs. It revealed a thonged cusp of ass that was nearly too much to grasp. As they usually did, his biological desires quickly overtook his emotional reservations.

Standing at the hot plate, Mikhail put a spork-full of tubbed margarine into the wok and sat down. He had to work through his lunch in order to get where he was in time for dinner. And he was exhausted for it. Thankful to sit again—especially after the two bottles of wine they had shared, but he had mostly drank—he pushed all the doubts about their relationship from his mind. Katya's cozy apartment was on the Lil' Rectangle's affordable strip, nestled between working families and steadfastedly single professionals. Of the latter she saw herself, working towards the former.

"Help me."

Mikhail stood back up. After she drained the leftover broth from the Styrofoam soup cups into the sink, he poured the noodles into the bubbling butter substitute with assembly line proficiency. She started chopping iceberg lettuce with a pair of scissors and when his job was done, he sat down again.

"How did all this start?"

"Well, I made you like me after months of persistence," she said. Katya shook her ass a little bit, her cheeks persistently peaking out beneath her negligee. It was playful, but it was wearing him out. "I finally won you over, flirtation by flirtation, systematically making you fall in love with me."

"Nah, I'm not talking about us—and that's not at all how it happened—but, I mean, this system of buses. And all the great fuckin' abyss that keeps cats scared of searching out some fresh air...what did I ever do to The Internet?"

"I'm not going to say that Sandy Bullock opened Pandora's Box when she made The Net, but someone did. I don't know...infrastructure was built and we've always lived here. I'm not going to question existence with you tonight, not while I'm making you dinner, not tonight. It just doesn't make sense."

"Somewhere, sometime, more than a minute ago, somebody screwed up. This guy, and I'm pretty sure it was a dude, was cleaning his room and his thoughts drifted too far into the realm of alternate reality and the whole shit blew up."

"He opened the box," she said, smirking.

"There was no box, it just happened. He wasn't trying to open anything, but it opened up all the same. He tapped into something."

Katya scraped the lettuce from the cutting board into the wok and gave the whole mess a whirl. She tapped a saltshaker, repeatedly, over it all. Then she mumbled something in Russian that Mikhail didn't understand.

"But I'd really like to blame a monster."

"A colossal squid, I'm sure," Katya said, continuing to flip the mound of noodles and lettuce with the scissors.

"They were too smart to allow the end of oceans. No one knew they were there, but no, despite their three hearts and freakishly large nerves, no, it wasn't a squid. It couldn't be. It was a social outcast. Someone who wasn't enough of an outcast to be noticed, but just enough to know it himself. He stayed in his room and typed lines and lines of binary code. He typed and typed. And typed. And typed. No one loved him and he wanted revenge and he created a portal that got out of hand. He only wanted to suck away particular troubles, but shit got out of hand. That seems like a dude-only problem."

"He opened a box."

"No, he deliberately opened a portal. He just didn't understand its power. He hacked into a government fail safe and then nothing was safe, it all failed. And he watched his enemies get sucked through and then he watched the select few people he actually cared about get sucked through, and maybe there wasn't even anyone standing in that line. So he stood in front of his portal and then the whole thing imploded, except for the people who knew how to write the software..."

"...and build the bus system that beat the box," Katya said, sitting down. She looked at him like he was a maniac.

Mikhail stood back up and started stacking the now-empty Cups O'Noodles, reaching his hand into each container that dared house a straggling strand of cold carbohydrates. He put the few noodles he found in a pouch at the side of his jaw, like a squirrel storing acorns for a supposed winter. He wanted to see how long it'd last until everything turned to mush. Except *for the two cartons that they'd later use for bowls, he put the remaining stack of Styrofoam into a plastic bag that hung on the handle of a cabinet door.*

"There are two sides. Either someone opened a box full of maliciousness and malcontent or accidentally did it in the daily walk of his life. It was a trip into malice or an absolute accident. I don't know which is better."

"Are you rooting for evil, Mister?"

"Does it even matter?"

Mikhail burned his fingers reaching into the wok. He blew furiously on the grip of noodles and wilted lettuce before barely chewing and quickly swallowing the recipe. He then sucked on his burning fingertips, feeling blisters already arise. Bringing them out of his mouth, he wiped them dry on Katya's inner-thighs. She was still seated and Mikhail dropped to his knees in order to kiss the wet spots on her legs. For every drop of salted cooking inhaled, he left three in passionate saliva. She softly moaned and he kissed harder, leaving his lips on her pale hamstrings before moving forever upwards.

She made him stand up and then pushed him back in his chair. It was the same chair he sat in while breaking up with her twice—once in the past, once in the future. They held so many serious conversations around that wicker-edged table. She untied his shoes and took off his jeans. It was then that he received his one-time gift of kitchen table head before moving to Katya's bed. They started to make love, but finished by fucking. Mikhail held back his true desires and she probably refrained from asking for what she really wanted. Regardless, it was a short ordeal that climaxed with them eating out of a single Cup O'Noodles container and sharing a spork.

"I love you," she said.

Naked under the sheets, Mikhail ate the room-temperature concoction and smiled. He wanted to light a cigarette but had already told her he had quit. He hadn't and there would've been something wonderful about ashing into the remnants of their dinner while lying on his back. Her body was sweating upon his and he started to worry that their skin would fuse together. It made him want to move, but he wasn't sure how to do it without pissing her off. Thankfully, she jumped out of bed before slowly somersaulting twice on her thick carpet and then standing at attention in order to hit the spacebar and jump-start iTunes. The Zombies' "Care of Cell 44" played. She hopped off the rug and back onto Mikhail. They were only separated by a sheet, but it allowed his skin to breathe.

"What if the colossal squids overtook the electromagnetic spectrum and then dialed up into space? They migrated out of the water to find freedom somewhere besides Los Angeles," she said, smiling a smile bigger than he'd ever seen.

"Maybe they started a chat room susceptible to higher bit rates than the network could handle. Perhaps they played puppets with the streaks of Wi-Fi radiation. Something leaked and it messed everything else up."

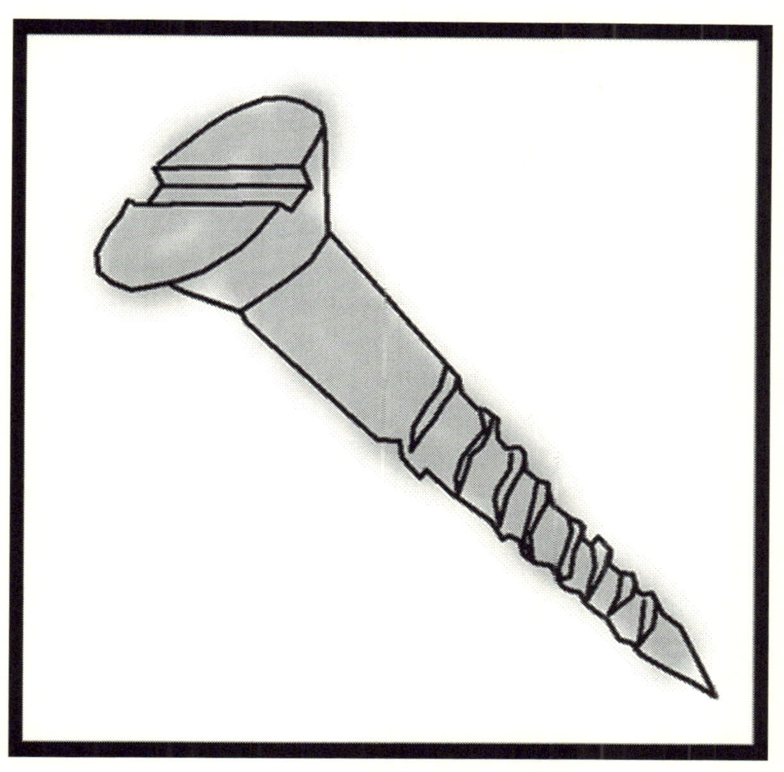

Visit **http://PleaseUseRearExit.net/home/Mibbs**
for a deeper look into the psyche of Hawthorne Mibbs

Chapter Thirty-One
The Alley Cat Plays Him Off

Mikhail leaned up against the exterior wall of Mr. Sallow's hallow and changed right in the middle of the #720's hustle and bustle. It was such a relief to kick off his dripping Converse then peel the once-white, since-blackened socks from his ankles. His jeans had shrunk with the moisture and it was a bitch to get them off his calves, but oh-happy-days once his legs were freely breathing. He used whatever dryness was left in the denim to scrub the shit off his shins and feet. The putrid concoction was caked in the hairs on top of his feet, both left and right.

Comers and goers, mostly drunkards moving from one bar or club to the next, kept walking by and Mikhail kept not caring. He stood in boxer briefs between a neatly folded pile of clean clothes and a disgustingly disregarded disposal of decomposing cloth.

He leaned to the left and put on the pair of clean slacks. Daintily bringing the black shirt around his wounded back, Mikhail then found a way to button the cuffs and subsequently, the shirt's center. The real revelation, however, was the socks. He had never worn black socks before, and these were cushioned with a knit thickness. It immediately dried his barking dogs and warmed his wounded soul. He wiggled his toes, enjoying the simplicity of their soft cocooning. It was almost a shame to put on shoes, but once he did, Mikhail felt like he was walking barefoot on Internet-issued grass before he even took a step. Mr. Sallow's blazer was donned, but the feelings it created didn't compare to heaven on foot.

Mikhail's attention was stolen by a natural redhead sauntering east. He'd never seen one before and thought they were all but extinct. Her blue dress—raining down in folds of ruffled elegance—clashed with the auburn rouge cascading from her head. Mikhail gathered up his tattered clothes and followed her. She walked unaccompanied and he watched from afar, keeping in-step without stepping up to her plate. Finding a garbage can, he emptied his load into a rubbermaid container full of plastic cups and various refuse. His clothes seemed to sit comfortably, as if they were home with friends and resting tired feet on a worn ottoman. When he looked up, after only a few seconds, the redhead was gone. He didn't even have time to name her Jen or Jenny or Jeni4.

Once she was gone, once his old clothes were disposed of—his Dipset scully and boxer briefs the sole remaining items from an outfit of a past life—Mikhail had no idea what to do. The only option that made any noise at all was to smoke a cigarette. It made sense to move forward, just by doing something, anything, even as logic pushed him back to bed. He knew why he still paced the #720—a mission had been created for him—but Mikhail wanted to be home. The alcohol in his blood pushed him towards a redhead he could no longer see in hopes that she might have a freaky friend. She vanished though, leaving a stone-cold path to The Smoke in her diminishing wake. Her direction was the Camel Light that'd break Mikhail's back. He told himself he needed a cigarette and then believed it.

He walked on the inside of whatever trail he could blaze, hugging any wall that'd hug him back. In the bars that had closed up shop for the night, Mikhail tried to catch a glimpse of himself in the mirrors of shadowed glass, but was always walking too fast. Sure, he saw his reflection, several times over, but it was never enough to gauge the image he truly projected. Mr. Sallow's suit felt right, but he hadn't yet seen its fit. Obviously better than what he'd just thrown away, he would have to find comfort in the fleeting impressions of fleeing glass. That most of the windows reflected visions of warped fun-house mirrors was without importance. He let out a fart because he knew no one was around to hear it.

Shirley, the lounge's door woman, checked his stamp and asked after Chevy. Mikhail didn't know and mumbled something about getting separated after the concert. Chevy's presence would have meant that Mikhail's concentration would be free to wonder who to approach, what to do, where to go, when to continue, why to stay and, sometimes, how to find new friends. But Mikhail knew by then that he alone was supposed to make those decisions until he gave up and went home. A choice that he wasn't far off from making.

The double-doors into The Smoke were crossed without comedy this time. A second-hand toxic event had piled up since Mikhail's last visit, even as the vents tried loudly and vigilantly, but ultimately failingly, to remove the billowing smoke inside. The Smoke was more crowded, but nothing that Mikhail hadn't dealt with all night. He silently barreled through the silly conversations and found the exact spot he had once shared with Chevy and Jayson.

Mikhail lit up—in a suit that couldn't be tailored any better—and wondered what he could invent and whether he could do it without aging. He had finally ended it with Katya. Saffron had made her choice. CGI wearily made him itch. Bridget dangled somewhere and Sara(h) moved through The Internet with or without an H, but definitely without him. The redhead had disappeared. Just like his friends. He hoped that his life would figure out its own path, not that a hope for such simplicities made the questions stop.

What the fuck am I even doing here? Mikhail thought, wondering if the squid was still listening, *I should be home right now. He inhaled and exhaled and leaned and looked around and inhaled and exhaled again. I should be in bed. This is completely disgusting. I'm in no shape to be charming. I should be in bed... trifling springs in my ghetto mattress and all. It'd be better than this. Why am I still here smoking...alone? How much money do I have left? I need another drink...I need to go to bed...*

But the cigarette was good. It filled him with something tangible at a time when an undisclosed nothingness left him only with a void. The only girls near Mikhail were pitifully entranced by guys with muscles. Everywhere he looked, there was nothing but proof of steroids. Masses of testosterone were talking about push-ups in the #7's booths, folding sweaters at their job on the #2, and the boring girls that did back-flips in bed but Mikhail would never meet. He didn't know the talkers or their sweaters or shawties or jokes...and he'd never worked out a day in his life.

New digs, I should have a new lease on life...but I'm too drunk to even deal. I should hold onto this railing so I don't fall, maybe just walk my way home...will Mr. Sallow be pissed if I fall asleep in his suit? Tupac won't really kill me if I don't get out there and get that threesome, especially if I hang the blazer up in my closet before I go to bed. What else could I really want... other than sleep? Everything else is nothing but a wolf ticket... or a squid beat down...

"I know what you want," said a cat. She wasn't in a hat, but her feline features and feminine voice gave her away as a she. "And it'll only cost you a cigarette."

Instinctively knowing that he only had one left in his pack, Mikhail took out the crushed box with a single Camel, and shook the lone smoke from corner to corner, corner to corner. He looked up from the one-party mosh pit of potential cancer and saw that the talking figure in front of him was indeed a cat. Walking on her hind legs and with three heavily-hairsprayed, dyed-red twists for bangs, her appearance didn't bother him. Something about it was, in fact, calming.

"It's cool," the cat said, non-chalantly refusing Mikhail's half-hearted offer. "Watch me totally blow these d-bags' minds."

She tapped a young fellow in a backwards white hat and then faked like she was going to punch him in the gut with her paw.

"Your name is Jacob and Katy was the first girl you ever kissed, it was the Friday after your Facebook Prom. The next night you got a hand-job from her. And by Sunday afternoon you caught your first blow job...but it'd be three months before you actually got laid. Your friend here once made out with a tranny and then pretended like it was an accident. Both of you smoke menthol cigarettes and you're each gonna give me one."

"..."

"..."

The cat looked at Jacob's friend and tugged on his crimson USC shirt, "Don't fret Trojan, I won't tell anyone."

"..."

"..."

She turned back to Mikhail, spreading two cigarettes between the claws of her paws like a #winning poker hand. "You have to give me at least a quarter if I'm going to tell you what you want. It's only protocol."

The two college boys were too stunned to protest and too scared to stick around, even once her attentions had moved back to Mikhail. The three foot feline had known everything about them and they had known only enough to hand over a few smokes in order to get away. Mikhail decided to hang around for further examination.

If you're so fuckin' psychic, Mikhail thought, partly amazed, wholly stunned, *why didn't you know that I only had one cigarette? Seems like the parlor tricks of an alley cat...And this is why I should already be asleep.*

"Alley cat? Are you fuckin' serious? Hello McFly! I can still hear you..."

Chapter Thirty-Two
The Master & Margarita

"Just because you can hear what I'm thinking doesn't mean you know what I want," Mikhail said. "I don't even know what I want, I'm just trying to survive a Friday night."

"If survival was truly the case than I'd be talking to you from the foot of your bed or maybe even one of the hospital routes. And yet, you're thinking about sleep when the night ain't over," the cat said. Her eyes were a divisive green and he couldn't tell where she was looking or even if her eyes were actually crossed. "Strike that. I wouldn't be in your bedroom. I refuse to step foot on Compton's Circle. The Brown BTWN makes me nauseous. The smell of that place is worse than a litter box."

This cat is so full of..."I don't know a damn thing about Compton's Circle either, I've only been there once and it was to visit a sick friend," Mikhail said. The cat was wearing a vest and it was starting to creep him out.

"You don't like my vest? Whatever, this shit is snazzy and the fit is right. I don't trust your opinion anyway, you can't even admit where you live. You think I have sympathy for you? I know everything, Mikhail. Let's just get past that and move on."

"Well then, I'm sure you're sick of being called *the cat* inside my head...what's your name? You know mine."

The cat stood a hair above three feet tall. She walked on hind legs without a hunch in her back and carried herself like a woman sexually confident about XXL stretch pants. There was no paunch to the cat, she just gave that air, especially while exhaling a menthol cigarette without purring.

"Roxanne Shanté. It'd be best if you called me by my full name," Roxanne Shanté said. She tugged on her vest and then flicked her cigarette. "Mr. Sallow agrees with me, you know, that you should keep going. It matters to people if you do or don't. Pastor Shakur is betting 3:1 odds that you won't meet his challenge...as we speak. Jay-Z is doing the Jay Face right this minute because he likes the odds so much."

"What's it matter?"

"Saffron was counting on you and you gave up like some kind of pussy. Now, you're trying to pull the same shit again... thinking about how you just need to go home and forget all these troubles. Is it that much easier to avoid conflict than to just pull your boot straps up and face what's in front of you?"

"What're you trying to say, Puss 'N Boots? I fought off a goddamn squid tonight! What else can I do to stay standing?" Mikhail asked, obviously embittered. "You want me to walk forward too? It's been a full night of that advice and I'm getting ready to be as lazy as I can. Let me lay in my bed and enjoy the battles I don't have to fight. There are battles on my screen every night...I can pick Avon Barksdale's or Hunter Thompson's or Murakami's, it doesn't matter. It's easier to watch than to do.

"I'm starting to think that not giving a shit is actually helping me out here. The ordeals I've been through tonight— well, you know—I didn't make any of them happen but I survived nonetheless. And I don't even want to put that much effort into it anymore. Who has the energy to chase down girls and be charming when you're busy getting drinks or running from club to club and always standing in line, the entire time?! I certainly don't, but I'm supposed to find it twice over while finding the right combination of mythical hotties who can play nice and share me. Pastor Shakur has to be out of his damn mind about this. Is there even enough of me to be shared?"

"There is hardly enough for me to care whether or not there is, but it's still more than my interest in most of the bores on this bus."

Mikhail scanned The Smoke for anyone he knew, but there was no easy way out from such a conversation. Roxanne Shanté said nothing and just stared at him. She didn't even bob her head to TopBananas's "Waiting For My Time To Come," which had just come over the speakers. It was the second time that Mikhail had heard the song that night. Roxanne Shanté's cat ears must've picked it up, but like so much, it didn't matter.

"Well, if you don't care about their stories then what's your deal, Ms. Shanté?"

"Mine is a breeze compared to yours, Mikhail. I know where people's minds are at, so I get to pick the conversations that I want to avoid. And thus, my night was completely uneventful. But yours was better than that with far more questions. For example, why did you fight the squid and not Robert Horry?" Then she paused and coyly added, "Do you get that yet?"

"Get what?" Such a weird remark from such a suspicious character. He was exasperated with the sudden accumulation of random expectations, and drunkenly decided to take it out on Roxanne Shanté. "Am I crazy? What's Saffron want with me? Why didn't Tupac's goons just beat the shit out of me and forget about it before smashing the next broad? This was supposed to be a night and that's it...you can read my mind, why so many questions? I don't know why I fought the squid and not Robert Horry, do you?"

"How drunk do you feel right now?"

"Enough."

"Enough then...just focus on what's next. Forget about Robert Horry, I'm already bored by it and you'll surely see Saffron again if you choose to. What are your options for what's next? I'm ready to click to someone else's page if you don't grab my attention again."

"I'm sick of replaying my options," Mikhail said, wearing all the truth in his shoulders that such sentiment could bear. "Why don't you tell me?"

"Somewhere you already know, otherwise I wouldn't. And because of that nugget I just revealed, I'll save you the details. The night has been long and now my energy is spent."

"You already spent nine whole lives?"

"Other than my energy, your joke is the only thing spent," Roxanne Shanté said. She straightened her whiskers like an ancient villain might frisk his mustache. "Say you're a quarterback and you've already looked past the play's top two options. There's a blitz and things are getting hairy. You have three-quarters-of-a-second before getting sacked and three choices to ponder until that crushing reality: loft it out of bounds, drop to the ground like Chris Everett, or hope to squeeze in the perfect throw to your running back in the slot. The first option is probably text book and as long as you get it far enough out of bounds, you'll be alright. Jim Rome is a smarmy bastard in that second clip, so you don't wanna be like either of those d-bags. You have to wear your Manning-face if you wanna be the hero and go for the final option. I'm talking about the serious Manning-face and not the sad Manning-face. There ain't much room for error on the play and you have to wear your game mask so tight it becomes your own skin. Someone gets a fingertip on that ball over the middle and you could be looking at an easy pick-six, but there's a lot of green around your running back. What do you do there, huh Mikhail?"

"I think I just proved myself in the Brown BTWN with that major task...you know, staying alive and keeping Saffy and Jayson out of The Internet too."

"You're just the offensive lineman if my metaphor rattles around your brain on that old business, we're way past that, Mikhail. Horry was the MVP and pretty girls don't date the left tackle. The Calamari Bowl is over now...you've already changed uniforms."

Mikhail was a little hurt with the overall accuracy of her analogy. He tried to think of a rebuttal but his mind kept going blank. And then he started worrying that Roxanne Shanté would see his thoughts as the static gray screen they were. The channel suddenly changed back to life... "Why are you helping me?"

"There seems to be so much at stake with tonight's outcome, and I like to use my talents in entertaining situations. I've seen every video on YouTube and there's only so much kitty porn or cheezburger a cat can haz stomach. Take my uncle for instance, Behemoth—no, literally take him, LOL—he ran between the legs of Pontius Pilate and Jesus Christ during their whole ordeal. He once watched this famous poet get decapitated by a train, frightened into suicide by my uncle's citizen colleague. Later that week, Behemoth emceed a circus-style art-installation which ended with rich housewives horrified in the streets, confused in their underwear. This was back when there actually was an outside, so you better believe it was cold. He was doing things that actually mattered, not just playing with string in an adorable matter."

"That's quite a life."

"That isn't even the whole shebang. He's the one who got cats to be The Internet's official animal. It's all gotten so twisted since his retirement, so many cats doing the same tricks. Alas, that's another story for another day."

Like a slow-motion coin-flip, an unlit cigarette flicked from her paw to behind Mikhail's ear on a graceful arc of somersaults. There was nothing else hiding under Roxanne Shanté's vest-length sleeves until a cell phone started humming an Aloe Blacc acapella.

"Right now, think about the time it takes to make plans. Go ask more advice, or don't. Maybe you should look up or maybe down, find J Hova or the first bus home...because one will be there before there's enough time to drunkenly find your lighter for that come-on-bus cigarette that you think speeds up life. That bus will always come. A lot of people are rooting for you, Mikhail, but all the pull in the interwebs won't make up for pussy-footing around."

Roxanne Shanté covered one of her calico ears and finally answered the phone call that hadn't quit ring-toning since its first hum. It too appeared out of nowhere and then she disappeared into thin air, answering the call of a bus that finally came.

"Bottom line, Mikhail, score that touchdown," Roxanne Shanté said, with only her voice as evidence of an existence. Mikhail wondered if CGI was visible to her in this invisible state. "And while you're moving down the field, steal all of the emperor's clothes. Come to think of it, it might be a positive that you still think survival and a notch on your bedpost are the only things in play right now, but even more likely, some further analysis of the game tape could be the extra help you need. If only you had time for that tonight. You might not get that you do or what the haute couture fashions of the wealthy have to do with it all, but one day you will. Just go after the goal line tonight."

And with a loud bang, Roxanne Shanté's voice disappeared just as her body had seconds prior. The exit was both impressive and startling, even for a clever cat like her. It jostled Mikhail out of a trance. He made sure his last cigarette of the evening was firmly tucked behind his ear before walking off towards Something. He'd have to confront Tupac Shakur sooner or later and if anyone would know where the B-I-T-C-H's were at, it'd be the Pastor.

Visit **http://PleaseUseRearExit.net/home/JAYSON**
for a good old-fashioned, hard-working American
of a bonus chapter

Chapter Thirty-Three
Hide Your Kids, Hide Your Wife

"What the media doesn't say about the Tupac Shakur Association of Being Dastardly Dapper is that we urge mature men to hunt for a compatible woman, someone he wants to share his years with. We may recommend that she likes giving head, but we don't mandate it. A man and his woman should have their boo-berry pie and eat it too. We should all be so lucky to find that. The brothers that come in here and know that they want permanent female companionship, we give them guidance on how to be real husbands and fathers that last the test of time. That's what it's called, 'Please Your Wife and Still Love Your Life 101,' you know what I'm saying? We're only thinking about adding a second level course, but each new idea means a new URL. You smell me?"

"M-V-P!"

"M-V-P!"

"M-V-P!"

Pastor Tupac Amaru Shakur was holding court. His back surrounded by a meticulous stack of sandbags and three-foot thick brick, he sat smiling in a corner, absolutely mesmerizing four of the TSABDD's top members. Jay-Z was already gone, having decided with 'Pac that the outcome of their wager was to be Tweeted, but Armstrong, Wood, Woody and Brother Bret Easton Ellis were all there. The Pastor's suit jacket donned the back of his chair and his dress shirt's sleeves were rolled up. His new custom suit was 97 percent Merino wool and 3 percent cashmere. He had pleated pants with a 1 1/2-inch cuff and the whole suit would cost about $1,500 off the rack. The knot in his tie was casual and a hand-woven earthy piece of fabric was the order of the day. The top two slots of his statesmanlike button-up were without restriction, but still hid Shakur's motive close at heart.

"We teach men how to be men when they're ready to be men. How to buy flowers just to let her know your trust in her is out of love. Not out of convenience or a Hallmark registered holiday, but because you really want to do the small things that make her smile. Whether it's a 50¢ bag of peach rings on a Tuesday or 50 minutes of yoga on a Thursday, that shit'll get a dick happy and make damn sure that a pussy never cheats. But only if it's genuine and a brother is really ready. The TSABDD turns dogs into men. Reprimanding us because we have to turn boys into dogs first, it makes me think that the media can't even bother to meet us at a half-way point."

"I don't even need a half-way point with the bitches out there, I just ask 'em if I can stick the tip in," Armstrong said. He was the only man to hold a die in the table's game of LCR and the first to interrupt the Pastor in 13 minutes. Shakur was the only other person with a chip. "They ask for more the minute they get the gist...and then I deliver my jizz on their tits."

"This is the problem with The Man right now. He's telling me that I should have Babyface over here on the campaign trail. Seriously," 'Pac turned to Armstrong, "can you look me in the eye and really turn 13 minutes of my campaign's philosophy into a dick joke? Not even one that encompasses my whole argument in some sort of political cartoon, but just the last five seconds of the whole damn speech? Motherfucker...O'Reilly doesn't wear glasses. Where's Dame and Cam when I need them? Talking heads will rip this dude to shreds..."

Armstrong slowly jangled the cube. It was nearly stale in his hands mainly because he didn't know how to respond.

The stray strands of green felt on the table were charged with the electro-radiation of modern Wi-Fi and it almost caused Armstrong to roll. Either the Wi-Fi or the tension in the room. All six men at the table were focused on the soft clink the cube made against his wedding ring. Armstrong had $10,000 on this hand and needed the die rocking in his fingers to come up a dot. L, C or R would make him miss a mortgage payment on his Westside condo. The electrical charge on the table left him void of any positive energy. It made it tough to roll. He started mumbling, "Shit, the pussy I passed up back when I was pro ballin—"

"Shut the fuck up and roll!"

"I haven't had a chip in 25 minutes because of Blow Job's stories."

"We're trying to get back in the game, motherfucker... just do something, so this shit can start again already."

Armstrong rolled and it was an L. His lone chip went to Shakur and the game was over in an explosion of fist-pumps.

"This is what I'm talking about," Shakur said. Despite the immediate victory, there was a quiet anger in his tone, like the stillness inside a tornado. He wasn't thinking short term. "Why is this round-rimmed brother sitting at my table? I know that they think I need polished-looking brothers like him speaking for me, but having Blow Job in front of those flip-cams will lead to this campaign's death in November. Other than them Polos, what qualifies you, Armstong?"

"Three championship rings before my card and 132 bitches afterwards," Armstrong said. He didn't like the "Blow Job" nickname, even as he tried to convince himself that it was something positive. The game over, he took the shot that sat in front of him, the other matching glasses having already been overturned. After originally placing his glass on the table upside right, he haphazardly flipped it, making a hell of a racket in the process. The heavy shot glasses were sand-blasted with the TSABDD logo and didn't fall quietly—even on electrically-charged green felt. It was a scramble to make his look like theirs, but eventually, it was turned right-side upside down. "I've been playing LCR with you for over an hour. Sir, please, you know that I'm down for the cause."

"He's down for the cause? You hear that Ellis? FUKS News may think I need a more white-acting representative in the Spin Room—without ever saying something that could be misconstrued as so racist—but is this the best we got? He's young, wears a Polo and tries to say the right things, but holy shit, is this it? Find me someone who gets it. Brother Bret, get this goof out of here before I puke, and set up a meeting with him for the start of next week. We need to go over a few things, but not now." Shakur was dismissive with his request, moving onto the next thought before Armstrong could be escorted out of the room.

"They are going to bring the shit to us this fall... or whatever their calendar tells us is September, October, November, whatever, whatever. Who's to know anymore? It all looks like another bus to me. Every lyric I ever wrote will stamp campaign ads for those government goons trying to brainwash the confused souls of Los Angeles. You better believe they'll try to spin 'Brenda Got a Baby' into some message of infanticide. 'I Get Around' will become proof that I'm trying to put STD's into the drinking water. It's going to come back around—all of it backwards, but they'll try. They're gonna think that outspending me will be enough; little do they know I was a multi-platinum rapper and Oscar-winning actor. I have money that I'm willing to spend and, more than that, the only thing out-earning my royalties is the power of the people. And maybe people are finally sick of looking up and seeing only metal.

"Their slander won't affect me, even as their standards for me aren't the same as the next man," Pastor Shakur continued. "One rapper can say, *'I'll kill you/Cut your heart out/I put this gun to your pregnant belly/And blah blah blah blah,*' and they all get love. All I say is, 'We don't need these B-I-T-C-H's to be running our life,' and I'm the one hating females. This is the type of warfare we need to prepare for, gentlemen. They are going to come at me hard—everything with Sister Pinkett-Shakur, the whole Janet Jackson AIDS-test thing—it's about to get fast and furious, and if brothers can't keep up then they need to keep out. I'm 38 years old, I don't need some wire-rimmed brother stuttering over the indiscretions I committed in my early 20's.

"The young crackers who introduced crack into the 'hood to ward off scary-dressing organizations of the peaceful black man, they're now the same decrepit and cantankerous rednecks who are nervous about rap finding its voice. Those career-government-types that were staking out Black Panther meetings way back when—sweating bullets and ready to pull triggers—are the same WASPs ordering around baby WASPs today. They're the ones making the decisions and they still fear the black man. They fear the assertive man. They don't want a single passenger on this damn bus thinking for himself unless he's in the top 1% of the pyramid. But I threaten what they hold dearest to their bitter shriveled hearts: white women and green cash. I get more than they think I deserve. I grew up on Compton's Circle. They know where my Moms has stayed at her whole life—including the prison line that housed me as a fetus.

"Think about the Internet heroes we have that help run this bus. Eli Porter, Latarian Milton and the Hide-Yo-Wife-Hide-Yo-Kids-They-Rapin'-Errybody guy. That's our contribution to the science that makes these buses move. That doesn't make an ounce of Internet-damned sen—"

"Excuse me, Pastor Shakur, with all due respect," the pillar said.

"What is it, Ivan? Go ahead and smile because, yes, I remember you—but turn that upside down if you're about to waste my time."

"Mikhail has been using your name again, sir," the pillar said, unable to hide a curious, almost flirtatious smirk. His nine-foot frame had shrunken considerably over the night and suddenly he had picked up the facial tick of a school girl. "He's well out of earshot, sir, but ahhhh, do you want me to bring him up or just break his ribs?"

"Praise The Internet, Ivan knows to keep that fire cracker at the bottom of the stairs. He don't need to hear the words coming out of my mouth, but he doesn't need the shit kicked out of him, either. Not yet anyway," Pastor Shakur said. He sounded like a disappointed den mother, especially compared to the spitfire he spewed at Armstrong. "There's an empty seat at the table, go grab him."

The TSABDD council sitting around the card table simultaneously raised their eyebrows at Pastor Shakur's summons. A paranoid man, it was highly unusual for a non-member to find a seat at his table. The pillar soon threw Mikhail onto the floor and Mikhail immediately knew that it was the same room as before. The furniture had been swapped around or replaced, but Mikhail could never forget the burn in his thighs after such a specific spiral of stairs. The walls hadn't changed, only the interior.

In a clean suit and having already survived this ordeal once—as well as an equally dangerous encounter with an invertebrate—it was a little easier to comfortably sit up without a directive to do so. Or maybe it was because he had slept with CGI since the last time he was up there. He knew that he had to keep that quiet for as long as possible, but just the knowledge of it made Mikhail feel like he belonged. It might have been an even more impressive score than the threesome required of him and Mikhail wondered if that nugget of fact would be enough. Mikhail had also surpassed a tipping point on a seesaw made of whiskey-emptied tumbler glasses. The tantamount moment however, was seeing Armstrong's babyface in full-on pout before Mikhail entered the staircase. Watching him run out of the door behind the bar, Mikhail was overcome with a warm feeling, especially as Armstrong might've been in tears.

"Wipe the snot from your eyes and sit down, take a load off," Pastor Shakur said, motioning with his arms. The rolled sleeves of his dress shirt were like flag markers waving Mikhail down. "In honor of our new guest, Ivan, why don't you get everyone a Jameson-rocks? One for yourself, too...a healthy pour all around. We're all alive and we deserve portions meant for the breathing. Sit, good sir, sit," he motioned again towards Mikhail. Pastor Shakur smiled, all pearly whites and charm. "What brings you back here?"

Mikhail stood and then sat, and focused on the physical memory of CGI's flexing ass in his hands. He thought about Roxanne Shanté's reinforcements and Mr. Sallow's well-tailored suit. Then all that disappeared. Mikhail's mind was once again drawing a blank. He stayed quiet and tried to appear like he was paused in the middle of thought—which he just was but no longer could create. He hoped the tightening of his jaw signaled a strong contemplation without trying too hard. Pastor Shakur was intimidating, especially with the adlibs from "Hit 'Em Up" floating silently through the air. He should've thought more about what he was going to say, but Armstrong's frown had dominated his brain while walking up the stairs. Fortunately, he knew how to play LCR.

"You told me to come back tonight, and I have a lonely $30 bill in my wallet that needs company."

"Now this is the ballad of a dead soldier I can dance to!" Pastor Shakur said, slamming his hands on the table. All was silent until Ellis started laughing, settling back into his chair after escorting Armstrong out. Wood Harris soon chimed in with the LOLs, and then Woody Harrelson. Mikhail started laughing too, if only to keep Avon Barksdale and Mickey Knox from kicking his ass. The characters of their past were haunting his present. "This man is terrified and yet he makes an effort to be anything other than nothing. We have to appreciate that, it has to be appreciated. Say money bring bitches, bitches bring lies. One nigga's gettin jealous, and motherfuckers died. Hot damn, that's why he's sitting there. No man that scared speaking shit that ain't true, and that's how I know I can trust lying-ass Mikhail. But before I get carried away, in all seriousness, did you do me right or did you come up here to die?"

"Is this a matter about the wetness of my dick or your Tweet bet with Jay-Z?" Mikhail asked. He grabbed his glass of Irish whiskey from the Pillar before it left the beige tray, and held it high for a toast before anyone else could grab theirs. Mikhail wondered if it was the high point of cool on this twisted night of FAILs and WINs. Tupac grabbed his—then Ellis, Wood, Woody, and the Pillar, respectively—and laughed before finally letting all five whiskeys trade clinks.

"This is why I love this guy...he answers my question with a sarcastic question of his own, like I'm not 100% serious. Drink up, fellas, drink up."

And everyone did. The Jameson was the least watered down he'd had all night. It was crisp and biting while the ice was a foreign collision against his teeth. Each sip was more valiant than the gulps he took from a certain booze-cart's perfect pour, and every jab was a more significant blow to his palette. The whiskey tasted so good, Mikhail wondered if it was a specialty label and that reminded him of something Hawthorne Mibbs had said earlier: "Rich motherfuckers drink green label and you blackies don't even have a label to peel from your piss-warm Budweiser." Mikhail wasn't sure what it meant, but that's what Hawthorne Mibbs had said.

"Sex is mathematics. Individuality no longer an issue," Ellis said. "Intellect is not a cure. Justice is dead. And those dice are equally soul-less. Are we playing or just sitting on our thumbs?"

"$30 is the bet, then," Woody said. Or maybe it was Wood. Either way, someone else had finally spoken up.

Chapter Thirty-Four
Left Center Right

Mikhail let the dice roll around in his hand a little bit. With only two chips left, the third die chilled unattended near his shifting wrist.

"Let's go, CL Smooth. Center and Left, sucka," Pastor Shakur said. "I got Pete Rock beats that you wouldn't even believe! Make them dice rhyme C and L, don't let me down, Mikhail! They reminisce over you!"

"It's about time you took an L," Wood added. He wore a Louis Vuitton visor that probably only left the design room a few times. "But throw a Right in there too...get scary for me, R.L. Stine or some shit."

"If I throw snake-eyes, you guys are going to let me beat up Horry without stepping in, aight?"

"You might be getting a little too darn comfortable here," Woody said, sitting directly across from Mikhail. There was something of a tick to the snarl that came from beneath his cowboy hat. "You can't be adding prop bets at the last minute like some rodeo clown. That just ain't right or left, it's just plain wrong."

"Woody, c'mon man, it's not the worst of provisions," Pastor Shakur said.

"Ain't no one have any chips left other than you two! I have to hope that you or Brother Bret get one just so you might be able to roll it my way and I have a chance of getting back into this darn game. Provisions sound like collusions."

"Chance is the game, Woody, just chill. Let him make this. If he rolls snake-eyes, we'll just have to let Horry fend for himself," the Pastor said, one emotion shy of relaxed. "Please, you have to see the humor in it, no?"

Mikhail let the dice roll and they revealed a pair of dots.

Woody shattered his empty glass against the wall and Pastor Shakur doubled over in laughter. Wood just stared in disbelief, while the Pillar rushed to find a dust pan. Whenever he got to Horry, it'd officially be a one-on-one contest. Mikhail repeated this silently a few times, in case the top-shelf Jameson kept pouring and he crossed over to black-out drunk land. He could feel his memory getting hazier with each sip.

"I need this third dot like I need the third eye," the Pastor said, further loosening the tie around his unbuttoned collar. Only one chip left, Shakur very specifically picked up the die Mikhail hadn't rolled. Mikhail wondered if there was more on this game than just the $150 tossed into the pot. But 'Pac was probably just that competitive, even for the comparatively low stakes. "No homo—but go ahead and dot me!"

And Tupac was dotted and everyone celebrated. The Pillar came back around and topped off everyone's drinks before sweeping up the rest of the glass. Mikhail pounded the table, so drunk he wasn't sure what he was doing. A pair of dice was thrusted at him. He dropped one and picked up the other; it just felt better.

"I know now what it's like to get shot," Mikhail said.

"Mosey on out of here with that nonsense," Woody said. "You ain't never been shot just as I ain't never been outside this bus or dunked a darn basketball."

"Not with a gun, no, but definitely by an eight-tentacled bullet that bit and scraped and slimed unlike any gun I've ever encountered. Real talk."

"Walk it out like Ushurrr, if you say real talk than I prolly won't truss ya, if you want to go to war, the guns, my pleasure," Wood said, slurring even more than Three Stacks. "Besides, them bitches have eight arms and two tentacles, there's a diff—"

"Is this lying-ass Mikhail or the Mikhail that doesn't give a what?" Pastor Shakur asked, interrupting Wood's would-be lecture on cephalopods. It was like the conversation had finally caught up to him, but he was already bored with the superfluous details and ready for point of it all. "This happened tonight?"

Mikhail opened his collar to reveal the long gash that snaked down his neck like the burn of a passing grenade. The table's quiet surprise was enough to confirm his assertion that he had indeed survived a squid attack.

"Maybe you are the one They speak about. I'm not sure if that makes me trust you more or less, but I'm impressed—even if I know you haven't gotten to that other thing we spoke about. There's only an hour or so left on this bus, has your luck run dry? We'll see, we'll see. In fact, I might add an additional wager and won't even ask you to put anything else up. I know that the last of your loot is already on the table," Pastor Shakur said. He then turned to the Pillar who was leaning against a bar stool by the door. "Why don't you bring out those shorties? They gotta blow on Mikhail's dice before he rolls them. Let's test that luck."

Ivan walked across the room and opened a door that Mikhail had assumed was spackled shut. It had certainly looked that way, but the Pillar was able to open it with ease—and not just because of his absurd size. Mikhail couldn't see into the room, but two young women slid out at the door's slightest crack, as if they had been intently listening, cupped ears on the thick plaster. They wore varying shades of pink and black in tube tops and skirts and high heels and one of them immediately looked familiar to

Mikhail. This wasn't an additional good deed wager, this was a potential game changer. Either way, Mikhail had to keep playing. He held up his pair of dice, jangling his hand, and waited with a flutter in his pulse for Bridget to blow on his fist.

"I wasn't good luck when your ex was around, what makes you think I'm lucky now?" Her earrings still dangled, even as her outfit had changed. Pastor Shakur, The Pillar, Brother Bret, the other girl, Woody and Wood…they all took a back seat to her dangles. The line between Bridget's neck and shoulders was devastatingly naked without losing a touch of her dignity. Then she gently blew on Mikhail's fist and it all started to melt away.

Pastor Shakur started talking again, but his spiel quickly turned into a throw away track, one of those songs that was probably the fourth or fifth of the day's studio session. His banter about bitches began to blend in with the beat—an instrumental that started sounding especially C-grade. There was still the probability of a gem lying in the mix, but Bridget's presence was too much of a distraction for any of the necessary concentration to pierce the meaning of Pastor Shakur's current song. Whatever was special about his highlights suddenly became very middling… or maybe he was just out-shined by the track's surprise guest.

It was probably the booze pushing his buttons, but Mikhail had to bite his tongue to keep it from declaring his love for Bridget. The night had kept on spinning, but his heart had stopped, letting it all rotate around each non-existent beat. Her words from earlier in the night kept ringing through his head— "you'll have to be real charming the next time around"—and the pressure behind his response under this new stroke of luck started to build up. With the ticking of each millisecond, he was getting more and more afraid that his tongue would out-wrestle his teeth and say what it so absurdly wanted to utter. He frantically searched his mind for that time, seemingly months ago, when their back-and-forth was infectiously flirtatious. One minute prior, he had felt in control, a bad ass revealing war wounds, but just then he could only hope she had heard what was quickly dispersing into nothingness.

"It's nice to see that we both changed outfits for the occasion," he jested. "Let's see how lucky you are or aren't."

Mikhail tossed his pair of dice right as Pastor Shakur shouted "LL Cool J!" The Pastor was only half right, as Mikhail's roll revealed an L and a dot. He got to keep a chip, but Shakur got the other. The reception was still rowdy, but a little less so. Bridget then stole Mikhail's Dipset scully and placed it over her tantalizing curls. The action stole some of the table's wind, especially once she started running her fingers through Mikhail's now-exposed hair. Pastor Shakur noticed the swinging momentum and picked up two dice that represented his two chips and quickly tossed them against the table's green felt.

"Railroad motherfucker!" Mikhail gasped as the dice were still spinning.

When it all settled, R and R were all that showed.

"If that ain't Rest and Relaxation, gentleman, I don't know what is," Mikhail shouted, barely audible over the eruption of cursing, laughing and stomping that resulted from Pastor Shakur's errant throw. He stopped trying to be heard once Bridget kissed him on the cheek, so close to his mouth that it hurt. The kiss of a pretty girl and the sweet sex of $150, his squid attack started to feel like a victory. Even his run-in with Robert Horry turned from a total affront to a sign that he and Saffy were not meant to be together. After their general hysteria died down and the laughter subsided, when Wood and Woody's bitching went quiet, Pastor Shakur placed his hand on Mikhail's shoulder.

"In all my years playing LCR, this is the first time I've ever seen someone end an epic game with all three chips. Maybe you do have some of that chosen one in you," he said, still shaking his head in disbelief. "But just because you got cash in your pocket, doesn't mean you've paid off your debt. The house is still on-top and I'm the bank that owns your mortgage."

"Me and my girl got Mikhail," Bridget suddenly said. The table was slightly more aghast at her statement than Mikhail's WIN, but no one said anything. "I don't know about his payments, but there's just something about him that makes me feel like he needs to be taken care of. And besides all that, his ex needs to be served."

"Well, I'll be damned. Why do I feel like giving you this easy lease on life was worse than if I had wagered the keys to my crib or secrets from my campaign files?" Pastor Shakur slowly shook his head, still managing to pierce Mikhail with intense eye contact: "You just better close the deal. Repo can be worse than the po-po, and you know this bank doesn't mess around."

"Agreed. So you don't mind if I steal Dangles and her friend? It's getting late and the night can only be young for so long," Mikhail said. "I mean, only if they want to go grab a drink elsewhere. Their choice, your choice, I'm just suggesting it."

"I think you deserve it and what's-her-name is certainly trying to serve it," Pastor Shakur said. "Just remember that I'm paying attention, and not just Twitter feeds or Facebook updates. I'll give you 50 feet. Defeat might not be your destiny, I'll release you to the streets. And keep whatever's left of thee. Jealousy is misery, suffering is grief. Better be prepared when the cowards fuck with me."

Visit **http://PleaseUseRearExit.net/home/SacredSaffron**
for a bonus chapter's true-to-the-word epiphany.

Chapter Thirty-Five
O Rly?

Mikhail walked down Something's set of stairs for a final time and pushed real hard to find a bit of conversation that would continue his winning streak. Two beautiful women pranced behind him, and even if he only knew one of their names, something magical was in the air. He promised himself that he'd say anything at all, as long as it didn't involve dangles.

"Without the shine off your dangles, Bridget, I'm pretty sure I'd FAIL down these stairs."

They laughed, and he felt his hot streak continue even if he'd officially tapped the same joke of a well one too many times.

"We're not going to really meet until we can see a damn thing, but what's your name anyway?" Mikhail asked, shouting out behind him while his hands felt through the darkness. "It'd be good to know at least one thing about you before the light exposed too much data."

"@_Asia," the non-Bridget voice said. "And don't think you've won me over so easily."

"I didn't even think I was playing for you," Mikhail said. "Didn't even know I was playing at all. But at this point of the night isn't it all house money anyway?"

"Is that what it is?" Bridget asked, as her heels clunked downward one by one.

"Oh, Mikhail, you won a dice game and nothing else," @_Asia said. "I can see those bruises even in the pitch-black of these spirals. It looks like you lost a few times over the past few hours."

"I think you're just remembering my bruises from when you saw me in the light," Mikhail said. "For all you know, I healed during the walk down all these stairs. Maybe darkness is my photosynthesis, and it's fixing my wounds as we speak."

"You're so weird and cute, Mikhail, I don't get it. Bridget doesn't know how lucky she is to—"

"Shut up, girl, you don't know what you're talking ab—"

"What?" @_Asia asked, genuinely incredulous. "I'm just talking, B, what'd I say? He's just really interesting, and you know, what was Pastor Shakur saying about him up there? It didn't make a whole lot of sense, but then BAM, he was sitting there...it's just interesting, that's all."

Mikhail thought he heard Bridget roll her eyes, but before he could even comment the light beneath the stairwell's door signaled the end of this particular leg of his journey. He pushed through the steel portal and let in a brightness that was wholly familiar. Once again, Mikhail felt better coming down than he did going up. New life had been breathed into him, as it had before, but this time he was a little more confident about who he'd recycle that breath back onto—Bridget and @_Asia. Dangles and her hot friend. He didn't know what destiny meant, he was just happy to be on the upside of it at the end of the night.

Once all three were basked in light—and doing their best to look cool while rubbing it out of their eyes—he formally met @_Asia. Shaking her hand, he could feel the lotion on it. Vaguely floral scented, the lotion was more sensual than greasy. Mikhail could feel it heat the areas of his skin that came into contact with the chemical reaction exploding from her epidermal layer. He started to get an erection, despite being at a point in his drunken night where he thought such arousal couldn't occur without direct stimulation. And that was just from a hand shake.

"So what makes you so important that you were sitting at that card table?" Bridget asked.

"No one was playing cards up there," Mikhail said. "And besides, you got to the party before I did. Apparently y'all were talking about me."

"Oh, you know damn well why we were up there," Bridget said.

"Yeah, stop trying to be adorable," @_Asia added.

Mikhail did know the reason for the girls' presence in Something's hidden tower, but he didn't know what lead a woman to make such choices in her life. And at this point, such a conversation would only lead to an awkwardness of FAIL proportions. He could sense that they were relieved to be out of there, but still wondered (as did they) if the ladies had blown their unlikely chance at making one of the powerful men upstairs fall in love.

"So are we getting a drink here or going back to Compton's Circle to drink some whiskey?" Mikhail reached out and grabbed Bridget's elbow, a move so natural he forgot what it had once meant. Whatever wager was being discussed above didn't matter, not when he felt her elbow and traded inspecting eye-contact with @_Asia. Bridget leaned into him—her hand squeezing his thigh with both affection and curiosity—giggling as she prepared to say something.

"Are you trying to show off some kind of ghetto pass, Mikhail?" Bridget asked, pausing everyone near Something's exit.

"No ma'am, it's just where I keep my whiskey," he said, trying to skip the show and get straight to the prove.

"You don't really live on The C, do you?" @_Asia said, in a bluster of surprise and suspicion. "Where at? And I'll know if you're bullsh—"

"Been there long enough to know that no one calls it 'The C' anymore. I'm equidistant from Magic Johnson's park and the infamous Penny Porn Palace, on a happy little block in the Lower Left. Where do you shawties stay at?"

"We have a spot on The Square," Bridget said, pointedly staying in the conversation, "near the rec center." She wasn't interrupting, only making sure that interruption wouldn't be necessary. Possessively, she would never allow the trialogue to devolve into a dialogue. It made Mikhail excited to see that passion play out between the sheets. "We have whiskey, but where's your air conditioning?"

They obviously had it and he didn't. And he didn't need to imagine the sweat box his place had turned into over the past seven hours either. He certainly didn't need another excuse to avoid the Brown BTWN. And surely, Bridget and @_Asia's apartment on The Square would smell like angels. Having passed through Something's doors and standing in the middle of the #720's stragglers, it had become apparent that someone would need to make the decision Mikhail already knew.

"I don't have anymore A/C than the Brown BTWN does," he admitted. "Jameson is in the freezer, though, and cold as hell. As far as I can tell, we're pretty much in the middle of the Blue and Brown BTWNs, what do you want to do? Whoever has to go home tomorrow morning has a long trip ahead of 'em."

"Isn't it a little presumptuous to think any one of us will be spending the night?"

"It's presumptuous to live according to The Internet's rules of afternoon, evening and night. Shit, even by their standards, it's almost two in the A.M. By the time we get to anywhere, it's going to be morning."

"OMI," @_Asia squealed, staring in disbelief at her Blackberry, "the Brown BTWN was attacked by squids tonight. Three people died, I'm reading it right now, it's a #Trending topic, I'm not even lying and I'm definitely not going on the Brown BTWN."

"Maybe you shouldn't either," Bridget said to Mikhail.

As much as he liked to brag about his residence, he still didn't want to go back there when most of it was almost empty. They were scared of squids and so was Mikhail. Drunk as he was, he wasn't sure if mentioning his survival of said Tweeted attack would work in his favor or against it. The bravery of fighting off those vile beasts might've been overshadowed by the disease he could have picked up by wrestling them. Every hero can still lose to a virus, especially in the eyes of pulchritudinous women. If the threesome on everyone's mind was going to happen, it had to be between feminine sheets. And just because Katya had done his last load of laundry, Mikhail's still didn't count.

"If squids are already on the prowl tonight, I might feel better if I can walk you ladies home, at the very least," he said smiling. Mikhail could feel their collective warmth wrap around him, especially as he walked between them. Everyone fully clothed, there was a static electricity that was left unsaid but continually sparked through their bodies. "No presumptions, I swear. Besides, I haven't been on the Blue BTWN in months. It's always good to be reminded how bad the Brown truly is."

"You don't think squids will actually attack the Blue BTWN, do you?" @_Asia asked, huddling closer to Mikhail.

"Of course not," he said. "There's a reason all those rich elitists pay all those taxes and it's to keep squids from getting at their innocent children. Which is completely fortunate for you two, because I'm pretty sure you don't have an innocent bone in your bodies."

"Hey!"

"O Rly?"

"Guess there are a few sensitive bones in there," Mikhail said, happy they were joking and that he was joking with them. The connection he had felt earlier with Bridget had carried over and actually spilled into @_Asia. "Shall we walk?"

And walk they did. The girls discussed their night and Mikhail did his best to charmingly chip in while trying to avoid crashing the slumber party. As they talked about questionable outfits on silly adversaries and who-said-whats, he was successful. The imagined smell of their apartment was already infecting his nostrils and he'd never known an infection so lovely. His drunken noggin once found reason to laugh because @_Asia wore a pink top/black leggings combination while Bridget peacocked in a black top/pink leggings outfit, but Mikhail admirably shook it off when they asked about his chuckle.

The lonely men who lulled past Mikhail's new-found trio were totally confused and butt-hurt by his monumental (and momentary) station in life. The jealous walked by cursing his luck, as he wrangled with his blessing. An hour before, he was a reflection of the solitary loner. They might've been right about his end-of-the-night wealth, but they were wrong about how he got it. Regardless, their negative energy was both futile and far between. Most of the #720 was empty and what was left was emptying out.

"FYI, Mikhail, our apartment is a crazy mess, we had a little Thirsty Thursday party last night and it got out of hand," Bridget said. "It ain't awful, but maybe it's not what you expect."

"Lucky for you, I just expect a place that's cozily lived in, and the remnants of a Thirsty Thursday seem to fit the bill," he laughed. "Besides, it's better than my sweat box on Compton's Circle. At least y'all have air-conditioning, right?"

They laughed too, and grabbed Mikhail ever closer. @_Asia put her forehead to his chin and it completely warmed anything in him that was ever cold; Bridget's curls tickled his neck and sent shivers through his entire body. Covered in their collective Icy-Hot, he had no choice but to hug them back. So tingling, so good, he almost didn't notice when Katya ran by them crying. She skirted by so quickly in such a quiet hush, that Mikhail probably wouldn't have noticed if she wasn't trailed by such a whiff of familiarity.

She's alone but she has to get used to it, Mikhail thought. *I can't always be there for her, maybe the next guy can. Hopefully she doesn't drive him crazy.*

"Wow, that girl had a bad night," @_Asia said. "LOL, she took whatever news came her way poorly, that's for sure."

That's when Hawthorne Mibbs limped by with a spot of crooked in his one un-crossed eye. Mibbs shied away from Mikhail and the ladies, sticking close to the shadows, but he seemed to be on a mission. Without question, he was following Katya. Despite his limp, Mibbs was deceptively fast...and unfortunately, Katya's sobs came quicker than her footsteps. Bridget and @_Asia didn't notice Hawthorne Mibbs—few ever did—but Mikhail certainly saw him.

"What's wrong?" Bridget asked. "Why are you stopping?"

"The Blue BTWN is right up here, Mikhail, let's go... there's no reason to miss it, it comes in five minutes. We don't want to wait for the next one, you know that."

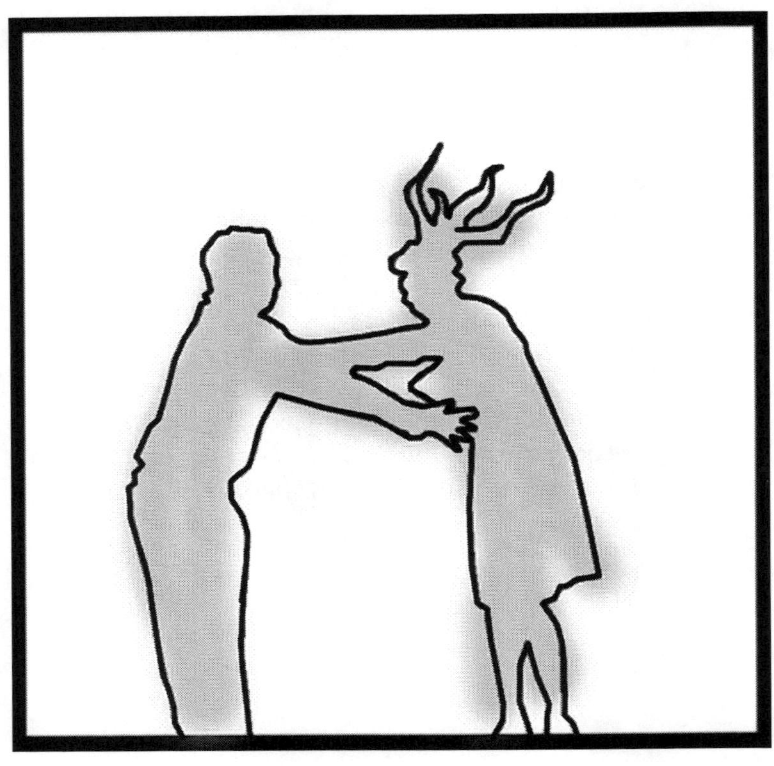

Visit **http://PleaseUseRearExit.net/home/GoingHome**
to watch "Not Goin' Home" featuring
Fat Tony, Apathy, The Machine & Spirit Animal
(beat by Evidence)

Chapter Thirty-Six
It's Yourz

Mikhail looked longingly at Bridget and @_Asia and did his woozily best to understand the two options in front of him. His desires were reinforced with the wants of others, but his consciousness just piled upon itself. The orange behind Bridget's eyes burned brighter and their teal seemed to plead a deeper kind of importance than Mikhail could understand. @_Asia smiled and tugged on his hand, supplanting her thumb below his; it was a digital relationship that Katya had always refused. But Mikhail absolutely knew that he had to go.

"Take the bus if it comes, I'm so sorry," Mikhail said, pissed off at the words leaving his mouth. "To paraphrase my best friend, I gotta see a man about a horse or maybe a squid about a man, I forget. I just know that I'm sorry. I'll be right back, but don't wait for me if I'm not...please, don't."

"What are you talking about?" Bridget asked.

"Apparently I'm talking about what I need to do. Trust me, I like it a whole lot less than you do. Think you'll be OK waiting for the Blue BTWN without me? I'm sure you will... but the reason I'm going, it's because I'm sure things won't be well there."

"What are you talking about?" @_Asia asked.

"The same hunch that got me to you is taking me away," he said. And he believed it. Mikhail individually kissed both of their hands; @_Asia's lotion left a numbing reminder on his lips and Bridget's essence left a longing in his heart. "If I don't see you on the Blue BTWN than I only hope to see you around."

Mikhail walked quickly in Katya's direction, disgusted with every self-hating step. He knew it was right, but it felt incredibly wrong. Bridget shouted something about how charm wouldn't save him the next time, but he knew there wouldn't be a next time. Unlike the initial moment he had stepped away from her or even when she angrily left him with Katya, this shift in direction felt final. Unless of course, he arrived before the Blue BTWN...an absurd outcome in itself.

It was at this realization that he ran for the first time since he was a child. Mikhail wasn't going to rebound from this—not with Bridget or @_Asia or Pastor Shakur's dictated threesome—unless he acted with the utmost speed. Perhaps the Olympian effort was a result of his best—his inner heroism actually chosen and not just called upon without option—or maybe it was his worst. He ran past a quivering Mibbs, who hid the minute he heard chasing footsteps, and caught up to Katya quicker than he could think of something to say.

"What the fuck are you doing in a suit?"

"I really don't know," Mikhail said. "Pastor Shakur and Mr. Sallow and a talking cat all said I shouldn't be here, but I don't know."

"You shouldn't be here. I don't need anything," Katya said, concealing a chuckle and wiping the make-up from below her eye with the sleeve of a man's hoodie. "I'm alive and well and my heart's still ticking."

"You were running and crying and a sketchy guy was chasing you," Mikhail said, already ready to leave. "If you don't want me here, I'll go right back to what I was doing."

"Wait...no...stay. He's been following me all night, Mikhail, I'm scared," she said. "I'm so sorry, this isn't how I want you here. I want you here—just not like this."

Mikhail couldn't admit to her that he didn't want to be there in any shape or form, like "this" or not. Instead, he let the silence vouch for him. His steps moved pointedly with hers and that was all he could allow himself to say. Still sniffling, Katya didn't overtly object to his closed mouth, nor did she take offense from it. Part of him just waited until she found something to start an argument over. More than ever, he just wanted to go home. And he definitely didn't want to be looking over his shoulder for another fight.

However, Hawthorne Mibbs seemed to be long gone, and Mikhail was furious with jealousy over an absence that should've been his. Walking Katya to the Brown BTWN was an action with a snail mail's pace in an email world. She dragged her feet and he was enraged about the drag. Every time he picked up the pace, she asked him to slow down. They walked along solemnly, as Mikhail's steps mixed with anger at the escalating realization that Bridget and @_Asia would be Westside Square bound before he could escort Katya to her transfer. Half a mile away, Mikhail could almost hear the #720 connect with the Blue BTWN. Maybe he was imagining it, but quite possibly it was happening. And maybe that's what drove Mikhail to start the inevitable fight before Katya could. Either that or all his bitterness finally boiled over.

"You do know you acted a fool tonight, right?"

"I'll take tonight if you take the last year and a half," Katya smiled.

Her joviality put Mikhail back on his heels. He had been ready for a full-on collision—an explosion even—but not for a light-hearted volley. Through the smeared make-up, Katya's eyes smiled brighter than her perfect teeth, teeth he knew she took great care in maintaining. He almost had to remind himself that he was mad.

"C'mon now, that's hardly fair," he said, allowing himself to smile just a bit. "I'll own a few foolish conversations, but I can't keep a year of our problems all to myself."

"Who's starting shit now?" Katya laughed. She bumped into Mikhail and he would've brushed it off as accidental if her bump didn't linger. They were always at their best when pretend fighting, coyness and sarcasm overlapping into some sort of connection. "You never said your opinion about anything when we were together. It's kind of refreshing to hear you say something that might get you yelled at."

"You found reasons even when I didn't."

"That's who I am, Mikhail. I probably would've yelled less if you gave me anything to be passionate about once in awhile. Our whole relationship, it was always me talking. Even when things were good, did you ever say anything that you actually felt? You were very convincing with your I Love You's and random bouquets of flowers and cute little notes, but on hindsight, wasn't it all a little empty? I always had to make the effort. I get the introvert thing, I fell in love with the introvert thing, but it has its breaking point. Was I just bending something already broken? I told you everything, Mikhail, and you told me nothing."

"Sometimes, I just don't have anything to say," Mikhail said, with an empty mind. "How many questions did you just ask without giving me a chance to respond?"

Completely silent, Katya was searching for the right comment. Mikhail couldn't remember a similar moment in either part of their relationship. The Blue BTWN long having left its station, he started walking slower than her and observing the #720 emptiness more and more. With a jolt of electricity, the blood hid from his face and he was flushed with the chills, startled by a sudden rush of shadow.

Maybe he was a little jumpy from everything that had happened, but it took a few seconds for him to realize that the shadows creeping from behind him were his own. The speckling of overhead lights were causing chaos without the line's normal throng of passengers. Mikhail could see three silhouettes of himself, cast against the ground, all stemming from his feet and swaying with his steps in varying levels of darkness. At their peak, they joined into a single shadow, but quickly dissipated into three separate entities in three separate directions, until they circled around and met again. Their opening and closing continued to make Mikhail's muscles tense. He was scared that his own shadow would come from behind in full-on attack-mode.

"Three," Katya said, "I asked three questions, and I didn't give you a chance to answer any of them. I'm sorry I do that. But the stage is yours. I'm quiet until you respond how you see fit."

"What were the questions again?" Mikhail laughed. If his night was one giant FAIL, he might as well have some fun with it. And be honest with Katya, no less.

"Was I bending something that was already bro—"

"I know it's frustrating. It pisses me off too. I'd like to be all sorts of talkative and revelatory with you, but it's just not in me. The only thing I could ever do is be honest, faithful and supportive, while doing the best to figure myself out. I fucked up that last part, but I never cheated and did my damn best to be there for you."

"Something happened with Saffron and I know it was—"

"We danced in the break-room and our lips kind of touched once," Mikhail said, fully exasperated. "You know the exact run-down, from me and everyone else at the OeEP. This path has been treaded...deaded."

"You sound like Chevy now," she said. "It's almost like—"

"No crackers, this is what it's like!" Hawthorne Mibbs said, jumping out from one of Mikhail's shadows. He was loosely brandishing a rusted knife in Mikhail's direction and wearing a crazed look in his twisted eyes. His hands were shaking.

"I'm sick of you Saltines eating. I'm hungry and I'm brown, so listen up, give me your money. That's what the news wants me to do, right? So this is what I'm doing. Don't make me get all touchy-feely with a white bitch in the process, yessir, 'cause you know I'll do it! I'm the angry black man—boogity boo! Give me your money. I want it all. Cell phones too, why not? Give me those. Anything I can touch, I want. This is my grocery store and you ain't in the cracker aisle."

"Hawthorne, I don't really know you, but I know who you are. I live on Compton's Circle and I've seen you sleeping on my sidewalk," Mikhail said, trying to bring an element of calm to the sudden insanity. His hand was out in front of him—a firm and soothing gesture. The déjà-vu was palpable and he hadn't even gone to sleep yet. "I know enough to not give a shit. Go home, man. Go to sleep. This isn't what you want. I'll give you a bit, but you ain't getting it all."

Mibbs made a stabbing motion that he didn't at all mean and Mikhail easily ducked away. It was aggressive enough for Mikhail to rethink his laissez-faire approach to the situation, but not enough to give away his wallet.

"Bend over for a blackie once in your rich life. This is how the black man wins, by fucking! Not by bending over. Boogity boo!"

"You're so right on so many levels, Hawthorne, but no," Mikhail said. Katya then pinched the arm she was grabbing on and she pinched it hard. "Ow, what the fuck?"

"Just give him what he wants, Mikhail, please," she whispered.

"Listen to your girl, bitch. You don't want this. I'll turn white to red if I don't get green. Don't get me thinking, you know how white folks hate a brown man thinking, why else do you keep trying to kill Tupac? You scared—now do as scared does and give it up. Boo motherfucker!"

Mibbs took a step back as he lazily pushed the knife forward. Mikhail looked at him and then looked at Katya. Her face was clenched, fighting back tears as he kept up a fight, begging him to just hand over whatever cash he had left in his pocket. She was always so scared and that made him feel all the more confident that Hawthorne Mibbs wouldn't do anything he really didn't want to do. Katya mustered a wink and a terrified glance at her purse, as if to say that she'd pay for dinner if Mikhail just handed over his money. She thought that Mibbs would be happy with Mikhail's money and then leave them alone. Mikhail could only think about those tangents of hers, the ones where she'd implore that a man's man always paid for dinner. She called guys who wouldn't pay cowards. He wouldn't be a coward.

"I may have an apartment and you don't, but we live on the same line in this same Internet-forsaken city. I'm not your enemy. Go towards the Blue BTWN and rob motherfuckers there, they're the ones with money to spare. I ain't got shit except this," Mikhail said, taking out two $30 bills with his left hand. There was some more cash in his wallet, but he wasn't about to give up all of his winnings to a lost cause on a lost night. "This is enough for me and maybe her to get a bite to eat and I haven't eaten anything since this morning. I'm not the fat cat you need to be robbing."

"White money is the best money."

"That's probably true, but this ain't—"

Hawthorne Mibbs surged forward, reaching for the two bills with his knife hand and Mikhail grabbed him by his skinny little wrist. He pulled Mibbs' twisted body towards the ground and swiftly came around with a tightly clenched fist in a singular motion. Mibbs had leaned in to snatch a bounty, but he had found something else entirely. He was caught with the weight of Mikhail's night and all its absurdity and the stone knuckles immediately broke Hawthorne Mibbs' jaw and shattered his cheek bones. The screw of a man promptly crumpled to the ground and twisted into himself like a towel that found the free will to wring itself dry.

Mikhail twice stomped on Hawthorne Mibbs' hand, just enough for him to let go of the knife. He then kicked it as hard as he could, careful to clip his scapegoat's chin in the come around. The knife disappeared into the shadows and Mikhail raised his fists against Mibbs' cowering face. He didn't feel the pain that punching men often confide about their aching knuckles. He didn't know that his black-out rage switch had long been flipped; he didn't even know what he was doing. Mibbs was crying for mercy as the back of his head repeatedly lifted up and slammed back down against the #720's tile, as his face continued to find new ways to bleed, as Mikhail found new lows in which to sink. Mikhail didn't feel anything at all—not his hand breaking and not the anger that would break hearts—not until he felt Katya try to restrain him.

She was kissing his cheeks, wildly sobbing and shouting, "Squeazle, please stop, please stop, squeazle, please, please baby, please." She wrapped her arms around his chest and pulled him back and even if he didn't know what a squeazle possibly could be, Mikhail finally stopped. He looked down and saw the evil of his wrath—Mibbs' eyes were already swollen shut, his nose was bleeding into his mouth or the other way around, a bone had found its way through his Vitiligo skin stained purple and red—it was a hell of a first punch. Katya said something about going home and Mikhail recognized just enough to let go. He kicked Mibbs in his already broken ribs one last time. As spiteful and merciless as it was, Mikhail felt like he had finally become a man. Perhaps the first to feel his punch wasn't the most worthy, but he certainly wasn't as innocent as he was helpless.

Mikhail didn't have these thoughts as he stepped over Mibbs' shattered body, as Katya muttered something about her loss of an appetite. There were so many things that crashed upon the shores of his night that it'd take some time for their impact to fully connect among his synapses. He could only look up and see that the Brown BTWN entrance was just a few steps away, bringing him full circle on this constantly spinning merry-go-round. The Brown BTWN's buzzer announced that the bus was only a minute away. Not knowing which way was up, he knew that Katya's was the first stop. From there, he only had three options:

(1) Go all the way, back to Katya's apartment, and succumb to joyless, guilt-filled, missionary-position sex...but sex all the same.

(2) Go half-way, walk her home only to wait until Katya went inside so that he could find a proper bench to pass out on.

(3) Go the half-assed way, by letting her walk home alone, so that he could continue on the Brown BTWN towards his own apartment—hungry and horny and worrying about failed missions, but happy to finally fall asleep.

The End.
(of Book One)

Skinny B Publishing, LLC
Facebook.com/PleaseUseRearExit
@SkinnyB | @PleaseUseBooks

Made in the USA
Charleston, SC
21 November 2012